Nurture

I Found My Heart in San Francisco Book Fourteen

Susan X Meagher

Nurture

I Found My Heart In San Francisco: Book Fourteen

ISBN (10) 09832758-7-4
ISBN (13) 978-0-9832758-7-9

This trade paperback original is published by Brisk Press, Brielle, NJ 08730

First printing: May 2013

By Susan X Meagher

Novels

Arbor Vitae
All That Matters
Cherry Grove
Girl Meets Girl
The Lies That Bind
The Legacy
Doublecrossed
Smooth Sailing
How To Wrangle a Woman
Almost Heaven
The Crush

Serial Novel

I Found My Heart In San Francisco

Awakenings
Beginnings
Coalescence
Disclosures
Entwined
Fidelity
Getaway
Honesty
Intentions
Journeys
Karma
Lifeline
Monogamy
Nurture

Anthologies

Undercover Tales
Outsiders

To purchase these books go to
www.briskpress.com

Dedication

To the people and the legislature of the state of New York, for supporting the right to marry whomever we love. And to my wife, Carrie. It took many years to be able to call you that, but it was very much worth the wait.

her body to rise. Teetering on rubbery legs, eyes tightly closed, she started to make her way to the bath. "Where the fuck are we?" she grumbled after banging into an unexpected wall.

"We're in Ryan's room in Noe." Jordan was immediately at her side, guiding her into the bath. "Let me help you."

"No way. God only knows what's gonna come out of me. I don't even want you to hear me, much less see me."

"You're really wobbly. I'm worried about you."

"Well, I'm worried that you'll dump me if you come into that bathroom. Put on some clothes and go upstairs. I'm sure our chipper hosts are already chowing down on a big breakfast—the bastards!" With that, she grabbed the door handle, hanging onto it to gain her balance, then closed the door, the lock snapping into place with a thud.

After rummaging through Ryan's closet, Jordan found some acceptable sweats and headed upstairs. As predicted, the cheerful clan was gathered at the dining table, with neither Jamie nor Ryan looking any the worse for wear. Martin jumped up. "What'll it be, Jordan? I can make anything your heart desires."

She beamed a smile at him, then nodded to Kevin, Conor, and Maeve. It was always a little disconcerting to be around the big O'Flaherty clan. Having six boisterous people at breakfast was so far beyond her ken that she doubted she'd ever be entirely comfortable in the group. But they were so good-natured and accommodating it was churlish not to try. "I'll take whatever's easiest. I'm not very particular."

"Will Mia be up soon, darlin?'"

"Not if she can help it." She gave Jamie and Ryan a pointed look, then sat down next to them. "Do you have anything for a hangover? Mia's in bad shape."

"I'll fix her up," Ryan said, going into the kitchen. She returned a few moments later, with a giant glass of something orange and some toast. "Your breakfast is just about ready, bud. I'll take this down to her."

"Oh, you don't wanna do that. She's beyond grouchy."

"I don't mind. You should eat while it's hot. Be right back." And with that, she took off.

Jordan gave the remaining guests a sheepish look. "I should have argued more, but I wasn't really looking forward to going back down there. I was ordered to stay away."

Jamie gave Jordan a pat. "Ryan'll fix her up. If nothing else, she'll give her one of her famous knock-out massages, and you won't have to deal with her for a few hours."

"That's not ideal, either. My flight's at three, and we have some pretty important things to discuss."

"Be careful what you wish for. Depending on how grouchy she is, you might prefer to spend the day looking at her while she sleeps. She has a tendency to bite your head off when she's hung over."

Blinking in surprise, Jordan said, "She's grouchy, but she'd never do that."

Jamie threw her head back and laughed. "God, you two are on best behavior, aren't you?"

"I thought she was just even-tempered."

Martin came in with Jordan's breakfast as Jamie was speaking. "No one's even tempered all of the time, love. Even my beloved Maeve can rain down fire and brimstone if the mood strikes."

His wife grabbed his belt loop and pulled him close, then hauled him down by the ear and whispered something.

"My mistake," he said, looking as innocent as an altar boy. "I was thinking of another."

Much sooner than Jordan expected, Ryan returned, with a disheveled Mia in tow. "I tried to get her to go back to sleep, but she insisted that she has too much to do."

Jordan raised a questioning eyebrow, then swallowed her bite of pancake.

"I have to go home and pack." Mia gave Jordan a very perturbed look. "I was the one who got drunk, not you; you should have remembered a thing like that."

"I…I…I thought that was the tequila talking. Were you serious?"

That comment made every head rise, but only Conor had the nerve to ask, "Where are you going?"

Narrowing her eyes, while staring at her partner, Mia said, "I thought I was moving to Colorado, but maybe I'm not wanted."

Stuffing the remaining half of her last pancake into her mouth, Jordan got up and took Mia by the hand. "Let's go downstairs and talk this out, okay?"

"There's nothing to talk about. Either you want me or you don't." She practically had to drag her, but Jordan got her downstairs before everyone heard what was probably the beginning of their first major fight.

As Mia's voice drifted away, Conor gave his sister an outraged look. His cheeks colored when he demanded, "What in the hell's going on? Aren't you guys still in the middle of the term?"

It was time to pull back out of this one. There was no way she was going to get into an argument with Conor. Ryan gave him an intentionally blank look. "Yes, we're in the middle of the term. If you want any more information, you'll have to ask Mia or Jordan."

"Don't be a jerk. I'm asking a simple question."

Ryan blinked at him, but didn't comment further. For some reason his temper was talking instead of his brain.

"Jordan's in Colorado Springs, right?"

"Right."

"She's on the Olympic volleyball team, right?"

"You know this, Conor. Don't play around asking rhetorical questions."

"I know that Jordan's supposed to be there. But why in the hell is Mia going? Especially now! That doesn't make any sense."

Conor's voice rose with every word, and Martin gave him a disapproving look. "Keep your voice down, son. This has nothing to do with you."

"The hell it doesn't!" He pushed his chair away from the table and stormed up to his room.

Martin, watching him leave, finally let his questioning gaze move from Jamie to Ryan. "What's bothering him?"

Jamie didn't say a word, and Ryan just shrugged her shoulders. "PMS?" she suggested ingenuously.

Mia was once again locked in the bathroom. Jordan's knock was met with a curt, "Go away."

Unable to hide her hurt, Jordan said, "I have to leave in two hours. But if you want me to, I'll go now."

"I...I...thought you wanted me to be with you!" Mia's sobs echoed loudly in the small, tiled room. "I gave up my family for you!"

"You're talking crazy! What have I said to make you think I don't want you? I want you more than I've ever wanted anything in my life!"

The lock turned, and soon the door opened just a crack. "You didn't even believe that I was serious about moving to Colorado. Did you think I made up the whole story?"

"Jesus, why would I think that?" Jordan pushed the door open and latched onto Mia's T-shirt to pull her into an embrace. "Look," she murmured into the tousled curls, "I know you're hung over and that you feel like crap. I also know that you're very, very sad about what happened with your parents. But I'm on your side, sweetheart. I love you, and I want you with me more than I want air."

Looking up at her partner with red-rimmed, bloodshot eyes, Mia's angry façade began to crack, and soon she was crying piteously. "I love you, too," she choked out, her words hard to understand because of her tears.

Hugging her even tighter, Jordan nuzzled her face into Mia's soft brown hair. She spoke quietly, but clearly. "I love you enough to do the right thing for our future, even if it's not what we want right now."

Mia froze, then slowly pulled back and stared. "What do you mean by that?"

"I meant just what I said." Jordan took her by the hand and led her back to the bed. Getting in first, she pulled Mia onto the mattress and settled her between her legs. Starting to slide her fingers through the tangled curls, Jordan soothed, "I want to make sure that we've thought this through, that's all. We're making some very big decisions, and I want to do the right thing at the right time."

"So you don't want me to come," Mia snapped, then started to cry again.

"No! I don't mean that at all. But it does mean that I care for you too much to have you make a decision that you'll regret."

"How can you even say that I might regret a decision to be with you? You sound like my mother!" Mia struggled to pull away.

"No." Jordan tightened her hold. "You're gonna stay right here and listen to me."

"Do you want me in Colorado or don't you? That's all that matters."

"Yes, I want you in Colorado, but that's not all that matters. I want you to think about this for a minute."

Slowly, Mia stopped struggling, then lay still. She didn't speak, but she seemed attentive.

"We have to consider the facts. You've got about eight weeks of class left. I know that sounds like a lot, but if you finish school now, you'll never have to worry about it again."

"I don't want to finish. I want to be with you!"

"I know that, and I want that, too, but does it make sense? We both have to finish at Cal because of the residency requirement. That means that we'll both have to spend a full semester here at some point, and my guess is that we'd want to do that right after the Olympics."

"Yeah? So?"

"So, if we're both in school full-time, how will we live? We'll both have to have part-time jobs just to be able to afford rent. But if you were already finished, you could work full-time while I finished school, and that would let us have our evenings together—rather than both of us working our butts off for minimum wage."

"I haven't thought past today. I can't get past what happened." She let out such a sad sigh that Jordan almost gave in and focused only on the present—on Mia's wounded feelings. But that wasn't smart. You could only get what you wanted if you planned for it.

"If you come to Colorado and get a job, you're gonna need your car. And if you come with me today, we're gonna have to make another trip back here just to get it."

Glumly, Mia said, "So I'm supposed to stay and finish school, then drive to Colorado."

"No, I'm not saying that. I'm pointing out the downside of your coming right now." She leaned over so Mia could see her eyes. "I don't tell you what to do. I never will. I'm just telling you my thoughts, so there's no misunderstanding. We're gonna make this decision together, sweetheart, but we've gotta hurry since I have to leave for the airport by one thirty."

It took a few minutes. A few minutes of stomach-churning anxiety for Jordan. But finally Mia spoke in a voice that sounded much more normal. "You're right. It's crazy to think we can figure everything out in a couple of hours." She turned in Jordan's embrace and kissed her on the cheek. "I'm sorry I've been such a bitch this morning." Her lower lip began to quiver, and soon tears were pouring down her cheeks again. "I'm scared, Jordy."

Jordan smoothed the hair from Mia's eyes. "Tell me what scares you."

"I've never been this alone before," Mia sniffed. "I've always had my parents behind me—always. No matter what I've done, they've stuck by me. It hurts so much to have them turn their backs on me." Her whole body shuddered. "To think of you leaving without me terrifies me.

I was only able to be strong with them because I knew you and I would be together. But if I have to stay here..." Overcome with emotion, she buried her face against Jordan's chest and cried until she began to hiccup. "Oh, fuck, this makes my headache worse."

"Let me go get you something to drink. You'll feel better if you stay hydrated."

"Don't leave me. Just lie here and hold me."

Jordan did as she was asked, holding on tightly until Mia calmed down. Finally, her hiccups left, but she still seemed very, very shaky. "I do need something to drink. And I need a shower. That usually helps."

Jordan untangled herself and started for the stairs, then turned and gave Mia a small smile. "We'll work it out. I promise."

Standing under the shower helped a little bit, and she was starting to feel human when the door opened. "When did you dye your hair?" she asked, peering through the clear shower curtain.

Ryan leaned on the vanity. "It's always been black."

"Bigger question. Why are you in the shower with me?"

"I'm not. If I were, I'd be wet," Ryan said in her usual, annoyingly logical style. "Granted, I'm in the bathroom with you..."

"Spill it, O'Flaherty. Subtlety isn't your strong point."

"Well, Jordan gave us a synopsis of your dilemma, and we thought maybe we could help you reason this out. Jordan's getting you something to drink, Jamie's making you something to eat, and I'm...well, I'm not sure why I'm here, but this is where they told me to go. I'll wait outside."

Mia turned off the water. "Nah. You can dry my back. It's not like you haven't seen me naked."

"More times than I can count." She handed Mia a towel, then took another and performed her assigned task. "Are you dating a woman or a leech? You've got marks all over your body."

"I like it when she bites me." Wrapping herself in her towel, she gave Ryan a half grin. "I've seen more than a few on Jamie, wise guy. And I bet I could find a couple on you after the way you two were carrying on last night."

Clutching the placket on her shirt, Ryan wrinkled up her nose. "You'll never know." Then she leaned over and kissed Mia's head. "It'll be okay, buddy. It'll all be okay."

When Ryan emerged from the steamy bathroom, Jamie was sitting on the bed, one eyebrow raised to dangerous heights.

"Uhm…I was just showing her where the hair dryer was." Ryan gave her partner her most charming grin.

"Likely story," Jamie sniffed, but her smile betrayed her. "Good thing I'm not the jealous type."

"I thank God for that every day." She got onto the bed and snuggled up next to Jamie. "I have a tendency to get myself into some pretty incriminating positions."

"I'd like to get you into a certain position right now." Jamie dropped a section of orange into her mouth. "You revved my motor so high last night that it's still in the red zone."

"Mmm…mine, too," Ryan purred. "Let's help these two figure this out and head right back to bed. I hated having to be quiet last night so Conor didn't hear us."

"Better us than Mia and Jordan. If he'd heard them howling like they usually do, he might have stabbed them!"

"I've got to have another talk with the boy. He seems quite delusional."

Jamie tweaked her nose. "I think he's just like his sister. He's so unfamiliar with rejection that he doesn't know how to react."

"Hey, I've had a pretty serious rejection. Don't forget Sara."

"Oh, I didn't. How many since?" Jamie asked, eyes twinkling.

"I'm sure I would have had a few if I'd kept going. Maybe another by the time I was twenty-nine…thirty-nine. Somewhere around there." She grinned and hoisted herself up to place a soft, moist kiss on Jamie's lips. "Luckily, the only woman who ever mattered didn't reject me. I would have been a hundred times worse than Conor if that'd happened. Hell, I was worse than that when you were seeing Jack again. The boys were afraid to come downstairs."

"Well, that'll never happen again. We're stuck together like green and grass."

"Hey, that's my expression!"

"What's yours is mine." They kissed for a minute or two, keeping the fire that had burned so brightly the night before at a low burn. "Is Mia okay?" Jamie asked when she pulled away.

"Yeah, I think so. I don't think she's gonna be with us long, though. I can't see her staying 'til the end of the term. Neither patience nor delayed gratification are strong points of hers."

"You never know. Jordan might be able to work on her this week."

"Uh-huh. And I might be able to change into a couch potato this week…but I doubt it."

Mia felt marginally better after she'd showered, finally feeling well enough to have a discussion about their tactics. The foursome convened in Ryan's room, where Jordan laid out the situation. "What would you guys do if it were you?"

Jamie jumped right in. "I'd quit school and fly to Colorado this afternoon."

Mia high-fived her, knowing James would see things the proper way.

"But Ryan," she continued, "would stay in school and finish her degree. By the time she left for Colorado, she'd have a list of places to interview, and she'd have a job by the end of first afternoon. I'd be tasked with looking for an apartment for us, and she'd expect it to be ready by the time she got there. Oh, and she'd drive the car, rather than fly. Much cheaper."

"Must be a jock thing," Jordan said, giving Ryan a wry look. "That's just what I think we should do."

Ryan cocked her head. "Am I that transparent?"

"Yes," all three women answered.

"Fine," Ryan said, pouting a little. "But that doesn't mean that's what you guys should do."

"No, but maybe there's a middle ground." It was almost possible to see an idea form in Jordan's head. Her eyes lit up and she began to nod, as if she could see the logic in what she was about to say. "Why don't you see if you can explain the situation to your professors? They might let you skip classes if you showed up for the final. I know it'd suck to try to finish from Colorado, but wouldn't it be better than wasting half of the term?"

"Yeah, I guess," Mia grudgingly agreed. Jordan's logical approach was maddeningly hard to refute.

"Then you'll at least be making a more informed decision. If your professors won't cooperate, then you can look at the whole picture and decide what to do."

Logic was fine, but it had its limits. "If I can't get 'em to work with me, I'm leaving."

Jordan held her hands up in surrender. "That's fine. You can drive your car and be there for the weekend."

"This coming weekend?" Mia could feel her dark mood lifting. Just thinking about being in Colorado was like a balm to her aching head.

"Yeah, this coming weekend." Jordan leaned forward, resting on her hands and knees on the bed. She kissed Mia tenderly, then murmured, "I'd love to have you in my bed by next weekend."

"It's a deal! I'll see if I can work my magic on my profs. But one way or the other, I'm gonna be in Colorado Springs this weekend. You'd better rest up, girlfriend."

Chapter Two

Mia sat in the O'Flaherty living room, with Jamie at her side. "I hate being an adult."

Jamie put her arm around her and pulled her over for a long hug. "It does suck sometimes, doesn't it?"

"I made such a big deal about how mature I was when I was freaking out with my parents last night, and an hour later I was ready to go to Colorado with no plans at all. I hate it when they're right. I *am* just an immature jerk."

Hugging her tighter, Jamie placed a kiss on her temple. "You're not immature or a jerk. You were upset—justifiably upset last night. But as soon as you and Jordan talked it out, you decided to slow down and think it through. That was a very mature thing to do."

"I only did it because Jordy talked me into it," Mia admitted. "That shouldn't count."

"Sure it should. If you were immature, you'd stick to your guns no matter what. Don't cut yourself down. You don't deserve it."

Mia gave her a half-hearted smile. "I'm just pissy today. I can't bear to have my Jordy leave me."

"I know. I really do. I'd be a mess if we were in your shoes." Jamie checked her watch. "You guys had better get going. It's one thirty."

"Damn," Mia sighed. She got up and saw Ryan and Jordan standing in the corner, speaking quietly. "What do you think they talk about when they're alone?"

"I think they have their own little jock way of saying goodbye. I'm sure we'll never know."

Ryan leaned against the wall, deep in thought. "I don't know. I guess we could have improved if one of us had been a middle-blocker last year, but I still think having a dominant pair of outside hitters is the way to go."

"I did, too. But seeing what kind of damage we're doing with our middle-blocker cheating on the weak-side has convinced me that we could've done better against schools with a big girl in the middle."

Ryan caught sight of their partners getting up. "Time to go."

Jordan wrapped her arm around Ryan's neck, getting her in a surprisingly good headlock. She roughly pushed and pulled her in various directions, with Ryan laughing as she allowed herself to be manhandled. Jordan thunked her head like a cantaloupe, then let go.

Ryan stood up and pushed her hair out of her eyes before bending over, grabbing Jordan by the knees, and sweeping her off her feet. Then she stood, holding her in her arms. "How much do you weigh?"

"Not enough," Mia said as she and Jamie walked into the room. "She's skin and bones."

"Put me down!"

Ryan placed a loud, wet kiss on her cheek then deposited her onto the floor. "Don't they feed you?"

"Yes, they feed me," Jordan looked embarrassed to have been picked up like a child. "About six people tell me what and when to eat. I feel like a lab rat."

"Tell 'em to finish their studies before the rat dies of malnutrition."

"I'm fine. The point is to be in peak shape in September, not now. They pay a lot of people to think for us. Don't try to upset the system." She was smiling, but it was clear that there was an edge to her comments.

"I'm sure they know what they're doing." Ryan clapped her on the back. "Maybe they're trying to make you into a stealth outside-hitter. You'll be so thin your opponents won't even see you."

"I wish my teammates didn't have to see me tonight, but I've gotta go. Thanks for everything." She opened her arms and Jamie nestled in for a hug. Jordan kept her arm around Jamie, and the foursome walked to the front door. Ryan squeezed her shoulder, then ruffled her hair a little. "You two take care of yourselves."

"We will," Jamie said. When she moved away from Jordan, Ryan slipped an arm around her waist. They leaned against each other, watching Jordan and Mia walk down the open staircase, with Duffy escorting them to the sidewalk.

"C'mon back, Duff," Ryan called out, and the obedient pup trotted back up and sat at her feet, waiting for a head-scratch.

"Yes, you're a good boy." Sighing, she closed the door, already feeling out-of-sorts at having Jordan go. She made for the loveseat, stretching out as well as she could.

Jamie leaned against the front door, looking pensive and a little down. "I'm worried about them."

"Yeah, me too." She arched her back and let her head dangle over the arm of the sofa for a moment. "I hate to see Mia act so impulsively, but I can understand wanting to get outta town after the way her parents treated her."

Jamie stuck her hands in her pockets and rocked back and forth for a moment. "I know her parents, and they love her as much as your father loves you."

Ryan looked up, surprised.

"I know it sounds like they were total assholes, but they're not. She and her mom yell at each other, but it always blows over quickly. It'll be a big mistake if she doesn't try to work things out with them before she leaves."

"But you said you'd leave today if you were her."

"Yeah, I'd want to, but I'm not sure I really would. I'm afraid she's really gonna damage her relationship with her mom, and her mom means an awful lot to her."

"But so does Jordan."

"Of course she does," Jamie agreed. "But what's she gonna do in Colorado? Jordan's busy all day. Mia doesn't know anyone there. You know how social she is. Imagine her being alone all the time."

"Damn, it's hard raising a family." Ryan chuckled at her own joke.

Jamie laughed as she crossed the room. "It sure is. I'm beat."

"Long morning."

Jamie sat on her thighs, making Ryan giggle. "I think we need a long nap and..." She ran her hand from Ryan's knee to her thigh, resting right on the seam of her sweats. "A little more lovin.'"

Ryan pumped her hips, a happy grin on her face. "Sounds good." Jamie got up and held out a hand to help her partner to her feet. "But I promised Tommy we'd watch the baby this afternoon."

"What? When did you do that?"

"Yesterday…I think. I'm not sure. He and Annie wanna go look for a new apartment." She returned her partner's look. "Why? Don't you wanna see Caitlin?"

"Well, sure, I always want to see her, but I thought we could have some down time today. I'm kinda beat."

"Oh." She hated it when they weren't on the same page. From the look on Jamie's face, they weren't in the same book. "I could watch her by myself."

"I wanna chill with you." Jamie put her hands on Ryan's shoulders and looked into her eyes. You didn't need to be very perceptive to see how disappointed she was. "I wanted to spend the rest of the afternoon just napping and making love."

Ryan felt a little sick. How did she get into fixes like this? "I guess I could cancel…but it's a little late for that."

Jamie shook her head. "It's fine." She patted Ryan's waist. "No big deal. Let me get my phone and put my shoes on."

"You sure? 'Cause I could cancel." She would rather have slapped herself, but if Jamie really wanted her to…

"No, it's fine. But tell me when you make commitments like this. I can adjust my expectations."

"I'll try. I just don't think sometimes."

"Oh, you think all the time. You just don't always think of yourself first. Your default answer to any request is 'yes.'"

They'd been at the Driscoll house for a few minutes, and Ryan was already on her knees with Caitlin, chasing her through the small house. Jamie took the opportunity to talk with Annie and Tommy. "Got any houses in particular that you're looking at today?"

"We can't afford a house if we're gonna stay close," Annie said. "We're trying to find a two-bedroom apartment that we can afford."

"But Caitlin loves her little back yard."

"I know she does. But we'll really be strapped if we stay here. The rent went up three hundred a month. Adding thirty-six hundred dollars a year to our budget is a big bite for us."

"Damn." Jamie looked around the tiny house. "They've got some nerve."

"They sure do," Tommy agreed. "All of my friends in the department are moving way, way out so they can have a decent-sized house, but if we did that we'd have to put Cait in daycare."

"And your mother would kill you."

Annie nodded. "So would mine. My mom threw a fit when I said we might try the Mission. Everybody wants us to stay in Noe, and so do we, but it's getting harder and harder to do."

"Niall says there are still some bargains in the Mission," Jamie said. "But they're all fixer-uppers."

Ryan looked up from her game. "Hey, why don't you guys buy the first house that the cousins are gonna fix up?"

Tommy shook his head. "They wanna make money. I don't blame 'em, but it'll be out of our price range when they're finished."

"Aren't you gonna help with the project?" Jamie asked.

"Nah. I would if we didn't have Caitlin, but I can't be working on a house every weekend I have off." He laughed, showing a charming smile. "I say that like it's my decision, but the truth is that Annie won't let me."

She bumped him with her hip. "Caitlin needs to have time with her daddy. That's more important than having a nicer place to live."

"I agree completely." Jamie reminded herself that it was easy to agree with the sentiment, even if she couldn't be sure she would have made the same choice. Having never had to worry about money put you in a different position. One she was sure none of the O'Flahertys would ever truly understand.

Three hours later, Jamie sat in the little living room, idly reading the Sunday paper while Ryan lay on her back on the floor with Caitlin sprawled over her body. They were both sound asleep, and Jamie was tempted to join them. But she wasn't much for sleeping on the floor, and the sofa was too short for her to stretch out on. She considered going to nap on Annie and Tommy's bed, but that felt a little forward even for the casual O'Flaherty/Driscoll clan. Instead she fished one of her books out of her purse and tried to do a little reading to get a head-start on her class work for the week. Longingly, she looked at Cait's little body stretched out entirely upon Ryan's, deciding that if she was going to be a successful member of the family she'd have to learn how to drop off anywhere—anytime.

Chapter Three

At six forty-five that evening, Jamie sat in her car, revving the engine while she waited for her partner. Finally, Ryan jogged down the stairs of her family's home, uncharacteristically late. "What's up with you?" Jamie asked when Ryan was seated and buckled in.

Ryan gave her a slightly confused glance, then turned to stare out of the windshield. "Nothing's wrong. Why?"

"Well, you were poking around for a good fifteen minutes, then you didn't want to drive, even though your car's right across the street, then you took forever to come down. That's not like you."

Giving her a cherubic smile, Ryan said, "Maybe it's the real me I've kept hidden for all these months. From now on, I'm gonna be late and inconsiderate."

Apparently Ryan wasn't going to give her a direct answer. Since she didn't feel like playing detective, Jamie put the car into first gear. "Who should run this meeting?"

"Niall, I guess, even though Brendan would do a better job."

"Then why Niall?"

"Mmm..." Ryan made the soft, musical sound she made when she had an opinion, but wanted to edit it before she spoke. "I think the lads will be more amenable to listening to Niall than they would Bren."

Jamie snuck a quick glance at her lover, trying to read her face. The strong features were impassive, so she let it slide. "You've got something going on in that pretty head, but you're gonna make me work for it, aren't you?"

Ryan turned and smiled. That guileless, open expression always melted Jamie's heart. "I'm as blank as a slate. You always think I've got a million things going in my mind. But sometimes the only things going on up here," she tapped her temple, "are the basic requirements for existence. No thoughts…no feelings…just breathe in, pump blood, digest food."

Even with the amped up power of her smile, Jamie wasn't fooled. Ryan was indeed working something over in her head. But she shared her feelings only when she was good and ready, especially when they concerned her family.

"Forget I asked. But this deal is pretty complex, and if your cousins are on the ball, they'll have a lot of questions."

"I've never claimed that my cousins were on the ball." She laughed, then leaned back against her seat and passively observed the city while the Boxster worked its way to the Sunset District.

When everyone was settled, Niall took a swig of his beer and tried to explain the details of the plan Jamie had come up with. Brendan and Maggie had worked on the raw idea, trying to make it as simple as possible. But as Niall talked, it didn't seem simple after all.

Ryan was sitting on the floor in front of Jamie and fidgeting so badly that Jamie wanted to pinch her. But the only time Ryan opened her mouth was to suck on her beer like a baby bottle.

When everyone was thoroughly confused, Jamie couldn't stand it any longer, and stepped in. "If I can say a few things?" She was surprised to find herself feeling tentative. All eyes turned to her, and she looked at her notes. "This is really simple, guys. We form our own company to buy distressed homes, fix 'em up, and sell 'em. Niall will make two hundred thousand dollars from the sale of this place, and he's agreed to use that money as the seed money for all of the houses we buy. So all we have to do is take out construction loans to pay for materials. When the place is finished, we sell it, use the two hundred thousand as another down payment, and use the profit to pay for materials on the next house. By the time we've done a few houses, we should have enough money to start distributing income."

"But how do we split up the money?" Donal asked.

"That's what we have to agree on tonight," Jamie said. "Since everyone has already agreed on the idea, we just have to hammer out the details. The big one is how to pay out profits."

Declan spoke up. "I didn't understand the stuff Brendan gave us. It didn't make sense at all."

"Yeah," Padraig chimed in. "Why are the girls and Brendan not getting paid? Aren't you all part of this? And why does Rory only get a half share?"

Jamie shot a look at her partner, but Ryan didn't come to her rescue. She was looking at her with the same blank stare that nearly everyone else in the room had. Jamie could see that Brendan wanted to say something, but he didn't speak either, leaving her to carry the ball. "Well, we're in school and both doing our sports until June. Then we're getting married and going on a honeymoon."

"That's the last thing you two need," Kevin mumbled, just loud enough to be heard. "You've been on a honeymoon since you met."

All of the boys laughed at that, and Jamie tried not to blush. "True. But we're taking one anyway. So we won't be able to help until fall. We thought we'd meet again in September and see how things stand. We'll help out before then, but I don't think it'll be very often."

Now Colm got involved. "But if you work, you should get paid."

"I helped you work on Niall's kitchen," Jamie reminded him. "Would you have been willing to give me half of your pay for that day?"

"Sure," he said, always gallant.

"Well, that's because you're generous."

"That's because he thinks you're fine," someone from the back of the room said.

Ryan got to her knees and scowled in the direction of the comment, making the boys laugh even harder.

"Anyway," Jamie raised her voice, trying once again not to blush. "We're not skilled in any of these jobs. We like to hang out and help a little, but we're not even good enough to be day laborers."

"You would be if you kept at it," Colm said. "And Ryan's plenty good enough to be paid a wage."

Ryan finally broke her silence. "There's a big difference between lending a hand once in a while and being part of the team. If we drop by to have lunch and drink a few beers, that's one thing. If we commit to giving up our nights and weekends, that's quite another. We're still at the beer and lunch point—so it's not fair to pay us."

"And I'm gone for half the year," Rory said. "So I should only get a half share."

"Why couldn't you work full-time for half the year?" Dermot asked. "What else have you got to do?"

"Well, nothing during the day, but it'd have to be an eight to four kinda thing, since I play a lot of gigs at night."

Dermot was insistent. "You should get a full share. S'only right."

Rory nodded. "Okay. You fellas can make sure I'm pulling my weight."

"None of that!" Frank's deep voice carried over the crowd. "Nobody keeps track of nobody else! You're in or you're out. And if you're in, you keep an eye on yourself, nobody else."

His proclamation was met with heads nodding and mumbled agreement.

Jamie smiled, thinking back to Ryan's prediction that the cousins would behave in just such a manner. "Okay, so everyone who wants to commit his weekends and some nights to the project gets a full share. That makes it very, very simple."

"Why not you, Brendan?" Kevin asked.

"I could use the money, but I can't commit to evenings. I have to work late too often."

"And I'm in charge of him on the weekends," Maggie said, wrapping her arm around his neck. "He's off limits."

"Women ruin everything." Niall gave Maggie a wink.

"How would you know, when you've never had one?" another man from the back of the room called out.

Niall pointed. "I know you're back there, Kieran. You're the only one I can't see, you moron."

Kieran's dark head popped up from behind Frank. "Just trying to keep the party lively."

"Are we finished?" Niall looked to Jamie for confirmation.

Jamie was quite sure that almost nothing had been settled, but she knew that was the O'Flaherty way.

Frank piped up again. "Is everything in these papers, Bren?"

"Yeah. Maggie and I worked on it together to make it as straightforward as possible. We'll file the papers to get a DBA and all of the other details. But you should all read and understand everything before you sign."

"You wrote it. That's good enough for me." Frank got up, took the bunch of papers from the dining room table, signed his name every place indicated, then handed the pen to the next cousin in line.

Jamie watched, amazed that no one questioned anything. It seemed they were significantly more concerned with taking advantage of each other than they were of being taken advantage of.

Ryan looked up at her and smiled. "This bunch would be a great target for a swindler, wouldn't they?"

Despite her words, Jamie could see the pride in her eyes. She knew that Ryan valued harmony much more than keen business sense.

As they were getting ready to leave, Maggie pulled Jamie aside. "I saw the comments your father made about prohibiting gay marriage." She paused, looking a little unsure of herself. Even though Maggie had been at all of the recent family gatherings, she and Jamie hadn't had any alone time to speak of, and it was clear she was unsure of how frank she could be.

Jamie squeezed her arm and gave her a warm smile. "My father is..." She trailed off, shaking her head. "He's a series of contradictions. I never know what he'll say next."

"I can only imagine being the daughter of a politician is hard for you. If you ever want to talk about anything..."

"Thanks. It is hard sometimes, and it's probably worse for me than some since I didn't grow up around politics. I'm not used to it."

"I don't know how you get used to your father's saying you don't have the right to marry. That's gotta hurt, no matter who you are."

"It does. And thanks for saying something to me about it. It's always nice to know that people understand."

Maggie gave her a hug. "We do."

Jamie smiled at her, charmed that she was using the plural pronoun to refer to herself and Brendan. Maybe there would be two O'Flaherty family weddings in the offing.

When they got into the Boxster, Jamie asked, "Wanna go get your car before we head back to Berkeley?"

"Nah. I don't need it this week. Besides, I'd rather go home with you."

"Sure you don't wanna drive? I'm not used to turning to my right to look at you. I feel like I'm upside down."

"It'll be good practice." Ryan rolled her seat back and let out a sigh. "Chauffeur me."

"Will do." Jamie put the key into the ignition and started the car. Checking the traffic, she pulled out and headed for home. "I had a little chat with Maggie right before we left."

"I saw you talking. I know where you are every minute, so don't get any ideas."

Laughing, Jamie said, "How can I get tired of you when I hardly ever see you?"

"You see me now." She put her hand on Jamie's thigh and gave it a good scratch. "What's up with Maggie?"

"Nothing. She just wanted to empathize about my dad. Said she figured it must be hard for me to have him be such a jerk."

Ryan's eyebrows shot up. "She said that?"

"No, of course not. That was the message—not the words."

"Whew! We like to be honest, but that's a little too honest."

Jamie snatched a quick look at Ryan's face. "He is a jerk, isn't he?"

Ryan turned and met her gaze, holding it for a moment. "Sometimes he does some pretty insensitive things. He usually thinks he's right, even when he isn't, and he can be single-minded. But I don't think he's a jerk."

"Sounds like you're describing a jerk."

"Not really. In my book, a jerk is someone who hurts people and doesn't care. Cassie's a jerk. Your dad does some dumb things, but I think he feels bad when he sees that he's hurt people."

"But that doesn't stop him from doing the next dumb thing."

"I agree. He doesn't seem to learn from his mistakes."

"So he can hurt me and hurt you and hurt my mom, and we all just have to forgive him, huh?"

Ryan fidgeted in her seat, clearly not about to put her position out there. "You have to make that decision for yourself, Jamers. It's a tough one."

"I have to set some limits. I can't let him come to our wedding if he's gonna parrot the administration's stupid position on gay marriage. I just can't." Sighing, she said, "Aren't the Democrats supposed to be for expanding civil rights?"

"Sure. As long as they don't lose any votes by taking that position. It's all politics—not principles."

"It just slays me that Clinton went out of his way to support a federal law to prohibit us from ever having our marriage recognized. The federal government will stomp all over states' rights by doing that. And my stupid father trots right along—like a lap dog."

Ryan didn't say anything. She just let her hand rest on Jamie's leg, silently showing her support.

The couple walked into their house just as the phone started to ring. Ryan looked at the caller I.D. "I don't recognize the name."

They waited to hear a voice on the answering machine announce, "Hi, I'm trying to reach Jamie Evans. This is William Fisher from the Gay, Lesbian, Bi-sexual, Transgendered and Queer Defenders Against Defamation."

Giving Ryan a puzzled look, Jamie picked up. "Hi, this is Jamie."

"Hi, Jamie, as I said, this is Will Fisher from GLBTQDAD."

"Uh-huh."

"We'd like to make you a proposal."

"A proposal? To me?"

"That's right." He sounded much like the people who called to beg for contributions from one of the local charities she gave to. "Even though we're a national organization, we realize that state propositions can have a significant impact on the entire country. We think that the defeat of Proposition 22 has to be our most important fight right now."

"Uhm…Will? I already donated to the fund for the state effort to defeat the proposition, and it's a little late to—"

"We're not looking for money," he interrupted. "We'd like you to write an opinion piece concerning your feelings on the proposition and the administration's support for 'don't ask, don't tell' as well as the Defense of Marriage Act."

She let his message sink in, then gave a puzzled-looking Ryan a wry smile. "Are you calling all of the gay people in California to offer them this opportunity? Just up to 'E' now?"

He laughed nervously. "No, you're the only person we've called. Your father's comments sparked the idea. I don't know you personally, but I can't imagine that you're very happy with his position."

Ignoring his statement, she said, "I'm not the politician in the family. And if you've paid much attention in the last few months, you would've noticed that I don't like to make my private life public."

"I realize that, Jamie, really, I do. Actually, your name came up in discussions we had in January, but we decided not to even ask then. It's just that your father's comments are going to hang out there if we don't respond to them. We have a hell of a time getting coverage in the mainstream press, but if you were to write the article…"

"The legitimate press would print it because of my celebrity," she finished wearily. "Being car-jacked and almost murdered makes you print-worthy."

"That's about it. Look, I know this is asking a lot of you, especially after all you've been through this year, but if there's any part of you that thinks making a public reply to your father is important—here's your chance. We have sources at the *Chronicle,* and they're confident they can get the article on the opinion page on Monday. We'll help you write the piece if you want, or you can take a stab at it yourself. Just give the idea some thought, will you?"

"Okay, I will. Give me your number and I'll call you tomorrow."

He did as she asked, and Jamie hung up, giving Ryan an aggrieved look. "Some days I wish my father and your father could change jobs."

After discussing Will's proposal with Ryan, Jamie decided that she needed to think the issue through on her own. "I'm going to have to live with this no matter which way I go, so I need to let this settle for a bit. Let's go to bed and forget the whole thing, okay?"

"Works for me." Ryan scratched her head and gave her partner an intentionally befuddled look. "What thing?"

Chapter Four

On Monday morning, Mia was up early, determined to find a way to get to Colorado before the week was up. She'd had her cell phone turned off all weekend, and when she'd returned to Berkeley there had been at least a dozen messages from her parents. She'd already made the decision not to speak to them until her plans were set. Punishing them for the way they'd treated her was only a secondary motivation for the snub. Even though she was confident that she was doing the right thing, this decision was a major turning point in her life. Their disapproval could easily make her waver, and she was intent on taking that power away from them.

Her mind had been racing all night long, and though she'd gotten very little sleep, her energy hadn't flagged. She'd used her sleepless hours well, coming up with a number of plans; reworking some, scrapping others. She had a few ideas that she wanted to try out, and her first class was the perfect place to start.

Leaving home early, she was the first to reach her classroom. She stood outside and made a list of everyone she knew by name. Nineteen names were on her list by the time the grad assistant arrived to begin the lecture. *That had to be enough people.* During the class, Mia wrote out requests to each of the students she thought would cooperate, asking if they'd share their notes with her for a specific week. There were eight weeks to cover, and she figured there was a good chance many would flake out on her, so she asked two people to cover each week—in hopes that one of the two would not only agree, but would actually attend the class and take notes.

Just before the class was scheduled to end, Mia snuck out the back door and waited. Her first victim walked out right after her, and she put on her most engaging smile. "Hey, Steve!"

"Hi," the young man said. "What's goin' on?"

"I'm not gonna be in town next week. Would you take notes for me?"

"Uhm…sure. Okay."

She handed him five dollars and an envelope that was pre-stamped with Jordan's address. "Here's some money to pay for copying them and an envelope so you can send 'em to me."

He looked surprised. "Send 'em?"

"Yeah. I'm gonna be in Colorado."

"Can't I just give 'em to you when you get back?"

"Well, yeah, you could." She saw another person on her list and tried to cut it short. "But I don't wanna fall behind. Can I have your e-mail address and cell phone number?"

He gave her a smile that was a little on the flirtatious side. "Sure." She dutifully wrote down his information, then kissed him on the cheek and ran to the next person, performing this ritual until her calendar was full.

She was breathless when she'd finished, but several people had offered to share notes for the whole term if she needed them. Since this subset seemed most willing to go out of their way, she arranged to call each of them every week to obtain class assignments and get information about the final exam. *At least one of them would know what they were talking about—probably.* The good news was that the grad student who ran the class didn't seem to care if people showed up or not, and class participation wasn't part of the grade. Being in Colorado wouldn't hurt a bit.

Her well-laid plans went off without a hitch for her next two classes, and she called Jordan with the good news, unable to go more than a few hours without hearing her voice.

"Being friendly has really paid off for you," Jordan teased. "I didn't know more than one or two people in any of my classes."

"It always pays to be friendly. If I hadn't been friendly with you, we wouldn't be together now, and God knows I'm glad we are."

"I'm glad too, babe. Our lunch break's just about over. I'll call you when we're through for the day, okay?"

"Okay, sweetheart. Don't let 'em work you too hard. You're gonna need your strength when I get there this weekend."

"If that's what you decide to do," Jordan added, ever the realist.

"You can believe me when you see me. Talk to you later, baby."

Mia's next class was the one she'd been dreading, and as the professor began the class discussion, she realized she'd probably be lucky to even be able to arrange for an incomplete.

The prof was young, and he seemed to believe that class discussion was the most important part of the learning experience. He allowed only two misses. Mia had only missed one so far, even attending when she'd really been sick so she could use her last cut for something fun.

Getting class notes wasn't going to be very helpful or get her around the attendance requirement, so when class ended, she took in a breath and approached the man. "Hi, Professor Norris."

"Hello," he said, giving her a rather blank look. "What's up?"

Even though Mia was gregarious and exuberant in most settings, she kept a low profile in most classes. She'd learned long ago that the best way to get through college was to be neither seen nor heard.

"Something very unexpected has come up, and I'm going to be in Colorado for the rest of the term. Is there any way that I can complete the class if I'm not able to attend?"

Suddenly, Mia had his full attention. "Not attend? How can you learn the material if you don't share your thoughts with your classmates? The free flow of ideas is what cements the concepts in your mind..." He trailed off, possibly searching for her name, which he obviously didn't know.

Nobody cements the concepts anyplace. We just tack 'em up at the last minute so we can stick 'em in a blue book during the final and never think of 'em again. But she was sure he wouldn't agree with her philosophy on higher education, so she tried another tack.

"I'd be happy to write a term paper, do independent research...anything. I've learned a lot so far, and I can show you how well I know the subject in another way."

"That's the problem. You can show me what you get out of the reading, but you can't hone your ideas without the input you get from me and the rest of the class. I'm afraid you wouldn't have a complete grasp of the subject, and I can't go along with that."

She looked at him for a minute, trying to determine any exploitable weakness she could mine. But it was clear he really believed in what he was saying. His beliefs were odd, but obviously strongly held. "Okay, is there any chance of getting an incomplete? Then I'd just have to sit in for eight weeks next term."

"No," he said, shaking his head. "That won't work. Each class is different, and part of the experience is seeing how ideas develop over the term. I'm afraid you'll have to withdraw."

"No other options, huh?" She wasn't going to flirt with him, mainly because of Jordan, but also because she could see it wouldn't work.

He looked genuinely regretful. "No, I'm afraid not."

"Well, I'm not certain I'm going, but if I do, I'll withdraw. You'll get a note from the registrar."

"I hope you're able to stay… Uhm, I'm sorry, but what was your name?"

"Jessica Alba," she said, never one to give her real name when a pseudonym would do.

Jamie was at home later that morning, getting ready for her afternoon classes. She answered the ringing phone, concerned to hear her mother's voice—sounding horribly upset. "Did you read the paper today?"

Thinking back a few hours, she replied, "Uhm, yes, I read the *New York Times* and the *Wall Street Journal*. Why? What's wrong?"

Catherine didn't speak immediately. The few seconds she waited had Jamie's heart beating fast with anxiety. "The *Chronicle* had a gossipy little blurb about my divorce. I'm so sorry to pull you into the spotlight again, honey, but they mentioned your name too. Then, just a few minutes ago, I had the television on, and they reported on it. They're talking about my divorce, but they had to include a picture of you and Ryan."

She sounded so anxious and distressed that Jamie immediately tried to soothe her. "It'll be okay. This kind of thing doesn't last long. It'll blow over by tomorrow. Dad's only famous enough to hold the public's attention for a few hours. You'll be fairly anonymous really quickly."

"Oh, I'm not upset about having my name mentioned. I'm upset because they're dragging you two into the whole mess."

"Mom, don't be silly. It doesn't bother us to have our names mentioned; we just don't want people chasing us. That hasn't happened to you, has it?"

"No, not at all. I just don't want you to be harassed any longer."

Jamie soothed her. "We're fine. Once you've been the top gossip story in the country for a few weeks, you really do get used to it. Which brings me to the reason I was going to call you."

"I don't like the sound of that. What's wrong?"

"I might be jumping back into the limelight, and I wanted to talk to you a bit before I made up my mind."

"You might voluntarily jump back in?"

"Yeah. Hard to believe, right?"

"So far, definitely."

Jamie talked about the phone call, and her instincts about writing the article. When she finished, Catherine asked, "Do you want advice, or are you just letting me know?"

Even though her mom couldn't see her, Jamie smiled. "That's such a perfect way to respond. When you put it that way, I guess I just wanted to let you know that I'm thinking about doing it. If you have any major objections I'm glad to listen to them, but if not, I'd like to make up my own mind."

"Go right ahead. This is between you and your father."

"And my community. I hate to be put into the role of representing the gay people of California, but I probably have more weight with the media than anyone else right now. I hate that, but I can't ignore it."

"I understand that, dear, but you don't have to let your notoriety run your life. You should only do this if you want to, not because other people want you to."

"It's hard to ignore the pressure. Speaking of communities, how has yours reacted to the news of your divorce? Have you heard from many people?"

"My phone has been ringing all day with condolence calls." She laughed mirthlessly. "Most of them merely want me to speak badly of your father, which of course I won't."

"They don't know you very well, do they?" Jamie smiled as she thought of how much she'd learned about her mother in the past year, and how nearly every bit of information she's gleaned had increased her love and respect.

Now Catherine's laugh sounded genuine. "I suppose that's a good point. I don't really want that type of person in my life, anyway. Thanks for reminding me of that."

"That's my job."

That afternoon, Mia shared the results of her struggles with Jamie. "It was kinda humbling to find a teacher I couldn't have my way with." She was sitting at the kitchen table with her head resting on her stacked fists. Her normally bright eyes were a little dull, and she'd been uncharacteristically listless since she'd gotten home.

"If you could charm everyone in the world, that would make life way too easy. Isn't it more fun when you have to work for it?"

"No! This is a hell of a time to come up against a teacher who actually cares if I learn the subject. Why'd I have to take a class from a newbie?" She frowned, clearly thinking. "I remember. This was the only class that fit my schedule, didn't require any papers, and just had a take home exam at the end of the semester." She sat up and banged on the table with her hand. "This woulda been so perfect!"

"Well, at least you can get out of your other classes. When you come back to Cal, you'll only have to take one class."

Mia nodded glumly. "You can bet your ass it's gonna be from someone who's about to retire."

While Ryan was at softball practice, Jamie went outside to think. She sat in a chair in the quiet, cool yard, trying to sort through all of the ramifications that writing the article could have. It came down to the damage it would do to her relationship with her father, versus the good it could do for her community. In this instance, she decided that her community needed a boost—even at the cost of more dissension.

On a whim, she called Ryan, surprised to have her answer. "Can you talk?"

"Seems like it. What's up?"

"I've got to do the article. I don't want to, but I have to."

"I understand. Really, I do."

"I've got to call my father right now." Her stomach was already in knots, and the thought of talking to her father just made it worse. "I'm not going to have a minute's peace until I get it over with."

"Wanna wait for me? I can't be home until seven, but I'd love to be able to hold your hand while you do it."

"Thanks, honey, but I have to get it over with."

"I'm just shagging balls in the outfield. I could sneak away, and no one would miss me."

Jamie smiled at the image of her partner sneaking away from the field, running across town, listening to a phone call and running back. "That's okay, honey. You go shag. I'll see you when you get home."

"I love you," Ryan said. "I respect you, too."

Jamie could feel herself starting to choke up, and she whispered, "Bye."

She walked up the stairs, head bowed. Moments later, a rush of anxiety mixed with sadness hit her when her father answered his cell phone. "Hi, Daddy."

"Hi, honey," he said quietly. "I'm at a benefit dinner. Can I call you later?"

"Uhm…sure. I'll be here."

She heard rustling and he whispered, "Hang on." A minute passed, and he said, "I stepped outside. You don't sound like yourself. What's wrong?"

"I…have something pretty serious to talk to you about, but it's not urgent or anything. I just wanted to—"

"I always have time for you, Cupcake. I'm not the guest of honor or anything here. They'll just think I'm conducting state business. Now, what's the matter?"

They hadn't spoken since their fight over his comments to the *San Francisco Chronicle* revealing that he supported both "don't ask, don't tell" and the Defense of Marriage Act. The telephone line seemed to buzz with the tension that lingered between them.

Jamie took a breath. "I'm sure you realize how upset I was over your comments in the paper."

"You've made your feelings very clear. And I hope I was clear about how sorry I was that I upset you."

"You were. But sometimes you have to do what you think is right—even when it hurts someone you love."

He paused before he spoke, and when he did it sounded like he was going to cry. "You have no idea how it makes me feel to have you realize that's true. Just because I vote a certain way or support a certain policy doesn't mean that I love you any less. I'm very proud of you, and I'm very pleased to see that you're creating a good life with Ryan. I can see how happy you are, honey, and I swear that's all I've ever wanted for you."

"I know that, Dad. I hope you know that I love you, too."

"I do. I truly do."

"If that's true, you'll understand that what I'm about to do is out of principle, not anger."

"What are you talking about?" She could hear the trepidation in his voice.

"Some representatives of a major gay and lesbian political action committee have asked me to write an opinion piece about Prop 22.

Specifically, on my feelings about the administration's two-faced approach to gay rights."

"It's not two-faced!"

She let that sit out there for a moment. "They've made some wimpy comments against Prop 22. Lovely. So they're against California prohibiting gay marriage. But they proposed the law forbidding the federal government from recognizing same sex marriages. That's bullshit."

"No, it's not. States have full autonomy to allow gay marriage. But the federal government shouldn't be required to recognize them. They just shouldn't."

"Why don't you say that more emphatically? You've got no logical argument for that ridiculous position; go with bluster."

"I have plenty of arguments—"

She cut him off. "I've agreed to do it, Dad, and it's going to be published in the *Chronicle* next Monday."

She heard the breath he exhaled, and waited expectantly for him to reply.

His voice was weary and thin when he responded. "How can you say you're not just trying to get back at me?"

"Because I'm not," Jamie said emphatically. "Not at all. I'll admit to being really angry, and at first, I thought about doing it because I was so furious with you. But I've thought about it a lot, and realize this is something I have to do. I won't get many chances to reach people in this way, and I have to seize the opportunity."

"Will you at least send me a copy of the article so my staff can prepare a response? I'd like to minimize my embarrassment as much as possible."

She wished she could think of something to say that would make him feel better but knew that she couldn't. "I'll send it to your home e-mail account. I'd really appreciate it if you could call me after you've looked at it. I'm willing to make changes if there's anything you find objectionable."

"All right. I'll call you after I read it." He switched off without saying goodbye, leaving her feeling even worse than she had before she'd called.

Arriving home after softball practice, Ryan went upstairs and found her partner lying on the bed, staring at the ceiling with a vacant look in her eyes. "How'd it go?"

"It went briefly. I told him, he asked if I'd send it to him, then he said he'd call me after he read it." She turned to her partner. "He was really hurt."

"Makes sense," Ryan nodded. "Maybe he'll feel better when he actually reads it."

"Maybe. Maybe not. Mind if I take a nap?"

"No, of course not." She ruffled her fingers through the soft blonde hair. "Do you feel like going out to dinner, or would you rather stay close to home?"

"Carry-outs?"

"No problem. We'll just cocoon tonight."

"Okay. Thanks, honey."

"Want me to rub your head to help you sleep?"

"Nah. I'm fine. Go order dinner."

Ryan started to walk out of the room, but something held her back. Crossing back to the bed, she sat on the edge and placed her hand on Jamie's cheek. "It's gonna be all right. He'll be angry, but he'll get over it. This is politics, and he understands that."

"You sure?" she asked softly, obviously craving reassurance.

"I'm positive. I really am. He loves you, and he won't let this little thing change how he feels about you."

"Ryan?"

"Hmm?"

"Could I have that head rub? And maybe a cuddle?"

Ryan smiled, really glad she'd stuck around. "Absolutely. There's nothing I'd rather do."

While stroking her head, Ryan heard a heavy sigh leave her partner's body. That sigh was usually the last sound she made before she fell asleep.

"Go to sleep, sweetheart. You'll feel better when you wake."

Jamie snuggled tightly against Ryan's body. "No, I feel better when you hold me. That's the key."

"That makes two of us."

Chapter Five

Ryan had a short day on Tuesday and found herself with three hours between her last class and practice. There were a million things she could have done, but she started thinking about Proposition 22 in a way she hadn't done before. Something about the whole thing had been bugging her, and she wanted to get a few things straight in her mind. She made a call, set up an appointment, and raced across the Bay Bridge, considering while she drove what she wanted to get out of the impending discussion. By the time she arrived, she was resolved.

A short time later, she settled her long frame into a straight-backed wooden chair in Father Pender's small office. She'd spent too much time at her old parish priest's office in the past year, and being there again was unsettling. "Thanks for seeing me on such short notice," Ryan said. "I know how busy you are on Sundays, so I thought this would be a better time to talk."

"My pleasure, Siobhán," he said, then corrected himself. "I mean Ryan. I know it's what you prefer."

"It is, but as I've gotten older, I've come to like Siobhán again."

"I suppose I've always referred to you as Siobhán since that's what your father calls you," the priest said, looking down at his hands. "How is he?"

"He's good. Married life suits him."

"That's hardly a surprise. Some men are born to be good husbands and fathers. He's one of them."

"That he is. I hope I'm half as good a spouse. I don't have much time to work on my skills, because Jamie and I are going to have our union blessed in August."

As he often did, Father Pender just smiled at her and nodded politely—leaving her room to expound on the thought if she chose.

Having a different agenda item in mind, she didn't pursue it. Her face grew serious as she posed the question that had been on her mind since she'd heard the rumor. "Something's been troubling me, Father, and I wanted to see if you could shed some light on the issue for me."

"I will if I can. What is it?"

"I heard that the bishops in California have pledged several hundreds of thousands of dollars to support Proposition 22. Is that true?"

He leaned back in his chair, a pensive look on his face. Rocking slowly, he finally nodded. "Yes, it's true." He waited a moment, obviously waiting for a follow-up question, then spoke again when she merely stared at him. "The Church supports many propositions, and it's perfectly legal to do so. We're not supporting a political party here, so it's not a question of separation of church and state."

Puzzled by that strange bit of obfuscation, she said, "I don't give a damn about the legality of the donation. I'm sure the church knows what it can get away with. I'm questioning it, but not on legal grounds. I'm upset because my church is using funds that my family contributes to support a proposition that we strongly disagree with."

"I can see that it might bother you, but the Church has to take stands that it feels are supportive of the greater moral good—even if they're unpopular. Our stand opposing the death penalty and abortion has taken a heavy toll, causing us to lose many parishioners. But we have to do what we think is right. It's the only moral path."

"I don't disagree with that either, Father. I understand that the Church is in the business of taking moral stands. And I support that, even though the Church's position differs from mine on things like abortion. My complaint isn't so much the stand you're taking, even though I'm confident it's misguided at best and intentionally discriminatory at worst. My complaint is that you're using our contributions to join up with the far right. This proposition is nothing but posturing—and I think you know that. If my guess is right, I'd say it's probably Archbishop Levada who has pushed this proposition along, and that just sickens me."

The priest nodded soberly. "I don't know what to say. Archbishop Levada has some very strong views on the sanctity of marriage, and he believes that Proposition 22 will help strengthen the institution."

"I hope for his sake that he's not that stupid," Ryan snapped. "The guy is the leader of a city with more gay people than anywhere on earth, and he's more antagonistic to us than someone from the most remote backwoods village in the country."

"That's hardly fair," Father Pender said, scowling at her. "Calling him antagonistic to gay people is ridiculous. He loves all of God's children. Just because he believes your conduct is against God's will doesn't mean he's antagonistic to you as people...as Christians."

She could feel her cheeks getting hot and knew they were flushed. "He's not antagonistic, but he's willing to spend my money to deny me my civil...and I do mean civil...rights. This isn't about whether the Church will let me marry; this is a proposition to prevent the state from marrying me."

"That's true," he admitted. "But many issues cross into the secular." He leaned back in his chair and rocked slowly for a moment or two. "Look, I'll admit there's a large gap between your beliefs and his, but he comes by his beliefs from a position of prayer and contemplation. You can't fault a man for disagreeing with you."

"Of course I can!" She got to her feet and paced behind her chair, too agitated to remain still. "When he's making decisions that are not only offensive, but morally wrong, I most certainly can fault him." She stopped abruptly and gazed at the man, trying to remember how close they had all been for so many years. "Look, Father, I think it's obvious we're never going to see eye to eye on this. I just want to make a few points."

"Of course," he said calmly. "Why don't you sit down?"

"I think better when I move."

"I know that, Ryan, that's why I suggested it." He tried and failed to suppress a grin.

She smiled back begrudgingly, but kept moving, covering all of the available ground in two long strides, then turning to go in the opposite direction. "Here's the deal. I don't know of many groups that need the support of the Church more than gay people. So many of us are tossed away by our families, and because of that, we desperately need a place that accepts us and loves us unquestioningly. In my opinion, that should—no, that has to be the Church, if the Church has any intention of following in the footsteps of Jesus. But not only do you not welcome us, you go out of your way to discourage us from belonging. I know for a fact that you wouldn't be comfortable with my being a Eucharistic minister."

The accusation hung in the air for a moment before he answered. "No,

I wouldn't," he said quietly. "You're in open dissent with the Church, and it wouldn't send a good message to allow you to dispense Communion when it's common knowledge that you're a practicing lesbian."

"I've been practicing since I was seventeen," she said, making him flush. "I think I've got it right by now."

"There's no need to be snide."

"Yes, there is! You allow single people who live together to hand out Communion. Why is their sin less grievous than mine? What about all of the people with only one or two children? Are they all infertile? Of course not! They're using birth control, and everyone knows it. But that's okay. You're willing to ignore those sins. It's only homosexuality that rises to this level of censure." She stopped and gripped the back of her chair with her hands, her knuckles turning white from the pressure she applied. "You're singling out gay people for particular discrimination. This is an archdiocesan-wide practice, and I'm sick of it."

"I don't think we do that," he said quietly, his eyes locked upon hers. "It's not the fact that you're gay that's the problem. It's that you're so vocal about it. You introduce Jamie to everyone as your spouse, making it very clear that you're sexually intimate. You can't expect to act like that and then have me ignore it. Of course I know that people live with their boyfriends and girlfriends, but they don't make an issue of it. They're discreet," he insisted. "The entire point is your discretion…or lack of it. You act like having Jamie around is perfectly normal, but it's not. I've gotten more than one complaint about the way you two behave in church."

"I have nothing to be ashamed of." Ryan's voice was quiet but full of anger. "I love Jamie with all of my heart. I desire her sexually. I express my love for her in a carnal fashion, and I will continue to do so until I'm carted away by the anti-gay police!"

"Ryan, you're taking this to extremes," the priest said patiently.

"No, I'm not. If you're able to limit my participation in the Church—which is my birthright, as a matter of fact—you're, in essence, supporting other institutions in their efforts to push homosexuality back into the deepest, darkest closet imaginable. You can't discriminate and then say that you're opposed to discrimination. It's untenable!"

"I'll admit that this is a complicated issue and that there are many views, but I assure you that I welcome you at Mass. I welcome both you and Jamie. I wish you'd be more discreet, but even if you won't, I'll defend your right to attend Mass."

"Big of you," she snarled. "But you wouldn't bless our union."

"You know I'm not allowed to do that."

"You're boxing me into a corner. I want to have a relationship with an organized church, but the Catholic church is making it very, very difficult for me to stick with them. Jamie's grandfather is going to perform our commitment ceremony and I think it's time we considered joining his church. It hardly makes sense to belong here and go to the Episcopal church to bless us before God."

His head cocked quizzically. "Her grandfather is an Episcopal priest?"

"Yes." She leveled her gaze at him and said, "Jamie's an Episcopalian. She comes to church with me because I've been happy here, and because it's where the rest of the family goes. But we're going to have to think long and hard before we continue to financially support this parish. I just don't think I can participate in my own oppression." With that, she nodded her head once and left the room, leaving an obviously befuddled man behind her.

Pissed off and agitated, Ryan found herself automatically heading over to her Aunt Maeve's house. She knocked perfunctorily, then opened the door. "Anyone home?"

"Is that my Siobhán?" Maeve's soft, lyrical voice called out.

"Sure is," Ryan called back, smiling at the always-warm welcome her aunt had for her. "Am I disturbing anything?" She took off her jacket and hung it on the front door knob.

Maeve walked into the parlor and put her hands on her hips. "When will you believe that's not possible? A visit from you is preferable to anything I could have possibly been doing."

Ryan went to her and hugged her tight, feeling a little ungainly when she felt her aunt's much smaller and frailer body in her arms. "You say I throw the blarney around," she said, laughing. "You're not bad at it yourself."

"Every word is true. Now go say hello to your father. He's outside trying to make a vegetable garden out of that sorry excuse for a yard. I swear the Aran Islands are better suited to gardening."

"Oh, it can't be that bad."

"Yes, it is," Maeve insisted. "Thirty-odd years of the pounding of children's feet, and what seems like the remnants of a quarry. Your father says there isn't a wheelbarrow full of good soil in the whole patch."

"I'll go give him my expert opinion. He loves to be second-guessed."

Maeve laughed. "Oh, you know him well, sweetheart. Have fun." Ryan had only gone a few feet when Maeve asked, "Will you stay for dinner?"

"Thanks, but I can't. I have softball practice tonight. I just stopped by because I've been to see Father Pender."

Maeve's eyebrows rose. "Father Pender?"

Ryan made a dismissive gesture with her hand. "I had the crazy idea that I might be able to have a rational discussion with him about this ridiculous Proposition 22."

"Oh, dear. I'm so embarrassed about that whole affair. After Mass on Sunday, they tried to get us to take signs and put them in our yards. I thought your father was going to take the whole lot of them and rip them to shreds."

"Then we're probably in the same mood. Ignore any cursing you hear, okay?"

Maeve playfully put her hands over her ears. "Hear no evil."

Ryan stood on the stairs and watched her father work on a small patch of the tiny yard, hefting spades full of dirt into a wheelbarrow. "Trying to grow rocks?"

Martin turned, and his determined expression immediately grew into a wide smile. "There's my favorite girl! What brings you to the western part of the bay?"

She could feel her smile die. "I was visiting a former friend of yours."

He looked confused for a moment, then scowled. "What's your business with that blackguard?"

She put her hands into the pockets of her jeans, then rocked on her heels. "I was in a hurry to waste some time. Sometimes I think that reason and logic rule the world." She gave him an abashed smile and added, "They don't."

He wiped his brow, then took off his leather gloves and twitched his head towards the picnic table. "Take a load off, love, and tell me what happened."

She kissed him when he got near, smiling when her lips touched the fine dusting of earth on his cheek. Taking a seat, she said, "I went to talk to him about Prop 22." She shook her head in disgust. "I must have been delusional to think he'd see my point of view."

"He's an idiot," Martin said. "I don't know how he hid it for so long, but the man is a complete and utter fool."

She smiled, knowing that her father didn't have the ability to see many shades of gray. "He acted that way today. He wouldn't give an inch."

He looked at her for a moment, clearly puzzled. "Why waste your time, love?"

"I wanted to check something out. And even though I know he's not on my side, I knew he'd tell the truth."

Martin scowled again and scoffed, "You trust him more than I do. I wouldn't believe him if he told me it was raining during a monsoon."

"He's not that bad, Da. And I think he did tell me the truth. Not that it helped. Now I'm angrier than I was before."

"What now?" he asked, sounding angry himself.

"The archdiocese gave several hundred thousand dollars to support Prop 22." She braced herself, getting ready for the fireworks, but the blast didn't come. Her father was looking at her with a surprisingly calm expression on his face.

"We've got to leave," he said, and his tone indicated that the topic wasn't open to discussion. "I heard about a mostly Spanish parish in the Mission we might try. They have an English service, but it's with a Vietnamese priest, and no one can understand a word he says. So even if he's spouting the same malarkey that Pender is, we wouldn't know it."

Ryan looked at him for a moment, trying to determine if he was serious. "What's the point? If we have to find a Mass where we can't understand the sermon, we might as well quit altogether."

"Quit the Church?" He looked at her as if she'd grown another head. "We can't do that!"

She nodded, understanding his position without his having to utter a word. "Can we let it ride for a while?"

"Why should we?"

She tried not to look as pathetic as she felt. "I can't take a lot of change right now. Leaving St. Philip's would be a very big deal for me. I don't wanna upset my apple cart." She smiled. "I've just gotten all of the apples into the damned thing, and it's still hard to keep it level."

He got up from his side of the table and walked around to stand behind her. Without speaking, he began to rub her shoulders, applying his usual firm, deep pressure. She felt her body relax, and within a few moments, her neck felt rubbery. "I'm okay," she said to reassure him. "I just don't want to ask for trouble. I'm trying to keep things simple."

He kissed her head. "Simple it is. We won't talk about it again until you bring it up."

"That's a deal. I've gotta go soon. Do you think Aunt Maeve has any cookies lying around?"

"That's why I'm still here," he said, laughing when she nudged his stomach with her head.

Martin took off his dirty boots at the door, then wrapped his arms around his wife's waist and said, "It's teatime, love. Want me to start the boil?"

"That'd be lovely," she agreed. "I was just making some scones."

Ryan snuck her head around her aunt's shoulder. "What kind?"

Maeve reached behind her and swatted Ryan's butt with a wooden spoon. "If you had called to say you were coming, I would have made your favorite—chocolate potato cake. But since you're always a last-minute-lassie, you'll have to suffer with sultana."

"I love sultana scones," Ryan said, kissing her aunt's cheek. "But I love chocolate potato cake even more. I've got to start coming by for tea more often." She went to the refrigerator and took out some honey, jam and butter. "We never have tea. I'm gonna have to train Jamie better."

Martin laughed at her. "You know how to make a proper tea, my little princess. You don't want to have an English girl mucking up the whole process."

"She's not very English, Da. Her people were in America when our people were still making peat fires in thatched-roof houses."

"That's even worse. American tea is a travesty."

"I've just about finished the first batch," Maeve said.

She was cooking the scones on the stove top using a cast-iron pan, Ryan's favorite method. They were crisper and lighter than a baked scone, and her mouth was watering just imagining how good they'd taste.

Martin was in charge of the tea. "Irish Breakfast, assam or green pekoe?"

"Green tea?" Ryan asked, her brows lifting. "Since when do you drink green tea?"

"Even though it does taste a little like hay, we're not above branching out a bit," he replied smugly.

Maeve smiled at her niece. "And Doctor Terry told him green tea's good for him. You know how compliant he is."

Ryan gave her father a fond look. He was remarkably independent and usually scoffed at every health fad. But if his doctor told him something might be good for him, he adopted the habit at once. "I'll have the green," she said. "I drink espresso in the morning, but I like a nice cuppa green in the afternoon."

Martin started to make the pot, while Maeve gazed at Ryan. "So tell us what you're working on now, Siobhán. How's your independent study going?"

"Fine. I'm making progress, but it's a lot of work."

"Tell us what the topic is again, sweetheart," Martin asked.

Ryan made a face. She loved to talk about her work, but she knew that her family didn't have a clue what she was talking about. To avoid insulting their intelligence, she tried to give them a summary. "Well, it's pretty technical, but the bottom line is that I'm trying to use some physics principles to predict trends in the stock market."

Martin shot her a look. "Physics? Like gravity and things like that?"

Smiling, Ryan said, "Yeah, that kinda physics. Actually, it's a mix of physics and statistics and engineering and computer science, and of course, math."

"We know all about these things, don't we, darlin'?" Martin asked his wife, giving her a sweet smile.

"Oh, my, yes." She set the piping-hot scones on the table, laughing when Ryan brushed her hand aside to get at them. "Don't act like a hungry dog, dear. I can make more."

"You'd better. I'm weak with the hunger." She tossed the scone back and forth, letting it cool just enough to be spread with butter. "How about this? I can't really explain how I'm doing it, but here's what I want to do. The stock market has gotten so crazy that people are starting to doubt the analytic methods they've been using to predict trends. I mean, really unpredictable things are happening, and it looks like they'll continue. I want to try to find a model that might work even in a crazy market."

"What sorts of things are happening?" Maeve asked. "We know about the ridiculous amounts of money people are making from the Internet, but the details are over our heads. Give us an example."

Ryan took a bite of her scone, then went through her usual paroxysms of delight, making her aunt laugh. When she could contain herself, she continued. "Okay. There's a company you probably know called 3Com."

"The idiots who put their name on Candlestick Park," Martin said. "They'd change the name of the country if someone offered enough money."

"Right," Ryan said, trying to avoid that particular discussion. "Well, they make a product called Palm. That's the electronic organizer that Jamie uses."

"Ah, yes. She's always looking at a tiny little thing, trying to decide if she has the day free."

"Right. Well, 3Com is spinning Palm off, making it its own company."

"Why would they do that, dear?" Maeve asked, looking befuddled.

"That's not the important part. We can't get bogged down in details." Both Martin and Maeve nodded, waiting for her to continue. "Companies do things like that all of the time. But the funny part is that people expect Palm to be worth a lot more than 3Com was, even though Palm was only a part of the original company."

Martin stared at her for a minute. "I must not understand. It sounded like you said that 'a' plus 'b' equals 'x'. But 'a' minus 'b' is greater than 'x.'"

"That's exactly right," Ryan said, proud of her father for catching on so quickly.

"That's ridiculous. It's not just ridiculous, it's not possible."

"But it is," Ryan said, feeling her excitement rise. "That's why the market is so volatile. Things that seem implausible are happening every day!"

Martin took a bite of his scone, pausing to kiss his wife for making them. "That's not volatility, that's insanity. And it's not implausible, it's impossible."

"Well, maybe," Ryan said. "But that's what makes it exciting—you never know what'll happen next."

"Siobhán," he said patiently. "The world has been spinning for a long time. In all of that time there's never been a situation where something is worth more once it's been devalued. Just listen to the word, child! The only time you benefit from losing something is if that something is harming the host…like…a cancerous growth. Does losing Palm make 3Com a better company?"

"Well, no, not really."

"Does Palm benefit from not having 3Com associated with it? Is there some horrible 3Com scandal that makes Palm guilty by association?"

"No, no, not at all. That's why this is such a crazy market. That's the point, Da."

He pursed his lips and shook his head firmly. "It doesn't make sense. And when things don't make sense, you're well advised to stay away from them."

Ryan scratched her head. "Well, when you say it like that, it does sound kinda silly."

"The emperor has no clothes. Just because everyone says he looks nice, doesn't mean he's not naked."

Deep in thought, Ryan ate some more and sipped at her tea. The vague buzz of voices surrounded her, but she couldn't focus on them. Luckily, her aunt and father knew better than to try to engage her when she was deep in thought. They'd learned to carry on their own conversation, waiting patiently for her to return to them.

Chapter Six

The next night, after she'd returned from softball practice, Ryan ran up the stairs, calling out, "Hey, Mia! Your doppelganger's downstairs. Want me to send her up?"

Mia leapt to her feet and ran over to Ryan. She was nearly bouncing with excitement. "Do you really think she looks like me?"

"Yeah, I wasn't kidding. She doesn't look identical, but you could be sisters."

Mia threw her arms around Ryan's neck and kissed her. "You're the best!" she yelled, running down the stairs at breakneck speed.

Ryan stood in the doorway, scratching her chin while she tried to figure out what had just happened. She finally gave up and went back downstairs, deciding that she was just happy that Mia was showing some signs of life again.

After her guest left, Mia went into the living room and collapsed into a chair, smiling smugly at her roommates.

"I'd recognize that smile anywhere," Jamie said. "That's the 'I got my way' smile."

"I did," Mia said, giggling. "It cost me two hundred and fifty dollars, but it was worth it."

Ryan looked from Mia to Jamie. "Can I be let in on this scam? Are you paying someone to steal your identity? 'Cause I think most people are willing to do that for free."

"No, silly. I was paying her to finish a class for me. One of my teachers is being all honorable, and he won't let me finish from Colorado. So I spent yesterday and today searching the campus for someone who looks like me."

She looked very satisfied with herself, but Ryan didn't grasp the full meaning of her story. "How does that help?"

"She's gonna go to class for me and tell me if anything unusual comes up. She's more like me than I thought, 'cause she got me to increase my offer from a hundred and fifty dollars to two-fifty. I shouldn't have let her know how desperate I was."

"But how can that work?" Ryan asked. "Won't she have to study and be prepared for class?"

Mia looked blank. "I never did. Why should she?"

Ryan smiled indulgently. "My mistake. I keep thinking like a real student."

"Don't put those weird values on me, O'Flaherty. College is just a way to keep us off the streets for four or five years."

"Right. I'll make a note. But how will you make sure she follows through? She might screw you."

"Nope. I have a friend in the class, and I'm gonna call her every week to check up on my employee. I'm paying Hannan by the week, in case you're wondering."

"Hannan? That's an unusual name. I noticed she had a pretty thick accent. Where's she from?"

"Lebanon. She's only a freshman, but I think she has potential. She knows how to hustle."

"It must be nice to know you leave your reputation in such good hands," Ryan said.

"Sure is. And now I'm doubly glad I never spoke during class. Hannan sounds like she's been taking English lessons for about fifteen minutes!" She got up and fluffed her curls, posing for her friends. "I'm gonna go call my woman and tell her to warm up the bed for me."

Ryan's stomach lurched. "When are you going?"

"Well, I've got a lot to do to get organized, and Jordy's only day off is Sunday. I guess I'll leave on Friday morning so I can get there on Saturday night."

"That's so soon," Ryan said, annoyed with herself when her voice came out significantly higher than normal.

"It's not soon enough. I'd leave tonight if I could possibly get ready." She scampered up the stairs, giggling with anticipation.

Jamie looked at her partner. "Our little girl is growing up, Ma."

"I liked it when she was little and still believed in Santa Claus."

Jamie scooted over and snuggled up next to her lover. "Ohh…it won't be so bad to be alone in the house. We'll have a new room to make love in."

"Hmm…" Ryan could feel the corners of her mouth curling into a reluctant grin. "I guess it won't be all bad. We can finally have this place be 'clothing optional.'"

"That's my tiger." Jamie chucked Ryan under the chin. "Now let's get some dinner going. You must be starving. I noticed you didn't eat all of the leftovers before softball practice."

"Oh, I went over to the city and stopped by Da's. Aunt Maeve made me a bunch of scones."

"What were you doing over there?" Jamie opened the refrigerator door and pulled out some cold cuts and condiments.

"I went to see Father Pender." She took the baguette that Jamie had purchased on her way home and started to slice it.

"I can't imagine why you did that. Not getting enough frustration in the East Bay?"

"Why don't I ask you about these things first?" Ryan said, feeling disgusted with herself. "Sometimes I'm such a Pollyanna. I thought he would apologize for the Church's giving so much money to support Prop 22."

Jamie's eyes opened wide. "Apologize? He was probably the chief fundraiser."

Ryan's head dropped as she mumbled a few choice words.

Walking over, Jamie put her arms around Ryan. "What's wrong, babe? Did he upset you?"

"Yeah…no…I don't know." Ryan didn't turn around. She hated to have Jamie see her looking so wounded.

"Come on," Jamie said, tugging on her. Ryan let herself be turned, but she immediately put her head against Jamie's shoulder, effectively shielding her face. "Tell me what's going on."

"Nothin'. I just feel stupid. I shoulda known I was wasting my time." She took in a deep breath. "I don't know why I always think the best of people."

Jamie tightened her hold, squeezing her hard. "I love that about you. I hope you never get jaded. Don't feel bad about hoping for the best."

"It's one thing to hope. It's another to expect it."

"That's what's so sweet about you." Jamie rocked Ryan in her arms. "Don't change, baby, and don't feel stupid. You just have a good heart."

Ryan rubbed her face in Jamie's hair, letting the soft strands and floral scent soothe her. "Maybe I'll feel better after I eat."

"That's my girl. A little food always makes the day seem brighter."

After dinner, Jamie and Ryan retired to their respective study spots, with Ryan working in their room until nine. She went downstairs to get a drink and stopped by the library for a moment. "How's it going?"

"Not well. I'm trying to write my opinion piece, but I'm clearly not in the mood."

"Can I help?"

"No. I don't think I need to talk about it, I just need to get started. All I've been able to do is write an outline."

"That's something," Ryan said, giving her an encouraging smile. She walked into the room and sat down, putting Jamie's feet on her lap. "I didn't ask if you've told your mom you're doing this."

"Oh, yeah." She blinked. "Didn't I tell you that?

"Nope."

"Damn, we're both so busy we're starting to lose track of each other." Jamie had a very glum look on her face. Her expression turned even more sour when she added, "I probably didn't say anything because she wasn't very enthusiastic."

"Really? That doesn't sound like her."

"Oh, no," Jamie quickly replied. "She's supportive, but she's worried about my drawing attention to myself after spending two months trying to get away from the press."

Ryan smiled and nodded her understanding. "That does seem a little counterintuitive, doesn't it?"

"Do you think I'm doing the right thing?" Jamie propped herself up on one elbow. "I know you said that I should do this if it's important to me, but you haven't said what you really think."

"That's a tough one." Ryan started to massage her partner's feet while she considered the question. "I don't like publicity, and my privacy means a lot to me, but making a statement about discrimination means a lot, too. I guess I'd sacrifice my privacy to take a stand, even one that put me in the limelight again. So, if I were you, I'd do it." She pulled Jamie's feet up and hugged them close, giving her a playful grin. "But I'd feel bad about putting my father in an awkward position—even though he's the one who stirred this all up to start with."

With a small grin tugging at the corners of her mouth, Jamie lay back down and gazed at Ryan for a moment. "Are you sure you're not me? 'Cause that's exactly how I feel."

"Makes perfect sense. Just because you're angry doesn't mean you want to publicly humiliate him."

Wincing when she heard those words, Jamie asked, "Do you really think he'll be humiliated?"

Ryan nodded. "Yeah. I think he might. You're going to officially come out very publicly. And you're doing it in the legitimate press. I'm sure all of the major dailies will pick up the story as well as the newsweeklies." She rolled her eyes and added, "Some cable channel will probably devote a week to it. And you're not just coming out—you're coming out to publicly chide him and all of the other lawmakers who've voted for these stupid bills. That combo is probably going to hurt and embarrass him."

An unhappy grunt was Jamie's only reply. The silence continued for a couple of minutes. "I think I need to talk to my grandfather about this. Maybe he can help me figure out if I'm doing this just to get back at my dad, or to do something that I feel is right."

"If you're going to do that tonight, you'd better do it now. He goes to bed early."

"You look pretty tired yourself, stretch."

Ryan stood and twisted around, loosening her muscles. "I am. I was thinking about getting into bed and reading until I fell asleep."

"Go ahead, honey. I'll call Papa and then try to write again. I'm not in the mood to sleep yet."

Walking to the door, Ryan lingered, then raised an eyebrow. "Sure?"

"Yeah. Really. I'll kiss you when I come to bed."

Ryan walked back to the sofa and kissed Jamie, their lips touching softly for a few seconds. "I need a kiss while I'm awake," she whispered. "But I'll take one later, too."

"It's a deal." Jamie waved at her, then got up to make her call.

Chapter Seven

The squeak of the hinges on the front door woke Jamie. She sat up quickly, realizing she wasn't in her bed. She stared at the blanket that partially covered her, not knowing how or when it had appeared. An annoying itch made her rub her eyes. When she took her hands away she noticed a note written in large font on her computer screen.

> *Sleeping in the library is unacceptable! I need my cuddles!*
> *XXXOOO*
> *R*

My girl loves me, Jamie thought, smiling to herself as she went upstairs to shower.

Catherine returned from her early morning walk feeling less invigorated than she usually did. After walking in the back door, she smiled reflexively when Marta greeted her.

"What can I fix you for breakfast?"

"Oh, nothing special. How about some fruit and coffee?"

"Let me make you an omelet or some hot cereal."

"No, fruit is enough." Catherine sat down at the breakfast table and started to read the paper.

Marta set a cup of coffee next to her, then gently laid a hand on Catherine's shoulder. "Are you not well?"

Catherine started, then shook her head. "I'm fine."

Not moving, she gazed at Catherine with a penetrating look.

"Okay." Catherine sighed. "I'm feeling a little down today."

"It's more than today," Marta said sternly. "It's been weeks now."

Catherine pointed to the coffee pot. "Get a cup of coffee and sit with me."

"Let me make your breakfast first."

"Please, have a seat. Maybe I'll be hungry in a few minutes, but I'm really not in the mood right now."

Marta got out a cup and added generous amounts of cream and sugar before she poured the strong, black coffee. Then she sat and waited.

It was amazingly hard to get it out, but Catherine managed. "I'm lonely."

Marta didn't say a word, but she reached over and put her hand atop Catherine's, sympathy showing in her eyes.

"I've made a lot of changes this year, and even though they were right for me, I feel lost a lot of the time."

"Lost? I'm not sure what you mean."

Catherine nodded, taking a sip of her coffee. "Rootless. I think that's the better word."

"How can I help?"

Smiling at the offer, Catherine said, "I don't think you can. I have to get myself back on track."

"It's hard having Mr. Evans gone, isn't it?"

Catherine bit her lip, knowing she could burst into tears with very little help. "Yes. It's been very hard." She sat back and reflected for a few moments. "It's odd. In so many ways, he was a terrible husband, but in other ways, we had a nice relationship. He was always fun to go out with, and he could be so funny," she said wistfully. "We'd be at some boring dinner, and he'd keep saying witty little things that made the time pass so quickly." She looked at Marta, embarrassed that she'd started to cry. "Why did he have to be such a cheat?"

"I don't know," Marta said, holding Catherine's hand. "But you deserve a man who wants to be with you."

"I know I do. That's why I divorced him. But sometimes…sometimes I wish we could have stayed together. I know he'd never have been faithful, but I miss him." She wiped at her eyes with a napkin. "I miss the way it was after I'd find out about an affair, and he'd romance me just the way he did when we first met." She gave Marta a watery smile. "He can be very romantic, you know."

"Does it feel romantic when he only does it to apologize?"

Catherine nodded. "Yes. If you want it badly enough, you can convince yourself of anything." She stood and walked to the counter, gesturing for Marta to stay seated. She poured another cup of coffee and returned to the table. "But it's not just losing Jim that has me down. No one calls me. No one asks me to lunch. I've lost all of my so-called friends."

Marta started to speak, but Catherine stopped her. "I know. I know. They weren't real friends. Jim wasn't a real husband. But that was my real life, and it's gone now."

"You still have your charities."

"I know I do, but they aren't enough to make me feel…important. I don't mean that the way it sounds. I mean…vital. Feeling like I'm needed."

"But Jamie and Ryan and Ryan's family…"

"Oh, yes." Catherine smiled at the thought. "I'm so happy when I'm with them. Honestly, I don't know how I'd make it without their support. But they're so busy now. They're gone every weekend, and I don't feel comfortable showing up on Martin and Maeve's doorstep looking for company."

"They'd love to have you," Marta said.

"You're right. But that's not my style. I'm a woman who needs an invitation, and they're a family with an open-door policy." She took in a deep breath. "It would be different if I lived in the neighborhood. I could drop in just like everyone else does."

"Why don't you buy a house or an apartment near them?"

Catherine thought about the idea for a moment, then shook her head. "I could, of course, but it's not…it's not my type of place." At Marta's inquiring look, she added, "It's a lovely neighborhood, and perfect for the O'Flahertys, but I'd never fit in there." She took another sip of her drink. "I have to find my own way, Marta, and moving in next to the O'Flahertys just to have built-in friends isn't the way to do it. The South Bay is my home. I simply have to find new friends down here. There has to be someone who isn't a back-stabbing monster."

"I'm sure of it. There are many, many people who live down here. Some of them have to be without knives."

While Catherine was talking about her sadness, Ryan was at her therapy group, silently wrestling with her own demons. "Ryan," Ellen, the group leader, said, "you've been awfully quiet today. Would you like to contribute?"

"No." She looked up, flashed a very brief smile and looked back down, staring at the button on her jeans.

"Sometimes the best days to talk are the days you least feel like it."

"Mmm," Ryan grunted, unmoved.

Ellen was clearly undeterred by Ryan's silence. "Since you don't want to talk, why don't I guess how you're feeling?" The best Ryan could offer was a shoulder shrug. "Given what I know about you, I'd say that you're angry with yourself."

Ryan's didn't move her head, but her gaze shifted to Ellen.

"I'd bet you get angry with yourself fairly often. And I'd also bet that you don't cut yourself much slack."

A tiny smile started to break through, and Ryan nodded, having been called on that trait too many times to deny it.

"Since we know that much, why don't you tell us the rest? Why are you angry?"

Ryan slapped her thighs with her hands, regretting her impulsivity when everyone seemed to start. "I'm sick of this! It's March! March! And I'm still weirded out by the car-jacking."

"It only happened at the end of December," Ellen said gently. "That's not very long at all."

That was about the stupidest thing she'd ever heard. "It might not be long in your book, but it's a long time in mine. I've got a very busy life to live, and I don't have time for this shit!"

"What shit?" Ellen asked, the soul of patience.

Ryan blew out a breath. "I have to go on a road trip tomorrow, and I'm freaking out because Jamie can't go with me. I'm an adult woman, and I need my girlfriend to hold me or I can't sleep." She was filled with disgust for herself.

"Does Jamie know it's still hard for you?"

"I don't know," Ryan said irritably. Then her voice softened. "Probably not. We don't talk about it much."

"Maybe you should tell her—" Ellen began.

Ryan cut her off. "She's got a big paper due on Monday. She can't be sitting in the stands watching me play softball for three days."

"Oh, I see."

"No, you don't," Ryan snapped. "Our roommate, Mia, is moving to Colorado tomorrow. Mia's part of our family." She emphasized the word so strongly that everyone looked up. "I can't stand it when my family gets screwed up!"

"I understand," Ellen said. She looked around the group. "I think we all do. When you're dealing with the after-effects of trauma, the last thing you want is change. Especially in your immediate family."

"I'm gonna miss her," Ryan said, beginning to sob, her stone-like demeanor now destroyed. "I'm gonna miss her so much."

That night, the roommates sat around the dinner table. Jamie had rushed home to make Mia's favorite dinner, but one of the guests was clearly not feeling very festive. Ryan was slumped down in her chair, barely picking at her food. Jamie didn't question her about her mood, since she looked like she was ready for a fight. With as much false cheer as she could muster, Jamie said, "How's the packing going, Mia?"

"Great!" She was bubbling with energy and excitement, as much a contrast to Ryan as was physically possible. "I'm remarkably organized." She laughed and added, "I guess I can be on time if I'm going somewhere I really wanna go."

Ryan shot her a sidelong glance that Mia didn't see, but Jamie caught it. She knew her lover was down about Mia's leaving, but it surprised her to see how upset she was. *I've got to get her alone and find out what's behind those moody blue eyes.*

As soon as dinner was over, Jamie said, "You two both have some packing to do. When do you leave, baby?"

"I have to be on the bus by seven. Our flight's at nine."

"Where are you going this time?" Mia asked.

"Fullerton."

"Where's that?"

"Nowhere." Ryan got up and started for the stairs.

As soon as Ryan was out of earshot, Mia whispered, "What's wrong with the princess?"

"I think she's sad you're leaving. She hates change."

"Ooo..." Mia winced. "I'd better not act so fucking giddy about going. But I don't know how to stop." She gave Jamie such a dazzling smile that it was impossible not to return.

"You don't have to change how you feel. Just don't be surprised if Ryan's really quiet or acts withdrawn. That's how she shows she loves you."

"She must love me a lot," Mia said, looking towards Ryan's room with concern. "'Cause she looks like she's about to jump off a bridge."

Jamie went upstairs and peeked into the bedroom Ryan used for her computer and her clothing. She was sitting in front of her computer, her fingers flying over the keys. Seeing that her partner was being productive, Jamie went to Mia's room and stood in the doorway for a moment, watching her try to jam nearly everything she had into three large suitcases.

"That's never gonna fit," Jamie said, stating the obvious.

"I know, but I can't decide what to take."

"Why don't you just take your warmest things right now? It's still pretty cold in Colorado. I'll pack up your lighter clothes and send them to you."

"Will you really?"

"Of course. I'd be happy to. Just let me know what you want and when you want it."

"Done deal." Mia started pulling things from her suitcases.

She was so happy that Jamie couldn't help but catch a little of her enthusiasm. "You don't have any second thoughts about doing this, do you?"

"Hell, no! I'm amazed I stayed this long."

"You know, I am, too. You're not the most patient girl I've ever known."

"Do you think you and Ryan will be able to visit before school's over? Jordy says we can ski until June this year because of the great snow pack."

Jamie pursed her lips, then shook her head. "Wish we could. But Ryan's got a softball tournament every weekend until the end of May. I'd come alone, but I've got a lot of golf left. I don't see how I can swing it."

Mia gave her a quick hug. "Swing it? You kill me, James."

At Jamie's blank look, Mia said, "Golf…swing…get it?"

"Puns aren't your forte, but that was mildly amusing."

"You're just not able to laugh because you're sick about my leaving," Mia said, pinching her friend. "But don't worry, you can come visit after graduation. With you two having the whole summer off, you'll be itching to visit."

"That's the truth. I still can't believe Ryan agreed to take a year off, but

I'm not gonna complain. It's gonna be so nice to spend some time with her where we're not always worried about the other things we should be doing. I'm so sick of school I could scream."

"That's because you made the mistake of caring about it." Mia gave her a fiendish grin. "You let 'em hook you."

"True. I've never been able to copy your devil-may-care attitude, and sometimes I wish I had."

"You're relaxed when you're with Ryan. I can see how content you are just to be with her—even when you're not doing anything special."

Jamie smiled, a wide, satisfied grin covering her face. "That's the best time. When we're just together, talking and holding each other."

Mia looked thoughtful for a moment. "You know, it's like that with Jordan, too. I've never been with anyone who made me feel that going out was almost unnecessary."

"That's because you're finally in love. Being with her can fill you up."

Mia took in a deep breath and let it out in a rush. "My heart races when I think of seeing her on Saturday."

Walking over, Jamie put a hand on her shoulder. "I know you don't want me to give you money, but you've got to let me pay for your car insurance. I'll worry myself sick if you're uninsured."

Mia looked like she wanted to refuse, but she eventually nodded. "Okay. My dad handled all of that stuff, so I'll call him when I get to Colorado and ask for the details."

"Your mom called my cell phone today," Jamie said. "I didn't answer when I saw your home number, but I felt like a jerk."

"I'll call them when I get there. I know they're worried, but I don't want to talk to them until I'm with Jordan."

"I don't wanna get in the middle of this, but if your mom calls me again, I'll probably take the call. I know how much she loves you, even if she's harsh with you sometimes."

Mia sat down heavily on her bed, remaining perfectly still for a full minute. When her shoulders began to shake, Jamie sat next to her and wrapped her in a hug. "It hurts, doesn't it?"

"So much," Mia whimpered. "She was so cruel, James. You know we've always fought, but she's never been cruel before. And my dad was such a stooge! I know he didn't agree with her, but he sat there like her puppet. I talked to Peter yesterday, and he said that Mom called him and was just like she was on Saturday. She told him she refused to support me while

I was being so immature." She lifted her head, her tear-streaked face and red-rimmed eyes nearly breaking Jamie's heart. "How can she say that? Loving Jordy has made me a better person, James, and it kills me that she can't see how I've changed."

"She's not around you much. You didn't go home for a while there, and she hasn't seen you and Jordan together."

"Whose fault is that?" She got up and walked over to her desk, where she picked up a picture of her family that they'd had taken over Christmas. Flicking the glass with her fingertips, she said, "I don't even recognize these people anymore. This happy family stuff was just bullshit." She dropped the photo face down and left it there.

Mia took several things from her desk and packed them, leaving the photo where it was. When she'd finished taking the things she needed, she put the top on the box and said, "That's it. I'm ready to go."

"When are you leaving?"

"Early. I want to be out of town before rush hour. I'll probably take off at around six."

Jamie looked at her watch and saw that it was nine-thirty. "Get ready for bed, and I'll rub your back. I'd snuggle with you all night, but Ryan would get jealous."

The last words were a little shaky, and Mia went to her and hugged her. "I'm gonna miss you, too, James." She pulled back in her friend's embrace and gazed into her eyes for a few moments. "We haven't been apart for more than a month since we started high school. It's gonna be so weird not to have you close by."

"The house is gonna be so empty without you," Jamie cried softly. "But I know that you need to be with Jordan now. This is right for you."

"Thanks, James." She squeezed her tightly, then went into her bathroom to brush her teeth.

When Mia came back, Jamie was sitting on the bed, waiting. Mia got under the sheet and hugged a pillow when Jamie started to massage her shoulders.

"I know you want to be independent," Jamie said, "but I called American Express and told them to put you on my account. They're sending a new card to Jordan's address."

Mia started to turn over, but Jamie held her still. "You don't have to use it. But if you get into a pinch, I want you to have it. I know you won't use it foolishly. I trust you."

"I won't use it at all. I really think I'll be fine."

"I know you will. Honestly, this is more for me than you. I can't stand to think of your having car trouble or something and not being able to get around."

Mia nodded then reached behind herself to rub Jamie's leg. "As much as I love Jordan, you'll always be my best friend."

Jamie leaned forward and kissed her on the cheek. Laughing a little she said, "Don't tell Ryan, but I feel the same about you."

Mia was almost asleep when Ryan entered the room. "I've gotta keep an eye on you every minute," she said to Jamie. "After tonight, you're not gonna have any options—you're gonna have to sleep with me."

"Not much of a burden there, sport," Jamie said, smiling at her lover.

Ryan walked around and squatted by the head of the bed. She looked into Mia's sleepy eyes and said, "I love you." Then she kissed her gently and got up, leaving quickly.

Mia watched her walk out the door. "Poor baby. She looks so sad."

"She is," Jamie agreed. "I'll go rub her back next. It's a full-time job around here."

Much to Jamie's surprise, Ryan was in bed and sleeping peacefully when she went into their room. She brushed her teeth then quietly got undressed. When she slid between the covers, Ryan instinctively moved toward her, wrapping her arms around her while she made a soft, purring noise. Jamie hugged her back, holding her close and breathing in her familiar, calming scent. After just a few minutes, both women were asleep, safe in each other's arms.

Chapter Eight

The next morning, having been unable to sleep for more than an hour at a time, Mia got out of bed at five o'clock. She was physically tired, but her mind was running at full speed and had been even while sleeping. A quick shower cleared out some of the cobwebs, then she put on a pair of sweats and a T-shirt. Remembering that it would be colder as she got closer to Colorado, she grabbed a Cal sweatshirt and draped it around her shoulders. A satisfied smile settled on her face. Being organized and making note of little details like the changing temperatures made her feel like a fully qualified adult, a status she'd never been in a rush to claim.

It took three trips to carry her stuffed bags outside, but she was able to wedge everything into her trunk. Jamie's cooler, filled with Diet Coke and ice rested on the backseat. In the front, on the passenger seat, she put the case with her favorite CDs, the printout for the quickest route to Colorado Springs, and a paper bag filled with gum, mints, candy and pretzels.

Her excitement was building, but she took the time to go back into the house one last time to make sure she'd collected everything on the list that Jamie'd insisted she make. Satisfied that she had everything, she started to walk out. But something stopped her, and she turned around to look at the still-dark parlor.

Unexpectedly, her mind flashed back to the first time she and Jamie had seen the house. They were just about to graduate from their prep school and were so excited about having their own home for the next year that they were giddy. They'd driven to Berkeley with their mothers and had spent about an hour in the place, running from room to room like a pair of terriers, making so much noise that Anna Lisa told them to quiet down and act like adults.

Neither girl had felt like an adult that day—at least Mia hadn't. She'd felt like a kid who was going to be able to run wild the next year—and that's exactly what she'd done. Jamie and Jack had started to spend all of their free time together, and by the time the girls had moved into the house, Jamie was already acting like a mature woman. But Mia's childhood had continued unabated.

Upon reflection, she realized that it was only when she'd met Jordan that she'd started to settle down. And even then she'd had a few less-than-mature indiscretions. But when she looked at the house now, she felt a mix of tender emotions—not for the house itself, but for all of the milestones that had occurred during her time there. Her eyes clouded with tears, thinking of the boyfriends whom she'd sworn she loved, the heartbreaks, the insecurities, the joys and the pains of growing up—most of them had happened right there. And all of them were linked to Jamie.

She'd never known what it was like to have a sister, but she was sure that a blood relative wouldn't have had a more secure place in her heart. They'd been through some trials together and had shed many, many tears. But most of their days had been nothing but fun. And since Ryan had moved in, they'd truly become a small, same-sex family. It was very hard to leave both her birth family and this one that had been cobbled together, but it was time to go—to move on with her life with Jordan.

Knowing that she had Jamie and Ryan's full support made the leaving easier, but it still filled her with a sense of loss, the intensity of which surprised her. She'd been so preoccupied with the break from her parents that she hadn't considered how leaving Berkeley would affect her. It was hitting her hard, and she felt like going upstairs and climbing into bed with her friends for one more hug, but it was time to go.

The door sounded a weighty, reassuring click when she turned the deadbolt. Kissing her palm, she placed it on the oak and let it rest there for a moment. Then she wiped her eyes and sprinted for the car, determined not to look back. This was a day for looking to the future—a future with the woman who'd helped her to grow up enough to make this decision and suffer the consequences.

As she pulled away, she didn't see the tall, dark-haired woman looking out of her bedroom window, crying silently.

Jamie stretched and fought the temptation to stay in bed for a few extra minutes when she heard Ryan start the shower. Forcing her feet to the floor, she walked into the bathroom and snuck into the back of the shower, surprising her lover by wrapping her arms around her steamy, hot body.

"Where'd you come from?"

"Our warm, soft, cozy bed. I wanted to be with you for a few extra minutes. Don't ever say I don't love you." She squeezed Ryan, expecting to hear a laugh in response to her teasing. But Ryan dropped her head, her black hair falling forward. Her belly began to shake, and Jamie turned her around and saw that her face was contorted with sadness. "Baby, what's wrong?"

Ryan put her head on Jamie's shoulder, causing the hot water to hit Jamie right in the face, but she stayed right there, tilting her chin so the water didn't pummel her eyes.

"I don't wanna go," she whimpered.

"I don't want you to go," Jamie soothed. "I'd much rather have you right here all weekend." She kissed her wet, warm cheek then whispered in her ear, "I always want you with me."

Ryan nodded then stood up and started to wash—first her partner, then herself. She didn't say anything else, but Jamie knew she was holding back. Usually, when Ryan was upset, crying a few tears cleaned out her system and let her get back to normal. The only time she didn't snap out of it was when there was something that she was reluctant to admit.

Grabbing a towel, Ryan started to dry Jamie's hair, giving it a rough rub. Then she draped the towel over her own head, took a fresh towel and dried her partner's body.

This was all done in silence, but that wasn't odd for them. Jamie wasn't usually very talkative until she'd had her coffee, and Ryan had come to respect her natural inclinations.

Today, though, it seemed that Ryan was brooding over something. Knowing it would be tough sledding, Jamie tried to get to the emotional truth. She took the towel from her shoulders and started to dry Ryan's back, being gentle and loving with her. Every part she dried got a soft kiss, and she held on to Ryan's warm body when she was finished. "Tell me what's bothering you. Is it Mia?"

Ryan nodded. "I don't want her to move away."

"I don't either. It's gonna be very lonely around here for a while." She looked at her lover. "Especially this weekend. I wish you didn't have to go on a road trip."

Ryan started to cry again, sobbing so hard that she stumbled blindly back into the bedroom and sat on the edge of the bed.

Jamie followed and held her, running her hand through Ryan's wet hair. "Honey, please tell me. I know it's not just Mia's leaving."

"I don't wanna go to Fullerton."

It was a little hard to understand her since she was crying so hard, but Jamie managed. Simply understanding the words didn't help her understand Ryan's mood, though. "You've gotta tell me more, baby."

"I don't wanna go on a road trip today," she said, still sniffling, but more in control. "I…just don't want to."

Jamie was confounded. Ryan almost never complained about her obligations, and she'd never said one bad word about the softball team. "Is there something about Fullerton that…" She trailed off, not even knowing what question to ask.

"No!" Obviously exasperated, Ryan got up and started to pace across the room. "I'm tired of being gone every other weekend. It seems like you're gone when I'm home and I'm gone when you're home. I want you…I need to be with you more."

Jamie walked over to her and put her hands on her shoulders. "Are you…thinking of leaving the team?"

Ryan's head shook, and Jamie could see how frustrated she was. "No! I love being on the team. I just don't want to go this weekend."

"Could you call in sick or something?"

"Of course not!" Now Ryan looked like she was about to explode. "Isn't it obvious? I don't wanna be alone!"

"Well, Jesus! Why didn't you tell me sooner? I could've arranged to come with you."

Calming noticeably, Ryan said, "You have a paper to write. You can't spend the whole weekend sitting on a bench." She tried to avert her eyes, but Jamie wouldn't let her.

"It's not fair of you to decide what's best for me." Ryan's eyes went round at her sharp tone. "It's not," she repeated. "The only way to have a real partnership is if you tell me what you need. Then we figure out a way to make it happen, or we jointly decide that we can't manage it. But your deciding what I have to do and where I have to do it just isn't fair."

"I'm sorry," Ryan said quietly.

"I don't want you to be sorry." Jamie gently kissed her head. "I want you to understand. We each have to tell the other what we need. Even when it's hard." She pulled Ryan down and kissed her.

Ryan's hands rose and encircled Jamie's back, and they kissed for a long time. Soft, gentle, sweet, love-filled kisses.

Jamie reluctantly pulled away. "Promise me that you'll try to tell me when you need something."

"I promise I'll try," Ryan said, kissing her again.

Patting her back, Jamie said, "You'd better get moving. It's six-thirty, and you haven't dried your hair."

Walking towards the bathroom, Ryan mumbled to herself, "I should have cut it off before volleyball season. I'd save myself ten minutes every morning."

Jamie started for the kitchen, determined to give her partner a proper breakfast. "Cutting hair is a joint decision, baby, and my vote is no."

As soon as Ryan left the house, Jamie got on the phone and called Jennie, pleased that she hadn't left for school yet. After speaking to Sandy, the housemother, for a few minutes, Jennie got on. "It's Jamie. Is anything special going on at school today? Any tests or quizzes?"

"Uhm…no, nothing special that I know about. Just another day. Why?"

"How would you like to ditch and go to Fullerton with me for the weekend?"

"Yeow!"

Jamie pulled the phone away from her ear and let the ringing subside. "I guess that means you're in?"

"Where do I go? What do I do?"

"I haven't figured that out yet. I just now decided to go, and I thought you'd be the perfect person to go with me. Let me get on the phone and figure out which flight we can make, then I'll call your school and tell them you're with me."

"We're gonna fly?"

"Yeah, I don't want to drive that far."

"Do you need my teachers' names?"

"Nah. I'll just call the office and speak to Sister Mary Magdalene. Don't worry about it."

"I'm not worried about anything," Jennie said, giggling nonstop. "I'm so excited I could die."

"I'm excited too. You pack a light bag and stay by the phone. I'll call you when everything's set."

"I won't move."

Jamie had a feeling she meant that literally.

Late that afternoon, Ryan's biggest fans sat in the dugout of the softball complex in Fullerton, California, watching Cal warm up on the neatly tended grass field. They were the only Cal fans in attendance, and when Jamie said hello to Coach Roberts, he invited them to sit in the dugout. Because of their position, Ryan couldn't see them, and Jamie was able to indulge in her favorite sport of watching Ryan when her partner was unawares.

Even though she'd attended many games, Jamie hadn't spent much time watching warm-ups, preferring to sit at a nearby picnic table and read. But since Jennie was with her, she felt she should be more social and consume the total experience. While watching the women prepare for the game, she decided that it was a surprisingly fun experience.

The focus of her attentions was, as always, one particular player. This woman, significantly taller and more substantially built than most of the others, caught and held Jamie's attention completely.

The team was wearing shorts for the first time that season, and Jamie marveled at the expanse of leg that was revealed by Ryan's dark blue pants. The shorts covered some of the other players nearly to the knee, but Ryan's exposed more than a foot of tanned thigh, much to Jamie's approval. She'd been a little worried when Ryan reported that they sometimes wore shorts, assuming that her partner would be a mass of scrapes and scratches by the end of a game. Much to her pleasure, everyone wore long white socks topped by navy blue kneepads, which Jamie was certain would protect Ryan's lovely long legs.

The players assembled in a large circle and began to toss the ball around lazily, just letting their arms get warm. Even though they were stretching, the more important activity seemed to be chatting, and Jamie noted that every player was involved. It seemed more like a sewing circle than a group of athletes preparing for a contest, but Jamie was enormously pleased that Ryan was able to share her sport with such a nice group.

One of the things Jamie really liked was that the coaches let the players warm up at their own pace. They remained on the bench, idly commenting about things they observed, but not closely supervising. After Ryan's unpleasant month with the basketball team, she knew that her partner reveled in the fact that the coaches treated the athletes like sentient beings.

When everyone was warm, the outfielders got to work near the left field fence. Even though Ryan had only played first base in games, she was the primary replacement for all of the three outfield positions, so she stayed with the starting fielders to work on the long throw.

Surprisingly, the four women began to toss a football back and forth, and after a relatively short time, they stood at least fifty yards from each other and threw the ball lazily, continuing to loosen up their arms for the more stressful long throws.

Jamie could see the trajectory of the throws getting progressively lower, and she heard a bit more pop when the ball was caught. By the time the fielders were throwing tight spirals, they switched to softballs and started to throw the balls in to the catcher. They had about fifty balls in a big bag, and by the time they had fired them all in, they came in for fielding practice.

"She's coming in," Jennie said, elbowing Jamie. "She's gonna be so surprised!"

"She sure is," Jamie said, gulping as she spoke. A big part of her feared that Ryan would cry when she saw her, and she knew nothing was worse for her partner than crying in front of her teammates. Fortunately, Ryan spied them before she hit the infield. Jamie saw her flinch, then dash back to the outfield fence and do a few wind sprints, running from the second base bag to the fence and back at full speed—obviously just to collect herself.

When the lanky woman was composed, she ran by the dugout, nodding towards Jamie and Jennie. "Isn't there a rule against groupies?" she asked the coach.

"You wouldn't hear me bitchin' if a pair of good looking girls followed me around," Coach Roberts said, chuckling.

"Be sure to let us know the first time that happens." She traded her outfielder's glove for her first baseman's mitt and ran to catch up to the start of infield and batting practice.

"Isn't she glad to see us?" Jennie asked, looking a little put out.

"She's thrilled," Jamie said. "Trust me."

Organized chaos reigned during the next fifteen minutes. Everyone got to take ten pitches, then the starters had another round. The players not batting were far from idle. Ryan was on first, working with the back-up shortstop and second baseman on fielding quickly thrown grounders; another knot of women stood in the outfield waiting for batted balls; and a third group of pitchers went to the bullpen to warm up.

Heather spotted the fans and ran over to say hello. "I didn't know you guys were coming."

"We just decided today," Jennie said. "I got to skip school!"

"Cool. I gotta go warm up." With that, she dashed over to the bullpen and started to work with the other pitchers.

Once batting practice was finished, the starting infielders took the field, with Coach Roberts hitting sharp grounders to all spots, really making them hustle to reach them. Since Ryan wasn't a starter, she went out to the edge of the field and ran sprints again. She was out there as long as fielding practice lasted, and when they called all of the players in, she was sweating freely.

Coach called them all together for some last minute tips, then the team lined up along the baseline for the playing of the national anthem. Ryan ran over to the dugout and tugged Jamie and Jennie along with her, and Jamie couldn't help sneaking an admiring look up at her partner—singing at full voice, with her cap held over her heart.

Chapter Nine

The weather forecast called for rain the entire weekend, and by the third inning it became clear that they'd be lucky to get the game in. Very dark clouds were gathering, and a few scattered droplets of rain started to fall. Ryan seemed oblivious to the weather, however. Her attention was fully engaged by watching the pitcher and the catcher, and seeing how the fielders positioned themselves for the various batters.

She barely spoke when her team was at bat, unless someone was on base. Then the entire team joined together to repeat some form of cheer or chant that had them all laughing. Even though she was mostly silent during play, between innings she was quite voluble, chattering on like she hadn't been quiet for the previous ten minutes. "You know what I like best about softball?" she asked Jamie during one such break.

"Nope. Don't have a clue."

"It's the only collegiate sport where you can eat during the whole thing." She laughed. "That's epic."

Jamie looked down at the pile of spent sunflower seeds under her lover's feet. "At least I know why you always smell like nuts after a game. Why do you do that, anyway?"

"Do what?"

"Spit the seeds out that way. It looks like you're chewing tobacco."

Ryan just grinned at her, ignoring the look of distaste. "It's a great tension reliever. I've gotta have some way to vent."

Jamie waited for the punch line, but she soon realized that Ryan was serious. Even though she rarely played, she was perched on the edge of the bench like she was waiting for the fire bell, and when she wasn't tapping her cleated feet against the concrete, she was spitting sunflower shells onto the ground. Try as she might, Jamie couldn't understand why her partner was so agitated. Watching softball was akin to watching grass grow, unless, of course, Ryan was playing.

Suddenly, realization dawned on her. Ryan felt just like Jamie did, but instead of being interested in one player, she was interested in all of them. She growled in sympathy at every strikeout, moaned when a player was badly fooled by a pitch, and grunted in frustration at every hit the opposing team made. In short, she cared deeply for her team and her teammates.

Reaching over, Jamie gave her partner's bare thigh a squeeze. "I'm glad you have this, sweetie. This is the right sport for you—even though it takes you away from me too often."

Heather sat on the far end of the bench with the other pitchers. Jennie was clearly more than a little disappointed that one of her favorite players wasn't sitting with them, and she leaned over and spoke to Jamie the first time Ryan's attention was elsewhere. "Why's Heather ignoring us?"

Jamie winced, thinking of how she'd felt when a girl from her neighborhood started to ignore her the minute the older girl had entered high school. "I think it's a jock thing, Jen. Hanging out with your teammates and looking cool is all part of the image."

The younger girl nodded towards Ryan. "Ryan's not doing that."

"Oh, that's a girlfriend thing," Jamie said, smiling. "Being a girlfriend takes precedence over everything else."

Ryan heard her and nodded. "She's a wise woman, Jennie. Listen to her."

The rains finally arrived, and after struggling through the last two innings, the coaches got together and decided to call the second game of the doubleheader. The weather report said that lightning had been spotted in Buena Park, so rather than risk any lives, the thoroughly drenched crew headed back to the hotel.

After an early dinner, the team voted to take in a movie. When Jamie learned that they'd chosen a horror movie, she elected to pass.

Ryan nodded agreeably. "Okay, we'll just stay in."

"No, you should go," Jamie insisted. "You like that kinda movie, and I know you want to hang around with your pals. Besides, I need to work on my article. I'll be more productive without you around."

"Gee, thanks," Ryan said, feigning hurt.

"You know I love to have you with me, but I really do have to work on this. You've a very distracting presence, you know."

"I have my moments," Ryan agreed. "Okay, Jen and I'll go out and play. Work hard, babe."

Jamie watched her walk through the lobby, one arm draped around Jennie's shoulders, already joking and teasing with her friends. She really did hate having her travel so much, but there was no better antidote to the poisonous atmosphere of the basketball team. Having this experience would let Ryan leave college with fond memories—and for that, Jamie was very grateful.

Ryan was still chuckling when she returned to the room a few hours later. "You missed a funny one," she said, crossing the room to place a kiss on Jamie's head. "How's it going?"

"Fine. I still have a couple hours of work to do. It's going well, though."

"Does that mean, 'Be quiet?'"

Jamie bit her lip and nodded.

"Have at it. It's only ten o'clock." She picked up her room key. "I'll be down at Jackie's. Room 212. We're gonna play cards."

"Don't rob them blind," Jamie called after her. "They're your teammates, not your cousins."

An hour later, Jamie knocked on Jackie's door and heard a muffled, "It's open." She went in to find most of the team sitting on the floor playing poker or sprawled across the beds watching the game. Jennie was sitting on a pillow, obviously trying to learn the game by watching the others. Lupe was sitting directly in front of Ryan, holding her cards so that the significantly larger woman could see them. Ryan leaned over slightly and whispered into her ear, then Lupe nodded once and discarded one card and asked for another. Jamie walked over behind her partner, and Ryan leaned back against her shins. "Nice backrest." She grinned up at her.

"What are you two doing?" Jamie asked.

"Lupe's never played before, so we're playing together. I'm sure I'll regret telling her my secrets later in the year when she starts kicking my ass."

The diminutive woman slapped at Ryan's thigh with her cards. "That'll take many years of instruction, and you're graduating this year."

"Not if I keep skipping class to go watch Jamie play golf," Ryan predicted. "Oops…it's our turn, Lupe." She leaned over again and whispered something, then Lupe called, forcing the remaining players to show their hands. She won the hand with two pair, and beaming, she slapped excitedly at the long legs that surrounded her.

"We won! Let's play again!"

"That's the devil talking, Lupe. Let's quit while we're ahead." Ryan extricated herself from her place and took Jamie's hand. "We leave for the field at nine, and coach wants us to meet for breakfast no later than eight. Time for bed. You too, Jen."

With very little grumbling, the game broke up and everyone headed back to their rooms. Jennie was taking Ryan's spot in Jackie's room, so she was already in the right place. Lupe gave Ryan a hug, her arms barely able to encircle the large woman. "Thanks, Ryan. That was fun."

"We can team up whenever you want."

Heading back to their room, Jamie asked, "So, how much did you win?"

"Oh, we don't play for money—just bragging rights." They reached their room, and Ryan started to strip before she'd walked two steps.

"I'm still in the mood to write. If I'm up really late, I'll sleep in and take a cab over to your game."

"I was going to suggest you do that anyway."

"It's a deal. Now brush all of your cute little teeth and hop into bed. You're barely going to get your eight hours tonight."

"You know…" Ryan put her arms around Jamie and let her hands rest low on her hips. "You could skip the game entirely and work."

Jamie looked up and saw the spark of lust in her clear blue eyes. "What are you suggesting, slugger?"

"Well, if you don't have to go to the game tomorrow, you could go to bed right now. We could…" She squeezed Jamie's ass as she bent to kiss her. "Think of something to do to relax."

"That's the voice of the devil," Jamie said, wrinkling up her nose. "You know I'd love to, but I'm really in the mood to work. Besides, since Jennie is with me, I can't skip. She'd have a fit!"

Ryan let her lower lip stick out in a pout. "You do still like to…" she inclined her head toward the bed, "don't you?"

Slapping her hard on the bare butt, Jamie said, "You've got a lot of nerve to even ask me that."

"Just checking. It's been a while, you know."

"Almost a week. I keep track, too."

"Okay, okay." Ryan went into the bathroom and brushed her teeth. When she came out, Jamie was sitting on an upholstered chair, reading some of her research materials. Ryan stuck out her hands, then slapped them against her chest. "Last chance," she said, turning slowly. She twitched her ass as she turned, then smiled impishly at Jamie. "Sure you wanna pass this up?"

"No, I don't. But I have to."

"Fine," Ryan said, feigning hurt. "Kiss me when you come to bed."

"With gusto."

By two am, Jamie was in good shape. She had a little more polishing to do, but that would be easy to finish in the next two days. Too tired to write any more, but too wired to sleep thanks to the Diet Coke she'd been drinking all night, she knew she'd have a tough time relaxing. Nonetheless, she brushed her teeth and got into bed, snuggling up against her partner.

Ryan woke partially, patting her arm and mumbling, "Go sleep."

Now she wants to sleep, Jamie groused. *I'm wide awake in a motel room in Fullerton, with nothing to do and no one to play with. I wonder if they have a gym here? No...I can't leave the room. She'd freak out if she woke up.*

She lay there quietly, hoping that just being near Ryan would calm her down, but the opposite seemed to happen. Ryan's smooth, steady breathing made her more aware of her own alertness, and soon it began to irritate her. *Great. Now I'm mad at her for sleeping!*

Getting out of bed, Jamie went to her suitcase to look for something to read, but all she'd brought were things related to her article, and she'd had enough of that. Lying down on the other bed, her head at the foot, she turned on the TV, lying so close she could have the volume at a whisper. Idly channel surfing, she lit on a premium cable series of very soft-core porn movies made for people who couldn't or wouldn't buy the real thing. She and Ryan had on a few occasions laughed at the ineptitude of the stories, and at the surreal attributes of the women, but she lingered longer than usual this time. Try as she might to get interested, the silicone-pumped blondes didn't do a thing for her. The loveliest woman she'd ever known was lying in the next bed, and her thoughts turned to her partner's magnificent attributes, some of which were totally visible.

Jamie rolled over onto her side and gazed at her lovely partner, sleep rendering her more beautiful than usual. Her lips were slightly parted, and a thick lock of hair partially covered her eyes. Sitting up, Jamie pulled a pair of pillows down and slipped them under her head to aid in her observations. Concentrating, she stared at Ryan, feeling her libido spark to life. She thought about waking her, but couldn't countenance how utterly selfish that would have been. Even though she knew Ryan would be happy to participate, it still felt exploitive to wake her from a sound sleep.

Her temperature was rising, and watching Ryan's breasts rise and fall wasn't cooling things down. Jamie lifted one knee and started to touch herself, feeling just a little guilty. She knew that she had nothing to be ashamed of, but they'd had so few opportunities lately she felt like she was wasting one of them.

Reminding herself that Ryan wasn't lying there wanting sex, she continued to stroke herself, getting into it more than she thought she would. She couldn't remember the last time she'd masturbated, probably before she and Ryan had made love for the first time. *What a difference a year made!*

Ryan woke with the sun the next morning, but it took her a few moments to get her bearings. The TV was on, and Jamie wasn't in bed with her. Blinking, she saw that her partner was lying in the wrong direction on the bed next to hers, and that the TV volume was on very low. She didn't have a clue what had gone on the night before, but was very glad that she'd been able to sleep. It was the tiniest bit of progress, but being able to sleep without Jamie in the same bed was progress nonetheless.

Struggling against the heavy hand of sleep, Jamie forced one eye open at a sharp noise, expecting to find the maid trying to make up the room. Both eyes opened when she saw that her partner had returned, looking a bit like a drowned rat. "We got rained out," Ryan said, a big smile covering her face.

Yawning, Jamie mumbled, "And that's good, why?"

Ryan jumped onto the bed, her wet clothing soaking through the sheet in moments. "We're going to Disneyland!"

"Get off me, you lunatic!" Pushing her heavy partner with all of her strength, Jamie grunted from the effort. "Damn. I can't move you an inch."

"Not when I don't wanna be moved. C'mon, babe. Time's a wasting."

Rolling out of bed, Jamie ran a hand through her woefully disordered hair. "We're going to Disneyland in a driving rainstorm?"

"Yep. I bet there won't be any lines at all." Ryan started to hop around the room as if she were riding a pogo stick, which made her partner giggle at her antics.

"Did they put something in your breakfast, honey? You act like you've got ants in your pants."

"Nope. I'm just excited! I love Disneyland, and I especially love it when everybody else is too intelligent to go."

"Words to live by," Jamie mumbled, trying her best to capture some of her partner's zeal for the endeavor.

Much to her surprise, Jamie found that going on rides in the rain with her giddy partner was a hell of a lot of fun. Ryan and Jennie were clearly the most enthusiastic pair of the group, but Ryan's passion for the place and the rides quickly became contagious, and the rest of the team got into the mood as well.

All of the players except Ryan wore their Cal rain ponchos, which did a great job of keeping the rain off their torsos, but their warm-up pants quickly became sodden. Once she'd heard the weather forecast, Jamie had insisted that her partner bring her full rain suit, so Ryan and Jamie were both completely dry, allowing them to be oblivious to the elements.

It seemed that the only people in the park were young, local kids, who probably had season passes. Lines for the most popular rides were no longer than five minutes, and child-focused attractions like Toon Town were completely deserted.

They'd been at the park for two hours and had been on all of the best rides three times when Jamie pleaded hunger. After a quick stop, they took off again, managing to go on each of the roller coasters five times.

A few of the more prudent women, Jamie included, wanted to spend a couple of hours at indoor attractions and shows, and after a little negotiation, they agreed to split up into two groups. Ryan and Jennie wanted to keep going on rides until they threw up, which didn't seem to be very far in the future in Jamie's privately held opinion. So they agreed to meet on Main Street at five o'clock, when the bus was set to pick them up.

Ryan found Jamie in the biggest gift shop just before five and chuckled. "I had a feeling you'd have to stop to buy a few things."

"I saw this cute Hawaiian shirt that I thought Conor would like, but then I had to get something for Brendan and Rory. I couldn't leave out your father and Maeve, and since Caitlin's outgrown the sweatshirt we got her last time, I got her another."

"About done?"

"Yep. Are we ready to leave?"

"Uh-huh." Ryan had a ghost of a frown on her face. "My stomach's a little upset. Must've been something I ate."

"Yeah, that's probably it," Jamie agreed, mentally rolling her eyes.

Chapter Ten

By seven o'clock on Saturday evening, Mia was nearing Jordan's neighborhood. They'd spoken four times so far, with Jordan calling twice to check on her progress, and Mia calling just because she was too excited not to. Once again, she dialed her cell phone, smiling when Jordan answered on the first ring.

"Hello?"

"Hi, sweetie. I'm close to that shopping center you told me about, so I should be there soon. My next challenge is to figure out how to get around your apartment complex. It looks like a dozen streets go around in circles. Why couldn't you guys live on a nice, normal street?"

"'Cause it's cheaper to live in an ugly, industrial-looking, poorly-built dump that looks like a motel."

"Good point. But it's not easy for your guests."

Jordan laughed. "We don't get many. But don't worry, I'll run down to the main entrance and meet you. Besides, I can't stand still for ten more minutes."

"You don't mind?"

"Mia." Jordan's voice was soft and soothing, and Mia felt it wrap around her like a gentle hug. I'd have come to Berkeley to drive with you if I could have gotten out of practice. I'm so excited about seeing you that my roommates have been threatening to nail my shoes to the floor. I'm wearing a path in our cheap carpet."

Mia laughed, knowing how hard it was for her lover to sit still when she was anxious. "Okay. I'm getting off the highway now. I should be there in about ten minutes."

"That's what it'll take me to run to the gate. See you soon."

"Bye," Mia said, but Jordan had already hung up.

Mia pulled up to the main entrance of the Castle Pines Apartment Complex and smiled when she saw Jordan sprinting down the macadam. In the second it took her to slow down, three cars pulled up behind her, two of them aggressively honking their horns. After pulling over to the side of the road, she started throwing everything from the passenger seat into the back.

Jordan headed for Mia's side, but she obviously thought better of the idea when cars started whipping around the vehicle. She made a slight correction and skidded to a stop, spraying gravel into the air. Jordan opened the door and slid into the now clean seat in one smooth move. Smiling brightly, she reached for Mia, but the car started to move when Mia turned to meet her embrace. "Brake!" she called out, laughing at Mia's short but colorful explosion of profanity. "Kiss me, you crazy woman."

Mia melted into her arms, feeling the stress and strain of two full days of driving disappear when Jordan embraced her. Their lips met, then pressed tenderly against each other's. The kiss lasted for a long time, the soft sounds of lips touching and touching and touching filling the small car. Mia let her head drop back onto Jordan's arm, giving her a lazy smile. "Has it really only been six days?"

"Seems like a thousand." Jordan dove back in for another lengthy kiss. They stayed right where they were for almost ten minutes, neither woman wanting to let the other go long enough to drive to the apartment. "My room is more comfortable than your car," Jordan eventually murmured. "Barely."

Mia pulled away and pushed the curls from her eyes. She took a breath. "Do you have anything to eat? I'm starving."

"Mmm...not really. I ate at the training center. But there's a lot of stuff around here. Let's go get something right now, so we don't have to leave again."

"Ha! Like I'll let you leave once I get you inside."

"Then let's get you some dinner, 'cause you're not getting away from me, either."

They went to a nearby restaurant and settled into a booth. The place wasn't fancy, but it had a wide selection, and Mia quickly found a salad with grilled chicken that sounded perfect.

Jordan didn't order anything, which earned her a scowl from the server, but she didn't seem to notice. The look on her face showed such perfect contentment that Mia guessed not many things could upset her at that moment.

While they waited, Mia studied Jordan's face. "Are you losing more weight? You look even thinner than you did last week."

Jordan looked down at herself. "Yeah, I lost about a half pound this week. It's not by choice, though."

"Jordy, order some food if you're hungry!"

"No, no, I'm not hungry. I'm fine, really. I'm getting lean, which is good for me."

"You were lean before. You're starting to get skinny."

"Maybe you won't think that when you see me naked," Jordan said, batting her eyes.

Images started to flash through Mia's mind, and suddenly eating seemed much less important. "Change the subject or we're bolting," she said, dead serious.

"Only because I know you're hungry." Jordan leaned close and said, "You have no idea how hard it is not to take you in my arms and kiss you until dawn."

"I can eat tomorrow." Mia grabbed her bag and started to get up, but Jordan snagged her belt loop and tugged her back into place.

"You need to eat. It won't take long."

The salad was delivered, and Mia concentrated on her food for a minute. When she looked up, Jordan was gazing at her, a surprisingly serious expression on her face. "What?" Mia asked, mid-bite.

Jordan's expression gentled. "I was just thinking of how big a deal this all is. It's still hard for me to believe you've chucked everything to be here with me."

The fork was halfway to Mia's mouth, but it didn't finish its journey. It stayed in the air as Mia cocked her head and asked, "Wouldn't you do the same for me?"

"Yeah. Yeah, I would. I guess I'm still having a hard time getting used to the idea that I'm important enough to you to have you do this."

Mia put the bite into her mouth and gave Jordan a scolding look. She chewed for a moment, then said, "You're the last person in the world who should be insecure. I still have a hard time believing that you picked me when you could have had any lesbian in the country."

"Yeah." Jordan showed a good-natured grin. "That's absolutely true.

I hear from every lesbian in the country—all the time, as a matter of fact—but I keep turning 'em down. It's costing me a fortune in postage."

"That's not what I meant, and you know it. My point was that you don't seem to have any idea of how desirable you are, and that amazes me. A woman who looks like you and is as smart and thoughtful and talented as you are should have a huge swollen head."

"That would kinda ruin the looks part of the package," Jordan teased.

"Fine." Mia took another bite. "You don't have to accept the truth. But you don't have one thing in the world to be insecure about. You're a fantastic woman, and no one knows that more than I do."

Jordan reached across the table and took Mia's hand. "No one but you matters," she said, fixing Mia with her pale blue eyes.

"When you say that, I believe it."

Jordan matched Mia's smile. "You'd better, 'cause it's all true. Now finish that salad so we can go home."

"I like the sound of that. Home."

They arrived at Jordan's unit after a drive through a maze of identical apartments. Mia was sure she wasn't going to venture out alone until she learned her way around, and she feared that would take months. They each took a suitcase and climbed up the exterior staircase to reach the second floor.

"How did you avoid breaking your neck when these concrete steps were icy?" Mia panted, her fitness level having dropped since she'd stopped going to the gym.

"It wasn't easy. Good thing I don't drink much, huh?"

"Well, I do," Mia wheezed through a laugh.

They reached the apartment, and Jordan used her key to enter. "You need to lock the door, even if you're only going out for a minute. There've been a couple of rapes in this part of town, and the police think the rapist might live in the neighborhood."

"Nice. Any ax murderers?"

"Not that I know of. I don't think most murderers use axes any more. Too cumbersome."

They went inside, and Mia was pleased to see that the living room was empty of people, but dismayed that it was also nearly devoid of furniture. "Minimalist. Nice."

"Cheap. We hardly ever use this room." She lowered her voice, "We're with each other all day. At night we want to be alone."

There wasn't a television or a stereo in the room, and the single overstuffed chair didn't hold much appeal. There was a collection of brightly-colored floor pillows that looked like they might be comfortable, but since there wasn't a television, Mia guessed she'd have to use them to stare at the ceiling. "Maybe I should've brought some of your furniture from the garage."

"Nah. You'll be here alone during the day, so all you'll need is the chair. At night, we'll be in my room. This is enough."

Mia nodded, an unspoken "We'll see" held back.

A door in the hallway opened, and one of Jordan's roommates emerged. Mia recognized her as the woman who'd leered at Jordan during the tournament in Florida. "Hi," the tall, dark brunette said. "You must be Mia."

Mia smiled and extended her hand. "Yeah, I am."

While they shook, Jordan said, "Mia, this is Jill Hennings. This is her second Olympics, so she's an old hand."

She'd better keep her old hands off my Jordy, Mia thought, trying not to let her antipathy show. "It's good to meet you. I hope having me here isn't going to be a problem."

"No, no problem," Jill said. "This isn't much of a home, anyway. It's just a place to sleep."

The reality of that hit her. It was going to be her home, even if the other women didn't think of it as theirs. "You don't eat together?"

"No," Jill said. "None of us can cook, and we can eat for free at the training center." She paused for a second and made a face. "Ooo...you won't be able to do that."

"Don't worry," Jordan said. "I'll come home as soon as I can. We'll have dinner together."

"I'm not worried. I know it'll all work out."

"It's good to have you here," Jill said. "If you need any info about the city or anything, I'm your woman. I've lived here, on and off, for six years."

"Wow...that's a long time." The thought of living with a bunch of roommates for six days, much less six years seemed like a long time—especially when you didn't particularly like each other.

"Yeah, it is. But Colorado Springs is a nice place, and it'd be hard for me to train at home. Sometimes I wish I'd chosen an individual sport—but I love volleyball, so it's worth the sacrifice."

"It's worth it to me too," Jordan agreed, "but Mia isn't playing a sport she loves."

"No, but I get the benefit of being with the woman I love. That makes everything all right."

Jordan smiled at her for several seconds, her gaze unwavering. Clearly having had enough of the doe-eyes, Jill went back into her room. Jordan didn't react to her leaving. She looked into Mia's eyes and blinked away the emotion that was building. "I'm not sure how I'll do it, but I'll do anything in my power to make sure you never regret coming here." When she held out her hand, Mia took it and pulled her close.

Automatically, Jordan's hands rested on her shoulders, as hers palmed Jordan's hips—the pose now a thing of habit. They stared at each other for another few moments, their eyes saying more than either felt capable of verbalizing at that moment.

Jordan tilted her head and started to lean in. As she did, each woman encircled the other's body with her arms, then their lips met. Gently, tenderly, almost shyly, they kissed, the sweetness of the moment almost too much to bear.

It reminded Mia of their first nights together, when Jordan was so painfully shy and afraid. But this time it wasn't Jordan who was afraid, it was Mia. Standing in the living room of an unadorned apartment in a city she'd never visited and having to contend with four new roommates suddenly felt a little overwhelming, and she needed the safety of Jordan's arms to reassure her.

Jordan was right there with her, seeming to know that Mia was feeling a little shaky. "Let's go to our room," she whispered. "You can meet the other guys in the morning."

Mia nodded, and they each grabbed a suitcase and headed down the hall. "Jill and Toni are in the first room," Jordan said, nodding at the door they'd passed. "It's Jill's apartment, so she gets the room with the bathroom. Makela and Ekaterina are across the hall from Jill. We're behind Makela and Ekaterina and across from the bathroom. We're gonna have to come up with some kinda schedule, so no one's late in the morning."

Before the door to the bedroom was fully open, Mia decided they needed to move. The room contained a full-sized bed and a television sitting on the floor—and it was overcrowded. The bed was pushed against two walls, and even with that, the door barely cleared it. "It's not much, but it's cozy, huh?" Jordan asked, obviously trying to put a good spin on it.

Mia put everything else out of her mind and focused on the one thing that was worth more than anything in her life. "If we're together, anyplace is fine."

Jordan leaned over to give her another kiss. "I'm so lucky to have you." When she broke the kiss, she stayed in position for a moment, staring into Mia's eyes. She still looked surprised, maybe even amazed. Like she couldn't believe Mia was in her arms once again. "I'll go get the rest of your stuff while you start to unpack. I, uhm…don't have a dresser or anything, and this room doesn't have a closet, but it has two windows." Her expression showed that was a big selling point. "I keep my stuff in those plastic bins." Neatly labeled blue rectangles were stacked against the wall. "We can go get some for you tomorrow, okay?"

"It's fine, honey. Don't worry about it. I'll get my toothbrush out. That's all I'll need, right?" She gave her lover a sexy smile while fingering the buttons on her fly.

Jordan's eyes widened in delighted agreement. "You might need a T-shirt to go to the bathroom, but other than that—you're set. Be right back."

Mia watched her leave, then she walked to the closer of the two windows and looked out, seeing nothing but two-story, flat-roofed, dun-colored buildings. It was an awfully long way from their roomy, homey, Berkeley bungalow, but it was where they needed to be. One day they'd regale their kids with stories of their first shared apartment. It would be funny—then.

After a thorough tooth brushing and flossing, Mia scampered back to their room, glad that the other roommates hadn't seen her in her underwear. She wasn't shy by any means, but she preferred to meet people while fully clothed. Her moment of discomfort vanished when she saw Jordan lying in bed, her long legs tenting the sheet and blanket. Jordan was wearing a dark turtleneck sweater, her golden hair shimmering in the light of a large candle resting on more plastic storage boxes, this set serving as a bedside table.

"Going somewhere?" Mia asked. She stripped off her shirt and panties and jumped into bed, shivering from the cold.

"I'm just trying to stay warm. I usually wear sweatpants, too, but I'm gonna let you keep me warm down there."

"Not a problem." Mia snuggled close and buried her face between her breasts. "My nose is cold," she mumbled. "It's gonna take a minute for me to warm up."

Jordan stroked her back. "It's gonna take longer than that. Having two windows isn't always the perk you'd think it'd be. They're single pane, and I swear I can feel the wind whistle through the part where they meet."

Mia looked up at the cheap, metal windows, seeing frost covering the bottom half of each. "It's gonna take some time to get used to the weather. I've been skiing a lot, but I've never lived anywhere cold."

"I thought I knew what cold weather was, but I didn't. It gets kinda mind-numbing after a while. Hard to believe my ancestors came from Sweden, 'cause I don't have the cold weather gene."

"Sleeping together will make everything better." Mia curled her body around Jordan's even tighter. "Being with you always does."

Jordan tilted her head but didn't make another move. All of her anxious energy was gone. She now seemed fully content to merely gaze into Mia's eyes. Her lips parted, then closed, and she blinked repeatedly. Mia saw that her eyes were dewy, and knew that Jordan was having a hard time putting her feelings into words. But with Jordan, she didn't need to hear words. She could almost feel the emotion that coursed through her body, and she knew how much Jordan appreciated whatever sacrifices she'd made for them to be together.

Mia tightened her grip and held Jordan so closely that she forced some of the air from her lungs. She ran her hands all over her back, probing the thin layer of flesh that covered her lean body. After a long while, Mia's hands were finally warm, and she slipped a hand under Jordan's sweater, just enough of a chill remaining to make her flinch. "Mmm...I love to watch you twitch," Mia whispered. She heard someone walking down the hall, then heard voices coming from the next room.

"Hi," one voice said. "Where've you been?"

A voice with a heavy eastern European accent said, "To the movies."

"What did you see? Anything good?"

Mia sat up and stared, open mouthed. "What are the walls made of—tissue paper?"

Looking embarrassed and abashed, Jordan said, "I usually have my TV on for background noise. I mean...I knew I could hear 'em, but I guess I didn't really..." She shrugged helplessly. "I sleep really soundly because

I'm so tired, and they usually go to sleep pretty early, so it hasn't been a problem. I can…I can…"

Mia pressed a finger to her lips. "It's okay," she soothed, angry with herself for showing her alarm. "We'll just put on some quiet music."

"I don't have…" Jordan looked around the tiny room, apparently searching for a stereo system that didn't exist.

"We'll get something to play music on. I can bring my setup from Berkeley or buy a speaker."

Jordan looked crestfallen. "I didn't think ahead. I should have figured out how hard this would be."

"Don't worry about it." Mia rubbed her partner gently, her cold hand causing a riot of goosebumps. "We're together. That's what matters. That's all that matters, right?"

With her head tilted down, Jordan shifted her eyes to look at Mia through her fair lashes. Her eyes were hooded, and she looked like she expected to be scolded. "Yeah, I guess."

Mia grasped her chin with her fingers. "It's all that matters. To me at least. Isn't being together enough for you?"

"Yes, yes! Of course it is! I'm just so sorry that this place sucks so badly. You're used to your great house. And lots of privacy and your own bathroom and nice furniture."

"None of that matters. Being with you is all that's important to me. If you don't believe that, we're gonna have problems."

"We are?"

"Yes. This won't work if you're walking around apologizing all of the time. I want you to understand that I want to be here. I need to be here. Not to be in Colorado Springs and not to be in a nice apartment. I need to be here because of you. Only you. And if you're here—I'm happy."

Jordan's face relaxed and she smiled—a hopeful, albeit tentative, smile. "I'm happy with you. Very, very happy."

Mia gave her a pinch, then jumped out of bed and ran to her suitcase. "I'm happy, but I'm freezing!" She rummaged through her bag and found a baby blue fleece hoodie and a matching pair of pants. She jumped into the clothes, nearly shrieking when the ice-cold zipper hit her bare chest. After adding some thick socks, she ran back to bed, letting Jordan rub her body to warm her up again. "Why do you only have one blanket?" she asked through chattering teeth.

"Well, I only own one, and I haven't wanted to buy another."

"Why not? It must be sixty degrees in here."

"I know, but if I'm really warm, it'll be that much harder to get up in the morning. Now there isn't much difference between being in bed and getting up."

Mia kissed her partner, their cold lips meeting long enough to begin to warm. "You are one nutty girl."

Jordan laughed. "You get up at five thirty and tell me how easy it is."

"Thank God tomorrow's Sunday."

"Uhm…I have to train in the morning. Sunday's my light weight-training day." Her words came out in a rush. "But I'll be finished early, and we'll have the rest of the day together."

Mia looked at her watch. "What time do you have to get up?"

"Uhm…five thirty…every day. The coach likes us to stay on a regular schedule. We stay on Mountain Time even when we travel. So when we're on the east coast, we get up at seven thirty. Of course that means four thirty on the west coast, which kinda sucks."

Mia gave her a smile that took more than a little effort to fabricate. "I'll get up with you so we're on the same schedule."

"Oh, not tomorrow. You sleep late. I know you're tired after that long drive. Besides, there's nothing for you to do at that time of the morning. I couldn't stay awake if I wasn't lifting weights."

"Can I go with you?"

Jordan shook her head. "No, I don't think so. There's a strict rule against having anyone watch us. The coaches are always worried about someone stealing our training program."

"Yeah, that's what I'm all about. I want to start my own Olympic team, representing Miaville."

"I'll ask, but I wouldn't get my hopes up."

Mia hugged her hard. "Get your hopes up for what we're gonna do when you get home tomorrow afternoon." She pinched Jordan's firm ass, then filled her hand with the flesh.

"Not now?" Disappointment clouded her face.

"It's ten o'clock," Mia said, amazed by her own words. "Time for you to sleep."

The warm smile Jordan gave her almost made forgoing making love worth it. "I hate to agree, but this is late for me. I'm usually in bed by nine and asleep by nine-thirty."

"Nine-thirty it is," Mia said, forcing herself to smile. They kissed again, spending a few minutes luxuriating in their closeness. All too soon she pulled away and kissed Jordan's forehead, then turned on her side and squirmed around until her butt was firmly pressed against Jordan's abdomen. Long, thin but muscular arms enfolded her, and for the first time in a long while, Mia felt safe and secure. Chilly on the outside, but warm as toast in her heart.

Chapter Eleven

After their full day at Disneyland, Jamie stayed in the room while Ryan and Jennie went to dinner with the team. It took about an hour to put the finishing touches on her article, and when she was finished she brought up her e-mail program and sent it to her father. Her stomach was in knots, but she knew that delaying wouldn't make it any easier. It was eleven o'clock in Washington, and she knew he was usually up at least that late. Fighting the urge to call him to ask him to read it, she decided it was better to just wait it out.

There was nothing on TV to hold her interest and she didn't really feel like socializing, so she didn't try to find Ryan. Ordering from room service provided a mild distraction from her anxiety. She briefly considered adding a drink to her order, but she'd promised herself she wasn't going to use alcohol to get through emotionally tough periods. Instead she did her best to focus on a documentary on PBS, wishing with all of her might that her father would read the article and call her soon.

Mia woke with a start on Sunday morning when Jordan's shrill alarm rang at five thirty, but after a few gentle kisses and a nice back scratch she settled down again and went back to sleep. Hours later she woke, visited the bathroom, then wandered around the apartment, pleased by the silence. Jordan and her roommates were obviously working out together, so she decided to enjoy a leisurely breakfast.

Her investigation of the kitchen cabinets revealed only protein powder, nutritional supplements, powdered sports drink and vitamins. Four adult women had to have some form of food in their apartment, but further exploration didn't reveal any—just more performance enhancing drinks, potions and elixirs.

She wasn't in the mood to shower, so she put on her clothing from the day before and ran out to her car, shivering in the crisp twenty degree day. Jordan had assured her that the cold spell they were experiencing was very unusual for that time of year. Mia wasn't sure she believed her. Having spent her whole life in California, she thought fifty degrees was time to pull out the down comforter. In her mind, if you needed a coat—it was damned cold.

She was able to scrounge up a pack of Oreos, half of a Twix bar and a Diet Coke, although the Coke was half frozen. Running back towards the apartment, she stopped in her tracks when a man started to dart up the same staircase. *Oh, fuck! I didn't lock the door!* She was angry with herself for being careless, but also a little angry with Jordan for making her fear what was probably an ordinary guy going to his apartment.

Since this was the first time she'd seen the place in daylight, she didn't know how many apartments the staircase served. There were three more sets of stairs, and she guessed there were about twelve apartments on the second floor. Doing the math as she walked closer to the staircase, she calculated that it served three apartments. The man quietly opened and closed a door, but she couldn't tell if he used a key. It hadn't take him long to open his—or her—door. She hated to imagine drama when there wasn't any, but it was clearly possible he'd been watching her and had run upstairs when he thought she wasn't looking. She felt in the pockets of her coat and pants, hoping that her cell phone was there. Then she realized the police probably wouldn't rush to a report of a man walking up the stairs.

She was freezing, not so much due to the temperature as to her lack of acclimation. Going from fifty to twenty degrees was a big drop, especially with a bracing wind chafing her bare hands. She tossed the Coke from hand to hand, considering her options. Finally deciding that she was too afraid to go inside, she got into her car and turned it on, blowing the heater at full power until the cold air became blessedly warm.

The cookies and the candy were the first course of breakfast, and she nearly broke a tooth on the frozen Twix bar. She desperately wanted coffee, but Jordan's neighborhood didn't seem like an espresso kind of place, and she didn't have any idea where the latte and biscotti crowd gathered in Colorado Springs. She warmed the Coke up enough to drink it after managing to spray several ounces onto her windshield and dashboard due to shaking it during her earlier deliberations.

Mia's eyes never left the apartment door, but no one exited. She was reasonably sure that if the man she'd seen was a rapist, he'd leave the apartment when she didn't come back in. But that was more wishful thinking than gospel, so she stayed in the car and waited for a good idea to strike her.

Feeling out-of-sorts and a little scared, she looked around the car in search of more food. Surprisingly, her hand hit her cell phone, and she was pleased to see that it had nearly a full charge. Almost automatically, she called her mother, breathing a sigh of relief when she answered. "Hi, Mom," she said, tearing up at the mere sound of her voice.

"Mia! Where are you?" Anna Lisa's tone was harsh and angry, just like it had been when they'd had their big blow out. But in a few seconds she cooed. "Sweetheart, what's wrong? Are you hurt?"

"No," Mia said, her voice shaking. "I'm just sad."

"Oh, honey, I'm sad, too." Then she started to cry, the sound breaking Mia's heart. "Please come home so we can talk about this."

"I can't," she said, struggling to speak. "I'm in Colorado."

"What?" Now the tears stopped and the sharp tone was even sharper than before. "You're where?"

"I did what I said I was going to do," Mia said, her own tears evaporating. "Why should I stay in Berkeley and work for minimum wage to stay in school? It was hard enough being there without Jordan when all I had to think about was school. I wasn't going to work every spare minute just to be miserable."

"So you quit school because you didn't have money to spend on luxuries? Very mature. Very mature. I can see what you meant when you told us how much you'd grown."

Taking a deep breath, Mia reminded herself that she had grown up. "I didn't call to be yelled at. I know you're worried about me, and I wanted to let you know where I am. I'm going to be living with Jordan and her roommates until we can afford an apartment."

"And just how do you think—"

"I'm not asking for advice. I'm telling you where I am and what I'm doing. If you want to talk after you've calmed down, you can call me on my cell phone. But I'm not going to let you yell at me. I'm just not." She pursed her lips to steel her courage, then hung up.

Mia's head fell back against the headrest. Everything was different.

Strikingly different. The weather, the scenery, the harsh, industrial look of the complex. She was in a foreign place and had no one except Jordan to anchor her. Even though she'd been the one to leave, she felt abandoned by everyone and everything she'd grown used to in Berkeley.

It took a while to regain her composure, but she finally shoved the various junk food wrappers into her pockets and got out of the car. Marching up the stairs, she opened the door to her apartment and called out in a loud voice, "I saw you go into the apartment, asshole. I called the cops, but they're taking for-fucking-ever to get here, and I'm freezing my ass off. So I'm gonna walk back downstairs and give you a chance to escape. If you don't wanna spend the next few years in..." She searched her mind and realized she had no idea where the worst prison in Colorado was. "The slammer, you'd better run." She ran back down the stairs and hid behind a truck, watching the staircase like a hawk. No one emerged, and after a few minutes, she decided that the man had been going to his own apartment. Nonetheless, she dialed 911, waiting to hit "send" until she got inside. Feeling like the victim in a slasher movie, she left the door wide open, then methodically went from room to room, looking inside the closets, nervous as a cat waiting to be attacked. She also checked under every bed, reassured that most of them weren't high enough off the floor for a human to fit underneath.

Finally satisfied that she was alone, she locked the door and stripped off her clothes on the way to the shower, learning another lesson in the process. It was unwise to get into the shower during the winter without fresh clothes nearby. When she emerged from the bathroom, freezing, she heard her phone ringing and dashed to answer it, feeling her heart drop to her stomach when she saw her parents' number. "Hi, Mom."

"You can't hang up on me whenever you want," Anna Lisa said, sounding just past irate. "You have to show me some respect."

"I do respect you. That's why I called. But you have to respect me too. I won't let you yell at my anymore. Period."

"Don't you dare tell me what—"

Once again, Mia hung up. She got into bed and hugged both pillows to her chest, burying her face into the down while she cried herself to sleep.

Mia was in bed, her computer propped up on her legs when Jordan opened the door. Their eyes met, and both women began to smile. Without saying a word, Jordan started to strip off her clothing and was stark naked in a matter of moments. Mia's smile grew as she slid into bed.

The computer was lifted and removed, then Jordan's arms were around her. Suddenly, the world seemed safe and secure and full of promise. Mia took off her sweatshirt, her body feeling the chill immediately. But when Jordan's skin touched hers, the cold was forgotten.

Few things felt better than having Jordan's body pressed up against hers, and Mia spent a moment trying to get as close as possible. Her head was nestled between Jordan's neck and shoulder, and blonde hair covered her face. The hair smelled so good, so fresh and clean that she had no desire to move it.

Their breasts compressed against each other, bellies lightly touching, Jordan's heat warming Mia's body and heart. She slid her leg up over her hip, trying to have every part of their bodies touch.

Jordan's hands danced up and down Mia's back and settled on her ass. She filled her hands with the flesh, warming it as she stroked.

Mia purred contentedly while nuzzling her face against her neck. She lifted her head and shook it, letting Jordan's hair fall back to the pillow. Looking into the guileless blue eyes, she softly said, "I love you."

Giving her a half-smile, Jordan's lips opened, drawing Mia to them. They kissed, gently, with an almost leisurely feel to their movements. Between the kisses, Jordan lifted her head and spent a moment gazing into Mia's eyes, looking so perfectly content that Mia's breath caught. She was so remarkably beautiful. In every way.

Lazily, Mia lay still and let Jordan lead the way. Sometimes they rocked the house, nearly attacking each other, their lovemaking filled with wild abandon. As pleasurable and satisfying as that always was, she knew that wasn't what fed Jordan's primal need. What she needed was connection—touching and being touched slowly, methodically—letting the heat build up between them at a very deliberate rate. She'd often spend an hour or two studying Mia's body, kissing and stroking every part of it, seemingly unconcerned with trying to excite her. It was more akin to worship than sex, but it seemed to fill her up in a way that nothing else did.

Mia was the more orgasm-centered of the pair, but in their time together she'd learned to pace herself. Usually, like today, Jordan made it clear from the beginning that she was going to take her on a slow, sensual ride. So Mia stretched her arms out over her head and closed her eyes, silently showing that she understood and happily acquiesced.

Mia tried to clear her mind and let Jordan take her where she wanted. She knew they'd be touching each other for hours, and that once Jordan set this pace, there'd be no hurrying her. So she tried to tamp down her thrumming desire and open herself to the delightful sensation of being totally and thoroughly loved by the woman to whom she'd pledged her entire future.

The softball team arrived back in Berkeley late on Sunday night. Ryan was tired, finding it much more draining sitting in a dugout watching rain fall than actually playing the game.

Everyone but Jennie was a little down on the flight home. They all loved the team, but spending the weekend in a motel during constant rain wasn't much fun for anyone but a high-school freshman with a serious case of hero worship.

When they dropped her off at the group home, Jennie was as happy as Ryan had ever seen her. She thanked Jamie so enthusiastically for taking her that both Ryan and Jamie laughed about it on the way home.

"Sometimes I feel so old and jaded around her," Jamie said.

"You're seven years older. That's a long time during those particular years."

"Yeah, but I feel so parental with her. And she treats us more like parents than peers."

"We're not her peers. I've always tried to maintain an adult/parental role with her. The last thing I wanted was for her to get a crush on me."

"Yeah," Jamie said, smiling to herself. "That worked out well."

They arrived at their house a few minutes later. It was strange not to have the answering machine filled with messages for Mia, and Ryan started poking around the house in an aimless fashion, as she often did when she was a little melancholy.

Jamie's anxiety had started to build as soon as the plane landed. Her opinion piece was scheduled to run in the morning paper, and she still hadn't heard from her father. The need to call him was overwhelming. Even without knowing his feelings about the article, she felt thoroughly torn about her decision to publish it. In her heart, she knew it was the right thing to do, but that didn't make it any easier to face the consequences. And she knew there would be consequences—with her father and with her personal life.

Ryan passed through the parlor and sat down next to Jamie on the sofa. "Wanna take a long bath and try to relax?"

"Mmm...a bath does sound pretty good. What are you gonna do?"

"I've got a big day tomorrow. I'd better turn in."

"Why don't you hop into bed, and I'll come cuddle you when I'm finished."

They got up together and Ryan leaned in to kiss her. "No running off to another bed, okay?"

"I promise." Feeling embarrassed, she hadn't told Ryan the whole truth of why she'd fallen asleep in the second bed at the hotel. "If I wanna watch TV, I'll put headphones on and watch from our bed."

"Our bed," Ryan said, a goofy smile on her face. "Such a simple, but wonderful image."

Jamie patted her butt. "Go dive in, tiger. I'll be in to join you as soon as I feel able to sleep."

"I'll rub your back."

Jamie appreciated the offer, but knew it was for a limited time. Once Ryan was sound asleep, she'd have to shake her to wake her, and she hated to do that. "If I need it."

They kissed, holding each other just long enough to make Ryan sigh heavily and tilt her head to deepen the kiss.

"Mmm...maybe you wanna relax another way."

"I do." Ryan smiled wryly and kissed her again. "But I'm too tired. How old am I?"

Jamie rubbed her back. "You're younger than springtime. And your energy level is stupendous. You just had a long weekend."

Ryan leaned heavily on her, making Jamie struggle to keep her feet. "I used to be able to stay up until three and still make it to class on time."

"You still could. But you don't have to." She slapped her on the butt. "Now get to bed. I'll see you soon."

"Okay, but feel free to wake me up if you wanna get rockin'."

"You'll be the first," Jamie said, giving her one last quick kiss.

Jamie was just about to call it a night when her cell phone rang. Her heart leapt to her throat, and she ran to the table in the entryway to grab the phone. "Hello?"

"Is this a good time to talk?" Jim asked with studied politeness.

"Sure. Of course." They'd barely said a word and she was already miffed at his formal, distant tone. Not a good way to start.

"I read it, then I had Kayla read it," he began. "Just to make sure, I had another aide read it, as well as my press secretary."

It wasn't wise to be snarky. No one liked it. It never furthered an argument, and it created a wall that had to be broken through. But she couldn't stop herself. "What did the doorman at your hotel think?"

He paused for a few seconds. "That's a low blow. It's one thing to have a difference of opinion with me, and quite another to take your opinion to the *San Francisco Chronicle*. You can't play the political game and then be angry when I treat this as a political issue."

"You're right," she said softly. "That was unfair of me."

He replied in an equally quiet tone. "Thanks for saying so."

"I know this affects you as a senator, but I'm really only interested in how my father feels about it."

Once again he was quiet for a few moments. "Well, as you might guess, I have mixed feelings. Just one question. Did you write this on your own?"

"Every word," she confirmed. "GLBTQDAD offered to help, but I didn't want them to be involved."

"I see," he mused. "Well, I guess my reaction is that this could have been a hell of a lot worse. Most twenty-two-year-olds couldn't have written something like this, especially when they were really angry. Thanks for that."

"So?"

"I wish we hadn't fought about this, and I wish you hadn't agreed to write it. But given that you did, this was the best outcome I could have hoped for." He chuckled lightly. "As your father, I have to add that I'm really impressed with how well you write. You have a real talent for expressing your ideas."

"Thanks, Dad," she said, feeling surprisingly proud. She cleared her throat and said, "I guess I lied. I do want to know how this affects you as a senator. What does your staff think?"

"They don't think it will be a huge problem. Actually, Kayla's already figured out a way to spin this; it shows that even though you and I disagree on an important issue, we're still close. She thinks it'll make me appear compassionate as well as principled."

"It's all about appearances, isn't it?" she asked, trying to keep the sarcasm from her voice.

"It is."

"Well, I hope I haven't made things too difficult for you." She paused for a moment and corrected herself. "Actually, that's not true. I do want to make things difficult for you, and for every other lawmaker who tries to keep society from recognizing the validity of my love. But I still love you—even though I strongly disagree with your position."

"I understand that, Jamie. I hope we can continue to talk about this. Maybe, over time, you'll see why I voted the way I did."

"Or maybe you'll change your position," she said, smiling to herself.

"I guess one never knows, does one?" He laughed, sounding at ease and relaxed. "It's past my bedtime, honey. Good luck with your article."

"Thanks, Dad. I'll talk to you soon."

"I hope it's very soon. Give Ryan my regards."

"I will." It was on the tip of her tongue to wish the same for Kayla, but she wasn't able to do that yet, so she just signed off. "G'night, Dad."

Chapter Twelve

On Monday morning, Mia woke to the sound of voices. She lay still for a moment, hoping Jordan was just in the bathroom, but the front door closed loudly and then the apartment was shrouded in complete silence. It was still dark out, and she saw that it wasn't yet six o'clock. The last thing she wanted to do was get up, but if she was going to go to bed at nine she was going to have to get used to getting up by six. She pushed the covers away, pleased to find that it wasn't nearly as cold as it had been the day before.

Having the place to herself was preferable in some ways, since she didn't have to make conversation with strangers. But it was also lonely, and she once again felt completely adrift, as though she'd lost her compass and couldn't find true north.

A long shower didn't help her mood, but it did wake her up. She got dressed and found the coffee pot, but there was no milk and no sugar, only artificial sweetener. She realized that even if she could make fantastic coffee she had a need for some human connection. Logging on to the Internet, she found a Starbucks that was just five miles from the apartment. After writing careful directions, she got into her car and started to drive, feeling better to have some sense of purpose.

The Starbucks was connected to a Barnes & Noble, and she brightened at seeing two familiar stores. She bought a copy of the newspaper and drank two cappuccinos, spending the better part of an hour doing so.

By the time she'd finished her coffee, the bookstore was open, but instead of browsing she went back to the apartment and got her notes and textbooks from one of her classes. Returning to the bookstore, she found a comfortable chair, and took up residence, spending the next four hours studying. That was the longest time she'd spent on schoolwork since the previous term's finals but it felt surprisingly good. Like it was part of her new, adult regime. If Jordan could work for hours every day—so could she.

When Jamie woke, she rolled over and found not Ryan, but the neatly folded editorial section of the *Chronicle* bearing a note that read, "I'm proud of you, R."

That was a nice way to start the day, but actually having Ryan in the flesh would have been much nicer.

Already knowing the words all too well, she didn't bother to read the article. Not in a rush to get to school, she dawdled in the shower. On the walk over, even though she didn't run into many people on the street, she had the creepy feeling that people were looking at her. She knew she was being ridiculous, but their recent infamy still lurked in the back of her mind. Once you'd been exploited by the news media you were always waiting to be thrust into the spotlight again. Asking for scrutiny, as she'd done this time, made her doubt her sanity. But she'd done it and now had to deal with it.

Not many students read the *Chronicle*, but the few that did must have told others. By the time she was in the middle of campus, Jamie was getting a lot of looks, and this time it wasn't her imagination. Her cheeks were burning with embarrassment, and she was so angry with herself for putting herself into such a situation that she felt like running back home and staying inside for a week.

When she entered her classroom, the normal chatter died to a hush. Jamie was certain that people were talking about her, and she was sure of it when she saw one woman pass the editorial section to another. For a few moments, she felt the same sense of panic she'd felt when she and Ryan were being hounded constantly. Her heart was racing, feeling like it would burst from her chest. A glance at the clock showed that class wouldn't start for a couple of minutes, and she was torn between getting up and leaving or jumping out the window.

Her cell phone vibrated in her pocket, and she reached out with her shaking hand to open the cover. It was Ryan. Immediately, her heart started to slow, and she touched the answer button and held the phone to her ear. "Come get me," she whispered.

"Be right there." Not a moment's hesitation. Knowing that Ryan would drop anything at any time for her was sweet, sweet consolation.

"No," Jamie said with a little more volume. "I'm kidding...mostly."

"You don't need to put up with any shit today. You can just go home. I'm happy to come and get you, and I swear I'll pop the first person who stares at you."

"You'd better have your brass knuckles on. I don't want you to bruise that pretty hand." She could almost hear Ryan's smile.

"Are you gonna be okay? Tell me the truth."

"Yeah, I am. Thanks for calling, baby. It always helps to know you're there for me."

"Always will be," Ryan said, her conviction sounding rock-solid.

"Gotta go. My prof's here. I love you."

"Love you, too. Call me if you need me. Any time."

Jamie blew a quiet kiss into the phone then hung up, trying her best to listen to her professor. But the hour passed with little of the lecture getting into her head. Instead, she spent the time trying to tamp down the anger she felt at her father. Not just for the stand he'd taken, but for his getting into politics at all. She and Ryan would have still had more infamy than she'd ever wanted, but her being the daughter of a senator made the carjacking story last longer than it would have if she'd been an ordinary college student.

Even the divorce was now news because of Jim's position. Having a senator get divorced was a big deal in the entire state, not just the San Francisco legal community. By the time the class was over, she was steaming—angry for herself and her lover and her mother.

She left the classroom building and tried to scamper to her next class as quickly as possible. From the corner of her eye, she saw a guy start to approach her. Though she walked even faster, he caught up with her.

"Hi," he said, smiling brightly.

A polite smile flitted across her lips, and she kept walking. The man touched her shoulder, and she ducked away, ready to slap him. But he was still smiling, and his friendliness finally penetrated her fog. "Yeah?"

"Thanks for the piece in the paper," he said. "It meant a lot to me."

"Oh." She looked at him for a moment, not sure how to respond. "You're welcome."

"That's all," he said. "I just wanted to say thanks." He smiled again and took off in the opposite direction. She stood there for a moment, then started to walk again. A group of women passed her, and one of them said, "No on 22!" as they walked on.

When she approached her next classroom building, her professor caught her eye and approached. "You did a great job on that opinion piece, Jamie. It must have been hard for you to do."

She nodded. "It was. I don't think it'll do any good, but I felt like I had to give it a try."

They got on the elevator together, and he said, "You don't always know what good you're doing. Sometimes you help people you aren't intending to reach. You just have to do your best."

"True, but I hope I can be just another anonymous student after this blows over. I never knew how nice it was to be ignored when I walk across campus."

"One of the little things you don't know you enjoy until it's taken away, huh?"

"Exactly," she said, smiling and feeling much better when they entered the room together.

Ryan was hurrying home from practice later that night, dreaming of spending the evening with Jamie. Her hunger for uninterrupted time with her partner was growing with each day. Never before had she craved the simple satisfaction of doing absolutely nothing with someone she loved, but she longed for it like a powerful drug.

She was about halfway home when her cell phone rang. Expecting Jamie, she frowned when she saw "Vijay Khan" on the display. "Oh, fuck!" She said this aloud, startling a young mother taking her son for a walk. "I'm sorry," Ryan said as she rushed past them. She opened her phone and said, "Hi, Vijay."

"Where would you like to meet tonight? We didn't set a place when we spoke the other day."

"Uhm…I'd really like to meet another day, if that's possible."

He made a soft clicking sound with his tongue and said, "That's up to you. But I don't have another night free before your next progress meeting. Do you feel comfortable enough with your work to fly blind?"

"No, I guess I don't."

"I'd love to help you out, but I'm really over-scheduled this month."

"Tell me about it," she grumbled. "I'll come to your apartment. What's your address again?"

He told her and she realized she was just two blocks away. "Wanna have dinner together? Maybe we can finish early."

"Sure. Should we order in?"

"Yeah. Order me anything. I'm not picky."

"Thai okay?"

"Yep. Just order like three people are gonna eat."

Vijay laughed. "I've eaten with you before. I know the routine."

"See you in a few," Ryan said. She hung up and dialed her home, hoping that Jamie wasn't as disappointed as she was.

Jamie was in bed, reading from her econ text when the front door opened and closed. She checked the clock. Ten p.m. So much for Ryan making it an early night.

A few minutes later, Ryan walked into the room and flicked the book with her finger. "Sleep aide?"

"It works when I'm sitting in class. I thought it would work here, too." She laid the book on her lap and opened her arms.

Ryan sat on the edge of the bed and nuzzled her face into her neck. "I hate physics."

"Bad night?"

"Yeah." Ryan sat up and pushed her hair from her eyes. "Physics isn't my strongest subject, and it's not Vijay's either. It takes us longer to get through those parts of the problems than either math or programming."

"Maybe you should have a physics advisor, too."

"All I need is another person to have to meet with. It's bad enough that I have to meet every week with Vijay and every month with my prof. How stupid was I to commit to a massive independent study?"

Jamie knew that was rhetorical. She touched the blue-tinted skin under Ryan's eyes. "You look beat."

"I am. But my mind is racing. We weren't really finished when we quit, and I can't stop thinking."

"Back rub?" She gently ran her fingers across Ryan's back.

"Nah. I'll go into my room and jot a few things down. If I can get these ideas out of my head I might be able to sleep."

"Mind if I don't wait up for you? Six o'clock comes awfully early."

"No, baby, you go to sleep. I know it's hard for you to get up for practice as it is."

Jamie stretched and yawned. "It is. I've never understood the appeal of playing golf when the grass is wet with dew."

Ryan gently played with Jamie's hair while gazing into her eyes. "You doing okay? You sounded pretty stressed today."

"I'm fine. I think this bout of fame is gonna be fleeting. It's not salacious enough to last long."

"Thank God for that. I didn't notice anyone paying attention to me today, so I must not have hit the radar."

Jamie smiled at her. She'd never been anywhere with Ryan that the majority of people they encountered hadn't obviously or furtively checked her out. But Ryan was so used to people being intrigued by her physical presence that she didn't seem to notice it. Jamie wasn't sure what level of scrutiny would penetrate her fog, but she was happy that today didn't reach that point. "I'm glad." She kissed Ryan tenderly, then wrapped her arms around her and held her for a few minutes, finding herself nearly lulled to sleep by her partner's strong, steady heartbeat.

"Come on, sleepy," Ryan said. She took the textbook away and fluffed up Jamie's pillows. "Time for Mr. Sandman to visit."

Jamie scooted down under the covers and puckered up for another kiss. Ryan bent down and they kissed softly until she winced. "Bad angle." Sitting up, she murmured, "I love you."

"I love you, too, honey. Kiss me when you come to bed."

"I always do." Ryan blew her one last kiss and went into her room, grumbling loud enough for Jamie to hear.

Chapter Thirteen

Ryan opened one eye when her alarm rang on Tuesday morning. The sky was a flat, dull gray, and she could see the trees moving briskly in the wind. The weather matched her mood; stormy, gray and bleak. Jamie's blow dryer buzzed quietly, but instead of joining her, she went into Mia's bathroom. When she felt like she did this morning, she didn't want to have to summon up the strength to be pleasant.

She was still showering when Jamie poked her head in to say goodbye. One minor skirmish averted. Once dressed, she had plenty of time to make coffee, but she dawdled a little, turning on the radio in the kitchen to hear the local commentators talk about the election. Every word she heard made her teeth clench, so she put on her slicker and grabbed her book bag. It was only about forty degrees, and the wind was really whipping, making the fine drizzle feel like icy needles. It was clear she was woefully underdressed. *Fuck it*, she thought, even though it would have taken her mere seconds to go back in and get a warmer coat. She considered driving to therapy, but knew the traffic would be horrible because of the rain. Taking her motorcycle flitted through her head, but Jamie hated it when she rode in inclement weather, so she dismissed that idea out of hand.

After wasting time and brooding about her options, she was running a little late and didn't have time to stop for coffee or food. Two buses were required to get to her session, and by the time she arrived she was ready to take on all comers.

Ellen caught her eye when they all sat down. "Ryan, would you like to start?"

"Love to," she growled. "I'm pissed as hell that I'm gonna have to spend the day waiting to see whether the citizens of my home state think I should have equal rights or not. What kind of country is this when we have popular elections to vote on who to let in and who to keep out of the party?"

"I assume you're talking about Proposition 22?"

Ryan gave her a blank stare, and the therapist said, "In case anyone doesn't know about it, there's a proposition on the ballot today to forbid the state from ever sanctioning same-sex marriage."

"Really?" Helen, one of the older women asked. "I didn't hear anything about that."

Ryan glared at her and snapped, "Well, you still get to vote. Just flip a coin in the booth. It's only my *life*."

The woman recoiled from the rebuke, staring at Ryan like she'd been slapped.

"I'm sure you didn't mean that like it sounded," Ellen said.

"No, of course I didn't. I'm sorry, Helen. I'm pissed off and I took it out on you. I'm…I'm sorry."

"That's okay," the woman said, looking very uncomfortable.

"Why's this such a big deal?" A new member, a thirty-something Japanese-American woman named Ei stared at Ryan. "You can still be in a relationship. There are churches that'll marry you."

"It's a big deal because it's wrong to discriminate against people for being who they are," Ryan said, her edge coming back.

"Nobody has to know you're gay. Try having the wrong skin color or an accent for a day, and then you'll know what it feels like to be a real minority."

Ellen stepped in immediately. "We're here to support each other. Getting into issues like this isn't very supportive. Ryan's feelings are perfectly justified, and that's what we should be concentrating on—not politics."

"Sorry," the woman said, not sounding sincere in the least.

Ryan didn't say anything else, and when Ellen tried to urge her to continue, she shook her head. "I'm done." She was, in fact, finished for the hour. She turned off the other voices in the room and thought of as many witty, vicious, cutting, incendiary things she could have—should have—said to her peer, wishing she'd had just one more swipe at her.

When the session was over, she stepped outside and saw that her nemesis was standing in the rain, seemingly waiting for Ryan to approach her. She took one step in her direction, then turned and went towards BART. Given the way she felt, she worried that she might actually take a punch at the woman, and she knew she couldn't let herself get that out of control. As she walked in the cold rain, she considered something her grandfather had once told her. They'd been talking about some restrictions the government was putting on commercial fishing vessels and how some of his fellow fishermen were taking it very hard.

"But aren't the rules the same for everyone?" she'd asked.

"Sure they are, love. But if you beat ten men with the same rod, some of them would say it felt like it was covered in lamb's wool, some would say it had been soaked in brine, and some would say it had razor-sharp barbs on it. Everyone sees the world, and his place in it, differently, even if they all have the same experience.

"Why were the men being hit?" she'd asked, missing the point at the time.

"Just a little story I made up. I only mean that some people always feel hurt, and others don't let hurt bother them in the same way. If you have a choice, I think it's better to feel like the world's on your side."

She smiled, amazed that she'd remembered the incident at all, much less on this dreary morning. It had taken years for her grandfather's message to reach her heart, but it had lodged in her at exactly the right time. Right then, she decided. She was going to see the proposition as if it had been covered in lamb's wool. It hurt to be beaten, but she didn't have to make things worse for herself.

As soon as Mia woke on Tuesday, she started thinking of Jamie. For a change, she knew she'd be up first, so she turned on the news, trying to get some indication of how the pundits thought the vote would go. She was pretty sure the proposition would pass, but she hoped the vote was at least close.

At eight, California time, she dialed Jamie's cell phone, catching her on her way to school. "Hi," she said when Jamie answered. "I've been thinking about you, and I just wanted to see how you are."

"Ooo, who's my best friend?"

"I am. And I know today's gonna be tough. Have you gotten much feedback on the article?"

"A little. I was freaked at school yesterday, but I feel better today. No one said anything rude to me or anything, but I could tell people were talking about me again." She made a tsking sound. "Just like me to give people ammo as soon as they stop pointing at me when I walk across campus."

"You did the right thing, James. That's what counts."

"I know. At least I think I know. So what's up with you? How's married life?"

"This is like married life in a sorority house. We've got to get out of here as soon as possible. I can't tell you how awful this apartment is, James. I knew Jordy didn't care much about where she lived, but this is ridiculous!"

"What's so bad about it?"

"My list is so long I don't know where to start."

"What could be so bad? Is it really dirty?"

"No, it's not that. It's just so cheap. I mean that in every way. There's no insulation, so it's cold as hell even though it's only about forty degrees. The walls are paper thin. Maybe literally. The women next door can hear us breathing, much less making love. I feel like I did the first time I blew a guy in a dark room at the TKE house and found out that there were a bunch of guys hiding there, listening to us."

Jamie was absolutely silent for a minute. "Think about doing a lot of editing before you tell your children about your college years, okay?"

Mia laughed. "I'll tell 'em I was home-schooled. Our room is about the size of my bathroom at your house, and there's no closet."

"What do you mean? A room has to have a closet."

"None. Nada. Jordy thinks the third bedroom was designed for a baby or as an office. All I know is that I've got to fold all of my clothes and put them in plastic bins. It's like living in the Target kitchen organizer aisle."

"How…where…fuck!"

"Tell me about it. Hey, can you help me out? I wanna make a real meal for Jordy, and there's nothing here."

"Sure, I can give you a shopping list. Do you have a pen?"

"Yeah. Shoot."

"You should make something easy. How about spaghetti and meat sauce."

"Great. She loves spaghetti. What do I need?"

"Not much. Pasta, a can of whole tomatoes, some tomato paste, a little onion, garlic—"

"Back up," Mia said. "What kinda pot or pan do I use?"

"What do you have?"

"Nothing."

"What do you mean nothing? I thought the other women had lived there for a couple of years."

"They have. They've got nothing. Trust me. I have to buy plates and metal utensils. All they have are paper plates and plastic forks."

"Jesus! They sound like guys."

Even though Jamie couldn't see her Mia nodded. "They are. I've decided. Jocks are jocks whether they're women or men. They only care about their sport. Somebody else has to do everything for them. They eat at the training center because it's free, and they can't stand to wait to make a meal. Have I mentioned they're all cheap?"

"Yeah, I got that impression. Well, it's gonna cost you a little money, but I think I can give you a very bare-bones list of what you need to make very simple meals. The first thing you've got to do is find either a Costco, a Wal-Mart, or a Target."

"When did you learn Wal-Mart existed? You think Neiman-Marcus is slumming."

"I do not!" Jamie said, laughing. "My sweetheart has been initiating me into the world of bargains. It's kinda fun."

"Clue me in. And tell Ryan I owe her one for bringing you down to ground level."

Jordan arrived home a little before five, and she grabbed Mia and twirled her around in a circle before planting a dozen kisses on her face. "Damn, I missed you. I know you're just a half-hour away, but that makes it that much worse." She put her down, and her nose began to twitch. "What's that smell? Did you order carryouts?"

"That's the smell of food. Food cooked…at home…over real heat. No plastic, no microwave, no kidding."

"What? We have a kitchen?" Jordan asked, obviously pleased.

"Yep. Come with me, and I'll show you all of the new things we have. Oh, and by the way, the new things are mine. I don't want your slobby friends to start using them, because they'll ruin everything. I'm very protective of my little realm."

"No problem. They have to keep their hands off my woman and my woman's kitchen. I'll fight to defend you and your spatulas."

For the tenth time that evening, a graceful foot obscured Jim Evans's view of the television, and he finally reached out and grabbed a bare knee, holding it firmly so that he could read the election results scrolling across the bottom of the screen. "This is important," he said.

Twisting out of his grasp, Kayla pushed her crimson hair from her eyes and chuckled mildly. "It's not important, and you know it. Bob Washington should have been declared the Democratic senatorial nominee before the election was held. Calling that group of socialists competitors was merely semantics."

"I know," he agreed, shifting so he could see around her, "but I'm interested in the rest of the results."

Sitting up, she gave him a very serious look. "You don't honestly think that Prop 22 is going to fail, do you?"

"No," he said, grimacing slightly. "I just hope it doesn't pass by too much. I know this means a lot to Jamie."

She ran her hand along his arm and said, "It's gonna pass, and it's gonna pass by a wide margin." As she spoke, the ballot initiatives from California started to slide across the screen. He blinked when he saw the preliminary numbers.

"Did I read that right? Did it say seventy-five percent in favor?" Blanching, he didn't even wait for her answer, knowing that his eyes had not deceived him. "Oh, shit." He lay down and draped his forearm over his eyes. "Assholes."

Gazing at him, she tilted her chin and asked, "You're upset by the numbers? I've been telling you all along it was a cakewalk."

"What?" he said, his arm dropping to his side. "It shouldn't bother me to have seventy-five percent of the people of the most liberal state in the country say that my daughter shouldn't ever be allowed to marry?"

Kayla blinked slowly. "Who are you? You voted for the Defense of Marriage Act, but you're upset about Prop 22 passing? Explain the difference."

Grumbling audibly, he turned onto his side. "Turn off the TV, will you? I've seen enough."

"Come on," she insisted, grasping his hip and giving him a shake. "Don't pout."

"I'm not pouting," he said, pouting. "I just don't want to talk about it. I get yelled at enough by my daughter. I don't need you piling on."

"Jim," she urged, tugging at him again. "I'm sorry if I hurt your feelings, but you've got to admit the proposition and the bill were basically the same thing. Are you opposed to gay marriage or not?"

He rolled onto his back and nodded his head. "Yes, I'm opposed to gay marriage."

"Then how…"

Petulantly, he said, "I'm not really opposed to lesbian marriage."

"Uhm…wanna run that past me again?"

"Seeing Jamie and Ryan together makes me see how women need that kinda thing…it's part of who they are. And I've gotten used to seeing them hug each other or kiss. It…it seems pretty natural. And…I'll admit to watching my fair share of lesbian porn. It's…not so odd to see women together."

Kayla was staring at him with a look that should have warned him that he was treading in dangerous waters. But he was too engrossed in his thoughts to notice.

"But guys are different," he said, growing more confident of his opinion as he continued. "Why two guys would want to marry is beyond me. Totally beyond me. Every guy I know had to be talked into marriage. Marriage is for women. Guys just go along for the ride." He was really getting into his topic, and he continued to expound. "The guys who want to marry look like such queens. You know what I mean. The pictures of guys all dressed up in tuxedos or wedding gowns," he added unable to suppress a grimace. "They turn my stomach."

"Let me get this straight. You voted for the Defense of Marriage act because seeing guys together makes you sick?"

"No! Well…partly…no, no, that's not it," he grumbled. "Marriage has been between a man and a woman forever. I don't see why we should change it just because of pressure. Besides, the numbers don't support it. The majority of people don't want it. That should count for something." He was trying to think of another good reason when he saw the look on her face.

"Of all of the narrow-minded…" She jumped from the bed, giving him a lethal glare before she stormed out of the room.

"What? What did I say?" he called after her. "Don't be so sensitive!"

When he didn't get a reply he went into the sitting room of his apartment and found her in front of the TV watching CNN. "Why did that upset you?" he asked, perching on the arm of the sofa.

She looked up at him for almost a full minute, finally asking in a quiet voice, "Don't you have any sense of how important your vote is?"

"Well, sure I do—"

She cut him off. "You told me how you explained your position to Jamie, and that made sense. I didn't agree with you, and it angered me that you felt that way, but at least it made sense. But to hear you admit that you voted to take away the right of adult citizens to marry just because gay men give you the creeps not only astounds me—it sickens me."

"Kayla!" He stared at her with his mouth gaping open. "I…I…I'm sorry."

"For what? For the fact that you upset me, or that I called you on it?" She got up from the sofa, went into the bedroom, struggled into her clothes and found the card key to her own apartment. "I'll see you tomorrow," she said, leaving the room and slamming the door behind her.

"What in the hell was that all about?" he asked the empty space.

Chapter Fourteen

Mia and Jordan were just finishing dinner when their roommates arrived. Toni walked over to the pair who were sitting at the small, never-used dining table. "Where'd you get that?" She looked closer. "Since when did you start eating carbs again?"

Jordan shot a guilty look at Mia. "One night won't hurt. I've been dying for a good carb-loaded meal, and Mia was nice enough to cook for me."

"Cook?" Toni looked at her. "You can cook?"

"Sure. I can cook...for Jordan."

Toni gave Jordan a smirk. "You'd better not let Roman know you ate a big plateful of spaghetti. He'll have you run to Denver and back to burn it off."

"What Roman doesn't know won't hurt him. And if he finds out, one of you had to squeal." She gave all of her roommates an evil smile. "If he finds out, I'll make up something awful about each one of you. Hot fudge sundaes, whole bags of Oreos, candy bars hidden in energy bar wrappers. I'm very creative."

"Roman's gonna have to smell the carbs on your breath to find out," Toni said. "And he might." She laughed and went into her room, followed quickly by the others retreating to their spaces.

Mia stared at her partner. "Why didn't you tell me you weren't eating carbs?"

Jordan looked a little sick. "After all the work you went to? One day isn't a big deal."

"Why did Toni act like it was?"

"Because she likes to stir things up. That's just her style. She doesn't mean anything by it."

Mia got up and started to clear the table. Jordan jumped to her feet to help, but Mia brushed her off. "Don't bother. It'll only take a second. Go relax for a little while. I'll be right in."

Jordan stood there for a moment, clearly indecisive. She was always willing to stand her ground when an issue was important, but more than willing to back away when it was minor. She must have figured this one was minor. "Okay. I'll be waiting for you."

After she left, Mia spent the fifteen minutes it took her to clean up trying to get over her anger. She knew that Jordan was telling the truth and trying not to disappoint her, but it still made her angry that she hadn't been more forthcoming. Once she was finished, she went into their bedroom.

Jordan was sitting up, gazing expectantly at the door. "Mad at me?"

Mia sat, then lay down, taking Jordan with her. "No, I'm not mad. I guess I was a little embarrassed. I felt like you were just humoring me."

"No, not at all. It really did feel great to eat a normal meal. Didn't you see how my eyes lit up when I saw you'd made spaghetti?"

"Yeah." She reached under her shirt and drew her fingers along her abdomen. "I've been wondering how you got this thin. I thought it was from working hard." She rapped on Jordan's belly, half expecting to hear an echo. "Is it good to be this skinny? You're starting to look anorexic."

"I know. And, no, I don't want to be this lean. But I've got to get to ten percent body fat before I can start to put on muscle. We all underwent a lot of testing when we got here, and they told me I was skinny-fat."

"What in the hell is skinny-fat?"

"I have the kind of body that can't build muscle until it's down to an almost dangerously low body fat percentage. If I'm not extra, extra lean, any additional weight is just fat."

Mia laughed. "You don't have an ounce of fat on your whole body."

"Yes, I do. Actually, it's down to about a pound right now, and once I lose it, I can start building up again."

"A pound? You're really concerned about a pound?"

"Yeah. Well, Roman is. I'm at just over ten percent body fat. Once I get to ten, I can start working harder on weight training. I don't know if this is really gonna help my game or not, but he's sure it is. He's had a lot of success with the past teams, so I've got to trust him."

"So…run this past me again. What's the goal?"

"The goal is to be as lean as I can be by eating an ultra low-carb, low-fat, high-protein diet. Then I'll start to increase my weight-training and slowly increase my carbs. Right now, I'm doing no more than twenty grams a day. That'll probably go up to fifty or sixty, but only if I can handle it."

"This sounds like a load of crap to me," Mia said, "but if you trust this guy, I'll support you. Now, what can you eat?"

"Not much that I like. No sugar, no added fat, no butter or oil, of course, no cheese, no beef. Just skinless chicken, fish, green vegetables, and as many kinds of beans as I can stand. Too bad I hate beans, huh?"

"Sounds like a big chicken and vegetable salad with no dressing," Mia said, making a face.

"Yeah. I've been having grilled chicken or fish, whatever green vegetable they make and a plain green salad for dinner every night since I've been here. I don't even care about food any more."

"Well, I don't know how Jamie can fix this, but I'll call her tomorrow and see what she can come up with." Mia tucked her arms around her and kissed her tenderly. "We need to call them tomorrow and give 'em a little love. Prop 22 won by a landslide."

"We should each marry one of Ryan's brothers and live in a big house where all the girls partner up and the boys run around with as many women as they can get their hands on. That arrangement would be perfectly legal. Morons," she muttered.

"Ryan would have to go outside the family. I think incest is almost as bad as homosexuality."

"Right. I guess she can marry my brother. He'd be a wonderful husband."

Mia looked at her for a moment and saw the guarded, closed expression that Jordan always wore when she talked about her family. She gave her another gentle kiss and hugged her even tighter. "Let's just live in sin. We're too young to commit to marrying all of those O'Flahertys."

"Good point. But if you get married, pick Rory, okay? I get bad vibes from Conor."

"It's a deal." She wasn't sure if Jordan knew just how bad the vibes had been between her and Conor, and she wasn't going to be the one to bring it up.

During dinner, Jamie and Ryan left the radio on in the kitchen. It wasn't very loud, but each of them could easily hear it since they weren't talking much. Ryan didn't tell her partner about her blow-up at therapy, partly because she never talked about her sessions, and partly because she was embarrassed to have caused a scene. They both picked at their food and listened to the commentators report that over seventy-five percent of the state thought them unworthy of state sanction of their love.

Ryan looked at her partner, seeing how down she was. She thought of the little story her grandfather had told her and said, "Let's go be gay."

"Pardon?"

"You heard me. Let's get on my bike and go to the Castro and be way gay."

A smile lit Jamie's face as she asked, "How do we be way gay? I don't wanna be on TV again."

"Let's put on our dykiest clothes and go sit in a seedy bar and check out chicks. That's what most people seem to think we do on a regular basis. We might as well do it."

"You wanna check out chicks?" Jamie asked, raising a dark-blonde brow.

"Sure. We scary homos can't have real, meaningful relationships. Let's go shopping so we can have the next victim lined up."

"I can't tell how serious you're being." Jamie reached out and put her hand on top of Ryan's. "To be honest, I'm having a tough time reading you lately. Do you really want to go out?"

"I meant everything but the shopping for the next victim thing. I'm gonna stick with you—just to screw with people's minds."

Jamie got up and held out a hand. "Let's go. We don't even have to clean up. I think lesbians are supposed to be sloppy."

"That's my girl. Always willing to adapt."

An hour later, they were seated on a pair of barstools, looking out at the mélange of people passing by the Twin Peaks, a venerable Castro bar. The place was located right at the epicenter of the neighborhood, the corner of Market and Castro. Even though it was mostly populated by forty-something men, she felt comfortable there. There were large plate-glass windows that allowed for a very good view of the passersby, and Jamie was taking full advantage.

She sat with her forearms resting on the wooden ledge, her beer in front of her. Trying to look as stereotypically lesbian as possible, she wore most of the outfit Ryan had bought her for the Dyke March—

camouflage pants, a tight, dun-green T-shirt, and a pair of black Doc Martens. Her distressed leather jacket was draped across her bar stool, and she intentionally kicked it every once in a while, just to add a mark or two.

Ryan matched her style, wearing faded jeans, an old jeans jacket that she had turned into a vest, and a skin-tight, black tank top. She didn't copy the Doc Martens, however, choosing her buff-colored work boots for a little variety. Her hair was pulled back into a ponytail, and she wore a black baseball cap pulled low over her eyes that read "Rough Trade" in bright red letters. Her motorcycle jacket was on her chair, just like Jamie's was.

They decided to girl-watch, and they spent a pleasant hour doing just that. To neither woman's surprise, it was established that Jamie liked big women, while Ryan preferred a smaller, more petite size. Ryan liked her women to be quite clean-cut, preppy looking if possible, while Jamie had much broader tastes. Ryan's eyes got wide when she commented that she fancied some pretty tough-looking characters, but she merely nodded her head, showing a half smile.

"Oh! Oh!" Jamie's eyes lit up, and she elbowed Ryan in the ribs. "There she is! That's the woman for me."

Chuckling, Ryan tore herself away from gazing at Jamie and looked outside. There, casually posing in front of the window, was a woman who looked like she'd just come from splitting a cord of wood. A blue and green flannel shirt covered her torso, the sleeves having been completely removed. Very well-cut arms extended out of the snug shirt, which was tucked into tight black jeans. Her hair was glossy black and straight, just ticking the collar of her shirt. Cocoa brown skin, flawless and smooth, perfectly complemented the nearly black eyes that darted up and down the street, obviously searching for someone. "You want her, huh?" Ryan asked, leaning over to whisper into Jamie's ear.

"Uh-huh," Jamie purred, gleefully engaging in the fantasy. "I'd make good use of those big muscles."

"So...does she replace me, or do you want us all to party together?"

"Mmm..." Jamie growled, still staring at the stranger. "I want you both. Since you're my favorite, you can pick which half of me you want. She'll take the leftover."

"Okay. Works for me." She got up and strode out the door, leaving a nearly apoplectic Jamie behind.

It was obvious that the two women didn't know each other. The stranger moved back a step and looked Ryan over from top to bottom, not even a hint of a smile crossing her dark features. Ryan was speaking, and she slowly inclined her head towards her partner, who tried to compose her expression. Now both women looked at her, and the stranger nodded once, then followed Ryan inside.

Jamie wasn't sure if her best course of action was to hide in the bathroom or run out the front door, but since the two large women were blocking it she decided that the bathroom would have to do. She got about two feet when Ryan grabbed the back of her pants and held on tight. "Don't bother getting up," she insisted. "We can pull up another chair." Propelling her back onto the stool, Ryan said, "Jamie, this is Coco. Coco, Jamie." She pulled a stool over and urged Coco to sit. She sat on the other side of the new addition, acting like she couldn't see the lethal gaze that had to be burning her skin. "Jamie, don't you have a question that you wanted to ask Coco?" She beamed a smile Jamie's way.

"*NO!* I mean, no, I don't. I, uhm, can't think of a thing I'd like to ask."

"I thought you were…curious."

Coco turned her dark, intense eyes on Jamie and let her mouth slide into a fantastically attractive smile. Her white teeth gleamed in the dull light, and she asked, "Ryan said you were thinking about trying something new."

Her smile was mesmerizing, and Jamie found herself powerless not to return the grin. Shaking her head, she forced herself to say, "No, no help needed. Just fine here…yep…just fine."

"Come on," Coco urged, "Don't be shy. Take off your shirt and let me get a good look at you."

"What?"

"Yeah, Jamie," Ryan urged. "Let Coco take a look." She hopped off her chair and removed Jamie's shirt before the smaller woman could lodge a word of protest.

Coco leaned back and assessed her thoughtfully, finally nodding with satisfaction. "I think you look fine."

"Thanks," Jamie said weakly, simultaneously plotting Ryan's demise.

"Do you take any supplements? Amino acids, Creatine?"

"Huh?"

"Do you take supplements?" she asked again. "It's hard to build bulk if you don't."

Looking from Ryan to Coco and back again, she repeated, "Huh?"

"Jamie," Ryan soothed, now placing her hands on her shoulders, "Coco was Ms. California Bodybuilder 1999. If you want to build up your arms, you really should listen to her." Looking at their new friend, Ryan asked, "What do you take?"

Coco laughed heartily and said, "You're kidding, right? I don't give out my secrets to anyone. Besides, just because something works for me, doesn't mean it'll work for you." She smiled at Jamie. "You're just getting started, but there's no reason you can't bulk up if you really want to. Just do it safely. A pretty girl like you doesn't want to mess up her body with steroids."

Jamie was still staring at her, her mouth slightly open.

"Oh, she won't," Ryan said. "She's far too precious to me to ever let her do something like that."

Coco smiled at the pair and cast another look outside. "Hey, my wife's here. Gotta go. See you, and good luck," she added, extending her hand to shake Jamie's limp mitt.

The pair watched the woman leave, then Jamie got up and went to the bar, buying herself another beer. When she returned, Ryan was unsuccessfully trying to compose her face, the grin leaking out of the corners of her mouth. Jamie sat down and sipped on her beer, finally putting it down on the ledge and gazing at her partner.

Big blue eyes batted ingenuously. "Am I in trouble?"

Taking another long sip, Jamie looked at her thoughtfully. "I wasn't raised like you were. Mia teases me a lot, and Jack teased me quite a bit, but no one has really exposed me to practical jokes. I'll admit that I probably don't know the proper rules, but those are the breaks." She leaned forward so that their noses touched lightly. "I'm not only going to get you back...I'm going to get you back at least...at least...twice as bad. And I don't want to hear a word of complaint." Tapping her on the chest with a finger, Jamie vowed, "You have been warned."

Ryan gulped noticeably. "Like when you paid that woman to make it look like I was cheating on you?"

"Child's play." Jamie smirked. "That didn't come near to what I'm going to do to you." She leaned back and cocked her head. "I know that you won't stop playing your little games—it's too ingrained. So I'm not even going to ask you to. Even though I might remind you that in Las Vegas you promised you wouldn't pull another one. I just want you to recognize the consequences of your actions. You'd better make sure your joke is worth the payback."

Ryan nodded soberly, finally saying, "This one was worth a lot. You might have to remind me of that after you humiliate me in front of the whole city, but this one was sweet."

"Enjoy! Soak it all up—revel in it, love. Perhaps you'll take some cold comfort from it in the future." Taking another sip of beer, she turned her stool to gaze out the window again. "Now, where were we?" She looked up and down the street, then pointed, "Pretty redhead, nine o'clock."

Ryan grasped her beer and took a drink. "Nah, not your type."

As the woman moved closer, Jamie had to agree with her. Chuckling, she asked, "How do you know my type better than I do?"

"I don't. My eyes are just a little better than yours."

"Are not."

"Are too. What's the most distant sign you can read?"

Jamie sighed, realizing that the competition was never over with Ryan at her side, but that was just how she liked it.

It was fairly early when they left the bar, and since the night was clear, Ryan guided her bike to one of her favorite spots to view the city. Corona Heights Park was located between the Castro and Buena Vista Park, and was usually very quiet late at night.

They walked hand in hand, crossing the cropped grass to find some large rocks to lean against. Because the night was clear, it was also very chilly, with the wind blowing vigorously. Ryan sat on one of the rocks, with Jamie in front of her, her heavy leather jacket protecting her from the worst of the chill. Snuggling against the cold, they watched in silence as the city below them went about its business—unaware that it was being observed.

"Ryan?" Jamie asked after a long while.

"Hmm?" The deep voice tickled her ear.

"You didn't think I was serious, did you?"

There was a quality to Jamie's voice that made Ryan shift her body so that she could see her face. "Serious?"

"Yeah." Her head nodded quickly, then she hesitantly added, "About being with someone else…about being with you and someone else."

Tightening her hold around her body, Ryan began to shake her head, saying, "No, no, no and no! You're the last person in the world who would ever want to do that." She leaned back to let Jamie see her face. "I'm the second to the last, by the way. I can't think of anything we'd enjoy less."

Jamie's expression was remarkably earnest. "I want to make sure you know I'd never...ever...be able to..."

Ryan silenced her with a gentle kiss. "Honey, the thought that you might be serious never crossed my mind. I had a lot of fun tonight. I love seeing you develop and refine your taste in whom you find attractive—and that's all that you were doing. We were just playing, and fantasizing about things that we would never, ever do. That's what makes it a fantasy."

Jamie nodded, the concerned look still on her face. "Okay. I just thought that maybe that's why you played the joke. Like maybe you were mad at me, or hurt, and that you were trying to teach me a lesson."

Ryan's eyes closed, and she leaned her head back and filled her lungs with the fresh, clean air. "Sweetheart," she finally whispered, "I'm so sorry for playing that joke on you."

Jamie looked down at the ground. "When you do things like that, it doesn't feel like a joke. It feels like you're trying to make me look foolish, or gullible or to embarrass me." Gazing at Ryan with guileless eyes, she quietly asked, "Why do you want to embarrass me?"

Suddenly, tears were flowing down Ryan's cheeks, the cold wind chilling the hot tears before they traveled an inch. "I'm sorry," she murmured. "I'm so sorry."

Jamie held her tight, whispering, "Don't cry. Please, don't cry."

"But I hurt you. I hurt you...intentionally."

"Did you do it to hurt me?"

"No! Of course not! But I messed with your mind, and that hurt you. It's the same thing."

"No, it's not. It's really not. We just don't speak the same language here. I usually know you're teasing when you do things like that, but it makes me want to hurt you to get back at you. I hate to feel like that; I just don't know how to control my reaction. You O'Flahertys all know it's a game, and you respond in kind. But I want to go nuclear on you—and that scares me."

"We don't all know it's a game. Donal doesn't think practical jokes are funny...at all."

"Really?"

"Yeah. Over time we stopped making him the brunt of jokes. He just couldn't take it. In high school, he broke Declan's nose because of a really harmless prank."

"What was the prank? Your version of harmless and mine might be different."

"No, it was really small potatoes. They were both on their high school basketball team. Actually, Dermot was on the team, too, and knowing him, he's probably the one who came up with the idea. Anyway, it was a pretty conservative Catholic boys' school, and they wouldn't let them wear the big, baggy uniforms that everyone wanted to wear. Before the game, Donal was dawdling a little, like he always does, and either Dec or Dermot hid Donal's real uniform and left him an unused one that must have been an extra-small. Well, as you can imagine, Donal was never an extra small anything, but since they'd hidden every other uniform, he had to put on this tiny thing and run out onto the court when he was introduced. It looked like the darn thing was spray-painted on him!" She threw her head back and laughed, her tears forgotten in the face of this hilarious image.

Jamie, however, just looked at her, shaking her head. "He must have been mortified."

Ryan's laughter died down, then stopped altogether. "You really don't think that's funny? It was so harmless."

"No." The blonde head shook. "I just feel sorry for Donal. He's such a proud guy—he must have wanted to crawl in a hole and die."

Looking at her with confusion, Ryan said, "That's the point of the joke. The guy's supposed to be embarrassed. Then he figures out how to do the same thing to you."

"Is that what Donal did?"

"No, he sure didn't. He waited until halftime and sucker-punched Dec when he ran into the locker room. Popped him a good one. Dec didn't even see it coming. Of course, Donal got suspended," she said quietly, suddenly seeing that the situation didn't seem nearly as funny as it had before she'd started to analyze it. "Uhm…" She scratched the back of her head. "Maybe Da was right when he used to say, 'It's only a game until someone loses an eye.'"

Eyes widening in surprise, Jamie said, "Well, that's a little extreme, but I understand his point. Jokes like that can get out of hand."

Ryan nodded. "You can get me back for what I did tonight. I don't care if you put a bare-assed picture of me up on a BART billboard so that every person crossing the Trans-Bay tunnel sees it. But once we're even,

I'm gonna try really hard not to pull another joke on you. If you don't think it's funny, it's just cruel."

"Thank you. And I don't think I'll pay you back. I wouldn't do it for a joke—I'd do it just to be mean, and that's not how I want to be with you."

"Okay," Ryan said quietly. "Although I'd prefer it if you'd just get me back. Now I'll have this hanging over my head."

Shrugging her shoulders, Jamie smiled impishly. "Them's the breaks, sparky."

"You're going to let this ride just to torture me, aren't you?" Ryan asked, amazed. "That's…that's cruel!"

"Could be." Jamie still wore an enigmatic smile. "I'll never tell."

"You're truly diabolical. I never can win with you."

"Nope. Sure can't. Might as well stop trying."

Ryan gripped Jamie's hand and pulled her to her feet, then wrapped her in a warm hug. "Yeah, like that's gonna happen."

Chapter Fifteen

On Wednesday morning, Jim got up and called Kayla, not particularly surprised when she didn't answer either of her numbers. He couldn't afford to be seen knocking on her door, begging to be let in, so he left for work at the usual time, surprised to see her already at her desk. That lovely red head didn't lift as he passed. He couldn't afford to let anyone know they were fighting, so he went into his office and closed the door, determined to let her make the first move.

Ryan was walking out of her French class when her cell phone rang. Her heart started racing when the caller ID showed "Maeve Driscoll." "Anything wrong?" she asked, the words coming out nearly as one.

"No, sweetheart," her father's calm voice said. "I wanted to call to see how you were feeling after that horrible vote yesterday."

She let out a breath. "Oh. You've never called me on my cell phone. I assumed something terrible had happened."

"It did. A bunch of idiots have been allowed to decide who the benefits and obligations of citizenship should go to. That's a terrible thing, darlin.'"

Tears stung Ryan's eyes. "You know," she said, her voice shaking, "knowing that my family understands why the vote was so wrong makes everything better. I mean that, Da. It makes everything better."

"This has been hard for you, hasn't it?"

"Yeah," she said, turning to face a building to hide her crying from strangers. "I've been pretty…I don't know…I guess lonely is the right word."

"You're not home enough. You don't do well when you're away from home for too long."

"I know. Believe me, I know. I'm not home enough. I'm not spending enough time with Jamie. I'm not working on my independent study enough. I'm pulled in too many directions, Da. Things aren't clicking for me this term. I'm at loose ends."

"What can I do, love?"

Ryan sighed, her breath catching as it left her lungs. "I don't know. If I knew, I'd do something about it. I overextended myself...again...and now I'm paying for it."

"Would it help if we came over to your house for dinner more often, sweetheart? It breaks my heart to hear you sound so sad."

"I am sad." Even though she was right outside her classroom building, she broke down, tears flowing freely down her face. Through sharp gasps and hiccups she managed, haltingly, to speak. "I feel like I'm screwing everything up. I'm not able to concentrate like I used to. It's getting late and I still haven't made sense of my project, and if I don't finish it I won't graduate."

"There, there, sweetheart. If you can't finish it, you'll finish it this summer. It's not the end of the world. Don't let little things like that get you down. You've had a very stressful year, Siobhán. Taking care of yourself has to be your biggest priority."

"Yeah," she said, the bitterness obvious. "I'm the hot-house flower."

"No, you're not. You've never been fragile or delicate, and you're not now. But you have to listen to your body and your heart. And you have to let me know when you're not feeling well. It's my job to help you through hard times."

"I'm an adult, Da. I have to be able to take care of myself."

"Nonsense! You're my baby, and you will be as long as I'm breathing. Let your ancient old father feel like he's needed."

"Okay," she said, unable to keep from smiling. "I'd love for you and Aunt Maeve to come for dinner the first night you have off."

"When do you get home?"

"Usually between six thirty or seven."

"We'll be there tonight. Tell Jamie we'll bring dinner, so she doesn't have to do a thing."

"Really? Tonight?" She didn't try to hide the excitement in her voice. She didn't have to with her da.

"Yes. Tonight. Hurry home, sweetheart. Your father misses you."

Jim and Kayla kept a cool distance all day. When he asked her to join him for a conference call with Bob Washington, the Democratic nominee for Jim's senate seat, she looked like she was on the verge of refusing, but she went along and even contributed a few things to the discussion.

By the time Jim was ready to leave, she was already gone, and he didn't hear another word from her until almost ten o'clock. Kayla knocked on his door and entered without a word when he answered. Walking over to his wet-bar, she poured herself a scotch and sat down. "How long have we been seeing each other?"

"About a year and a half," Jim guessed, hoping he was right. She looked like she'd strangle him if he replied incorrectly.

"That sounds about right." She gave a curt nod. "I'd say we should know each other pretty well by now, shouldn't we?"

He looked at her warily. "Yes, I think we do."

Tilting her head, Kayla looked at him for a moment. "What do my parents do for a living?"

"Ahh…for a living?" Jim repeated, searching his mind for a clue. He had almost nothing in his memory bank.

"Yeah. What do they do for a living?"

"Uhm…I think your father is a doctor of some kind. But I don't recall what your mother does."

"Not much," Kayla snapped. "Being dead limits your professional opportunities." She raised her glass to her lips and drained it.

He blinked slowly, stunned. "I'm so sorry. I didn't know."

With a voice as cold as ice, she snarled, "Of course you didn't know. You didn't know because it's my life—not yours. If it doesn't directly impact you, you don't give a crap!"

"That's not true!"

"How many siblings do I have? Where did I grow up? Did my father remarry? What are my interests? What are my long-term goals?"

She fired the questions at him so quickly that he barely had time to comprehend them, much less answer them. "Just because I don't know those things it doesn't mean I don't want to know. You're very guarded around me, you know. I just…I don't want to pry."

"Fine," she snapped. "You want to know, I'll tell you the answers to these complex questions. My father is a psychiatrist. When I was two, my mother was killed in a car accident." Jim's heart raced. Kayla had never,

ever given a clue about having been though such terrible trauma. "She'd been drinking, and she drove off Mulholland Drive on her way home." Narrowing her eyes, she said, "I grew up in the Hollywood Hills, for your information."

"That's just horrible." It was a very trite expression, but he was too shocked to think of anything deeper.

"No, the Hills are actually very nice," she snarled, being intentionally obtuse. "I don't remember my mother, but from all reports, she and my father had a very unhappy marriage. He regrets having married her."

Jim started to speak, then held back. When she didn't continue, he said, "That's not a very kind thing to say about your late wife."

Giving him a look that questioned his intelligence, she said, "He regrets it because he knew he was wrong to marry her. He's gay." She let that hang there for a moment, then added, "He tried to ignore the truth, thinking he'd be able to make a go of it, but it didn't work out. They were both very unhappy, and she drank and ran around with other men, trying to make him jealous."

Seeing the pain that had settled upon his young lover's features, Jim just shook his head. "That must have been so hard for her."

"How about him?" she demanded, her eyes flashing with anger. "She knew about him before they married, but she wanted to be married to a successful young doctor. She used him as much as he used her. And if society wasn't so fucking narrow-minded, he would have faced up to the fact that you can't get over being gay, and she would have had to find a nice, straight man to marry. She might be alive today," she added with a sneer. Her expression changed, and Jim could see a dark look in her normally bright eyes. "She'd only be forty-four years old."

"I'm sorry," he said again, at a loss for a way to be more supportive.

"I'm sorry, too. I'm sorry that people like you can't see how loving and supportive two men can be. My dad and his partner Dan raised me. And I think they did a hell of a job. I just wish they'd been able to have me without getting my mom involved. Of course, if you had your way, they would never have been able to adopt a child, so they wouldn't have had me at all."

"Kayla, I really apologize for what I said last night. I was letting my mouth get ahead of my brain again. What I said was stupid and very narrow-minded." He reached for her hand and was only mildly surprised when she pulled it away. "I didn't know," he offered. "You never said anything."

She narrowed her gaze and stared at him for a few moments. "I learned a long time ago that I had to trust someone before I told him about my family. I got burned too many times." She looked so sad as she revealed this that he desperately wanted to hold her, but he recognized that his comfort would not be welcome.

"I'm very sorry," he repeated. "I'd really like to hear about your father and his..."

"My parents," Kayla said, her eyes flashing fire.

"Your parents," he parroted. "I'd like to hear about them."

Obviously taking him at his word, she nodded once. "As I said, my father's a psychiatrist. We have a funny kinda house. It's set way back in the hills, and rather than one big space, it's a group of small buildings. One of them has our kitchen, dining area and living room, another houses the bedrooms, still another is a small guest house. My father has a freestanding office, and Dan has a freestanding studio. He's an artist."

"Oh? What kind of artist?"

"He's a painter of some renown. Dan Buchard."

Jim's eyes widened. "Does he do a lot of very, uhm...unique portraits? Like a traditional figure study, but with a twist?"

"Yeah," she said, a small smile forming. "Do you know him?"

"Catherine's a big fan. I think we have...had...two...no, three of his paintings."

"I guess I should thank you," she smirked. "The outrageous prices his work has demanded in the last few years put me through UCLA Law—loan free."

"But who actually raised you? Did you have a nanny?"

"No!" she said, her eyes narrowing again. "My parents raised me. Dan likes to work early in the morning when the light's good, so he was ready for a break by the time I got up. When I was little, I'd play in his studio while he worked. They switched off, each of them taking care of me at different times of the day." She chuckled mildly and said, "Dan always got stuck taking me to shul for my bat mitzvah lessons. Strangely, we really bonded over the lessons, and he decided to convert."

Jim stared at her blankly for a moment. "I had no idea you'd had a bat mitzvah. You don't—"

She cut him off with a withering glare. "I'll stab you in the heart if you even think of telling me I don't look Jewish."

"No! No, that wasn't what I was going to say. I was just going to say that I'd never heard you say you were religious. I guess it surprised me that you had formal religious training."

"I was at home for the high holy days last year, so you wouldn't have noticed that I attended services. Passover fell during Easter week. You were with your family, and as I recall, you didn't ask me what I did."

"Oh," he said quietly. Trying to get back on topic, he commented, "I've never been to a temple. Maybe we could go together sometime."

"Maybe," she said tersely.

Trying to draw her out, he asked, "So tell me about what it was like to be raised by two men."

She was quiet for a moment. "It's all I've known, but from being at other kids' homes, it didn't seem very different. Dan's very maternal," she said fondly. "And I don't mean in a limp-wristed kinda way. I don't think he'd make you sick."

Her expression was challenging, and Jim tried to placate her once again. "Look, let me be honest. I admit that I don't know many gay men. I just…I've never had any gay friends. But that doesn't mean I'm a total homophobe."

"No, you look," she said, her anger flaring again. "You'd never vote on a farm bill or a foreign appropriations bill without trying to understand the impact of your vote. I've seen how you study things. I've seen how seriously you take those issues. But you voted for the Defense of Marriage Act for no reason whatsoever. I know the President didn't put any pressure on you, and you aren't running for re-election, so you had nothing, nothing to lose. You did it because you didn't think it was important enough to really study it and make a reasoned judgment. That's so fucking wrong. You owe it to your constituents to try to serve them all—based on fact, not your gut-level fears. You should have dealt with your fear of gay men by the time you were fifteen."

He nodded. "I was wrong to vote for that bill without really thinking it through. I'll try to educate myself. I really will try."

"That's all I ask," she said quietly.

"Uhm…could I meet your parents sometime?"

Kayla shook her head. "No. I'm a little…I'm a little ashamed."

"Hey, don't feel like that." He walked over to her and sat on the arm of the sofa. "You should be proud of them."

"I am!" She got to her feet and glared at him. "I'm ashamed of you. I'm ashamed of myself for sleeping with a married man. I was raised better than that," she said quietly, as a few tears slipped down her cheeks.

Taking her in his arms, he found himself whispering, "So was I, Kayla. So was I."

Chapter Sixteen

As expected, Martin and Maeve arrived in Berkeley at six, half an hour early. Jamie opened the door and hugged them both for so long that she forgot to invite them in. "Are we staying on the porch?" Martin asked. "It's a lovely one."

"My manners!" Jamie slapped herself in the forehead. "At least you know I'm happy to see you."

Maeve put her arm around Jamie's waist. "And we're happy to see you, too. I feel terrible that we haven't made more of an effort to visit."

They walked inside and sat in the parlor. "What can I get you to drink?" Jamie asked.

"Nothing now," Martin said. "We'll relax for a moment and then make up our minds. But you can put these bags in the kitchen. We brought Italian combos for the princess. Conor assures me that nothing makes her happier."

"Oh, my God," Jamie said, smiling brightly. "She hasn't had one in ages. She'll be in heaven." She went into the kitchen and put the bags on the table, then joined Martin and Maeve in the parlor.

Jamie looked at Maeve and said, "I don't want you to feel bad about not knowing what Ryan needs right now. I've let her down, too. I think we've all got to change our habits a little—including Ryan. She hates to talk on the phone, but she's gonna have to get over that and call you both more often. And I have to let you know when she needs you—since she won't."

"She thinks she's impervious from having needs, doesn't she," Maeve said.

Jamie nodded emphatically. "You know her better than I do. She hates to feel weak, and she feels weak when she has to ask for help." She shook her head. "She's so frustrating sometimes, I want to shake her!"

"It's the O'Flaherty side, Jamie." Maeve gave her a wink. "They must be descended from the Spartans."

"I can't disagree," Martin said, "even though I'd like to. I know Siobhán gets this from me. I regret trying to make her so independent. I raised her like I raised the boys, and that wasn't always good for her."

"You're a great father, Martin. Really. I think this is just part of Ryan's personality. Plus, I'm sure she didn't want to let her big brothers think she was a baby."

"At least she can cry now. She wouldn't cry in front of the boys when she was little. She could break an arm and not shed a tear."

"Thank God for small favors," Jamie said, laughing.

"So, what have you been up to?" Maeve asked. "Besides traipsing all over the west coast with your golf."

"Not a lot. My schedule's been easier than Ryan's, mainly since I have a regular course load. It's much easier to take a test than develop a complex formula like she's trying to do."

"Do you have any idea what it is she's doing?" Maeve lowered her voice. "We've asked her so many times it's embarrassing, but we don't understand a word."

Jamie smiled. "To be honest, I think I understand what she's talking about when she explains it. But I must not really get it, since I couldn't begin to tell you what she's told me. All I know is that it's hard, and it's not coming to her as easily as most things do. The only real course she has is French, and she's having a hard time with that, too. This just isn't her term."

"I hate to even bring this up," Maeve said, "but have you been training for the Breast Cancer Walk?"

Jamie put both hands over her eyes. "We haven't started! I'm afraid we're just gonna show up on the day of the walk and hope for the best."

Maeve's eyes widened. "Can you do that?"

"I guess we'll find out. I haven't been to the gym in I don't know how long, and Ryan doesn't go, either. It's hard for her to even find time to run, and you know how much she loves that. She told me the other day that she's in the worst shape she's been in since she was in high school."

"She's fit as a fiddle!" Martin said.

"Oh, sure, ninety-nine percent of the population would trade places with her, but she's not fit like she was for the AIDS Ride. She was awesome then. It's her aerobic capacity that she's ignored. Her softball skills are fantastic, but I don't think it's gonna matter how far she can throw a ball when we're walking for three days straight."

"I'm frightened to death, and I'm walking every day," Maeve said. "I keep dreaming about dropping to the ground and being left behind."

"If you drop, we'll drop right next to you," Jamie promised. "No one will be left behind."

"What if you drop first?" Maeve asked, eyes wide.

All three of them stopped talking when they heard Ryan's tread on the steps. She walked in, dropped her bag and smiled so brightly that it seemed the entire room lit up. But as soon as her father stood to hug her, she started to cry, hanging onto him for dear life as Maeve and Jamie looked on with sympathy.

Martin and Maeve left early, instructing the girls to ignore their schoolwork for the night and get to bed. Dutifully, Ryan marched upstairs and started to brush her teeth. Jamie sat on the tub and watched her, charmed by how utterly complaint she was with her father's instructions. It was just nine o'clock, but Ryan stripped off her clothes, went into the bedroom and pulled back the bedspread.

"Are you really going to bed?"

"Da's right. We both need more sleep. I'm gonna turn my mind off and get a good nine hours. That should help me feel more like myself."

"Okay. I'll brush my teeth and be right in." It took Jamie less than five minutes to get ready for bed, but by the time she walked into the bedroom, Ryan was sound asleep, a contented, childlike expression on her lovely face. All she needed was a good dose of fatherly love. That was the key to a good night's rest.

On Thursday afternoon, Jamie sat in the parlor, catching up on some reading. She'd been home from school for hours, and even though she hated having Mia gone and Ryan away every afternoon, she had to admit that she'd never been more prepared for class. She didn't have a lot of extra time, but for the first time since she'd met Ryan, she didn't flinch when one of her professors called her name in class. The phone rang right before Ryan was due, and she assumed her partner was on the phone. She didn't even look at the caller ID, just said, "Hello," in her usual friendly fashion.

"Hi, it's Daddy."

"Oh." She could hear the drop in enthusiasm in her voice, and she hated that it was so apparent. But she never knew how things would go between them, and she was more than a little cautious. "Hi."

"I want to apologize."

She waited for a moment then asked, "For what?"

"For several things, but first and foremost, for the way I've voted on some very important issues."

"Go on," Jamie said, thinking he could be referring to nearly anything.

"I'm sorry for my vote on the Defense of Marriage Act, and I'm sorry I voiced support for 'don't ask, don't tell.'"

She waited a beat, thinking of how he could benefit from being sorry. His angle wasn't apparent, so she tried to fish for more information. "Why the conversion?"

"Kayla called me on it. She made me tell the truth about why I voted the way I did, and she tactfully pointed out that I was an ass."

"Huh. I think I pointed that out, too," Jamie said, still not feeling very warm towards him. "You yelled at me."

He let out a short, nervous laugh. "I guess she gets a little more leeway. With you I still think I'm the dad and you're my little girl."

Jamie didn't point out that the little girl and the lover were contemporaries, but she wanted to. "So are you gonna tell me the secret? What was your real reason for voting the way you did." She could hear him breathing, and knew he was coming up with either a lie or an excuse.

"You know, that won't help us mend fences. Just know that I wasn't thinking…I was reacting, and I'm going to try to make sure I think before I vote from now on."

"Okay." She knew it wouldn't do any good to press him. "That's all I ask of my other representatives, so I shouldn't hold you to a higher standard. How are you going to educate yourself?"

"Oh. Well. I…I haven't given that much thought. But I'm going to try."

"Let me know if I can help. I did a lot of reading on homophobia for my lesbian psychology class."

He laughed. "It still amazes me that you can take a course in being a lesbian. Berkeley is a very unique place."

Once again, her anger flared. "It wasn't a course in being a lesbian. It was a course on how society is trained to react to lesbians. There's a big difference."

"Isn't trained a pretty strong word? I don't think most people are indoctrinated."

"I think they are. Actually, I'm sure they are."

"Fine," he said, "Let's not argue about semantics, okay?"

"All right. I don't want to fight. It's too stressful."

"I'm not catching you at a bad time, am I? I don't want to interrupt dinner or anything."

"No, this is good. Ryan's still at softball practice, and I haven't started dinner yet."

"Uhm…I don't know if this is the right time to talk about this, but something's been on my mind for a while."

"What's that?"

"It's the way you identify. I know you feel like you're a part of this group now, but sometimes you sound so strident. You could reach more people if you soft-pedaled it a bit. No one likes to listen to someone who sounds so shrill."

Her eyes were closed so tightly that she could see stars. "If having a well-thought out opinion that differs from yours is being strident, I'm guilty as charged."

"Now don't be defensive. I just want to counsel you to watch your language. Throwing labels around only makes people angry."

"What labels?"

"You said I was being homophobic, and nothing could be further from the truth."

"It's not a slur, Dad. It just means that you have an irrational fear of homosexuals. Since you can't tell me why you voted the way you did, I think the odds are that your votes were based on fear and ignorance. That's homophobia."

"Jamie, you're the same girl you were a year ago. But now you're a member of some angry special-interest group. I wish you hadn't adopted their attitudes. What happened to the girl who used to make her own decisions?"

Thinking that the only change was that she used to parrot his choices and was now making her own, she was close to cursing him and hanging up. But things had been so tense between them, she forced herself to finish the conversation. "You don't know much about this. Trust me."

"I can have an opinion, can't I?"

"Sure. Just like I can have an opinion about coming-of-age rituals in New Guinea. I don't know a thing about them, but I can spout my opinion."

He let out a breath, and she could hear the anger he was trying to contain.

"Let's put this to bed, okay?"

"Fine. Let me know how your research goes." She allowed her tone to show she believed his research would end when he hung up the phone.

Jim didn't seem to notice her snarkiness. "I will. I hope you take my apology seriously."

"I do." He said whatever he had to when he wanted to placate someone. That's all an apology had ever meant to him, and he'd never shown the slightest sign that would change.

Ryan bounded up the stairs at her usual time, and before she had time to put her bag away Jamie began to recount the conversation she'd just had with her father.

Ryan crossed her arms over her chest. Her cynicism about Jim was weighing heavily on her and she found herself speaking without thinking. "He sure does like to jerk you around, doesn't he?"

Jamie bristled. "What do you mean, jerk me around?"

"Oh." She didn't need a clearer sign that she'd been too frank. "I just meant that he…hurts you and then thinks about it for a while and apologizes. I used the wrong term."

"How is that any different from what you did with the practical joke? In Las Vegas, you promised you wouldn't do it again, and you did. Isn't that jerking me around?" Her hands were clenched into fists, and she looked like she would welcome a fight.

But Ryan was desperate not to have one. She'd had a long day, and she just wanted a nice meal and a little peace and quiet. "You're right. Apologizing isn't enough. I have to change my behavior. And I promise I'll try.

Jamie made a face, turned and walked towards the kitchen. Ryan stood right where she was, trying to figure out what had really happened to piss her lover off so much. Ryan knew she had her faults, but she would never like being compared to Jim Evans. There was a huge difference between playing a practical joke and voting to deny basic rights to a disenfranchised minority. But she wasn't about to make that point. She needed another fight like she needed another sport.

Jamie stood at the sink, trying to get Ryan to talk. "Everything go all right at school today?"

"Uh-huh. Nothing exciting."

"Practice?"

"Good. Ashley and Jennie were there. Today's the first nice day we've had for a while. It was good to have a few fans back."

"You don't mind that I don't come anymore, do you? I need the time to work."

"Heck, no. Watching softball practice is really boring. I don't know why Ash and Jennie bother."

"Well, Ashley goes because she has friends on the team, and I think she misses playing her sport. And Jennie…well, Jennie just loves to be around you guys. It makes her feel like she's part of something."

"Yeah, I guess you're right. Oh, I forgot that I had to take Jen to the clinic to have her follow-up HIV test and STD exam today. I had to skip class to do it." She put her head down and took another bite, chewing mechanically, not seeming to be getting much satisfaction out of the meal.

Jamie stared at the top of her head for a moment. "Doesn't that merit a comment? How is she?"

Ryan flinched, looking like she'd been slapped. "Who?"

Jamie spoke slowly, trying to make sure her partner could keep up. "Jennie. You took her to the doctor for a pretty serious test."

"I would have said something if there was a problem." She looked down at her food again, and moved some of her chicken around on the plate. "She's fine. No evidence of any STDs. She's a little worried about the HIV test, but I'm not. I'm sure her friend was clean." Her brows knit together. "What was his name? Ajax? No, no, Axel. Anyway, they didn't do anything that could have caused a blood exchange. I wanted her to have the test just to scare her."

"It's good that she's a little worried. That might make her think twice before doing something like that again. When will she get the results?"

Ryan had clearly moved on to another topic in her head. "Huh?"

Jamie waved her off, not bothering to ask again. Ryan went back to eating, putting all of her concentration into her meal. It was patently clear that something was troubling her, but also clear that she didn't want to talk. Jamie was about to get up and clear the table, but she recalled a question her mother had asked. "What time is your game in Sunnyvale on Friday? Mom wants to come."

It only lasted a second, maybe less, but Jamie saw it: a look of stark fear passing across her face.

Ryan composed herself as quickly as she'd let the emotion seep through. "Three o'clock. We're staying down there, right? With your mom, I mean?"

"Yeah, sure we are."

"I just...I was just checking the schedule."

"Everything's the same." She studied Ryan's expression carefully. "I have to leave at four on Saturday to catch the plane to Temecula, and you're gonna stay at Mom's that night."

The fear flitted by again, and Jamie realized what the problem was. She reached across the table and took Ryan's hand, then gently stroked her skin with her thumb. "Are you upset about being alone while I'm gone?"

Ryan held out for a second, then nearly shouted, "When I get home, no one will be here. No one. I don't think I've ever slept in an empty house my whole life." She started to cry, wiping at her tears with a vicious swipe of her hand. "You're mad at me, and I don't even know why, and I'm a big, fucking baby! I need a god-damned babysitter as much now as I did when I was two!"

Jamie got up and went to her, wordlessly urging her to move her chair back. As the chair slid back, she slid onto Ryan's lap. "I'm not mad at you, and you don't need a babysitter. I was mad at my father, and I took it out on you. I'm sorry for that, baby."

"It's okay."

Running her hand through Ryan's hair, Jamie said, "You're a very mature, very competent, very capable woman. The truth is that you're having a hard time right now, but it will pass. You need to keep things nice and simple for a while, and that's hard to do when we're both so busy."

Ryan gave her a look that made Jamie's stomach do a flip. "Why doesn't it bother you? You don't get upset when you have to leave. Doesn't it affect you at all?"

She knew her answer was very important, and she spent a moment trying to make sure she got it right. "I don't like to leave you. I hate to be away from home." She put her hands on Ryan's cheeks and moved her head so they were face to face. "I want to be with you. Every day."

"But you don't get upset when you're not." Ryan's eyes were dark, and Jamie knew that the ice she was walking on was very thin.

"Do you remember how you were when you were on the volleyball team?"

"What part?"

"You went on a lot of road trips, and even though you weren't crazy about them, you didn't mind. You weren't upset about traveling. That's how I feel. I'd rather be home, and if I can't be home, I'd rather have you travel with me. But I like to play, and travel is one of the bad things about the sport."

"So…I used to be normal like you, and now I'm not."

Jamie's eyes fluttered closed. Being with Ryan was usually such a joy, but helping her through these periods of vicious self-recrimination tested Jamie's soul. "I think the car-jacking has had a more lasting effect on you than it has on me. Life has been harder for you since it happened, baby. And that's made it harder for you to be away from me and your home and all of your routines."

The blue eyes were still dark and devoid of emotion. This was Ryan at her most frustrating: furious at herself and unable to cut herself the smallest of breaks. "We were in the car-jacking together. I've been through bad things before. I should have gotten over it sooner than you did."

"Sweetheart, it doesn't work that way." Jamie tried not to let her frustration show, but Ryan wasn't making things easy. "Anna and I have talked about this a lot."

"You talk about me?"

"Yes," Jamie said, knowing she probably shouldn't have admitted to this. "We talk about all of the people I love. I love you more than anyone, so we talk about you pretty often."

"So what does a woman I've never met think about me? Am I ready for shock therapy?"

"Of course not! Anna doesn't try to diagnose you. She's my therapist, not yours. We talk about how the things you're going through affect me." She kissed Ryan's forehead, but got no response. "I worry about you—a lot. I know how hard things have been for you and how angry you are with yourself."

Ryan ignored most of her statement. "I'm fine. I just don't like to travel right now. It's not the end of the world."

"I know that. I'm certain it's temporary. But it upsets you, and anything that upsets you upsets me."

Ryan's posture loosened up a little. "Why does Anna think I'm having a hard time?"

"Mmm…I haven't asked her specifically, but she did say that old traumas can get new life when something new happens. They build on one another."

"Yeah, I've heard that. But I should be able to use the things I learned before to get out of this. Experience is the best teacher."

"Not always, baby. Experience can be a very cruel teacher. Really bad things are still bad—even if they happen often. We suffered through a very traumatic event, and it's gonna take time, but you will get over it. You just have to have a little more patience."

"I'm sick of being patient! I got over being gay-bashed faster than this. I don't feel like I'll ever be confident again."

"Yes, you will," Jamie said, her voice louder and stronger. "I know you will. We both will."

"When does it bother you?" Ryan asked, her eyes suddenly filled with concern.

"In small ways. I cross the street whenever I sense someone behind me, I get up and leave Sufficient Grounds if someone particularly menacing comes in, I'm always wondering if some stranger will want to hurt me for no reason at all. I don't have that…that secure feeling I used to have."

Ryan tucked her face against her chest. "I'm so sorry," she whispered. "I'm so sorry they took that away."

"It gets better all of the time," Jamie assured her. "I feel lots better than I did just a month ago. Besides, it wasn't good to assume everyone was my friend. Over time, the fear will fade, and I'll just be a little cautious. That's not a bad thing."

"You feel better…consistently better…all the time?"

"Yeah, I do. Anna says that's most common. As I encounter things that upset me, I try to face them. Then we talk about them in therapy. It helps a lot."

"I don't feel like that. I don't feel much better than I did after we got back from Pebble Beach."

Jamie stroked her hair for a few moments, then slid her arms around

Ryan's shoulders. She brought her lips close to Ryan's ear and asked, "Does it worry you?"

Ryan's eyes closed and she nodded.

"It will get better. It's just taking longer than you want. But time will heal you, honey. I'm sure of it."

A heart-rending sigh escaped from Ryan's lovely lips. "Life can be so hard."

"And so good," Jamie whispered, tightening her embrace and feeling Ryan's solid body in her arms. She'd come close to losing her. Close to losing everything. But they were both whole and healthy. That was the reality, and for that, she offered up a prayer of deep, deep gratitude.

Chapter Seventeen

Ryan walked into the house on Thursday night, animatedly talking on her cell phone. "Tell the fellas we'd be there if we could. Make sure you tell 'em that, okay?" She nodded. "Just don't forget. Love you, too. Bye."

She clicked the phone off and walked over to Jamie, giving her a quick welcome-home kiss.

"Who was on the phone?"

"I was," Ryan said, giving one of her "I'll pull that trick on you for the rest of our lives" smiles.

Jamie swatted her on the seat. "Who were you speaking to, Ryan?"

"My brother. Rory," she clarified when Jamie raised an eyebrow. "Niall's moving this weekend. I'm really bummed that we can't help."

Jamie paused, trying to determine if Ryan was kidding. She'd never helped anyone move, and didn't feel that her life was made poorer by that fact. But Ryan looked entirely sincere. "Does he really need help?"

"Nah. All of the cousins will be there. But I hate to miss anything like that. You know what Da always says."

"No, I don't."

"He says your friends help you move. Your real friends help you move a body."

She had a perfectly straight face on, but Jamie could see the merriment in her eyes. "Does he really say that?"

"Nah. I heard it somewhere. I just thought it was funny."

"You're in a good mood. Feeling good?"

Ryan took a banana from the bowl Jamie was always careful to keep filled with seasonal fruit. "Yeah, I suppose. What's for dinner?"

"Nothing special. Just fruit and cheese. I got home late."

"So...this is an appetizer?" Ryan wiggled her banana.

"It fits with the menu." Jamie patted her side and started to gather the things she needed for dinner. Ryan jumped up to sit on the counter, as she always did when she was home in time to watch the preparations.

"Why were you late?" she asked, peeling her banana.

"I ran into Hannan. The woman Mia hired to impersonate her."

Ryan laughed. "I think about old Hannan every once in a while. I was wondering if she was getting away with it."

"Hannan says everything's fine. She claims the prof has been complimenting her on her class participation."

Ryan's eyes popped open. "She's participating?"

"Yeah." Jamie giggled. "She says she's gotten into it. If she wasn't sure the professor would recognize her, she'd like to take the class for credit."

"Maybe she can wear a disguise." Ryan shook her head. "That's a damned odd situation."

"Not for Mia. She's always spent more time figuring out how to get out of work than it would take her to do the work."

"Hmm...I see politics in her future."

Jamie looked at her partner for a second. "The most cursory background check would prevent her from running for sewer commissioner."

"Riiiiight."

After dinner, Ryan and Jamie went upstairs to work on their stock portfolio. The game had progressed to a point where they'd merged their assets, deciding that they'd get just as much enjoyment out of beating the market as each other. After a very bullish week, their combined assets now totaled $1.6 million.

As she watched Ryan's eyes light up when the totals flicked across the screen, Jamie decided that observing the joy Ryan derived from playing the game was one of the most enjoyable parts of her week. She knew that Ryan would never get the same satisfaction from real money, but playing with "funny money" as she called it allowed her to enjoy herself immensely.

"So, when do we get those shares of Palm from that spin-off of 3Com?" Jamie asked.

"Didn't I tell you what those rats did?" Ryan asked, her pique obvious.

"No, what?"

"They decided to distribute the shares six to nine months after the spin off. They won't be worth the paper they're printed on."

"Really? But people are jazzed about Palm."

"I know, but an IPO rarely lives up to its hype." She looked up at Jamie thoughtfully. "I think we should sell our whole 3Com holding. It's a bad sign that they're making us wait so long for the spin-off shares, and it really bothers me that they still won't say what the distribution's going to be. I don't trust a company that plays cat and mouse like that. Plus, I keep thinking about what my father said. He doesn't know anything about the stock market, but he has a firmer grasp on reality than most people who claim to be expert stock pickers."

"I see your point."

Ryan made the entry, and when she was done, Jamie looked at her and said, "Hey, wanna have some fun?"

"Sure."

"If you feel strongly about Palm being over-hyped, let's sell it short."

"Really?" Her eyes lit up. "I've never sold short before. How do we do it?"

"Well, if you're sure the stock will fall, you place an order to sell as many shares as you want at the current market price. But since you don't necessarily own them, your broker has to sell them out of his own inventory, or go out and buy them so he can sell them. You have to put up one hundred and fifty percent of the current value of the shares, either in cash or stock, then when the price reaches the point you want, you buy the shares and make good on the sale."

Ryan shook her head and said, "What's in it for the broker?"

"He gets one hundred and fifty percent of the value, and after he buys the shares, that extra fifty percent is his to play with or earn interest on. If you keep the transaction open for a while, that can really add up."

"This is pretty risky, isn't it?"

"Oh, yeah. If the stock goes up, there's no limit to the amount of money you can lose. You've gotta have big cojones to sell short, amiga."

"Let's do it!" Ryan said gleefully. "Let's go big, baby. It's a mortal lock that Palm's gonna go up like a bottle rocket and then crash just as fast."

"I'm in. We just have to wait until the day the IPO is issued."

"That's next Thursday. Can you come home for lunch that day? We can see how it does and decide when to sell."

"It's a date."

"Oh, shit! I've gotta go to Sacramento next Thursday. But we don't leave until three. Will we have time to do this if I'm home by one?"

"Sure. It'll just take a minute. It's not like we have to call a real broker, honey. We just have to take a quick look at the stock price, and make an entry on our books."

"Cool. We'll be rich, rich, I tell you!"

"We're already rich," Jamie teased.

"Yes, but now we'll be rich with imaginary money that we really earned. That's cool."

Ryan barreled into the house on Friday morning and took the stairs two at a time. Her bedroom door was open, and she motored in just as Jamie was coming out. They grazed each other, just missing butting heads. "Jesus! A little warning would be nice!"

Jamie clutched at her chest, fearing her heart would stop. "The house was empty two seconds ago. If anyone should warn anyone—it's you! Damn, my heart's still racing."

"I'm late," Ryan grumbled. She went to her closet and pulled out her Cal duffle bag, then started to add some clothes.

Jamie watched her put in some cotton slacks and tailored shirts, a few T-shirts, a pair of jeans and all of the compression shorts she owned. "What do you need those for?"

"Don't have any underwear," Ryan said, not looking up. "Got my last pair on."

"You have a full supply. I did your laundry when I got home from golf practice."

Ryan looked up and blinked. "You did? You've never done my stuff."

"That's because Maria Los does my laundry and I don't usually pay much attention. But yesterday she asked me if she could do yours, since it had filled the entire hamper." She smiled. "We were both a little amazed at how many pairs you have. I think she thought we'd taken in boarders."

Ryan looked a little embarrassed. "I've got about six pairs of really good undies. Then I start going down the ladder until I get to the ones that I wouldn't use as rags. I've never run out before. I didn't think it was possible." She started to unbutton her jeans, then shimmied out of them. "Now that I have good ones, I'm gonna put on another pair."

Jamie looked at the pale pink panties that looked like they were once white but had been washed with something red. The elastic was exposed on one leg, and when Ryan took them off, the skin on her thigh looked irritated. "Honey, I know it's hard for you to find time to do your laundry. Why didn't you ask me to help?"

Ryan shook her head. "It's my responsibility. I have to schedule my time better."

Walking over to her, Jamie put her hands on her partner's shoulders, steadying her while she put clean underwear on. "I'm going to start doing it for you. I'm home more than you are."

"But you don't like doing laundry. You don't even do your own."

Jamie shrugged. "So? I have the time, you have the need."

Ryan made a face, looking like she was going to spit. Then she sighed and said, "I'm gonna figure out a way to make the time to do it myself."

Jamie started to argue, then realized it wasn't worth the time. "Fine. Whatever."

"I'm sorry," Ryan said, clearly sensing Jamie's frustration. "I just feel weird having someone else wash my underwear."

Jamie looked at her, trying to figure out why Ryan relished having her mouth on every part of her that the underwear covered but was uncomfortable having her wash it. She quickly realized this was a quirk she wasn't going to able to understand. She nodded and put her hand on Ryan's waist. "I threw away every pair that had holes or where the elastic was exposed. I can't have my girl looking like she dumpster-dives for her undies."

A smile slowly bloomed and Ryan grasped Jamie and hugged her. "Thanks for doing my laundry. Thanks for caring about me. And thanks for putting up with me. I know I can be a pain."

Jamie patted her butt, and Ryan released her. "We all have our things, honey. One of yours is laundry."

Nodding, Ryan grabbed her bag and kissed Jamie quickly. "Gotta go. See you at your mom's tonight."

"Okay, Sparky. Play well."

When she heard the door shut, Jamie called her mother. "Hi," she said when Catherine answered. "Wanna meet me at the Stanford Shopping Center before the game? Ryan's in dire need of new underwear."

Late on Saturday afternoon, Ryan sat on the bed in Jamie's room in Hillsborough, watching her lover pack a bag for her trip. "I forgot to ask if your mom's going to fly down to watch you play."

"I didn't ask her to. I know she'd come any time I asked, but it can't be fun for her. She's just being nice."

Ryan nodded. "Maybe. But if you'd like her to come you should ask her."

"I think I'll wait for her to offer. Then I'll know she really wants to."

"*I* really want to." She was on the verge of tears, and she held onto Jamie's suitcase, unwilling to release it.

Jamie sat down and slipped an arm around her, gentle fingers probing the knots of tension in her back muscles. "How are you feeling?"

"I'm all right," Ryan said quickly. "It's only a couple of days."

"I know that." Jamie's voice was soft and calm. "But I don't feel very good about going, and I thought you might feel the same."

Ryan nodded. "You know I don't like it, but that's life." She laughed very artificially. "A series of calamities and disappointments, occasionally interrupted by moments of joy."

Jamie patted her and got up to finish getting ready. "Mom said she'd drive you home after the game tomorrow."

"I can take the bus. She doesn't need to go out of her way."

"She likes being with you, Ryan. And if you'll let her drive you, she might stay for dinner. Eating alone every night is hard on her."

"It is? Why doesn't she come to our house? She never has to be lonely."

Jamie walked over to her and kissed her gently. "You're such a find," she whispered. "How did I ever get so lucky?"

Feeling shy, Ryan shrugged her shoulders. "Dunno. Must be fate."

Jamie kept her arms around her neck and hugged her tightly. "I'll call you tonight when I get to Temecula, okay?"

"Okay." Ryan got up, and they held each other for a few moments, then walked downstairs together. After Jamie said goodbye to her mother, Ryan walked her out to the circular drive. She put Jamie's bag onto the passenger seat of the Boxster, then opened her arms to hold her for a long hug. "I'll miss you, sweetheart. Play well."

"Do my best." Jamie kissed her and got into the car. Ryan stood there for a long time, hands in her pockets, staring after the departing car.

Catherine and Ryan ate in the kitchen, and the pair convinced Marta to sit and eat with them. That was a rare accomplishment, and it was clear that Marta didn't feel entirely comfortable.

As soon as Marta had finished her last bite, she got up and started to clean the kitchen, politely, but firmly refusing help from Ryan.

Catherine could see that her daughter-in-law was fidgeting. She knew it went against Ryan's grain to have someone waiting on her, so she suggested they go into the living room for a while.

While Catherine turned on some music, Ryan sat on one of the sofas, taking up much of the space, as was her wont. Catherine recalled how the young woman had behaved the first time she'd visited the house, how she'd tried to blend in with the rather stiff Evans style. It made her happy that Ryan was now comfortable enough to kick off her shoes and lounge on the sofa, something she did at home. "You seem a little on edge tonight, honey. Is everything okay?"

"Yeah, yeah. Just a little…off my game. I think I'll feel better when Jamie calls. I…like to…I…" She looked adorably, childishly unsettled.

"It's hard for you, isn't it?" Catherine asked gently. "To have her gone."

"Yeah. It is."

She didn't say another word, but Catherine could tell she was anxious. "Do you worry about her?"

Ryan nodded, quicker this time, looking like she might cry.

"Since the car-jacking?"

"Uh-huh." The young woman made a fist and rubbed her mouth with it, her lips reddening from the friction. Catherine guessed she was trying to distract herself from crying, and she respected Ryan's need to save face.

"That makes perfect sense. I still have nightmares about it, and I wasn't even there. I have a low-level discomfort… I guess it's anxiety…that hasn't really left since that night."

"You do?" Ryan got up and settled herself close to Catherine on the sofa. "How can I help?"

Catherine smiled and put her hand on the younger woman's leg. "You're such a giver. I'm so glad you and Jamie found each other."

"Me, too," Ryan said quickly. "Now, how can we make you feel less anxious?"

"Oh…part of it is my trying to limit my drinking. I was downing an awful lot of anti-anxiety medicine on a daily basis. It's going to take me a long time to get a baseline on what my real feelings are. My psychiatrist has offered medication, but I don't want to take anything unless I'm unable to cope. I want to see if I can ride this out and calm myself down."

"You talk about this with your therapist, don't you? I know it's hard to ask for help, but you've gotta do it."

"It is hard," Catherine said. "Is it hard for you?"

Ryan nodded again, her lower lip quivering.

"How about a hug?" Catherine asked.

It was hard to ask for comfort, but Ryan was one person who offered it without question. They hugged for a minute and when Ryan started to pull away Catherine found herself reaching up to secure Ryan's arm around her shoulders. Feeling like a child burrowing against her mother, Catherine let herself be enveloped by Ryan's love and concern. It felt absolutely divine and only a brief stab of longing hit her when she realized she'd never actually felt this cared for by her own mother. They spent a long time sitting quietly, reflecting on how their worlds had changed in the last months—for better and for worse.

Chapter Eighteen

On Monday morning, Catherine drove down Castro Street in San Francisco, pleased to find that the parking situation was not bad on a weekday. Assuming she'd be walking a lot, she'd dressed casually, wearing tattersall plaid slacks in tan and brown, and a brown suede blazer covering a simple, cream-colored cashmere shell. Brown tassel loafers deducted two inches from her usual height. Even though she liked the extra height she got from heels, she was trying to get comfortable wearing more casual clothing. Being around the O'Flahertys had begun to rub off. One day Ryan might have her in one of those Cal warm-up suits she seemed to wear constantly.

After she announced herself to the receptionist, Catherine waited for just a moment before a man came out to greet her. "Mrs. Evans? Alex Joyce."

"Catherine," she said firmly, extending her hand. "It's good to meet you, Alex."

"Come on into my office," he said, leading the way. "I'll show you what types of places are on the market now, and you can let me know if any of them suits your needs."

They sat next to each other and began to look through his listing book. "You said on the phone that you were looking for properties for your daughter?"

"Yes, my daughter and her partner."

"Does she have children, or is it just the two of them?"

"They've only been together since summer, so it's the two of them for now, but they do plan on having children. Knowing Ryan, her partner, they'll have more than the two they're talking about."

"Ahh...he's in favor of big families."

Catherine blinked at him, puzzled by his choice of pronouns. "Oh," she said after a moment, "I didn't make myself clear. Ryan's a woman."

"Oh!" he said, blinking in return. "Well, I must tell you how nice it is to see a mother who's so supportive of her lesbian daughter."

Taking her turn, Catherine blinked again, and gave him a tentative smile. "You know, I don't think I've ever used that term for her. I'm so comfortable around them that I don't stop to think that they're lesbians." She shook her head and laughed softly. "But I suppose they are. The evidence is overwhelming."

The young man smiled back at her. "Any chance you could have a word with my parents? They seem to think that my being gay is the focus of my entire being. I only wish I lived the hedonistic lifestyle they imagine I'm embroiled in."

She patted his arm. "Give them time, Alex. They might come around."

"Maybe." He shrugged. "It's their loss if they don't. You mentioned that you're only interested in Noe and Castro, is that right?"

"Yes. Ryan's family lives in Noe, and she wants to stay within walking distance."

He looked thoughtful for a few minutes, then thumbed idly through his book. "There really isn't anything on the market in those neighborhoods right now that I'd waste your time looking at. Why don't we look at styles of homes, just so I can get a feel for what you think they'd like."

"That sounds fine. I think I have a pretty good idea of what the girls want." She smiled. "What they really want is a fairly modest house that can magically expand to accommodate fifty people for dinner."

He smiled back. "We have our work cut out for us then, don't we?"

"Catherine?" Alex said quietly. "Catherine?"

When he touched her shoulder, she started, turning to give him an embarrassed smile. "I'm sorry, I went off for a minute." Looking around the home they were viewing, she said, "This place isn't right for Jamie and Ryan, but I certainly wish it were."

"It is special, isn't it? I think it's one of the nicest properties I've ever listed."

"This is your listing?"

"Yes. The owner has been agonizing over listing it for months, and we finally put it on last week." He laughed softly. "He's an art director in Hollywood, and he's absolutely never home. I think he said he was here for a total of one week last year. It's silly to have a place like this sitting idle, no matter how much money you have."

As Catherine looked around again she said, "I would hazard a guess that he wants to renovate another place. People who do this kind of work are rarely satisfied to live in it once they've finished."

"You could be right. He's owned the place for three years, and it was an absolute mess when he bought it. It's only been finished for about nine months, and as soon as the last workman left, he was talking about selling."

"That's not uncommon. I have...had friends who live to decorate." She folded her arms over her chest and walked around the rooms on the first floor once again. "I don't know what it is about the place," Catherine mused quietly, "but something about it really resonates with me."

"Are you certain that your daughter couldn't be persuaded to range a little past her comfort zone? Pacific Heights isn't far from Noe."

"No," she said with regret. "This space wouldn't suit them at all. It's a good size, but it's not set up like they'd want, and it's so beautifully done that it would be a crime to knock down any of these walls." Catherine cocked her head and said, "Besides, it's a little elegant for Ryan's tastes. I think she'd feel intimidated here."

"You didn't mention how old they are."

"Jamie just turned twenty-two, and Ryan's twenty-four."

"Ahh...that is young for a space like this."

"Jamie's used to living in luxury, but Ryan's struggling to acclimate. She'd break out in hives when she saw the silk on the walls of the master bedroom. And I think there's more marble in the master bath than Michelangelo ever laid his hands on."

"Where do you live? Here in the city?"

"No, I've lived in the Peninsula my whole life. I'm fewer than five miles from where I was born."

"Thank God I can't say the same thing. I'd be in a corn field in Iowa."

"Are you happy in the city?"

"Very. I always say that everyone who loves cities should live in San Francisco at least once in his life. The opera, a world-class symphony orchestra, great museums, wonderful restaurants, and thousands of great-looking gay men—it's nirvana. I felt like my life began the day I moved here."

Not quite sure why she was sharing details of her personal life, Catherine said, "I'm starting my life over, in a sense. I'm in the process of divorcing my husband."

"I'm sorry to hear that," Alex said sympathetically. "I…uhm, figured out who you were when you talked about your daughter and her partner by name. I didn't know that you and Senator Evans were divorcing. That hasn't made the news, has it?"

"Yes, but it wasn't a very big story, thank God. We've kept it very quiet, and we're not fighting, so it should blow over quickly."

Alex gave her a sad smile. "I broke up with my lover a few months ago, and it's been hellish. I really understand how hard it can be."

"Yes, it is hard, but I have Jamie and Ryan, and they help a lot. Actually, I'm in the city more than I'm at home lately. My husband has an apartment on Telegraph Hill that's usually available, and I should stay there more often just to avoid the drive." She shook her head. "It doesn't suit me, though. I'd rather drive home than stay there."

He nodded. "I can't imagine how hard it must be to have your lives held up for the whole world to see. I know it's been very tough, but I must say that I've come to respect all of you for the classy way you've handled it."

"Tough is not a strong enough word. Having my marriage break up, and then having my daughter and her partner almost killed has really taxed my resources. I feel like I'm just getting by. I crave solitude, but when I'm alone down in my big house, I feel so lonely." She shook her head. "Well, enough of my complaining. I suppose we should go."

"Would you like to see the second floor again? I know the house doesn't suit your purposes, but if your daughter is going to remodel, the second floor balcony is one of the nicest I've seen. It might give you a few ideas."

"Yes, I would like to see that again, if you have time."

They went back upstairs and Alex opened the door, allowing Catherine to walk outside alone. The balcony, which was very generous in size, seemed like a veritable Garden of Eden, right on the crest of Pacific Heights.

Generously-sized concrete planters surrounded the space—each painted a matte black to allow them to stand out against the low, white wall. A lavish variety of roses filled them, spilling out a profusion of color and scent. Wisteria and clematis were just beginning to bloom from where they draped beautifully over a wrought iron archway, also painted black, which stood right outside the door. She sat down on an upholstered chair, covered in black with white piping, and gazed out upon the Bay, the wind ruffling her hair.

Even though the breeze was stiff, she wasn't cold, and realized that was because the space was well-protected from the wind on all sides. A six-foot-high glass wall surrounded the patio, the glass so clean that it was invisible. Looking up, she noted that the designer had also installed gas heaters every few feet, the appliances almost disappearing from their clever placement on black wrought iron posts.

A feeling of absolute peace settled over her, and she completely lost track of time. It wasn't until she began to chill that she looked at her watch and realized in amazement that it was nearly five o'clock. "Alex," she called as she went back inside.

He came back into the room, his cell phone up to his ear, and held up a finger, indicating that he'd be off the phone in a minute. When he hung up, he chuckled at her shocked expression. "Did you enjoy your afternoon?"

"How long was I out there?"

"A couple of hours, but it wasn't a problem. I've been busy the whole time. I've got my PC in my briefcase, and I was able to catch up on a lot of work that I can't get done at the office."

"But…Alex," she said again, thoroughly embarrassed. "I've wasted your entire afternoon on a house that I won't even bother to show Jamie."

"I promise you that I don't mind a bit." He smiled broadly. "I don't believe in rushing. If we're going to work together, I want you to feel free spending as much time as you need in a space. That's the only way to know if a home is right for you."

She blinked at him, and heard her mouth form a statement that shocked her as it registered. "This house isn't what the girls are looking for, but it's absolutely right for me. I've purchased three homes in my life, and I bought each one the first time I saw it. Let's get the owner on the phone and make a deal."

Late that afternoon, after their matches were over, Jamie got in the courtesy van that the country club had arranged for them. Christie, Crystal, Samantha and Valerie were already in the van, and they had room for another player or two.

Scott Godfrey, the coach, walked up to the van, asking, "Who were you paired with, Jamie?"

"Jaclyn. She was still in the locker room when I left. Should we wait for her?"

"No. Go on back to the hotel. I'll catch the stragglers in the last van."

"Okay." Scott closed the door, and the driver started the van. "How'd you guys do?" Jamie asked. "I didn't see the results."

"Not bad," Christie said. "I won my pairing, but only by a stroke."

"I sucked," Crystal said. "If I don't get my slice under control, I might as well drop out of school."

"Drop out? Really?"

"I'm just here for golf. My game's really suffered with all of the school work. I might quit and go on a mini-tour."

"But you're getting a free education," Jamie said, wincing when she heard how much like an adult she sounded. The look Crystal gave her confirmed their different perspectives.

"I could care less about a degree."

Couldn't care less, Jamie said to herself. *If you could care less, you would.* She sank back into her seat, barely paying attention to the other women talking about their scores. All of a sudden, she didn't care if they'd all shot their IQs, which, even though they were single-minded, were high.

Softball practice was short on Monday night. Since they'd played two games each of the previous three days, Coach usually let them coast a little on Monday—especially if they'd played well on the weekend. It was raining, and rather than risk an injury on the wet field, Coach kept the team inside and talked about the weekend games. They'd played very well, but he clearly had a thing about them growing complacent, and he picked every nit he could find.

"O'Flaherty," he said, his voice gruff, "you didn't take the safe option when you came in to pinch hit in the eighth inning of the first game on Saturday."

Ryan stared at him, knowing exactly what he was talking about, but finding it hard to believe he was chiding her.

"What's your excuse?" he asked, his tone a little sharper.

She looked down at the tile floor, staring at the pattern of beige splotches on the dark rose background. It didn't always work, but often she could stop herself from being snappish by spending a second or two focusing on patterns or counting something.

Coach didn't give her a few moments. "I don't have all day. What's your excuse?"

For some reason, she felt humiliated, even though he'd already called out almost everyone in the room. Her chin jutted out and she said, "I drove in the lead run. The run held up and we won. I don't need an excuse."

His eyes opened wide, and he really looked at her for a moment, something he never did. She knew she would curse or cry if he said another word, and she hoped against hope he shut up and moved on. He looked down at his clipboard as every other player coincidentally found someplace innocuous to direct her attention.

"Hernandez," he said, looking at a little-used player. "You didn't take a turn picking up bats on Sunday. Don't think I don't notice little things like that."

"Sorry," she mumbled.

"It's all right. I only bitch at ya because I care." He paused for a second and then laughed, breaking the tension in the room. "That's bull. I bitch at everybody."

Everyone laughed except Ryan. She stared straight ahead, her face impassive.

"Okay," Coach said. "See you all tomorrow. And don't be late."

In a flash, Ryan headed for the door and was outside in seconds. She was walking quickly, but when she heard Coach's gruff voice call her name she started to sprint, eating up the ground with her long stride. If he wanted to bitch at her some more he was gonna have to earn it.

As soon as she arrived home, wet and breathless, Ryan started to tear off her clothing. Leaving it where it fell, she was stark naked when she reached her room. Not knowing where she was going didn't curb her desire to get there in a hurry. She threw on a sweatshirt and a pair of jeans, then sat on the bed to put on some dry socks and shoes. The phone rang, and when the machine picked up she heard Coach Roberts' voice.

"Hey, O'Flaherty, I don't wanna make a big deal out of this, but I want you to know I wasn't really pickin' on you today. I was glad you didn't sacrifice on Saturday. I wouldn't have put you in to pinch hit if I'd wanted a sacrifice no matter what. I only asked the question 'cause I knew you had a good reason for taking a poke at it. I wanted the younger girls to hear what goes through a good hitter's head. That's all…okay? No harm, no foul, right?" He was clearly uncomfortable, but he continued, "You can call me back if you're pissed or something. Uhm…sorry," he mumbled, barely audibly, then hung up.

Ryan sat still for a few moments, feeling like she was on the verge of exploding, but not knowing why. Having Jamie gone always made her feel at loose ends, but this was bigger than that. The house felt confining, like the walls were creeping inward. She couldn't bear to be inside another moment. She shoved her feet into an untied pair of basketball shoes and grabbed her raincoat. When she got downstairs, she picked up her keys and dashed to her car, feeling better once she was inside the warm, confined space.

A CD turned up loud started to thrum and she took off, not having any destination in mind. The rain made traffic so ridiculously heavy that she didn't even have to make a choice about which direction to go. She just went wherever she had the opportunity. Her body had no plan, but her mind must have and about half an hour later she found herself in a gritty part of South San Francisco, near a place she hadn't been for many years.

The car slowed to a crawl and she saw that the Jackson Arms Target Range was still there and open for business. Inside, she approached the young man at the counter. "What've you got that'll put the biggest hole in the target?"

He placed a nine millimeter Ruger on the counter, the weapon that most women used to get out their frustrations at bosses, boyfriends and bullies. But when his eyes met hers, a black eyebrow had lifted and ice-cold eyes bore into him. Wordlessly, he turned and selected a Glock .45. Ryan picked up the pistol and wrapped her hand around the piece, then nodded at him. He handed her a box of ammo, and she said, "Gimme two." After producing her driver's license and credit card, she pointed at a shelf that held safety equipment for her eyes and hearing. "Those, too."

The clerk handed her the safety glasses and ear protectors and ran her card, leaving the total blank in case she wanted more ammunition. There was something about the woman that told him two boxes wouldn't get rid of whatever it was that brought her out on such a night. "Third lane," he said.

Ryan went into the range and immediately put on the ear muffs and glasses. She realized she hadn't taken off her coat, so she did that and pushed up the sleeves of her shirt.

Methodically, she inspected the firearm and made sure it was in good working order. Then she loaded it and felt the weight of it in her hand—almost three pounds. A small smile of approval creased her lips at the heft of the weapon. Reaching out, she stroked the cold steel, caressing the undulations in the metal with a fingertip. Feeling better than she had all day, she squared herself at the firing line, then extended her arm and clapped her right hand around her left hand and the weapon. Slowly, gently, she squeezed the trigger, the kickback soothing some place deep in her heart. Her lips parted, and her teeth shone in the poor industrial fluorescent glow, making her look like a fearsome animal about to take a large bite out of a small victim.

Chapter Nineteen

The golf team ate in a small private room at the hotel. The room was set up with a steam table and a number of cold salads. *I know I'm a food-snob, but wouldn't it be easier to let us go to the regular restaurant and order from the menu? This stuff looks like it's been sitting here for hours.* Jamie tried not to let her mood show, but she looked around and saw that each small table was filled with the usual cliques. Lauren, her roommate, sat alone, waiting for Jamie to join her.

Jamie took her tray and maneuvered through the room, then sat across from Lauren. "Hi," she said, trying to sound happy. "How'd you do today?"

The young woman was slowly coming out of her shell, and Jamie felt rather proud of herself for getting her to carry on a conversation. She knew that Lauren was ultra-shy, and if it were not for Jamie, she'd talk to no one.

The girl gave her a bright smile. "I did really well. You know how the landing area on the first hole was really narrow?"

"Uh-huh."

"I landed right in the middle! And my approach shot hit the edge of the green and rolled five feet from the hole. It's like that started my day off right, and things just kept going."

"That's great, Lauren. I'm really happy for you."

Lauren reached into her back pocket and took out her score card. "I made par on two. How about you?"

Dutifully, Jamie took out her own card, and she and Lauren replayed their matches—shot by shot.

As soon as Catherine was finished with her tiring negotiations, she got on her cell phone and started to call Jamie at home, then remembered that her daughter was in Temecula. She let the phone ring anyway, hoping that Ryan was home. Part of the fun would be seeing their faces when she told them about the new house, so she'd already decided not to tell them on the phone. But if Ryan were home, she wouldn't be able to avoid going over to share the news. She guessed Jamie would be surprised, and she knew Ryan would be very happy that she'd seen the light about the grandeur that was San Francisco. No one answered, so she hung up, not wanting to leave a message. She considered what to do, not having any desire to go home to her empty house. It was almost nine o'clock, and on a whim she called the O'Flaherty house, pleased to have Conor answer on the second ring.

"Conor? Catherine."

"Hi there," he responded brightly. "What's up?"

"Ryan's not there, is she?"

"No. She's coming over tomorrow night, though. She's probably in Berkeley tonight. Have you tried her cell phone?"

"No, but I called the house. She must be out."

"What's up? Is something wrong?"

"Wrong? Oh, no. I…I did something very impulsive today, and I'm so excited about it that I could just burst!"

"Don't even tell me what it is," he said immediately. "I want to hear about it in person. Where are you?"

"Oddly, I'm on Castro Street."

"Oh, no, not you, too! I'm not gonna let 'em have you, Catherine."

She laughed heartily, assuring him, "I haven't changed my sexual orientation. I was conducting some business here."

"Are you anywhere near Market?"

"Yes, just two blocks, I think. Why?"

"I'll meet you at Castro and Market in ten minutes. Don't talk to any strangers. Especially women!"

As promised, Conor arrived in just a few minutes and managed to find a space to double-park. He hopped out of the truck and loped down the street, smiling when he caught sight of Catherine. Giving her a hug, he warned, "People may stare at us, but just ignore them. Our kind is pretty rare around here, but we can't live in shame just because we're different."

She laughed gently and grasped his hand, letting him lead her back to the truck for the short drive to a legal parking space. They chose a lush little martini bar, and he escorted her to a small table. "Name your poison. They have every kind of martini ever conceived."

Ignoring the little voice that urged her to give in, she smiled up at him. "I'm in the mood for something non-alcoholic. I'll take whatever they have that isn't sweet."

"Done." He turned and sauntered over to the bar, then returned a moment later bearing a caramel apple martini for himself and a mineral water for Catherine. Clinking the rims of their glasses together, he gazed at her seriously. "Now, tell me what we're celebrating."

She tried to control the luminous grin that insisted on covering her face. "I bought a new house!"

"You bought a new house? I thought you were going to start looking for Jamie and Ryan." His face broke into a wide grin. "You are an impulse shopper, aren't you?"

"Usually not. But Alex, the real estate agent I worked with, showed me a house in Pacific Heights that I fell head over heels in love with. It belongs to a production designer who spends most of his time on location. It's right—"

"At the crest of Divisadero…looking down into the Marina," he supplied, beaming. "And it was recently beautifully renovated by one of the most talented carpenters this side of the Rockies."

"Conor! You renovated my new home!"

"I sure did," he said, smiling brightly. "I do good work, don't I?"

"It's a showplace! I've never been so impressed with a home."

"Well, I've got to admit that the owner came up with most of the ideas that make the place sing, and he also gets credit for going all-out on the moldings and trim. That's what makes a house look like it's built with care."

"I didn't think it was possible to be any more excited, but now that I know you worked on the house, I'm positively giddy."

"You've bought a great house, Catherine, and I know you'll love it there. I'm surprised you're going to move, though. I thought you loved Hillsborough."

She looked at him for a second, then decided to tell him the whole truth. "I love Hillsborough, and I love my house. But lately, I've been so depressed that I can hardly stand to be at home. I've spent more nights than I can count staying in hotels in the city. I'm...I'm...lonely. Jim was rarely home, and Jamie has been gone for years, but the ghosts in that house are about to drive me mad."

Immediately, he reached for her hand, chafing it between his large, warm, callused ones. "I'm so sorry," he said, his eyes filled with concern and empathy.

Her own eyes fluttered closed, and she nodded slowly. "I appreciate that. I think I'll keep the Hillsborough house—at least for the time being. I love my garden and the pool and it's calming to spend time outside. I just don't want to have to sleep there for a while."

"You let me know if you ever need a shoulder to cry on. I'm a very good listener, and I've had my share of heartaches. You're not alone," he said emphatically, locking his clear blue eyes on her.

"I know that, and I'm more thankful than you can imagine," she said, feeling a few tears welling up. "I might take you up on your offer, too. I don't like Jamie to see how upset this has made me. She's got enough to worry about right now."

Grasping her hand again, Conor said, "I meant what I said. If you're lonely or sad and you want to talk, just give me a call. Do you have my pager number?"

"I don't think so."

"Take out your cell phone and program me in," he instructed, giving her both his pager and his cell. "Don't be afraid to use them."

He said it with such emphasis that she believed him completely. "Thank you," she said softly. "I never would have guessed that having my daughter decide she was a lesbian could bring such unexpected joy into my life. Being welcomed into your family is healing for me in a way I can't even begin to express."

"We're very glad to have you. I thought we'd gotten the pick of the Evans family with Jamie, but I think the race is too close to call."

When he beamed a grin at her, Catherine spent just a moment thanking the heavens for bringing her into the circle of love that was the O'Flahertys.

When Jamie got back to her room, she called Ryan, but didn't get an answer. Checking her watch, she saw that it was almost nine, long past time for Ryan to be home. She called her cell, but the call went to voice-mail immediately, something that usually happened when Ryan was out of cell range. That was an all-too-common occurrence in the Bay Area, so she didn't let it worry her. Instead, she called home and left a message. "Hi, baby. I'm back in my room, and I'll probably go to bed soon. If I don't hear from you in a while, I'll turn off my phone so it doesn't wake me. So call my cell and leave a message so I can check it when I get up, okay? I love you with all my heart. And I miss you even more than that. Bye."

Ryan stayed at the shooting range for a long time, not even noticing how much time had passed until the lights flicked on and off to signal closing time. She didn't know where to go next, but she wasn't ready to go home.

She surprised herself by winding up in front of the lesbian bar in Berkeley. It felt like her car had been programmed to head to a safe place. A place where she would be with her own. Her hand froze on the door handle, and she wondered if she was asking for trouble. Jamie wouldn't approve, but her need for contact was greater than her desire to please her partner. So she went in, sat at the bar, and talked to a bartender she'd never seen before. The entire time she was there she nursed a beer, staring at the colorful liquor bottles on the back bar when the bartender was busy.

For the first time she could recall, no one approached her. She was glad for that, since she didn't want to strike up a conversation with anyone. But it was a little troubling, too, since it was so unusual. She took a long look at herself in the mirror behind the bar and decided she wouldn't approach a woman who looked like she did, either.

An aura of lonely, aimless need showed back at her. The sort of woman who'd glom onto you and talk your ear off. She blinked, hoping the image would change. But it didn't. All of her confidence, her cockiness, her spark, were…gone. She looked like the kind of woman she used to feel sorry for—a lonely woman with no one to speak to, the anonymous comfort of a tacky bar the closest thing she had to a friend. She took out a five-dollar-bill and slapped it down, then left without a word, knowing that neither the bartender nor anyone else would notice her departure.

Ryan walked into the house at midnight, wet and tired and emotionally spent. She played Jamie's message, a half-smile on her face as she listened to her soothing voice. But her smile darkened when Jamie said she'd turned her cell phone off. Her heart started pounding as she tried to decide what to do. Ryan knew she could call the hotel—she knew that Jamie would want her to—would be angry with her for not calling when she felt so low. But she couldn't make herself do it. It wasn't just that she didn't want to disturb her partner. The bigger issue was that thinking about how needy she was made her skin crawl.

She refused to examine her heart, to search for the darkest feelings, the ones she rarely forced herself to acknowledge. The feelings that made her guts clench in impotent anger. The ones that irrationally held Jamie responsible for her pain—for abandoning her with such ease.

Ryan dropped to the sofa and tried to decide what to do. For just an instant, she considered doing nothing—just going to bed without calling. But her conscience chided her immediately. So she got up and dialed Jamie's cell and did her best to leave an upbeat message. Then she went upstairs and logged onto her computer, poking around until she found one of her favorite math bulletin boards. There was a message from a student in Ireland who was having trouble with his homework assignment, so she shot him an e-mail, offering assistance. He replied immediately, and they met in an IRC chat room and worked on his trigonometry problems until two a.m. Richard was very grateful for the help, and Ryan knew she'd done most of the work for him, but she felt so much better to connect with someone—even a high school kid thousands of miles away—that she felt like she might be able to sleep. She lay down, fully clothed, not even bothering to pull the bedspread off. In minutes, she was fast asleep.

Chapter Twenty

On Tuesday afternoon, Ryan consciously tried to fit her usual softball demeanor onto her prickly psyche. She left the locker room and took a path to the field that led her near Coach Roberts. Trotting by him, she said, "You've gotta stop calling me at home. Jamie's the jealous type." She smiled to herself when she heard him chuckle, relieved that she wouldn't have to explain the previous day's meltdown. Briefly, she wondered if it would be easier to be straight. Guys loved to ignore emotional issues. She could struggle through her feelings for months without ever having to talk about them.

As soon as practice was over, she drove to San Francisco and met up with a bunch of her cousins at a local bar to participate in a well-known trivia contest. The boys had been going to The Bitter End for years, and they always played as a team. Ryan had only been there a few times, but Conor wasn't available, and they wanted to make sure they had someone good with numbers so Ryan was the obvious choice.

She was still in a strange mood, but none of the boys noticed, none of them being particularly sensitive to mood swings. Rory showed up just as the game began, and he was given a roaring welcome, since he was their music ringer. The first category was television shows from the seventies, and they all groaned in unison.

"We've got to get one of our fathers to come," Kieran said. "We're getting killed because we don't know jack before 1980."

"It's the first category," Colm said. "Don't get your panties in a wad."

"He's not wearing panties," Niall said. "He gave up cross-dressing for Lent."

Ryan signaled for another beer, keeping up with the boys. They started to click, answering question after question. "Damn, we've gotta have Jamie come some time," Ryan said when they were all stumped on what was probably a pretty simple American literature question. "She knows everything about books."

"Where is she tonight?" Declan asked. "How'd you get the handcuffs off?"

Ryan gave him a sickly smile. "She's playing golf in So Cal. She'll be back tomorrow night."

"Wow, it must be love if you don't have a date later," Dec said, grinning evilly.

"I won't dignify that with an answer. And, just for the record, saying that Austin had the biggest port in Texas was dumber than dumb. Stop guessing if you don't know the answer."

"Touchy," he said, taunting her. "Somebody gets cranky when she doesn't get any for a couple of days."

When she flashed him a lethal glare, he slapped her hard on the shoulder. "Lighten up, pup. I'll buy you another. Murphy's?"

"Yeah. Murphy's," she said, trying, ineffectively, to smile.

At eleven thirty, Ryan's cell phone rang, and she got up from the table and threaded her way through the tightly-packed chairs, stepping on many toes and kicking the odd shin on her way out. She stood in the vestibule of the bar and clicked the answer button. "H'lo?"

"Where are you?" Jamie asked. "I called you at home two hours ago and asked you to call me back. That's two nights in a row you haven't been at home when I expected you to be."

"I'm in the city with my cousins," Ryan said, deftly answering only the first point. The noise was nearly deafening, so she dashed outside, the cool evening hitting her damp cotton shirt and making her shiver.

"At a carnival?" Jamie asked. "It sounds like Times Square."

"We're playing trivia at The Bitter End. We won two-hundred and fifty bucks. I got the winning answer."

She sounded a little slow. Not very Ryan-like. "What was the question?"

"How many fifty pound cannon balls would it take to fill a two ton container. No…wait. How many two ton…No, that's not it. Uhm…it was something about cannon balls. Or bowling balls."

"I see," Jamie said. "Did you drive over there, honey?"

"Sure. Inner Richmond's too far to walk."

"Who's with you?"

"The usual suspects."

"Can I speak with Conor? I want him to do me a favor."

"Huh-uh. Conor didn't come."

Great! Now who do I ask for?

"Rory's here," Ryan volunteered. "Can he do your favor?"

My God, she's as high as a kite. I could never get away with this if she were sober. "Yeah. Either he can do it or ask Conor for me."

"'Kay. I'll get him." She went back into the bar and shouted, "Rory!" He looked up and walked over to her, putting his arm around her shoulders to get close enough to hear her. "Jamie wants you to do her a favor."

He gave her a puzzled look and took the phone, stepping outside with his sister. "Hi, Jamie. What can I do for you?"

"If you're as sober as you sound, you can drive your sister home. How much did she have to drink?"

"Sure, I'll be glad to do that," he said, smiling at Ryan's sloppy grin.

"If she doesn't fight it, I'd rather she slept at your house tonight. Think you can manage that?"

"No problem. Wanna talk to Ryan again?"

"Sure. Put her on and don't let her drink anymore! She has school in the morning."

"Easier said than done, but I'll try."

Ryan accepted the phone and winked at her brother when he went back inside. "I miss you," she said.

"I miss you, too, sweetheart. Now, pack up and go home. You have class in the morning, you know."

"Oh, fuck. I forgot. Gotta go. Love you."

"I love you, too," Jamie said. She lay down on her bed, her stomach doing a flip when she thought of the possibility of her lover driving home. *No, she won't do that. Rory won't let her, and if he can't handle her, the boys can throw her in the back of one of their trucks.* She sighed heavily. *It sure is nice to have a bunch of strong men in the family–even though they're the same ones who lead her into temptation.*

Ryan went back into the bar and signaled to Rory. "Gotta go," she said.

He jumped up and was beside her before she could make a move. "Give me a ride."

She was too slow to realize that he'd driven his own car, so she kissed all of her cousins goodbye and left with her brother. They passed his car on the way to hers, and when she failed to notice it he knew he couldn't let her drive even the short distance to Noe Valley. They were a few feet from the BMW when he said, "Mind if I drive?"

"I'm fine," she said, an edge to her voice.

"Fine for what? I just wanna drive a nice car for a change. Mine's about to fall apart." He hated to guilt-trip her, but he wasn't taking any chances with her safety.

She fished the keys from her pocket and tossed them to him. "You can drive it whenever you want, you know. Why don't you keep it for a while? I'd be happy to trade."

Damn, a little guilt goes a long way. "No, once in a while's plenty. It's a nice treat."

They got in and he adjusted the mirrors. "Big day at school tomorrow?"

"Nah. Just have my French class at eight. Then I'm meeting with my advisor about my project."

"When's that?"

"What? My meeting?"

"Yeah."

"Mmm…eleven or eleven thirty. I havta check."

"Why don't you blow your French class off and stay overnight? I miss having breakfast with you."

She gave him a sidelong glance, obviously suspicious. "You think I'm wobbly?"

He could see the sharp look in her eye, and knew he'd better tell the truth. "We've both had more than we should. I wouldn't feel safe going all the way to Berkeley." He was lying, but he didn't think she'd kept track of his drinking. He'd only had one beer. She'd had at least five.

"I'll stay over, but I'd better get up for my class. It's hard enough when I go. Skipping will only make it worse."

"Okay. I just thought you could use a little more sleep."

"I could," she agreed. "I could use a lotta things."

"Like what?"

She laughed, but her laughter was tinged with bitterness. "A thirty hour day would help. Having Jamie home more. Being away less. Seeing you guys on the weekends. Seeing Caitlin more. Having Duffy at my house."

He gave her a quick look, surprised at how swiftly she'd come up with her list. "Can you do anything about any of those wishes?"

"Nope. If I could, I would." She lowered her seat and stared out her window.

"You don't seem like yourself. I'm worried about you."

"Mmm. Yeah. I'm worried about me, too."

She said this so matter-of-factly that he was sure it was the alcohol talking. But he decided to make use of a rare situation. "Tell me what you're worried about."

She yawned noisily. "Oh, the usual shit. I'm worried about not finishing my project and not graduating. I'm worried about my relationship. It's really fucking it up to be away from each other so much."

"What about upstairs?" he asked, tapping his own head. "How are you feeling up there?"

"Shitty. Totally shitty."

He waited, but she wasn't more forthcoming. "Doing anything about it?"

"Yes, Rory," she sighed. "I'm in a crappy, useless therapy group. We get together every Tuesday morning and whine about how frightened we are." She gave him a wholly insincere smile. "It's a delight."

"Why are you going if it's not helping?"

"'Cause Jamie told me to."

"Jamie wouldn't tell you to go to something that wasn't helping. Have you talked to her about it? Does she know you don't like going?"

"Mama's dead," she snapped. "Aunt Maeve took her place. Not you."

Her words stung, but he knew she didn't mean to sound so sharp. He started to apologize for butting in, but she beat him to it.

She scratched his arm, letting her hand rest there for a moment. "Sorry I'm being such a bitch."

"You're not being a bitch. You're just down."

"Well, I'm sick of being down. Sick and tired of it."

"It's the carjacking, huh?"

"Yes. It's the fucking carjacking." She sighed heavily.

"Does it still bother you that you had to shoot that guy?"

She laughed. The sound so bitter and spiteful that it brought him up short. "I'd love to bring him back—so I could shoot him again. I think about emptying the weapon into him. I start off low and work my way up until I put the last slug right between his eyes."

He didn't say another word. Ryan had a smug, satisfied look on her face and Rory let her engage in her fantasy. But he felt significantly worse about her than he had at the start of the evening.

The next afternoon, Ryan was in her room reading when the metallic click of a key being slid into the lock sounded. Like a cat running for the kitchen when it hears the can-opener, she flew down the stairs, her arms open when the door was pushed. Ryan grabbed Jamie and held her tightly. "God, I missed you," she whispered into Jamie's ear, the salty drops of her tears falling onto strands of blonde hair.

Jamie dropped her shoulder bag, struggling a little in Ryan's clutch. "I missed you, too." She reached up and brushed her cheek when she felt something wet. Pulling back, she looked into Ryan's eyes and saw fresh tears. "Oh, baby, was it horrible for you to be alone?"

Ryan released her and let her head drop. It felt like her body was collapsing into itself. It was all she could do to wrap her arms around Jamie's midsection and hold on.

Jamie kicked the door shut and gently guided her to the sofa, where she sat on her lap.

Ryan tucked her arms around her and nestled her face so hard against Jamie's neck that she thought she'd bruise her. But Jamie pressed back, making her feel slightly less needy. They stayed just like that for a long while.

Eventually, she stopped crying and was able to breathe normally, but she felt incapable of moving. After a long time, Jamie tilted her head just enough to be able to kiss her cheek, and then Ryan shifted to reach Jamie's mouth. They kissed gently and slowly, both needing to connect physically.

No matter how long they kissed, Ryan didn't feel a flicker of desire. Instead of the beginning of lovemaking, this was more like a long, long welcome home kiss that neither wanted to end.

When it finally did, Ryan pulled back just enough to stare at her partner's lips for a full minute. A slow, sure smile blossomed, and she said, "Missed you."

Jamie had just finished calling for Thai food when the phone rang.

"Hello?"

"You have three guesses," Catherine said. "I did something very, very impetuous on Monday, and you get to try to figure out what it was."

"Hold on a sec, Mom, this is Ryan's favorite game." Holding the phone so that her mother could hear them both, Jamie said. "Mom did something very, very impetuous. She wants us to guess what it was."

"Hmm…went skydiving?"

"No, that's a little bold for me," Catherine said. "This isn't entirely out of character."

Jamie shook her head and relayed the message to her lover. "You bought something big," Jamie guessed.

"You're right—but not nearly specific enough."

Ryan's eyes grew wide, and she asked in a loud voice, "You didn't buy us a house, did you?" Ryan could hear the amused laugh coming through the receiver, and her heart started to slow its rapid beat.

"Tell Ryan she's half-right. I bought a house, but I bought it for myself."

"You bought a new house—for yourself?" Jamie gasped. "Since when… why would you…how long have you been…huh?"

Ryan lifted the phone from her partner's hand. "That's a very big surprise, Catherine. Where are the new digs?"

"Pacific Heights. Not far from your old school, as a matter of fact. Right at the crest of Divisadero."

"Ooh…I bet someone has a view of the Bay from her windows."

"A fantastic view," Catherine acknowledged. "Now, I don't want to keep you two. I know Jamie just got home."

"Don't be silly," Ryan said. "I'll always share her with you. I just have custody."

"As you should. Now tell Jamie not to worry. I'm not giving up on Hillsborough. This will be my city house. Really, I should have had one years ago since I'm in the city so often. We'll still have our big O'Flaherty gatherings down at the old house."

"I don't know if Jamie would be worried about that, but I was," Ryan said, chuckling softly. "I love that pool, you know."

"I do. You and Caitlin both have the same addiction."

"You have my sincere best wishes for your new home. I predict you'll never want to go back to Hillsborough. But the best part of your news is that we'll be so close to you on weekends. That's beyond great."

"I think so, too."

"I'm sure you're gonna love it, and I'm really happy for you. Here's Jamie, okay?"

"Bye, Ryan."

When Jamie had the phone back, Catherine said, "I honestly was trying to look for a home for you two, but something about this house spoke my name, and I had to have it."

"It's not the type of place we'd like?"

"No, it's in the wrong neighborhood, and it's very…uhm…not stuffy, but very elegant and refined. It looks like a home for a middle-aged person, not a pair of young women who plan on having children."

"Gotcha," Jamie said, nodding. "Well, I have confidence that you'll help us find the right place, Mom. But if I hear of your buying yet another house for yourself, I'm taking you off the job."

Chapter Twenty-One

After the pair had finished dinner, Ryan put her hand on Jamie's shoulder. "I can't study tonight. How about you?"

Shrugging, Jamie said, "I guess I could, but I'm not going to. What do you wanna do instead?" She was on the verge of suggesting they go straight to bed, but Ryan was still not putting out any sexual vibes, and she didn't want to push her.

Giving Jamie a lovesick smile, Ryan said, "I'd be happy to have you sit on my lap all night. I don't care what we do as long as I'm touching you."

Jamie linked her hands behind Ryan's neck, having to reach to accomplish the move. "Mean that?"

"Yeah. Of course. Why?"

"I'd love a massage. We were on some tiny puddle-jumping plane, and I didn't get much time to cool down after my morning match. I'm all knots."

Ryan lifted her chin and gazed into the distance, while moving her hands to a variety of points on Jamie's back. "Mmm…you do feel stiff. Let's get out the big guns."

Jamie cocked her head in question.

"I brought my massage table over here, and we've never used it. How dumb is that?"

"How dumb am I not to know you brought it?"

"Conor brought it over not long after I moved in. He said we had more room than they do, which is true. I put it in the garage."

"Go get it," Jamie said, slapping her on the butt. "And drink some caffeine. I want an all-night massage, Buffy."

Ryan set up the table in the parlor, mostly because she didn't want to haul the heavy table up the stairs.

Jamie had stripped to her underwear and walked down the stairs carrying an old sheet and a large bottle of vanilla-scented massage lotion. She wiggled the bottle in her hand. "I don't want you to stop until this is all gone."

"A modesty sheet?" Ryan asked, one eyebrow raised.

Jamie stood next to her and kissed her. "A 'don't-stick-to-the-vinyl' sheet. I'm the opposite of modest when I'm with you. I'm…bumptious."

Ryan drew a fingertip across her ass. "You have a very nice bum."

"Look it up later," Jamie said as she spread the sheet on the table and slid onto it, sitting upright.

"Underwear?" Ryan asked. "I thought you were bumptious."

"I am." She reached behind herself, unhooked her bra and tossed it aside. Then she lay flat on the table and lifted her hips while she shimmied out of her panties.

Ryan leaned over a little to watch, and when the panties were off, Jamie placed them neatly upon her head. Ryan smiled and adjusted them until she was satisfied with her mint green cap. "How do I look?"

"Like a woman wearing a hat with very large ear holes."

Ryan whisked it off and tossed the garment near where the bra had landed. "Every once it a while, I'm glad Mia's gone. Not very often, but this is one of those times."

Jamie nodded, laughing. "She had impeccable timing. No matter where she was or what she was supposed to be doing, she would have marched in here as soon as you got me covered in oil."

"I think she would have waited for this," Ryan said, tearing off her T-shirt and pajama bottoms. "She had a sixth sense for when I was naked. I can't count the times she caught me in the shower or changing clothes."

"I think she just liked to see you naked. Not that I blame her." She rolled onto her side and openly ogled her lover. "You are one gorgeous hunk of flesh, O'Flaherty."

Ryan slapped her on the hip, just a little harder than she had to. "You'd better not flirt with all of your massage therapists."

"Just you." She rolled onto her stomach and let her arms dangle. "Do whatever you want, baby. I'm all yours."

Ryan assessed her for a moment, thinking about Jamie's general complaint about her back muscles. "I think I'll start out with a pretty gentle Swedish massage, then get serious."

"Serious?" The blonde head lifted.

Patting her butt, Ryan said, "Relax. I won't hurt you any more than I have to."

Jamie dropped her head, muttering, "Very reassuring. You should really consider medicine as a field."

Ryan knew her partner was talking, but she was concentrating, making up her action plan. She knew Jamie would repeat herself if she were saying anything important, and if not, her babbling was nice background noise.

She warmed the lotion in her hands and started near the shoulder blades, making smooth, strong, long swipes with her palms, getting her used to her touch.

Jamie hummed with pleasure, always a vocal, enthusiastic client. After a while, Ryan started to knead the pliant flesh, working from head to toe with a very light pressure.

Ryan's touch grew more concentrated, and she made brisk chopping gestures up and down her body, energizing her while simultaneously relaxing her. Finally, Ryan started to stretch her out, beginning with her ankles and slowly progressing to her knees, hips, hands, elbows and shoulders.

"Ungh. More."

"Plenty more, you little piggy." Now that she was sure Jamie was limber, she began to work a little deeper, this time using her fingers and thumbs. Some of the points she probed caused Jamie to groan a little, but Ryan urged her to breathe through the pain and try to relax.

After a long time, Ryan was fairly satisfied, but there was a knot at the base of her right buttock for which she needed more leverage. Without warning, she knelt on the table and stood, surprising Jamie who let out a yelp. "You're gonna break the table!"

Laughing, Ryan said, "This table can take eight hundred pounds of working weight. I could jump up and down, and it'd be fine."

"What are you doing up there?"

"I need a little leverage. She squatted down, then put her knee right above the knot and began to press while she rotated her leg in a quick, circular motion.

When Ryan lifted her knee, Jamie moaned, "Thank you, thank you, thank you. I thought it was my back, but you found just the spot."

Hopping back onto the floor, Ryan started to rub her hands all along her partner's body, keeping the circulation going. "My pleasure. Want some more?"

"Duh…I think I do, but won't I be sore?"

"Probably—especially in your glutes. You had some real tightness built up there. We've gotta work on those muscles more often."

"Must be from shifting my hips in my swing. Maybe I'm not warming up enough."

"Or stretching when you're finished. Did you stretch today?"

"No." Jamie reached up and put a hand over her eyes, shielding them. "As soon as I finished my match I had to run into the locker room and put on a dry shirt. We almost missed our flight."

Ryan patted her on the butt. "I know how it is when your team's waiting, but try to stretch whenever you can, okay?"

"Deal." Jamie raised her head and batted her eyes. "Now why don't you give me a nice, gentle, fall asleep massage? I know you're good at those."

"Already warming up the lotion," Ryan said, rubbing her hands together. She started at her partner's feet, slathering the lotion around her toes and insteps.

The earlier work seemed to have energized her, and Jamie started chattering away, telling Ryan about each of her matches. Ryan tried to pay attention, but one golf match sounded very much like the next to her. She was sure that reaching the green with a driver from a bunker two hundred yards away was a wonderful thing, but she guessed hearing about it interested her as much as hearing about solving a quadratic equation impressed Jamie. She figured her job was to take her cues and make the appropriate sound of approval or dismay as Jamie talked.

Even though her words weren't spellbinding, Ryan noted that when her partner laughed her ass wiggled in the most adorable fashion, something she'd never noticed before. As Jamie explained a particular shot, she twitched her torso, and her cheeks grew as firm as a pair of melons. *What a fantastic view,* she thought, feeling a definite tingle in her clit. *Why haven't I put her on her belly more often? It's like having a whole new girlfriend.*

Ryan started working up one tanned leg, feeling the solid muscle in her calf. Going up the leg, she started imagining ways she could straddle it, dreaming up all sorts of shapes that Euclid had never considered.

There was something very appealing about watching her lover and fantasizing about her when she was completely oblivious. Even though she knew she could always talk Jamie into being sexual, it was fun to start to be sexual without her. Ryan wasn't sure why that was, but there was some part of her that felt a little guilty about it. That didn't stop her though, and she realized that part of the allure was that Jamie wasn't self-conscious since she didn't know she was being gawked at. Even though she'd come a long, long way, she was still a little skittish about Ryan's open appraisal of her body. When she didn't know she was being looked at, she behaved completely naturally, letting Ryan focus on nothing but her body.

While staring at her back, Ryan realized that she usually focused on Jamie's eyes and the connection that always built during lovemaking. Ryan loved that feeling more than she could say, but not having it let her stare at Jamie's ass—her very favorite spot. She'd seen asses of every shape, size and color, but there wasn't a doubt that Jamie had the *ne plus ultra* of asses. Firm, but with enough give to make a lovely pillow, smooth as an infant's, shapely—with a little dent on the outside of each cheek further defining it. There were a few faint freckles on the uppermost edge of her bottom, right where a low-cut bikini would leave the tender skin exposed to the sun. There was still the vaguest remainder of summer's tan line, and Ryan had to stop herself from sliding her tongue all the way across it.

Jamie rambled on, with Ryan guessing she was still on Monday's match. Ryan was barely acknowledging her partner's commentary now, just mumbling an "uh-huh" here and there. She was so lost in her thoughts that she was sure Jamie would notice, but she was managing to pull it off. She took her partner's left leg and stretched it at the knee, then pulled her thigh off the table, revealing one of Ryan's favorite places on earth. Her mouth began to water like a hungry tigress', and she pulled the thigh further away from the other, making her view all the more alluring.

Not noticing anything out of the ordinary, Jamie continued to talk when Ryan put her leg on the far edge of the table. Ryan switched to the right leg, once again starting at the foot and moving her way slowly upwards. By the time she got to Jamie's upper thigh, she was ready to eat her alive. Ryan's clit was throbbing, and a rush of warmth spread through her groin. She snuck a look at the lotion, quickly reading the label before she coated her fingers with it. Then, she placed Jamie's right thigh on the outside edge of the table, opened her lips with one hand while two fingers simultaneously slid inside. Ryan purred with satisfaction when her fingers found their depth, but Jamie squealed, her cunt closing on Ryan's fingers, making her wince. "Relax, baby," she soothed. "Just a little surprise."

"Mmm…" With a heavy sigh, Jamie's hips began to sway, and she opened up, letting Ryan slowly turn her hand, touching every surface. "Good surprise. Very good surprise."

"You sure? Should I have asked first?"

"Huh-uh. Surprise me anytime you want. It's yours," she purred, her voice low and sexy. "Anytime you want it."

The way her hips moved made Ryan's knees weak, and in a matter of seconds, she was sure she would fall. Her head was swimming with desire, and she found herself slipping out of her partner and climbing onto the table, covering her with her body.

She supported as much of her own weight as she could, but Jamie wanted more. "Lie on me," she demanded. "Let me feel all of you."

Ryan's hands slid up her slick body and grasped Jamie's hands, stretching them out over her head. Then she rode her, pressing her mound into Jamie's ass while they moved together on the table.

"Bite me," Jamie moaned, lifting her head to expose her neck.

Ryan complied, taking a mouthful of tender flesh between her teeth. She mouthed her, sucking on the skin while pressing into Jamie as hard as she could. Lost in a lust filled haze, she saw stars, completely unaware that she was biting down until her partner moaned.

"Damn, that feels good."

Immediately, Ryan released the skin, nuzzling and kissing the welt she'd made.

"Do it again," Jamie begged. "Come on, baby. Do it again."

Ryan had partially come to her senses, and she continued to mouth and suck on bits of flesh across Jamie's neck and back. But she kept her teeth covered, unwilling to give in to her partner's temporary desires. Still, even those tender bites were driving Ryan's need, and she slid down until she was straddling Jamie's slick thigh. She moved it about, trying to wedge it between her legs when Jamie let her muscles go loose, allowing Ryan to do whatever she needed.

It was tough, but Ryan supported her torso in a semblance of a pushup, then settled against the curve of Jamie's ass, letting the plump flesh press against her. Her hand slid down, and she opened herself, hissing out a sigh when her overheated clit touched Jamie's slippery cheek. She lay still for a moment, trying to control herself, but her cunt was throbbing painfully, and she couldn't wait another second. She started to snap her hips, rubbing against Jamie's ass with every ounce of her strength. Their skin slapped together, squishing with each rough thrust. Ryan shook her head and let it fall back, sucking in as much air as she could while she tried to hold out for just a few moments.

Jamie reached behind herself and slapped her hard on the ass. "Come on, baby. Come for me."

Groaning loudly, Ryan grabbed her around the waist and thrust hard, once…twice…three times, and then she came noisily, calling out a string of partially formed words before she collapsed upon Jamie, making the table squeak as it bounced on the wooden floor.

"I wanna hold you," Jamie mumbled.

"Unh," was all Ryan could manage. Finally, she forced herself into a state of semi-rational thought and slithered off the table, holding on to the edge for dear life while she got her sea legs.

Jamie rolled over, sat up and then scooted down the table, wrapping her arms around her. "My God, what got into you tonight?"

"I have no idea," Ryan mumbled thickly.

Jamie started to giggle, quickly shaking with laughter. "Make sure it gets into you again, okay? I don't know what the hell we were doing, but it sure was fun!"

Ryan gave her a half smile, feeling like she did when she'd had too much to drink. She took the sheet from the table and briskly dried her body, then folded it and covered the sofa with it. Wearing her sexiest smile, she lay down and curled a finger in Jamie's direction.

"Me? You want me?" Jamie asked, playfully looking around the room.

"You're the only one in the world."

Jamie walked over to her. "Where do you want me? I'm game for anything."

Making a quick decision, Ryan patted her lap. "Lie against me."

"Like this?" Jamie sat down and used Ryan's torso as a backrest. She had her knees raised, exposing herself fully.

"Perfect. Now I can touch all of the parts I didn't get to play with before."

"Always thinking," Jamie said. "You're a planner."

Jamie's ear was right beside Ryan's lips, and she spoke softly as her hands started to roam. "Have I told you lately how perfectly spectacular your breasts are?" She filled both hands with the silky-smooth flesh and moved her hands up and down a few times before giving them a good squeeze.

"Huh-uh. You're way behind on your compliment quota."

"I should be spanked," Ryan purred.

"I gave you a pretty good swat earlier. Was that okay?"

Ryan laughed wryly. "Made me come like a rocket. That's always a good thing." She started to flick her fingernails against the hardening nipples, making them like pebbles in moments. "Was it really okay that I snuck up on you?"

"Huh?"

"Before," Ryan said. "When I put my fingers into you."

"How did I act?"

Laughing again, Ryan said, "You seemed to get into the mood pretty quickly. I just wasn't sure how you'd feel about my fantasizing about you and getting hot when you didn't know I was doing it."

"Ooh…is that why you were so sizzling hot? I was wondering…"

"Well, you do make me hot in seconds, so that's not odd, but I had a real good head start this time." Ryan was lightly scratching Jamie's breasts, covering them in slowly growing circles, then going back to the nipples to plump them up again.

"Keep doing that," Jamie murmured. "You're such a little devil."

"Is that good?"

"When you're good, you're very, very good. But when you're bad, you're better." She grasped Ryan's hand and slipped it between her legs. Then she spread herself open and guided the fingers inside, a growl of pleasure accompanying the motion. "Show me your bad self."

"All night long, baby. I'm gonna study you like Riemann's hypothesis."

"Call it whatever you want," Jamie said, her voice like a tiger's purr. "Just don't stop moving those fingers for a good, long time."

Chapter Twenty-Two

The next afternoon, the fledgling stock moguls kept their planned lunch date and sat in front of Jamie's computer, watching the real-time stock ticker. "I can't believe how quickly Palm is going up," Jamie gasped. "It's absolutely amazing!"

"Offered at thirty-eight and it's at one-forty-five now." Ryan nodded slowly. "There are some very wealthy people out there if they get out soon."

"When do you think we should sell short?"

Ryan checked her watch. "It's gotta be now. I've gotta be on the bus in thirty minutes. Unless you want to take over…"

"No, no, this has to be a joint decision. Now's fine."

Ryan kissed Jamie's cheek and said, "I don't think this is the best way to time stock sales, but duty calls. Call me later and let me know how high it got."

"Will do, Ms. Megabucks."

Giving her one last kiss, Ryan said, "That's a title I'll never be able to wrest from you, sweet cheeks. See you later tonight."

"Can't wait. You, a cheap motel room and a dusty field in Sacramento. What more could a woman want?"

At the end of the workday, Catherine sat on her outdoor patio and watched as Conor, Kevin and Brian roared up to her new home in Conor's big, black truck. She'd seen him drive many times, and had yet to see him arrive stealthily.

The men emerged from the truck, each of them carrying a bag with the tools of his trade. Conor had a metal clipboard in his hand and he looked up and waved it at Catherine.

"We're ready to go," Conor said. "Kevin's going to check the electrical, Brian will look at the plumbing, heating and air conditioning, and I'll get up on the roof and do a water test."

"Oh, Conor, do you really have to do that?"

"Yeah, it's a mistake not to. A leaky roof can cause more damage than almost any other fault. I'll be surprised if this one leaks, but I'd feel like a fool if I didn't test it and you were putting out buckets during our first storm."

"If you're sure," Catherine said. "I just don't want any of you to risk injury."

"We risk injury every day," Kevin said. "We're tradesmen." He struck a heroic pose, throwing out his chest for a moment before Brian gave him a hard jab in the belly.

Conor took his extension ladder from the truck bed, and hefted it over to the side of the house.

As he got it into position and started to raise it, Catherine said, "I'll go into the house and show Kevin and Brian around. I can't stand to watch you climb that high."

"This isn't very high," Conor said, but Catherine had disappeared by the time he'd finished his sentence.

It took about two hours for the men to check every system thoroughly. Kevin wanted a couple of ground-fault interrupter outlets put into the kitchen, and Brian recommended replacing an old section of galvanized pipe with copper. Conor couldn't find a thing that needed fixing, and he'd looked as hard as he knew how.

"The few little things we found will cost under five hundred dollars to fix," Conor said. "You can try to negotiate for the seller to pay for them, or we can do the repairs for you. Materials will be about a hundred."

"I'd be happy to have you do the work, but only if I pay your normal rate."

"That's not how we do it," Brian said, his strong jaw sticking out just the way Ryan's did when she was being inflexible. "Materials only."

"All right," she said, smiling sweetly at him. "I'll ask my real estate agent to recommend someone."

"She's as hard-headed as we are," Kevin said, laughing. "She'd hire a guy off the street before she'd let us work for free."

"Just like Jamie," Brian said, shaking his head.

"Where do you think Jamie got it?" Conor asked. "She's a chip off the young, beautiful block."

Catherine bumped him with her shoulder and laughed. "I think it's lovely that you all help each other out, but you've all got skills that you use for each other's benefit. All I have is money, so it's only fair that I pay for what I receive."

Conor put an arm around her shoulders. "She does have a lot of money," he agreed. "It's only right that you two should help her lighten her load."

"Now it's your turn," Catherine said, turning to Conor. "I'd love to put an office in the house, and I'd like for you to help me plan it and get it done."

Conor put his hands over his eyes, crying, "No, no, not me!"

"Yes, you," Catherine said, poking him in the chest. "I need you to help lighten my load, too."

He let out an aggrieved sigh. "When do you want me?"

"How about tomorrow? I'm going to be here to have a termite inspection around noon."

"That's good for me. I'm gonna go to Sacramento to see Ryan play, but I think I'll wait and go over on Sunday."

"Great. That's when I'm going, too. See you tomorrow...anytime after one o'clock."

"Should I bring you lunch?" he asked.

"No, I never eat lunch. But feel free to bring something for yourself."

"He's always got a snack stashed somewhere," Brian said. "He and Ryan eat more than any two of the rest of us."

"Good metabolism," Conor said. "Although if I worked a desk job, I probably couldn't get through the front door."

At around six o'clock that afternoon, Jamie reached Ryan via cell phone while she was on the bus. "We sold three thousand shares at one fifty."

"Wow, we've gotta put $675,000 in our margin account. That's a lotta dough."

"Oh, no we don't," Jamie said. "It's already down to one twenty-five. We only have to put in $562,500.

"Only you could say 'only' when you're speaking of half a million dollars," Ryan said. "Hey, you're breaking up. Good job on the sale. See you later."

Jamie knocked on the door of room 215 at the Comfort Inn in Sacramento at eleven. As soon as the door opened, she put her hands on Ryan's waist and asked in sing-song fashion, "Guess how much our margin is?"

"I don't know," Ryan asked excitedly. "How much?"

"Four hundred and five thousand dollars!"

"Jesus! You mean the stock dropped all the way to ninety?"

Momentarily stunned, Jamie asked, "How do you do that so fast?"

"Uhm…math…me…you know the drill. That's off the hook, babe. We're making money hand over fist."

"When should we buy? Soon?"

"Nah. Let's let it ride for a while. I think it'll continue to drop."

"Well, you've been a damn fine prognosticator so far. 3Com closed at eighty-one today. We made over thirty dollars a share by selling when we did."

"Not too shabby."

"I'm really excited about this. We should celebrate."

"Okay. Let's drink some fine imaginary champagne and eat some of the best caviar that money can't buy—all paid for with our sham profits."

"Our profits might be fake, but the fun is real," Jamie beamed. "Now strip me and take me to bed, in that order."

They lay in bed, their bodies entwined. Jamie's head was on Ryan's breast and she was nearly asleep from listening to the slow, steady beat of her heart. "What would you do with the money if it were real?" Jamie idly asked.

"Oh, I don't know. Probably invest most of it. Give as much to my grandparents as they'd take…which isn't much. Help pay for my cousins to go to university." She chuckled, making Jamie's head bounce. "Hire someone to impersonate me when I have to take my language proficiency test for grad school."

"Mia could hook you up."

"I've been looking around school. It's hard to find a woman who's as tall as I am. I've had my eyes peeled."

Jamie turned her head and kissed Ryan's breast. "Why won't you send your grandparents money now? We've got a lot more real money than imaginary money."

Ryan's shoulders shifted. "Dunno. Still doesn't seem like mine, I guess. Don't think it ever will."

"I hate that. I thought we'd agree that we'd work on putting together a foundation to give most of our money away."

"We will. But that's different from giving money to my family."

"How?"

"I don't know. It just is."

"It doesn't make any difference to your grandparents or your cousins. If they need some help…"

"I know, I know. I'll ask my aunt if she can think of a way to slip my grandparents some cash without their going wild."

"Who'll be the harder sell?"

"Usually my granny, but I think my grandfather might have a harder time with accepting money—especially from one of his grandchildren. He never made a good living, but he wouldn't take any assistance—not even used clothes from St. Vincent de Paul. Poor Aunt Moira had to wear my mother's clothes, after Aunt Maeve had first whack, of course. I don't think she had one new piece of clothing until both Aunt Maeve and my mother had moved to America."

"Write to her, honey. If we can make them a little more comfortable we just have to find a way."

Ryan shifted her hips and sank lower onto the bed. "'Kay. I've gotta do what I promised and start writing to Cait more regularly. I've really let that drop."

"You can't do everything. You've written a couple of times, haven't you?"

"Yeah. But she doesn't tell me anything. I don't think she trusts me."

"Really?"

"Yeah. But she doesn't trust Aisling, either, so I'm not surprised. I've just gotta work harder at convincing her she can tell me her secrets." She let out a breath. "One more item on my to-do list." She lay down and turned onto her side, wrapping an arm around Jamie. "G'night."

Jamie kissed her, then turned onto her side. *Nice move. She's finally in a good mood, and you make her feel bad for more things she doesn't think she's doing well.*

On Friday night, the senior softball players went to a bar close to their hotel to celebrate St. Patrick's Day. Coach Roberts gave them permission, telling them to stay out as late as they wanted. The girls met in the lobby, and were just about to leave when they saw the coach reading a magazine while sitting in a chair near the door.

"Have a nice time, ladies," he said, not looking up.

"Thanks, Coach," Jackie said. "We'll have one for you. No curfew, right?"

"Right. I'm gonna sit right here and make out the lineup card for tomorrow. I have a hard time remembering names, so I'll probably just put down the first people I see as they come home."

"Eleven o'clock?" Ryan asked, smirking at the man.

"That's a lovely time," he said. "One of my favorites."

"We'll be here. Sober."

"That's one of my second favorite things," he said, taking in a deep breath as though he could smell it. "Ahh...sobriety."

"Are we gonna have to walk a straight line?" Ryan asked.

He looked at her for the first time. "What a question! You make it sound like I supervise you. You're adults."

"Yeah, right," she said, turning and giving him a little wave from over her shoulder.

Coach Roberts looked at Jamie, who was smiling at him. "I'm misunderstood."

"I don't know how you do it, but they understand you better when you try to confuse 'em."

"That's my secret," he said, winking at her. "I shoulda worked for the government."

Jim Evans stood at the window of his suite, looking down at the revelers streaming in and out of the hotel. "There must be a big St. Patrick's Day party here," he said to Kayla.

"I saw signs in the lobby when I came in. It's some ancient order of something or other."

He turned, a small smile forming when he saw that she was wearing nothing but a tiny white T-shirt and bright green bikinis. "Are you Irish?"

"A little. My mother was a mix of English, Irish and Scottish."

"You look Irish," he said, regarding her thoughtfully. "With your red hair and fair skin. Green's a very good color for you."

"For my ass?" she asked, turning and wiggling it.

"For all of you. But it looks awfully good on your ass. Of course, everything does."

She went to him and put an arm around his waist, and they stood together for a few minutes, observing the traffic and the people near the hotel.

"Looks like fun," he finally said. "Do you want to go out? I'm sure we could find someplace close that wouldn't be filled with kids."

"No, it's only fun to go out on St. Paddy's Day if you're with a group of friends." Her arm dropped and she moved away, going to sit on the sofa. She picked up the remote and started channel-surfing. "PBS has Great Performances. Les Troyens from Milan. Want that?"

He sat down next to her. "Sure. I'm always up for opera." He relaxed against the sofa. "Have you ever seen Les Troyens performed?"

"No."

"Are you interested? What would you watch if I weren't home?"

"I wouldn't watch TV," she said without hesitation. "When you're gone, I'm either on my computer or talking on the phone. Well, I might have the TV on," she amended. "But only for background noise. I put on MTV or VH1...if either of them actually has music on...which isn't very often."

"What do you do on your computer?"

She gave him a sidelong glance. "Why the interest?"

He blinked in surprise. "What?"

"Why are you interested in what I do when you're not home?"

He frowned at her. "You're my lover. Shouldn't I be interested in what you do?"

"Sure. You should be. But you usually aren't." She didn't blink, staring right back into his eyes as he looked at her for a few seconds. "What? You look surprised."

"I am. Don't you think I care about you?"

She put her hand on his thigh, gently stroking him. "Sure you do. But..." She trailed off and looked away.

"What? Come on, tell me."

"You care about me like I care about you."

He stood up, releasing her hand and letting it fall to the cushion. "What in the hell does that mean?"

"We use each other, Jim. We always have. That can't come as a surprise."

"I thought we'd had this out before." His anger was starting to bubble to the surface.

"We've skirted around it before, but it's time to discuss the future. I'm going to have to find a new job soon."

"What? Why?"

She sighed. "We've talked about this. I can't go back to the firm. Everyone knows about our affair. I'll never have credibility in the San Francisco legal community again. I have to stay here."

"Here? As in Washington?"

"Yeah. I don't think anyone will hold our affair against me." She laughed bitterly. "It might even help me."

"So this is a done deal? You're definitely not going back to San Francisco with me?"

"With you?" She blinked in surprise. "What are you asking?"

Suddenly he realized he'd been perilously close to the edge of a cliff. "Uhm…just that I thought we'd work together and live together. I'd love to have you as my deputy."

"Oh. Right." She shook her head. "No thanks. I've got ten years to make a name for myself while I'm young. Then, when I get older, people will stop looking at me like a piece of ass and start paying attention to what I know. I can't spend my prime time riding your coattails."

He stumbled a little as he grasped for a chair and sat down heavily. "Is that all I am to you? A vehicle?"

She glared at him. "Why are you playing the victim here? You knew just what you wanted when you started flirting with me. You wanted a young woman who was naïve enough to sleep with you and be discrete about it. You had a plan."

His glare matched hers. "And you didn't?"

Kayla was silent for a minute. She turned her head, gazing at a picture on the wall. After a few contemplative moments, she swept her crimson hair from the side of her face and lay her cheek against the back of the sofa. "Not at first," she said quietly. "I hadn't been at the firm very long, and I hadn't heard much gossip. I was…really flattered that I got to work with you when I was a new associate. I thought they'd picked me because they thought I had a lot of potential." She turned her head and stared at Jim for a few seconds. "You asked for me, didn't you?"

"Uhm…I don't recall. I uhm…might have mentioned—"

She cut him off. "Spare me. I'm sure your list consisted of Melanie Angelos and me. You lucked out. She's gay."

Jim turned away from her, striding over to the window, where he let his head rest against the cool glass. He didn't say a word, so she continued.

"I was so dumb." She let out a short, wry laugh. "I honestly thought that you and I had something special. I knew you were married, of course, but I assumed your marriage was in trouble. I thought it was only a matter of time until you divorced your wife so we could be together." She sniffled, and wiped a few tears from her cheek. "I'll never forget the day I was having lunch with a couple of people who'd been at the firm for a few years. One of the guys started warning me about keeping my distance from you. That's when I found out that I wasn't the first—and that I wouldn't be the last."

He turned and leaned against the window, staring at her in stunned silence. Finally he asked, "Why didn't you tell me to fuck off?"

"It wasn't that easy. I knew word would get out. And once people knew, it didn't matter if I'd slept with you once or a thousand times. So, I swallowed my pride and decided to get what I could out of the relationship. I think we've both come out of it pretty well. You wanted me because of how I looked, and you got a bonus because I also know what I'm doing. I got the bonus of coming to Washington with you."

"Do you care about me or not?" He felt like he might cry, but her eyes squinted in disgust as his cheeks reddened. She wasn't the kind of woman who had any sympathy for self-pity.

"I care about you just as much as you care about me. Do you want to get married? Have children?" She paused for a second and said with added emphasis, "Be faithful?"

Jim paled and moved to an upholstered chair, where he sat quietly for a moment. When he looked up, she was next to him.

She sat on the arm of his chair and touched his chin, lifting it so they could see each other's eyes. "Is that what you want?"

He shook his head. "No. I don't want to get married again, and I certainly don't want to have more children." He cocked his head and asked, "Is that what you want? You've never mentioned anything like that before."

She dropped her hand. "I want it if I can have it. If I can't, then I want a kick-ass career. I can't have either with you, and there's no use getting sentimental over it."

"Jesus, you sound so…hard."

Kayla got up and returned to the sofa. Looking at him for a long time, her eyes burning with intensity, she finally said, "You'd like it better if I threatened to hang myself, wouldn't you."

Her tone was bitterly cold, and Jim visibly shivered. "Why in the fuck would I want that?"

With a wry, astringent smile, she asked, "Am I the first one who played the game like you do?"

"What game?"

Kayla looked at him like he was slow and thick-headed. "The sex game. The cheating game. The 'I'll use you until I tire of you' game. Don't even try to tell me you don't think of this as a game."

"It's not," he said, indignantly. "I genuinely care about you."

She got up and went to the bar. Not offering to make anything for Jim, she spent a few thoughtful minutes making herself a margarita. When she was finished she sat down on the sofa and took a sip. Conversationally, she said, "I can name four women at the firm with whom you've had affairs. Each one is about four years younger than the last, and rumor has it that you dumped each of them when a younger, more…shall we say… malleable one came along." She took another sip. "Coincidence?"

"Yes!" He got up and stalked over to the windows, his back to Kayla. "I was married. I couldn't afford to have significant, long-term relationships with other women. It was just…fun."

"Fun," she repeated. "Kinda like a…oh, I don't know…a game?"

"You make it sound so conniving. Like I used them."

"You did. And they used you. All of them have done pretty well at the firm. I'd say they've kept up with the men in their peer group, and that's all a woman can hope for."

"But you say you can't return to the firm," he said, turning to look at her again. "If they've done well, why can't you?"

"Because I don't want to be number five on the list. I mean…I *am* number five, but I don't want that to be how I'm referred to at work. If I leave, people will forget me after a while and put your next conquest in the number five spot."

"People really refer to those women that way?"

She laughed, a bitter edge to her normally lilting tone. "Of course they do. Being your ex gives a woman a certain degree of security. No one knows many details, but everyone's a little leery about crossing them.

If you let them stay at the firm, you must still have a little place in your heart for them, and that's reason enough to steer clear."

Walking to the bar, he said, "I never knew. I swear, I didn't know."

"How many people tell you the truth?" she asked, cocking her head. "Does anyone?"

He stopped in the middle of pouring a glass of scotch. After a long moment, he said, "I guess you're the only one." He put down the bottle and walked over to her, then sat next to her on the sofa. "That's why I need you to go back to San Francisco with me. You're more than a fling to me, Kayla. I've really come to rely on you. I trust you."

She reached down and took his hand, then smoothed her thumb across his skin. "I'm glad to hear that. I really am. I trust you, too…about work."

"But not personally?"

"No, not personally. I can't trust a man who cheats on his wife."

"You cheated with me," he said indignantly. "You're as much to blame as I am."

She patted his hand as she would a child's. "That's not true. You were married, I wasn't. And even if you'd never met me, you'd still be a cheater. If I'd never met you, I wouldn't be one."

"So…you've…?"

"Never before," she said, her expression distorted with distaste. "And I'll never do it again. I still don't know why I did it. I guess I was genuinely attracted to you and thought we could be discreet enough to fly under the radar. I was just stupid," she said, without any rancor in her voice.

"Do you regret it?"

Once again she gave him a reassuring pat on the leg. "No, not really. I told you—I'm attracted to you. I think we work well together, and I've learned a lot."

"So, how do you think of me?"

"Mmm…I think of you as my boyfriend. I know it's not permanent, but I'm happy with you. I'd like this to continue until it doesn't work for one or the other of us, then we should let it go."

"Just like that?"

"Yeah. Just like that. I'll miss you, but I'm not in love with you, Jim. I put away that delusion when I found out about your history." She paused a moment, running her lower lip over her teeth. "I think your wife is the only one who ever really loved you."

Annoyed, he asked, "How can you know that? You've met her once."

"True. But she's very attractive, very youthful looking, and very wealthy. Maybe she has her own string of lovers, but it doesn't seem logical that she would have stayed married all of those years if she didn't love you."

"She did," Jim said solemnly. "I betrayed her time and again, and she forgave me each time but this one. I think she saw there was more between you and me than just sex."

"There is," Kayla said. "But she made a mistake in thinking that extra bit was love. It isn't."

"How do you know I don't love you? Would it make a difference?"

"No," she said immediately. "That wouldn't change my mind. Besides," Kayla added, gentling her voice, "if you can't love your wife, a woman you vowed to love, I don't know that you're capable of it. I'm sorry to say that, but if you don't love the mother of your child, you might just not be able to love any woman."

He didn't say a word. Returning to the bar, he finished pouring his drink then went back to sit next to her. He used the remote to switch to the PBS station and settled down to watch Les Troyens, thinking of the night he and Catherine had seen it performed at La Scala. He could feel Kayla's body next to his, but he consciously tried to recall how it had felt to have Catherine pressed against him in the narrow seats, the lovely music washing over them, the light, floral scent of Catherine's perfume that he noticed every time he turned his head to whisper a little something to her.

She's probably been there with her boyfriend by now. He sat up a little, his stomach aching each time he thought of her with that man. *She was mine. Only mine.*

Chapter Twenty-Three

At one o'clock on Saturday, Conor arrived at Catherine's new house. He had to park about fifteen blocks away, and while walking to the house, decided that he'd better borrow Ryan's motorcycle if he was going to be making a regular trek.

He knocked on the door and she answered, looking very, very casual for Catherine Evans. He took in the blue chambray, man-style shirt and the buff-colored Capri pants and waggled his eyebrows. "You look mighty fine today, Catherine."

"I thought I might have to climb up on the roof with the inspector."

He waited for a second, then realized she was teasing him. "You look dressed-up to me, but if this is casual, it really works for you. Is the inspector finished?"

"He left just before you got here. Ready to brainstorm?"

"Sure am." He opened his nylon briefcase and took out a legal pad and a pencil. "Tell me everything you'd like in an office and we'll see if we can get it done."

They spent the better part of three hours discussing which bedroom should be converted, what kind of lighting would work best, how many electrical outlets she'd need, and a dozen other details. At four o'clock she looked at her watch and said, "No wonder I'm tired."

"And hungry," he said, smiling.

"Did you have lunch?"

"Oh, sure. I always have lunch. I usually have a snack at three or four, so I'm right on time."

"You know, I'm hungry, too. Do you have plans for dinner?"

"Nope." He looked contemplative for a moment and said, "You know, I thought we'd go over to Maeve's for dinner all of the time, but Kevin and Rory and I wind up ordering pizza or stopping for burritos most nights. Things have really changed."

"Does it bother you?"

"No, not really. I'm almost twenty-nine. It's time for me to stop relying on my father to make dinner for me." He let out a low laugh. "Time to find a woman to take over for him."

"I have a feeling you're not ready to settle down yet," Catherine said, giving him an appraising glance.

"You never know. You don't have any sisters or cousins or..."

"No, Conor," she said, smiling at him. "I'm the only single woman in my family right now. Jim has a sister, though."

"No offense to Jim, but I think I'd like your side of the family better. That *is* where the fortune is, right?"

She patted him on the back. "That's right. I suppose you'll have to wrest Jamie away from Ryan."

"Like I haven't tried!"

Catherine refused to go out for dinner, insisting that only a natural disaster would compel her to appear in public in such casual clothes. Conor was happy to go to the Mission and pick up Mexican, but Catherine insisted on providing what she called a proper dinner. She called a service that delivered meals from some of the best restaurants in the city, ordering a selection of appetizers and two entrees.

The feast arrived quickly, and they set it out on the dining room table. The seller hadn't left any linens or dishes, so she set the foil containers directly on the wood. "My mother would turn over in her grave if she saw me doing this. Actually, she'd faint to see me dressed this way. This kind of outfit would only be acceptable at a picnic or the beach. Never for dinner."

"We always ate at the table, but there wasn't much of a dress code... except for Sunday dinner."

Catherine started to sit, but she stopped and stood up quickly. "Utensils!"

"Utensils," Conor said, nodding gravely. "Plastic won't work, huh?"

"I bought you a nice steak. I can't imagine a plastic knife will get through it."

"Knife...knife..." He brightened, saying, "Hold tight. I've got just the thing." He walked to his truck, grousing to himself about the dearth of parking in the city. When he finally reached the vehicle, he pulled out a small bag of tools he always carried, then ran back to the house. "Snap-off cutters," he exclaimed, holding them in the air. "We break off a couple of blades, and they're like brand new."

Catherine extended her hand and Conor dropped an orange one into her palm. "I've never seen one of these," she said, investigating it. "How does it work?"

He showed her, then they both sat down and started to eat. Catherine didn't need the knife, since she only picked at a couple of appetizers and ate a good portion of the salad Nicoise. But Conor made good use of his tool, ripping through nearly everything that Catherine didn't consume.

"Your appetite is even healthier than your sister's," Catherine observed, watching Conor eat his steak in a very determined fashion.

He grinned. "Da says we all eat like polite wolves." He gestured with his fork while he swallowed. "But it's his fault. He used to serve the food on a big platter, so the faster you ate—the more you got. He should have divided the portions in the kitchen. Then we wouldn't have gotten into the habit of eating like beasts."

"It's nice to see people who enjoy food. I still have a love/hate relationship with it."

Cocking his head, he gave her a puzzled look. "You hate food?"

She moved a tiny bit of seared tuna around on her paper plate. "In a way." She looked like she was going to avoid answering, but then looked him in the eye and said, "I debate over every bite."

"Huh?" His voice was a decibel louder than it had previously been.

"You heard me," she said, looking both embarrassed and shy. Her brown eyes were mostly downcast, and her chin was tilted away when she snuck a quick look at him. "I have a running argument with myself over every bite of food I eat. I always try to eat as much salad and vegetables as I need to satisfy my hunger, then I let myself have a few bites of something really tasty...like this tuna. It's divine," she said in a near whisper, her voice taking on a sultry tone. "But I'm fairly sure I'll be full enough without it. So I'm arguing with myself about whether I should eat it or not."

"Eat it," Conor said immediately. "When in doubt, give into temptation."

Catherine smiled at him fondly. "You sound so much like your sister."

"She sounds like me." Conor got back to the point. "You don't have to starve yourself. I...don't wanna get into your business...but you're awfully skinny...I mean, thin. You've lost a lot of weight in the last few months, haven't you?"

She nodded and gave him a brittle smile. "I was getting a lot of calories from vodka."

He ignored the import of her statement. "So eat a little more. You can't treat food like it's toxic. It's one of the best things about being human. There's a reason we have so many taste buds, you know."

"I have always—always treated it like it's poison. Being thin wasn't just encouraged in my family, it was required. My mother regarded extra pounds with disgust."

She was quiet for a moment, but Conor sensed that she wanted to continue. He could see her struggle for a moment, then she spoke again. "I was bulimic in high school and college."

"Is that when you..." He drew a line from his stomach to his mouth.

"Yes. I'd sneak into the kitchen and take a fresh box of cookies and eat every one. Then I'd go down to dinner and eat next to nothing, then vomit afterwards. It was the only way I could...I guess...rebel."

"Uhm...how long has your mother been gone?"

"It'll be twenty-three years in June."

Conor softened his voice and reached across the containers of food to gently touch her arm. "Isn't it time to start listening to yourself? Your mom didn't give you very good advice. You don't have to listen to her any more."

"I'll...I'll think about that," she said, shakily. She took a breath and managed a smile. "Catherine Deneuve has said that a woman has to make a decision when she reaches middle age. You have to choose your ass or your face."

Conor's eyes widened. He was sure he'd never heard Catherine use that word before. "Choose them for what?"

She laughed, a genuine one this time. "Which part you want to keep looking good. If you choose your face, you need to add weight to keep it full. You won't have as many wrinkles, but your derriere and hips will be bigger. If you choose your ass, you can stay thin, but you'll look your age. A thin face starts to look haggard." She gave him a rueful smile. "Of course, most women in my peer group stay thin and start having plastic surgery at thirty-five. I'm already overdue."

"You can put off that decision for a good ten years. And I hope you decide to leave that beautiful face alone. I think plastic surgery is a crock." He wasn't able to keep the grin off his face. "Except for breast implants, that is. Those rock."

She reached over and grabbed a lock of his hair and gave it a good tug. "You, Mr. O'Flaherty, are incorrigible."

"I'll take that as a compliment."

"That's exactly how I meant it."

After cleaning up from dinner, they gathered their things and started to walk to Catherine's car. They went slowly up Divisidero, both of them silent until Catherine said, "I've been thinking of asking you for a favor, but I want you to promise that you'll say no if you're uncomfortable with it."

"Okay, I think I can do that."

"First off—do you own a tuxedo?"

Conor chuckled. "The last tux I wore was to my high school prom. I think I weigh about thirty pounds more than I did then, so even if I did own it, I couldn't get it on."

"How would you like me to buy you a nice tux in exchange for putting up with some of the most two-faced, insufferable women in the entire Bay Area?"

"Boy, you sure would make a good salesperson." Conor scratched his head and made a face. "Before I give you my answer I have one question—will you be there?"

"Of course."

"Then it sounds like a blast, whatever it is. You don't have to buy me a tux, though. I can rent one."

"No offense to the rental houses, but those suits look like they're rented. This is a very elegant event, and I can't have my escort looking less than top-notch."

"I can pay for my own suit, you know. I can get one for a few hundred dollars, can't I?"

Catherine put her hand on his arm. "I'm inviting you as my guest. This isn't the kind if thing you'd go to on your own, so I'd really like to buy your suit. Is that all right?"

"Sure," he said, nodding. "A couple hundred won't do it, will it?"

"Sadly, no," she admitted. "Not for the kind of suit that will make you look like you belong with this superficial crowd. Now, the event's in a couple of weeks, so we're cutting it close. Can you make some time this week to go shopping? We'll have to work some magic to get the suit altered in time, but I think we can manage."

Thinking that Catherine could probably charm any tailor in town into working overtime, he said, "Sure. I can be free any day after four. Name the place and the time. Uhm...I can act like myself at this thing, can't I? I mean, you don't want me to impersonate a guy with class, do you?"

She took his arm. "Conor, I couldn't dream up a man who would be one shred more interesting than you are. Of course I want you to be yourself."

"Just checking." He gave her a smile. "Let's make a deal. I'll try to act like myself and not feel like a fish out of water, and you try to not give a crap about how much you eat or what your friends think of you."

Catherine opened the locks and put her things on the passenger seat of her car. "It's a deal," she said at last. "I'll do my best to go to one of these events and actually have a good time."

"It's guaranteed," Conor said, confidence nearly oozing from him.

Charles Evans was working on his sermon for the week when his phone rang. He was in the middle of a thought and was going to let the machine answer, but changed his mind on the fourth ring. "Hello?"

"Senator James Evans is calling for Reverend Charles Evans. Is this Reverend Evans?"

"Yes, it is," Charles said, smiling to himself.

"Will you hold one moment for the senator?"

"Yes, but just a moment. I'm a very busy man." But the secretary had already put him on hold, and he decided she probably wouldn't have gotten his joke anyway.

"Dad?"

"Senator Evans?" he asked, sounding excited. "Is it really you?"

"Okay, okay," Jim said, laughing. "I guess it is a little pompous to have my secretary make my personal calls."

"Just a little, son, but I'm always glad to hear from you, even if I have to get through a layer or two of the bureaucracy. How are you?"

"I'm good. A little bored, but good."

"Bored? My tax dollars are paying your salary. Get busy!"

Jim laughed. "I'm a lame duck. Everyone has turned his attention to the November election. I'm just keeping this chair warm until January when I hope Bob Washington is going to fill it."

"His competition is making things easier for him. The Republican candidates went after each other with hammer and tongs. They really injured each other during the primary. And I don't think the better man won."

"I don't either."

"I think Washington should win fairly easily."

"Yeah, I do, too. He's a good man. I think he'll fit in here."

"I'm sure you didn't call to get political advice. What's on your mind?"

"You have been. I miss seeing you, Dad, and I haven't been able to come home as often as I thought I would. So I thought I might be able to talk you into coming to visit me for a few days."

"I'm sorry you miss me, but I'm a little glad, too. Parents like to be needed."

"I'm serious. I know you can't get away on weekends, but I thought you might be able to come out on a Sunday evening and stay until Wednesday or Thursday. We could visit some sites, have lunch in the Senate dining room...do some touristy things I haven't done."

"You really want me to come?" Charles asked.

"Yes, of course I do. Why else would I ask?"

"I don't know. It just seems odd to think of visiting you. I guess having you live so close by all of your life makes this seem extraordinary."

"I think we'd have fun. But I'll understand if you're not able to come."

"No, I'd like to," Charles said. "I haven't been to Washington for many, many years. Have they finished the Lincoln Memorial yet?"

Laughing, Jim said, "Yeah, they have. There's a bridge over the Potomac, too."

"Well, that I've got to see. When do you want me?"

"Whenever you can make it. I don't have anything I can't get out of for the rest of the month."

"Then we should probably do it soon, so nothing comes up."

"Great. I'll fly you out tomorrow night."

"That soon?"

"Yeah, why not?"

"You have to buy tickets weeks in advance. You can't do things like this at the last minute!"

"Sure you can," Jim said. "Don't give it another thought. I'll make all the arrangements."

"Now, don't go to a lot of trouble. I can sleep on your couch."

"My couch? I was just going to get you a newspaper to keep the light out of your eyes. The lobby's really nice."

"You got your mother's sense of humor," Charles said. "But I'm still happy that you called. I'm looking forward to seeing you."

"Me, too, Dad. See you late tomorrow night."

Chapter Twenty-Four

On Sunday afternoon, Jamie and Catherine sat at the end of a row of spectators that included Maeve, Martin, Jennie, Conor and Rory. The Evans women intentionally tried to sit at the far end of a row during games so they could chat. They both loved showing their support for Ryan, but Jamie was only really interested when Ryan was playing, and Catherine couldn't even summon much enthusiasm at that point. But she loved to be with the family, and she took every opportunity she could to spend time with her daughter.

"Did I tell you about my dilemma in trying to find a date for the Opera Guild dinner?" Catherine asked.

Jamie turned to her with a puzzled glance. "No, I didn't know you were having trouble. Why didn't you tell me?"

"It wasn't a very big issue. As a matter of fact, I was thinking of asking your father to go with me just to make everything appear normal. But that gossipy little item in the newspaper about our divorce ruined that plan."

"Are you going alone? 'Cause I'd love to go with you." Jamie did her best to sound sincere, but she couldn't pull it off. She knew too many of the people in the Guild.

Catherine laughed. "That's sweet of you. But I know you'd rather watch paint dry than go. Besides, you've had enough people staring at you this year. And if you needed another reason not to go, Cassie's mother will be there. I can only imagine how much pleasure she'd get in saying something rude to you."

"Gosh, you sure do make it sound like a fun night. Do *you* have to go?"

"Since I'm the chairperson, it would be a good idea. But don't worry. I've found the perfect escort."

"Who's that?"

"Conor," Catherine said, looking very pleased with herself.

"Conor?"

"What?" the young man asked, leaning forward in his seat.

"Oh. Nothing," Jamie said. "I was just…I forget," she added, turning red.

He gave her a look that questioned her sanity, then sat back to watch the action on the field.

"Conor?" Jamie asked again, quieter this time. "You're taking Conor to the dinner?"

"Yes. Why does that surprise you so?"

"He's…he's Conor. People will think you hired him from an escort service."

Clapping her hands together, Catherine said, "Goodness, I hope so."

"Are you all right? Everyone will be talking about you."

"They will be anyway. I might as well give them something good to talk about. I think we'll have a great time, and that's all that matters to me. I'm not going to stand for re-election, so I won't have to meet with the vipers who most annoy me every month. I'm free!"

"Mom! You've been on the board of the Opera Guild…for…forever."

"Only since you were a child. I suppose that seems like forever, but it's really not. It's time for some new blood to get power."

"You're hardly a relic. Don't give this up if you don't want to."

"I wouldn't," Catherine said, confident about her decision. "I'm tired of seeing the same old faces and hearing the same petty gossip. I'll give more money to take the place of my labor. From now on I'm going to enjoy the opera as a spectator, nothing more. I'm sure I'll love it even more if I don't know about all of the squabbling that goes on behind the scenes."

"Wow," Jamie said. "I thought you'd always be connected to the Guild. This is really a big deal."

"Not for me. I'm trying to divest myself of the things that haven't been adding something positive to my life. I still want to do charity work, but I'm going to find programs that appeal to me on a different level. Maybe I'll work with literacy programs or music education or something more down to earth."

"Okay," Jamie said, a troubled-looking frown on her face.

"This is good news," Catherine said, sensing Jamie's doubts. "I'm getting rid of the things in my life that have been holding me back, making me feel stuck and unproductive."

"If quitting makes you happy, I'm happy. But I think I might have to go to the dinner just to watch Conor flirt."

"Laura Martin and I are the new girls in the Guild. The other women still call us that, by the way. Conor won't find many women from his generation."

"I've seen him flirt with octogenarians," Jamie said. "He flirts with anyone with a double X chromosome."

"Marvelous! That'll make people even more certain he's a paid escort." Catherine giggled, now truly looking forward to an event she'd been dreading. "This is going to be fun."

After the game, Jamie and Jennie stood outside of the players' dressing room. Ryan walked out with Heather, and they all said hello. "Want a ride back to Berkeley, Heather?" Jamie asked.

"Sure. If you have room."

"It's just Jen and me," Jamie said. "My mom brought Conor and Rory, and Martin and Maeve drove up separately."

"Great. I'm always happy not to have to ride on the bus."

Jamie tossed Ryan the keys, and they walked to the parking lot together, where they spent a few minutes speaking to the rest of the family. When they were finally ready to leave, Ryan opened the doors and put her and Heather's bags in the back, then she went to sit in the passenger seat. Surprised, Jamie looked at her. "You don't want to drive?"

"Nah. I'm tired." Jamie stood in front of the passenger door, staring at her, making Ryan finally ask, "What? I can't be tired?"

"Sure you can. But you don't look tired, and you don't act tired."

"I'm stealth-tired. It's under the radar. Let's go, okay? I'm also hungry."

"Well at least that's an indication of normalcy," Jamie said, accepting the keys.

She started the car, and after getting onto the freeway she noticed that no one was talking. Ryan looked fidgety for reasons she couldn't guess and both Jen and Heather were silent as stones. Jamie could hardly start grilling Ryan with their passengers watching them, so she tried to think of a safe topic.

Jennie finally broke the silence. "I got my test back, and I got an 'A'. Thanks for helping me, Heather."

"Hey, that's great, Jen. Ashley just asked me if you'd gotten it back yet. She's always worried about grades—even when they're not hers."

"My offer still stands to help you with French whenever you need it," Jamie said.

"I know. But one of my friends is from France, and we do our homework together. It's kinda like being able to do your homework with a teacher."

"She's not doing it for you, is she?" Jamie asked.

"No…not…really."

"Jennie…"

"She doesn't do it for me. Really. She's just there when I get stuck."

"Just make sure you do the work to get yourself unstuck," Jamie said. "That's how you learn."

"I'm learning a lot. We send notes to each other in French, and I have to figure them out. Sometimes it takes me all day."

"Ryan's taking French," Jamie said, sneaking a look at her lover, who was slumped in her seat, staring blankly out the window.

Giggling, Jennie said, "Yesterday my note said, 'Oh, la vache! Le paquet de devoirs qu'il fiche aux potaches, ce prof…ce n'est pas croyable! Je crois qu'il est sado!'"

Jamie laughed. "You're using some pretty good slang there, Jen. But will any of that be on your tests?" She looked at Ryan. "Did you get any of that, honey?"

"I heard, 'Oh, the cow.' But I doubt you were talking about farming." She said this with such a flat affect that Jamie decided she couldn't wait to get home to figure out what she was kicking herself about this time. So she took the first exit and went to a gas station. "Will you guys use my Speed-pass to fill up the car?"

"I don't know how," Jennie said, even while she eyed the key fob that Jamie handed her.

"You're smart girls. You'll figure it out. Ryan, will you come inside with me?"

"For what?"

Jamie gave her a sweet smile. "Because I asked you to."

Without comment, Ryan opened her door and got out, seemingly expending a lot of energy to accomplish the task. She followed Jamie into the bathroom, and stood there with her hands in her pockets. "What's up?"

"You're not," Jamie said, touching her on the shoulder. "What's bothering you?"

"Nuthin. I've gotta pee."

She walked into the stall, obviously expecting Jamie to leave the room, but she wasn't about to play into her hand. She stayed right where she was, asking again, "Tell me."

There was a prolonged silence, during which Ryan managed to produce about an ounce of urine. She came out and washed her hands while Jamie leaned against a sink and stared at her. "I'm supposed to be giving Jennie music lessons every week. I haven't done it twice since I gave her the damned clarinet."

Shoulders slumping in dismay, Jamie said, "She understands. I bet she doesn't have time anyway. And Rory's still teaching her theory. It's not a bad idea to learn how to read music before you play an instrument."

Ryan dropped her head and mumbled, "I promised."

Jamie knew there was no way to assuage her partner's guilt, so she didn't even try. She slapped her on the shoulder and said, "Then you'll have to make it up to her this summer. You and Rory will have her playing like a champ if you both put your minds to it."

Ryan nodded. "Yeah. I guess that's the answer."

Jamie put her hand around her waist and walked with her to the narrow door. "It'll be all right. No one expects as much from you as you expect from yourself."

With a thin smile, Ryan said, "You're not the first to mention that."

Jim Evans sat in the back seat of a Mercedes sedan with the car idling curbside at Reagan National Airport. There were signs decreeing that only "Official U.S. Government Business" was to be conducted, but it was commonplace for members of Congress and their guests to be picked up and dropped off in the spot.

He saw his father walk out of the terminal, and both he and the chauffeur alighted. Jim waved and caught his father's attention, and Charles got just a few feet before the chauffeur was at his side taking his bag. "Oh, you don't have to—"

The gray-haired man gave him a businesslike smile. "It's my job, sir. Allow me."

Charles released his bag and let the man carry it to the car and tuck it into the trunk. "Dad! It's great to see you!" Jim gave his father an enthusiastic hug, then opened the rear door of the car. "Hop in." He dashed around to the other side and let the chauffeur hold and then close his door. "Good flight?"

"Yes, it was very nice," Charles said. "But you didn't have to put me in business class, son."

"Oh, please. It's nothing. Really."

"I was glad I didn't wear my clerical collar. Don't want people to think I'm raiding the collection plate."

"If every minister were as honest as you are, more people would belong to a church."

Charles patted his son on the leg, "You're not running for office, but I'd vote for you if you were. You don't have to flatter me."

Jim looked at him, holding his gaze for a moment. "I'm not flattering you. I meant that."

Looking slightly embarrassed, Charles nodded. "Thanks. I appreciate that." They pulled out into traffic, the roads congested, as usual. "Nice car you have here."

"Just one of the perks."

"Where are the perks better? Law or politics?"

"Hmm…that's hard to say. They're different, that's for sure. I guess the perks were better for me at the firm, but I'm treated like a demigod in the senate. Each place is nice in its own way, but I prefer law."

"That surprises me," Charles said. "People give up an awful lot to win a senate seat."

"Yeah, they do. But it's never been a dream of mine. Politics is boring, if you ask me."

"Boring? Really?"

Jim laughed softly. "I shouldn't admit to that, but I'm used to getting things done. I could get on the phone with the president of a major corporation and work out a deal—just the two of us. Nothing gets done quickly in the senate. Nothing. It's all about compromise and waiting for the right time. If you were in office for thirty or forty years, you'd probably feel some accomplishment. But I'm just holding this place for Bob Washington. He really wants it."

"So you'll go back to your law firm?"

"Yeah. That's the plan, and I'm ready to get going. There's not much for me here."

Charles Evans poked his silver head out of the bedroom on Monday morning, surprised to see his son showered and dressed, sitting at a table by the window, sections from several newspapers spread out in front of him. "Good morning," the younger man said when he spied his father. "Sleep well?"

"Very well. What are you up to?"

"Just reading a couple of papers."

"I assume you've got to do a lot of work to stay informed."

"Yeah. I read the *Washington Post* and the *New York Times*, then I get a news summary for the world from my staff."

"The world?"

"Well, not the whole world. Just the places where something is happening that might affect our interests." Jim gave his father a wry smile. "I was thinking about the founding fathers the other day, and felt a little envious that it could take over a month to get news from Europe. There's not a minute's time lag now. We're on a twenty-four hour news cycle." He stood up and said, "I made some coffee. Take a look at the room service menu and we'll order breakfast."

"You order breakfast?"

Jim raised an eyebrow. "I'm very busy. My time's worth too much to spend it cooking."

Charles clapped his hands together. "I've got to remember that you're a big boy now. You don't need my advice on how to live."

"I'd be doing a lot better if I'd taken your advice on a lot of subjects," Jim said as he disappeared into the kitchen to fetch some coffee.

After her morning walk, Catherine sat down in her office and gathered some of her monogrammed stationery and a fountain pen. She played with the cap on the pen for a few moments, then checked the ink supply, a little disappointed to find it full. There wasn't one bit of her that wanted to write this letter, but it was time. The polite thing to do would be to speak to him in person, or at least on the phone, but he was very persuasive, and she didn't want to give him the chance to talk her into backing down.

After wasting as much time as she could, she uncapped the pen once more and wrote in Italian,

"My dear, Giacomo.

I hate to do this in a letter, but I've made a decision about us. I'm not able to see you any longer. It's not that I don't care for you, or find you a wonderful companion and lover. But I need more than you're able to give me."

Chapter Twenty-Five

After breakfast, Jim asked, "What would you like to do today?"

"I'd like to see where you work. Would that be all right?"

"Sure. I've love to take you. I'll just put on a suit and tie."

"Oh...we don't need to go."

"No, no, don't worry about it. I just don't like to be on the hill in casual clothes. I like to look like I'm working—even if I'm not."

"Are you sure you don't mind?"

Jim got up and put his hand on his father's shoulder. "I want to take you around town. I wear a suit and tie everywhere. It's my uniform."

Charles smiled at him. "A little different from California, huh?"

"Very. Washington is stuffy, proper and traditional. People on my staff make fun of me because I wear Italian suits and shoes. Most of my colleagues buy American." He smiled. "One of the perks of not running for office. I don't have to wear a single-vent suit and an oxford-cloth shirt like all of the other guys."

"Hey! I wear a single-vent suit and an oxford-cloth shirt."

"Only because you won't wear the shirts Catherine buys for you."

Charles made a face. "They're too nice. I hate to eat a bowl of soup if I'm wearing one of them. And they have to be dry-cleaned. My housekeeper can just run an iron over my oxford-cloth shirts."

"Well, I guess it doesn't matter any more. Catherine won't be buying us Christmas and birthday presents any longer. I'll try to think of something you'll really like, rather than something I think you should like."

A bit awkwardly, Charles gave his son a one-armed hug. "Bringing me here was the nicest present you could have given me."

Jim and Charles exited the hotel and stood in the bright sunshine for just a moment before their car arrived. The doorman helped them in, saying, "Have a good day, Senator."

Seated in the comfortable sedan, Charles asked, "Was it hard to get used to being referred to that way?"

"I still turn around sometimes to see what important person is behind me. I really haven't settled in like I would if I were gonna be here long."

The trip to the hill was relatively short, and they both spent the time admiring the flowering trees that dotted the streets of Washington. "I sure would enjoy having lovely trees like this," Charles said.

"Yeah, there are some definite benefits to living in a cold climate. But I wasn't crazy about the slush and sleet we had. Even though I didn't have to walk in it very much. I'm practically carried everywhere I go."

The driver guided the car through a gate, then showed some credentials to a uniformed officer. The man looked into the window, smiled and said, "Good morning, Senator Evans. Have a good day, sir."

"Thank you. Same to you."

Charles looked ahead, seeing a few black cars lined up. "Private entrance, huh?"

"We'd never get to work if we had to go through the main entrance. This makes things move along." The driver stopped and another police officer opened the door, once again greeting Jim by name.

The two men started to walk up the stairs together, but Charles stopped about halfway up. He smiled at his son, and patted him on the back. "I never thought I'd see the day my boy was a member of the senate."

"I wasn't elected, Dad. I was just picked out of a small crowd."

"Don't be modest. It's quite an accomplishment to be in that crowd, and you know it. And no matter how you got here—you're here—and I'm damned proud of you."

Jim smiled broadly, beaming with pleasure. "I hate to admit it, but I really wanted you to come so I could show off a little. I don't feel like I belong, but it's a fun club to be in—even for a short time."

When they got to the door, Jim could have sidestepped the security process, but he stayed in line and went through the metal detector with his father. They passed through a few doors, then entered the marble-clad halls of the United State Senate. "I haven't been here since…gosh, I think it might have been when I was still in college," Charles said.

"Let's go look around, and then I'll take you to my office."

"Sounds good to me. Show the way, Senator."

They spent a few minutes in the old senate chamber and took a peek at the president's room, which was now used for interviews and photo opportunities. The senate was in session, and as they got closer to the chamber, more and more people bustled past them. "Can we come back during a break?" Charles asked. "I'd love to see where you sit."

They were nearing the door and Jim said, "We're going in now. Follow me." Jim said hello to the guard, who opened the door for them. They didn't walk very far, since Jim's desk was close to the back, on the right side with the other Democrats.

Charles' eyes were wide, and he looked around like he was afraid he'd be thrown out. Jim could tell he was uncomfortable, so he said, "Take a good look at how few people are listening to the guy who's talking."

Looking closely, Charles saw that over a third of the desks were empty. Of the senators who were present, many of them were chatting with colleagues, some were reading, and some appeared to be dozing. "Is it always like this?"

"No, if we're debating something important, nearly everyone shows up. But even then, there are a million things going on." A young man approached and nodded to Jim. He put a pile of papers on the desk and started to turn away. "Jason, got a minute?"

"Uhm…sure." It was clear the man didn't have much time, and equally clear he didn't want to be rude.

"Just a sec," Jim said. "I'd like to introduce you to my father. Dad, this is Jason Farlington. Jason works with me."

The young man stuck his hand out. "Good to meet you, Reverend Evans."

"Nice to meet you," Charles said. "Did you come from California?"

"No, I'm originally from Iowa, but I was with Senator Somers for over six years. Senator Evans was kind enough to keep me on."

Jim laughed. "Jason was kind enough to stay on and keep things running. I'd still be looking for the dining room if it weren't for him."

Jason snuck a look at his watch. "Don't believe him, sir," he said, addressing Charles. "He's a very quick study. It takes most people a full term to really feel comfortable here."

Jim patted the man on the back. "Don't let us keep you, Jason. You look like you've got your hands full."

"Got a meeting with some lobbyists from the California Cotton Growers Association. Don't want to keep them waiting."

"Good to meet you," Charles said quietly, still nervous about talking in a normal tone of voice. As he watched Jason leave he asked, "Is that what your staff does all day? Take meetings?"

"Yep. A lot of the day. Everyone wants their share of the pot of gold."

"There's gotta be a better way."

"I'm sure there is, but I don't think any country has found it yet."

They left the senate chamber just after Jason did. Just outside of the room, Charles pulled Jim to a halt and stood there for a moment. "You had a pretty impressive office at the law firm, but it was nothing compared to this. I'm a little awestruck."

"If you think my desk at the back of the chamber is nice, wait'll you see my office. You'll want a tax refund."

They took a shuttle from the Capitol to the Hart senate office building, where Jim and forty-nine other senators were quartered. The building was modern—much more modern than Charles had imagined. "This hardly looks like a government building. I thought there'd be lots of old marble and statuary."

Jim twitched his head at the huge Alexander Calder sculpture in the center of a soaring atrium. "This building's not even twenty years old. We have nearly the same number of senators that we've had for the past hundred and fifty years, but now we need three buildings to house us."

They took an elevator to the third floor and entered a rather unimpressive door. A fairly typical office layout filled the space. High modular walls created semi-private workspaces for about ten people. They walked past the cubicles and went through another door, and Jim grinned when his father's eyes opened wide. Suddenly, they were in a large, opulent, high-ceilinged room—decorated in navy and a warm buttercream yellow. A woman, sitting behind a magnificent desk, spoke quietly into a nearly invisible headset. She gave Jim a friendly wave, then started to write on a notepad. "Nice digs, huh?" Jim asked.

"Good lord! What was that other room? The place where the people who polish the wood take a rest?"

Jim turned and pointed up. Charles followed his finger and saw that there was a second floor above the office they'd just left. The upper floor had a huge glass window that would allow the people on that floor visual access to the reception area. "My staff is on two floors. All of the senators have sixteen foot ceilings, and the staff quarters are divided in two to save a little space. The upper floor has all of my legislative staff and the lower floor has my schedulers, personal assistants and the press staff. Then I have a bunch of people who work in the mailroom. I get a lot of mail."

"I had no idea," Charles said, stunned.

"I've got over eight thousand square feet. That's a damned big office."

"I'm almost afraid to see where you sit. Or do you lie on a pile of gilt cushions?"

"I'm working on that. But for now, I just have a desk." He opened the heavy, painted door and escorted his father inside. "But it's a nice desk, isn't it?"

"Nice?" Charles put his hands on his hips and did a slow turn, taking in the huge desk, two velvet sofas and wooden table with six chairs. "I'm paying for this."

"And for the fresh flowers," Jim said, indicating two elaborate arrangements. "Those come every other day."

"Your office in San Francisco looked like a phone booth compared to this."

"I know. This is part of what makes people want these jobs. You get used to being important, and everyone here makes you feel very, very important." He gestured to one of the sofas. "Have a seat and I'll get us something to drink."

The words were barely out of his mouth when his secretary knocked and poked her head in. "Tea? Coffee? Soft drinks? Bagels? Danish?"

"Whoa!" Jim said, laughing. "You're going to make my father think I'm always treated this well."

The woman winked and said, "You are."

"Margaret Aimes, this is my father."

"Reverend Evans, it's so good to meet you," Margaret said, shaking Charles' hand. "It's so nice to put a face with a name."

"Same here," Charles said. "It certainly looks like Jim's being very well taken care of."

"We just love him," Margaret said, looking entirely sincere. "He's so much easier to get along with than Senator Somers." She clapped her hand over her mouth and said, "Forgive me for speaking ill of the dead."

"I can't forgive sins," Charles said, "but as sins go, that one barely registers."

"I can see where Senator Evans gets his charm from," Margaret said.

"You must pay her well," Charles said, laughing.

"Not well enough. And I'd love some juice, Margaret," Jim said. "How about you, Dad? Margaret can magically make anything you want appear."

"I don't want to be any trouble. Coffee's fine."

"What do you really want?" Margaret asked. "It's no trouble. Really."

"A decaf cappuccino?" he asked tentatively.

"Back in a minute. What kind of juice, Senator?"

"Surprise me."

Margaret left, and the men sat on opposing sofas. "If I were you, I'd hole up in here and refuse to leave in December," Charles said.

"I'm ready to go." He looked contemplative for a moment, then said, "I'm even more ready than I was a short time ago."

"Why's that?"

"Oh, things are…not going well between Kayla and me."

"Mmm." Charles just nodded. "I was wondering if you were still seeing each other."

"Yeah, we are. But she thinks she'll stay in Washington when my term's up. I thought we might go back to California and live together or at least work together. I really rely on her, Dad. She's…" He looked away, and shrugged his shoulders in an oddly adolescent way.

Margaret knocked on the door and brought in a tray with a tall glass of pineapple juice and a steaming cup of cappuccino. She left before they could finish thanking her and both men chuckled at the words that hadn't been said.

"Tell me more about Kayla," Charles said.

"It's not just Kayla. It's…all of the women in my life."

"There are…others?"

"Oh! No, no, just Kayla. I mean that I'm having a hard time with Kayla and Catherine and Jamie. I used to think I knew how to treat women and what they wanted, but in the last year…I've either gotten stupid or I was deluding myself."

"I don't think you've gotten stupid, son," Charles said, looking at Jim over the rim of his coffee cup.

"Smooth, Dad. Very smooth. So you think I haven't ever known how to deal with women?"

"Oh, you and your mother got along very well. Maybe too well."

"That's a little Freudian. Care to elaborate?"

Charles nodded. "I don't mean to analyze you. But you could do no wrong where your mother was concerned. I'm not sure it was good for you to be able to sweet-talk her into anything you wanted."

Jim took a drink of his juice, his forehead creased in thought. "I don't remember it being like that."

"It was. It certainly wasn't intentional, but I think we set you up to be a very successful man. Your mother treated you like a little prince and I set goals for you that you could never quite reach."

Waving him off, Jim said, "Don't be silly. You were great parents."

"No, we weren't," Charles said, his voice somber. "I was consumed by my career when you were young. Power and prestige meant everything to me. I put those same warped goals on you, son, and you did your best to make me proud of you."

"So you set goals for me. What's wrong with that?"

"I think you believed that I'd love you more if you met those goals." He felt he was about to cry. Looking back on those years was always hard, always painful. "And to be honest, I might have. It's only since I've had my spiritual awakening that I've realized love can't be attained or earned. It just is."

"Come on, Dad. You're being silly. There's nothing wrong with the way you and mom raised me. You have nothing to apologize for."

"You're wrong, Jim. We both made a lot of mistakes. And I think some of our mistakes have contributed to your problems with the women in your life."

Jim got up and went to his window, looking at the expansive view of The Mall. "That's a lot of psycho-babble. I don't believe in coming up with excuses for why I do things. I've made my mistakes and I need to learn from them."

"I can't argue with that, son." He paused for a moment, waiting for Jim to look at him. "But if you've learned from them, why do you keep making them?"

His face flushing, Jim asked, "What does that mean?"

"You heard me. You have a very difficult time allowing the women in your life to have their own lives…their own opinions…their own needs."

"Oh, Jesus," Jim snapped. "Now you sound like Kayla. Or Jamie."

Charles settled back into his seat and looked at his son until Jim reluctantly made eye contact with him. "I'm not a psychic. How would I know that Kayla felt that way?"

Jim grumbled quietly, then walked back to the sofa and sat down heavily. "Damn it, Dad, what am I supposed to do? How do I change?"

"I'm not sure, but I think you have to."

Chapter Twenty-Six

That night, Jim and Charles went to one of the restaurants populated with Washington insiders. Charles was not-so-discreetly looking around, trying to see if he recognized anyone. Jim joined him, his lips pursed. "Mmm…a couple of congressmen and a bunch of lobbyists. All those guys do is go out to lunch and dinner. I don't know how they don't all weight five hundred pounds."

"Then I'm with the most important man in the place," Charles said, with a teasing smile.

"Yeah, you're a lucky guy." The waiter came by and took their drink orders, and when he left there was a stilted silence.

"You've been pretty quiet this afternoon," Charles said. "Is everything all right?"

Jim didn't answer right away. He was obviously debating whether to reply, and he eventually let out a breath and said, "I'm thinking about what you said this afternoon."

"Mmm."

"I have a hard time believing you don't have any suggestions for ways to change."

Charles held up his hands. "I don't know of any shortcuts. And I'm sure you know the difficult ways to change behavior."

"What? Therapy?"

"That works for a lot of people. But it's a waste of time if you're not motivated and ready to be brutally honest."

The server set their drinks in front of them. Jim took a sip of his Manhattan, smiling slightly while he savored the expertly made drink. "I take it you don't think I'm motivated," Jim said while he played with the cherry stem sticking over the lip of his glass.

"I didn't say that." Charles sipped his wine, an enigmatic smile on his face.

"But you do think it."

"No, I don't. I don't have any idea how motivated you are. Only you know that."

"I could get motivated if I thought it worked," Jim said, scowling.

"Therapy does work—for the right person—in the right circumstances. It's worked for me. It's worked for Jamie."

"Yeah, it's made Jamie into an entirely different person," Jim grumbled. "She was a fantastic kid before she got involved with that lesbian class and started seeing that shrink."

"Ryan's not on your list of evil influences?"

Jim smirked at his father. "I honestly don't think Ryan has influenced her as much as that therapy has. Ryan seems like she wants Jamie and me to be close. She really seems to value family."

"She does. But she's been an integral factor in a lot of Jamie's changes."

Looking frustrated, Jim said, "Oh, the changes aren't all bad, and you know it. It's just that Jamie's so short with me. She's ready to jump on me for the slightest thing. I don't think she and I ever had a serious argument before this last year, and now it seems like all we do is fight."

"Maybe you're making up for lost time."

"What?"

"It's not normal for parents and kids to have a perfectly smooth relationship. If you're not having some ups and downs…someone's hiding something."

"She seemed perfectly happy to me before this all started. Perfectly."

"That's not how I saw her."

Jim waited for his father to continue, but he didn't add a word. Impatiently, Jim asked, "Are you going to tell me how you saw her? Or do I have to guess?"

"I'll tell you if you want to know."

"Of course I want to know. I *do* value your opinion, you know."

"You don't ask for it very often," Charles said neutrally.

Eyes narrowing, Jim said, "I'm asking now."

"All right." He pursed his lips and looked at a spot to the left of Jim's head. He thought for a few moments, then said, "Jamie always seemed like a girl who wanted to do the right thing."

"And that's bad?"

"Only when she's not the one who's deciding what's right. Jamie wanted to please you and Catherine—you in particular. She wanted to be the perfect daughter, the perfect granddaughter, the perfect student. But she didn't seem to get much pleasure out of striving for those goals. I'd call her lifeless, in a way. Like she was playing a role rather than making up her own mind about her life." He took a long sip of his drink and set it down with a thump. "I've seen more joy in that girl's face in the last year than I did in the previous twenty-one. And I'm damned glad for it."

"She still loves *you*," Jim grumbled. He was slumped in his seat, looking like he did when he was a teenager.

"She loves you too, Jim. The fact that she's hung in there with some of the pranks you've pulled proves that."

Jim slowly shook his head, looking completely defeated. "I don't know if she loves me or not. Sometimes I think we'll have one of those relationships where we get together just to argue."

"It doesn't have to be that way. I know Jamie doesn't want that."

Raising one dark blond eyebrow, Jim asked, "You know that for a fact?"

"I do. She loves you very much and she wishes you could get past some of the things that have been causing friction. But there's only so much she can do."

"So...the ball's in my court, huh?"

"Jamie hasn't said that. But I would."

On Tuesday morning, Ryan anxiously awaited her turn to talk at her group therapy session. As soon as Ellen looked at her, she said, "I can't drive anymore."

As always, Ellen waited a few seconds before she broke the silence. "How long has it been since you could get behind the wheel?"

"Oh." Ryan nodded to herself. "I can drive if I'm alone. I just can't do it if anyone's in the car with me. I think Jamie's gonna figure it out pretty soon, 'cause I used to drive every time we rode together."

"And you don't want to tell her?" Ellen asked. "She might be able to help you."

"How could she help me?"

Turning her gaze to the group, Ellen asked, "Does anyone have any ideas?"

Helen raised her hand. "I wasn't able to go to my husband's office to pick up his things after he died. They kept calling me, reminding me, and every time I felt so humiliated that I couldn't face it." She looked at Ryan. "I stopped answering the phone, just so I didn't have to explain why I couldn't come."

"What did you do?" Ryan asked, intensely interested.

"A friend was visiting one day when the office called, and she could tell something was wrong. She offered to go for me," she said, smiling fondly. "Just hearing how easy it seemed for her to go gave me some courage. I called the secretary back, and my friend and I went that very afternoon." She paused for a second, then wiped her eyes with the back of her hand. "There were some wonderful things in that box. I'm glad I got them."

Ryan smiled at her empathetically. "I'm glad you did, too."

"Do you think that Jamie might be able to go on some short rides around town with you? Just for a little experiment?"

"She would," Ryan said. "But I'm not ready. It's…too much. Too much."

"What is?"

Trying to keep the annoyance from her voice, Ryan said, "She already has to change her schedule around to go on my road trips. I don't want to ask her to do anything else. It's enough."

"But you need more," Ellen gently suggested.

"I don't want her to worry about me. I'm fine when I'm alone. I don't feel much different when I'm walking around town or driving. But when I'm with her or her mom, or especially my little cousin, I can't relax if we're outside. Everybody looks like a killer. If I'm a passenger, I can keep an eye on more things. Nobody's gonna sneak up on us again," she said, the strength of her belief burning in her chest.

Dinner was waiting when Ryan got home from practice on Thursday night. Her nose twitched, trying to guess what they were having as she went into the kitchen.

Jamie turned just as Ryan was about to touch her, and the smaller woman jumped. "You were sneaking up on me again!"

Ryan put her arms around Jamie and hugged her tight. "I was not. I'm just quiet."

"I think you learned how to be quiet so you can sneak up on people."

Jamie let her head drop back and looked up at Ryan. "Why haven't I been kissed?"

Rather than answer, Ryan's head bent and she kissed the soft lips that always made her feel like she was home. "Missed you."

Jamie hugged her, holding on tightly. When she moved away, she asked, "Did you really? You're usually too busy to miss me."

Ryan sat on a stool and rested her head on her hand. "Yeah, I did. I just found out that someone I really admire died, and I was bummed. You always make me feel better when I'm upset."

Jamie was holding her before Ryan finished her sentence. "Honey! Who died?"

Resting her head on her breast, Ryan said, "W.D. Hamilton."

"Should I know him?"

Nodding, Ryan said, "You should, but I'm sure you don't. He'll probably be a household name in a hundred years if his theories hold up." She looked at Jamie and saw total befuddlement. "I'm sorry." She pulled back. "He was a biologist. One of the most original thinkers…ever."

Squeezing her partner's shoulder, Jamie walked back to the stove to finish the meal. "Tell me about him."

"The sucky thing is that he was perfectly healthy," Ryan said. "Only about sixty-five. But he contracted malaria and died while he was in the Congo. He was investigating the theory that AIDS came from infected polio vaccines given in central Africa in the 1950's."

"Wow. Is that really possible?"

"Sure. I've got the book that explains the theory, but I haven't had time to read it."

Jamie shook her head. "There's so much we don't know. You try to wipe out one disease, and you wind up killing millions more."

Ryan gave her a thoughtful look. "That's one of the reasons I worry about being a scientist."

"What?"

"We know so little. Sometimes I feel like we're stumbling around in almost complete darkness. I mean, Hamilton was a big deal…a very big deal. But what was he able to do…to really *do* during his life?"

She folded her arms and lay her head on them, a pose Jamie found impossibly endearing.

"One of the great thinkers of our time, and even though his contributions to biology are huge, I don't think one life has been saved because of his work." She frowned and mumbled something to herself. "Sometimes I think I'd better stick with math."

"You don't have to decide tonight, baby. You just have to decide what kind of dressing you want on your salad."

Ryan got up and walked over to her partner. "Your choice. The chef knows best. All I know is that I'm hungry."

"That's my girl." She gave her another hug. "You'll feel better after you eat. You always do."

"Then why do I ever feel bad? I'm always eating."

The next afternoon, Ryan had an hour free before practice, so she found a sunny spot on the lawn near the softball field and pulled out her cell phone. Hitting the speed dial, she waited a minute, then said, "Hey. It's me."

"I thought you'd lost my number," Ally Webster said. "Where the hell have you been?"

"Running my ass off. I know this is hard to believe, but this is the first unscheduled hour I've had in weeks."

"Where are you? I hear birds chirping."

"I'm lying on the grass near the softball field. I have practice soon."

"Good job on your winning streak," Ally said. "Sara keeps me up to date. She gets an e-mail about your and Jamie's teams."

"You should come see us play. Although we probably play when you're working."

"My weekends are pretty booked. Makes it hard to spend as much time with Sara as I'd like."

"How's it going?" Ryan asked. "Still hot and heavy?"

Ally laughed. "None of your business, hot stuff. You know I don't kiss and tell."

"I wasn't asking about the sex," Ryan said, chuckling. "Sheesh! You do have a relationship outside of the bedroom, don't you?"

"Yeah," Ally drawled. "What do you want to know about it?"

"I wanna know how you both are," Ryan said, frustrated with her friend's reticence. "What's going on? Are you mad at me?"

"How can I be mad at you? I haven't seen you. Or talked to you. Or gotten a post card."

"Okay, okay. You've got me dead to rights. But I did send you an e-mail."

"After I called you. That's what I do when I don't wanna talk to someone."

Ryan was quiet for a moment, debating how frank to be. "I really don't want you to take it personally. I haven't had time for any of my friends. Hell, I haven't had time for Jamie. I'm…in over my head."

"Aw, sugar, tell me what's going on."

"Nothing bad. I'm just really over-scheduled. I'm not seeing my family enough, I haven't taken my poor dog for a walk in a month, Caitlin could've learned to read for all I know."

Ally laughed. "I kinda doubt you're that disconnected, but I get your message. And I won't take it personally."

"I feel disconnected," Ryan said, feeling a little uncomfortable when the words left her mouth.

"Tell me about it. I'm your friend."

"I know you are. But I can't explain it. Things aren't clicking for me right now. I'm just trying to hold on until we graduate. Then I can reconnect with Jamie. It seems like all we do together is eat and sleep."

"How's Jamie doing? We saw her piece in the paper. That must have been fun."

"Yeah. A real blast," Ryan said, chuckling mirthlessly. "She's good, though. Too busy, but good."

"We're gonna have to get together. When will you have more time?"

"After graduation. We're taking time off after that. I plan on sleeping through June."

"I know you, Rock. That'll last about one day, then you'll be itching to get going again. Face it, you're hyperactive."

"I guess I can't argue with that. You'd know better than most."

"Yeah, I guess I would. We had some great times together, baby, but it's nice to be in a relationship, isn't it?"

"Sure is," Ryan said. "I was about to blow a gasket."

Ally laughed. "I'm glad you're happily hooked up. But don't forget your old buddies, okay? We both love you."

"I love you guys, too," Ryan said, the words feeling strange rolling off her tongue. "We'll get together as soon as we can, okay?"

"Deal. Give my best to Jamie."

"I will. Same for Sara. Bye."

Ryan hung up and rolled onto her back again. There was something very strange about talking with Ally on the phone. She knew she could get used to it over time, but she wasn't sure they'd ever be able to be platonic friends. Feeling glum, she pulled out her laptop and started writing a long e-mail to her cousin Aisling, always feeling better when she vented her feelings to the person she could trust with every secret.

Chapter Twenty-Seven

On Sunday afternoon, most of the members of the O'Flaherty family attended Ryan's game at Stanford. The few who couldn't make it, mostly due to excessive carousing the previous night, managed to show up later in the afternoon for the barbecue-pool party at Catherine's house.

Nearly fifty people crowded around the pool, with most of Ryan's teammates playing with Caitlin, who was, as usual, the belle of the ball. The late afternoon sun was warm, the party noisy and getting noisier.

Marta and Helena had been working hard, and once all of the food was set up on the outdoor tables Catherine insisted that both women take a long break.

"I don't need a break," Marta said, indignantly. "I do nothing all week. I enjoy having these parties."

"I know you do," Catherine said. "But there's going to be a big cleanup job later on. I happen to know you've been on your feet since seven o'clock this morning. Even you get tired, my friend."

"I'm not tired," Marta insisted. She was standing with her hands on her hips, looking like a child refusing her afternoon nap.

Unexpectedly, Catherine hugged her, holding on until the older woman relaxed and returned the gesture. Catherine let her go, but not before placing an affectionate kiss on her cheek. "You don't have to rest. You can go join the party."

Marta narrowed her eyes, knowing she'd lost the battle. "I'll go read my book," she said, giving Catherine a faux scowl as she turned and left the room.

Marta and Helene were both ensconced in their rooms and Catherine was just about to leave the kitchen when the doorbell rang. She was puzzled, since all of the family members knew to walk around the side of the house to join a party in progress. It must have been one of Ryan's teammates. As she opened the door, she was struck mute to find not a fresh-faced young woman, but a suave, handsome, charming, sexy man smiling at her. A man she had hoped she'd never have to see again.

"Buona sera." He moved her limp hand to his soft, full lips to kiss it tenderly.

"Giacomo," she whispered, feeling she might faint.

"May I come in?"

The manners that had been drummed into her compelled her to step aside and let him enter. As he passed, his scent tickled her nose, and her body reacted as it always had when she was near him. Tingling, she followed him into the living room, where he was pointing at a sofa.

"May I?"

She nodded, still unable to manage even a fragment of a sentence. She sat in an upholstered chair, not daring to get close enough to smell him or feel his always-warm body.

"You are so far away," he said, giving her the little pout that always melted her heart.

She artfully danced away from his comment. "You got my letter."

"Of course I did. Why else would I arrive, unannounced? I knew you'd refuse my visit, but I had to see you."

Catherine gestured towards the rear of the house, where music and loud voices pulsed. "This is a very bad time. I'm having a party."

"I can hear that." A seductive smile started at the corner of his mouth. "There must be a lot of people here."

"There are."

"Good. They won't miss you. Let's go…" He looked around, probably trying to get a sense of the layout. "Upstairs. We'll have privacy there, no?"

"No!"

He blinked in surprise, but rose and crossed the room before she could say another word. Dropping to his knees, his hand slipped into her hair and cradled the back of her head.

Involuntarily, she leaned into his touch, the instinct so sweetly familiar that she was unable to stop herself.

"I've come so far." His warm, sensual voice sent shivers down her spine. "Don't send me away." He pulled her a little closer, and she didn't fight him. Soon they were a fraction of an inch apart. Catherine's eyes were half-closed and her lips parted just enough to invite his advance. Gently, he broached the distance and touched her lips with his.

She didn't want to give in. It was sheer madness, but he was so warm and tender and smelled so tremendously wonderful that she couldn't resist. Just like the first time they'd kissed, her stomach somersaulted and her head felt like it was filled with helium when their lips met. Her hand came to rest on his muscular shoulder, and she let it move across the silky feel of his suit jacket.

When Giacomo took in a deep breath, Catherine felt as if he were breathing her into his body. She reacted without a concern, sliding her arm around his back and drawing him close. Her mouth opened, and his warm tongue darted inside, making her whole body prickle with sensation.

Suddenly, her orientation changed and she felt him effortlessly pick her up. In a blink, she was on his lap, and he was kissing her with such passion that she forgot where they were or why he was in her living room. All she was able to do was move with him, feel his heart beat, follow his warm tongue, and purr when his hands moved over her body.

The zeal with which they kissed was nothing new. From the first, they'd instinctively sparked in just that way. A quick kiss usually led to many more—often to making love, just when they were getting ready to part after an entire afternoon of pleasuring each other.

It was the first time in her life she'd had such carnal hunger for a man. Their connection produced such a heady rush that, once they'd started to kiss, neither had any control. Having gone so many months without intimate contact, her hunger for his touch was omnivorous.

After a particularly incendiary kiss, Giacomo tightened his hold around her body and stood. He was momentarily indecisive, but then headed for the staircase. He was halfway up, with Catherine placing soft kisses along his jaw-line when he stopped abruptly. Gently, he placed Catherine onto her weak legs, tucked an arm around her and turned her.

Catherine turned as pale as a sun-bleached bone, and she grabbed Giacomo's arm for support. "Maeve!"

"Are you…is everything…?" Maeve was obviously not only stunned but uncomfortable. She was turning in the direction from which she had come, looking like she'd rather be anywhere else in the world.

"I'm fine. Just fine." Years of practice lying about her emotional state got Catherine through the sentence.

"I'll just go back outside. I came in to see if you needed...help," she added, looking mortally embarrassed.

Catherine took Giacomo's hand and tugged him down the stairs with her. He was straightening his tie and smoothing the wrinkles out of his suit when they reached the landing. "Maeve O'Flaherty, this is my dear friend, Giacomo Fontini."

Giacomo gave the woman a short bow and took her hand, giving it a quick kiss. "It is my pleasure to meet you. Are you related to Ryan?"

Catherine smiled at him, charmed that he'd remembered her daughter-in-law's name.

"Yes. I'm her au...step-mother."

"Ahh...you're the lovely woman who recently married Ryan's father. His taste is exquisite."

Catherine mused that his charm was so remarkably attractive because it never sounded forced or false. How that was possible was beyond her ken, but he always sounded like he was telling the full, unadulterated truth.

Maeve's face lit up and she blushed, yet another victim of the Fontini allure. "Catherine has told me about you, Mr. Fontini. Are you visiting from Italy?"

"Yes, I am." His white teeth glowed against his tanned skin. "And please call me Giacomo. Catherine is probably cross with me, since I didn't tell her I was coming, but she's too polite to admit it."

Catherine squeezed his arm, unable to stop giving him a goofy looking grin. "I'm not angry. I'm always happy to see you."

Turning to Maeve, she added, "I think we were a little too happy to see each other. I hope we didn't offend you."

"No, not at all!" Her voice was higher and louder than it needed to be. "I just hadn't seen you in a while and I...I told you this already, didn't I?"

"Let's go outside," Catherine said, relieving her friend from prattling on. "I'm sure Giacomo would like to meet everyone." *Ooo...this is going to be fun.*

The threesome walked outside, with very few of the guests taking notice. Maeve waved to Martin, who walked over to the group. "Martin, this is Catherine's friend, Giacomo Fontini."

"How are you?" Martin asked, shaking the man's hand.

"I am well. You are Ryan's father?"

"I am." Martin looked puzzled. "Do you know my girl?"

"I've spoken to Giacomo about the girls," Catherine said, wondering how she was going to get through the rest of the evening.

"I'd like to meet her, and Jamie, of course," Giacomo said.

"They're right over there," Catherine said. "See you soon," she added as they started to walk away.

"Who was that?" Martin asked his wife, a scowl forming. "What kind of friend knows about Ryan but has never met Jamie?"

Maeve knew more than she wanted to share, so she tried to give him an evasive answer. "He's a man she knows from Milan. She usually goes to Italy alone, so Jamie must not have met him."

"What's he doing here?" Martin asked, still giving the well-dressed man the once-over. "Is he in town on business?"

"I don't know, sweetheart. I didn't interrogate the poor man. Why are you so interested?"

He turned his back on the interloper. "I'm not," he said stiffly. "He just seems out of place." He took a sip of his drink, and Maeve could hear him mutter, "What kind of fellow wears a suit and tie to a pool party?"

Jamie was sitting on the edge of the pool, trying to eat a quick dinner so she could take her turn watching the baby in the pool. She turned when she heard footsteps behind her on the tile. Her smile froze when she saw Giacomo, recognizing him from a photo her mother had shown her. When she put her plate down, her hands shook. Giving her mother a quick look and seeing that she appeared calm, she turned her attention to the remarkably handsome man. Deciding to speak in Italian, she said, "Hello, I'm Jamie. You must be my mother's friend. It's good to meet you, Mr. Fontini."

He answered in English. "I'm very happy to meet you, Jamie. And please call me Giacomo." He gave her a charming smile. "I don't know where you learned Italian, but you have a beautiful accent."

"I was very young. I honestly don't remember learning it."

"That is the best time," he said, gazing at her so intently that she felt her personal space being invaded.

As was often the case, Ryan sensed her partner's discomfort and was standing at her side before Jamie knew she'd moved.

"Hi," she said to Giacomo, her smile warm and friendly.

"You must be Ryan," he said, shaking her hand.

"I must be," she agreed. "And you're…?"

"This is my friend from Milan, Giacomo Fontini," Catherine said.

Ryan looked more than a little surprised, and she made no attempt to cover. "Surprise visit?"

"Yes." He gave Catherine the intent look he'd just used on Jamie. "I hope it's a good surprise."

Catherine was still holding his arm, and she squeezed it close to her body. "It's always good to see you, Giacomo."

The man bowed slightly to Jamie and Ryan. "It was a pleasure to meet both of you. Your mother speaks of you so often that I feel I know you, Jamie."

She gave him a tense smile. "I feel the same. It's good to finally meet you."

His smile grew even more luminous. "I hope this will be the first of many, many meetings."

As the couple walked away, Jamie turned towards her partner. "I don't know what he's doing here, but he wasn't invited."

Ryan started to speak, but before she could get out a word, Conor was at her side.

"Who's the suit?"

"Friend of Catherine's."

"Foreign?"

"Italian."

"That explains it."

"Explains what?"

"Only an Italian would come to a barbecue in a thousand dollar suit and Bruno Magli shoes."

"How do you know what kind of shoes he's wearing?" Jamie asked.

Rolling her eyes, Ryan said, "Don't get him started. He knows more about shoes than Imelda Marcos. He's got a foot fetish."

Jamie squeezed her partner's hand. "Look who's talking."

Before the blush could hit her cheeks, Ryan dove into the pool, popping back up a good twenty feet away.

"She'll never change," Conor said, looking at his sister. "She's harder to corner than a scared cat." His gaze traveled to Catherine. "Is your mom okay? There's something about that guy that doesn't sit right with me."

"Yeah, I think she's fine. She wasn't expecting a visit, so that might be what you're picking up on."

"A guy drops in from Italy?" Conor looked more than a little suspicious. "What kinda friend is he?"

"I'm not sure," she said, lying. "I don't know him. He's an art dealer from Milan. Maybe he's here on business."

"He looks like he could play the lead in a movie about a jewel thief," Conor said, studying Giacomo. "There's something too smooth about him. Course, maybe it's the shoes. I'd kill for those babies."

"Just when I think I'm partnered with the quirkiest of the bunch, you surprise me." Jamie put her arm around Conor's waist and escorted him back to the buffet, knowing he'd always help empty the table.

Since all of the O'Flaherty men had to get up early on Monday, the family started to disperse at nine. The softball players stuck around for as long as they could, but when no one was left besides Jamie and Ryan, even the players changed clothes and took off.

Marta and Helena were just starting to clean up when Jamie and Ryan sat down near Giacomo and Catherine. "Wonderful party, as usual," Ryan said. "Thanks so much, Catherine."

"It's always a special day for me when your family can visit. I'm just glad the evening was warm enough for the girls to be able to swim."

"Me, too. Because Caitlin would have gone in anyway."

"The baby is terribly beautiful," Giacomo said. "It would be a blessing for her to grow up and look like her older cousin."

Ryan gave him a thin smile. She was always cautious about people who complimented her on her looks, and Giacomo made her uncomfortable even without doing so. "Caitlin used to look just like Jamie. That's when she was a real knockout." She gave her partner a smile, and Jamie took her hand and squeezed it.

"When do you have to leave?" Catherine asked.

Jamie looked at her watch. "My flight's at ten thirty, so I guess we should get going."

Catherine stood. "Let's go inside and make sure you have everything. I'd hate for you to forget something important."

Jamie face their guest and gave him a fairly genuine-looking smile. "It was good to meet you, Giacomo."

Ryan stood as well, "Same goes for me."

He said goodbye, kissed each of them on both cheeks, then sat back down, allowing them time alone with Catherine.

Once they were inside, Jamie put a hand on Catherine's shoulder, giving her a sober look. "Was this a surprise?"

Catherine laughed nervously. "A big one."

"If you want him to go...he's gone," Ryan said, her eyes focused and determined.

Laughing, Catherine touched her arm. "No, no, I just wasn't expecting him. I...I wrote to him and told him I didn't want to see him the next time I went to Milan. Obviously, he..."

"He's got good taste," Ryan finished for her.

Catherine kissed her on the cheek. "You're always good for my ego."

"No bull, Catherine. He'd be crazy to let you get away so easily."

Jamie was clearly not going to give up easily. "But if you don't want to see him, maybe you should ask him to leave while we're still here. You shouldn't let him talk you into anything you don't want to do."

"He's not going to overpower me, honey." Catherine fanned her flushed face. "My God, this is an uncomfortable situation."

"Do you want me to stick around?" Ryan asked. "Jamie can leave her car at the airport and you can give me a ride home tomorrow."

Catherine put both hands on Ryan's biceps and shook her a little. "It's all right. Now you two get going. And don't worry about me."

"But we do worry about you, Mom. Are you sure you're okay?"

"Yes." Catherine took her daughter and turned her towards the front of the house. "Now get going or you'll miss your flight and have to drive to El Cajon."

Chapter Twenty-Eight

Catherine walked back out to the yard and watched Giacomo as he sat on a lounge chair by the pool. How he managed to make sitting still look so graceful was beyond her. He was the type of man who was so self-assured that he looked at home nearly everywhere. Oddly, he seemed particularly comfortable sitting by the glimmering pool in his expensive suit and polished shoes. He'd made himself a drink, and had just taken a sip when Catherine drew near.

Immediately, he stood, and took her hand to ease her into the chair next to his. He picked up a second glass and offered it to her. "Campari?"

She hadn't had a drink all day, or the day before, but this one looked too inviting to resist. Accepting the tall glass, she took a sip, smiling when the sweet/bitter taste of the liquor mixed with sparkling water tickled the roof of her mouth. "Thank you."

He sat down, then reached over and took her hand. Giacomo didn't say another word; he simply held her hand while they gazed at the patterns the light made on the water. It was a little breezy, but warm, and the water danced and swayed gently with the wind.

Catherine wasn't sure how much time had passed when his low, soft voice broke the stillness. "Are you angry with me?"

Giving his hand a squeeze, she said, "No, of course not. It was rude of me to write to you the way I did, but I was…" She trailed off, not sure if she should say the truth.

"What were you, my treasure?"

She smiled at him, unable to resist the sweet gentleness of his voice. "I was afraid."

His eyes grew wide. "Of me?"

"No, of course not. I could never be afraid of you." Her thumb lightly traced along the back of his hand. "I was afraid to tell you in person, and I didn't want to tell you on the phone. A letter was the best idea I could come up with."

He brought her hand to his lips and kissed it. Holding it there for a moment or two, he warmed it with his breath. When he spoke, the vapor caressed Catherine's skin. "Why were you afraid to talk to me?"

For another moment, she debated whether to be frank. Finally, she said, "I thought you'd convince me I was making a poor decision."

"You are," he whispered. He moved her hand to his cheek and let her fingers rest there while he reverently kissed her wrist. "A very poor decision. For both of us."

Her heart was hammering in her chest, but she couldn't force herself to take her hand back. His cheek felt so nice. Rough, where his beard grew and soft as a whisper above. "What can I do?" she asked, even though she knew the question was rhetorical.

He slowly peppered her palm with kisses. "Is there someone else?"

"No. No one."

"Have you lost your desire for me?" He slipped her hand into his jacket and she felt his heart beating quickly. "You can feel how you make my poor heart race."

Her mouth was dry, but she managed to say, "No. I still…I…" She sighed, and took her hand away, resting it in her lap. "It's nothing you did. I just need…more."

"I'll give you more. Whatever you want."

Reaching out to caress his knee, she said, "You can't give me what I want. I want a man who's devoted to me. Only me."

His head dropped in defeat and a few locks of his black hair escaped careful grooming to fall across his forehead. Slowly he shook his head. "You are correct. I cannot give you that." He lifted his head and gazed at her for a long time. "Is there a man who wants to give this to you?"

"No," she admitted. "But I'm afraid I won't look for him if I have you."

Slowly, his head tilted and the barest of smiles touched his lips. "Because I make you happy?"

Catherine nodded, realizing that her excuse wasn't a very good one when it was held up to the light.

Suddenly, he was sitting on the end of her chaise, holding her legs on his lap. "You make me happy, too. Very, very happy." He spent a few minutes rubbing her legs, straightening the creases in her slacks, adjusting the fabric just so. "Is it wrong to be happy?" he asked, not looking her way while he worked.

Putting her hand atop his, she said, "Of course not. But I want someone who lives here, who I can see often—if not live with. Seeing you once or twice a year isn't enough."

"Then come to Milano more often." He gave her a look that made that seem like the obvious answer.

Catherine blinked, trying to stop herself from being so easily seduced. "I don't want to have to travel to be with a man. I want him here, and I want him to be devoted to me."

"We all have desires. Sometimes we only realize parts of those needs. Is a part worth nothing?"

She reached out and clasped both of his hands. "No, of course not. But I'm not ready to give up my desire. And staying involved with you seems like I'm...settling." She cringed, hating how harsh that sounded.

But Giacomo either didn't understand, or he was intentionally pleading ignorance. He shrugged his shoulders and looked puzzled. "Settling? What does this have to do with us?"

"I'm accepting less than I need."

"Yes, yes, I understand that. But don't we do that in every area of our lives? I want to live in Torino. I love the mountains, and skiing excites me more than anything else on earth. But I live in Milano. That's where my wife feels at home. That's where my children have their friends and their grandparents. It's a compromise, no?"

"Yes," she agreed.

"Does that mean my days in Milano are horrible? Do I wish for a quick death? No. Of course not." He slapped himself on the chest with both of his hands. "I make Milano mine!"

He said it with such fire and conviction that she felt herself inexorably draw closer to him. As soon as he put his hands on her shoulders to pull her close, she pulled away, shivering. "No, I can't, Giacomo. I can't continue to see a married man. I'm doing to your wife exactly what my husband did to me."

He smiled indulgently and stroked her face. "Catherine, you know my country well, but you have an American mind."

"I know you and your wife have an agreement, but you've told me that it's an unspoken one. My husband probably thought we had an agreement, too."

"No. No. No." He enunciated each word crisply. "We have an…" He squinted, searching his mind for the correct word. "Explicit agreement. She's willing to speak to you on the phone to assure you that she doesn't mind our seeing each other."

"You…you…asked her…about me?"

"Yes." He looked very proud of himself. "For you alone."

"But Giacomo…why?"

"Because I knew one of your reasons for not seeing me again was because of my marriage. I've made sure that isn't a problem."

"You want me to speak with your wife?" Catherine could hardly believe she was saying the words.

"If you want to." He touched Catherine's chin, lifting it so they looked into each other's eyes. "She's not happy with me. Having our private lives private was better for both of us. But I couldn't let you go." Desire flashed in his expressive eyes. "You mean too much to me."

Her mouth went dry, stunned by his passion. "What do I mean to you?"

"I care for you," he said, his voice growing husky. "You're the perfect woman for me. But I'm married, and I have my children. I can't…I won't hurt my family. But if I could do it over again, you would be the woman I'd choose. If I could touch only one woman…for the rest of my life… you would be that woman."

"Giacomo," she said, her eyes filling with tears. "I had no idea that you felt like that."

He put his hands on her waist but didn't pull her closer. Gazing into her eyes, he whispered, "Can't you feel it when I love you?"

She let out an enormous breath and nodded her head, tears starting to fall. "Yes. I *have* felt it, but I thought…I thought only I felt that way."

"No, no, my love, you are not alone. I cannot give you my body, but when we're together—you have my soul."

Catherine extended her arms and rested her hands on Giacomo's shoulders. They regarded each other for a few moments, speaking only with their eyes. Finally, her eyes fluttered closed and he closed the distance that separated them. Lips and then bodies met and merged in a tender communion. They showered each other with affection until Catherine took her lover by the hand and led him to the pool house. "We'll have privacy here." She locked the door behind them.

"Have you made love here?" he asked as he looked around.

"No, never."

"Good. I don't want to be in a place where you've been with another. This will be our special place."

She wrapped her arms around him and kissed him. "I remember the first time we met. I wanted you from the start."

He looked thoughtful for a moment, then cleared his throat and started to recite a poem that he obviously had once known well. "Benedetto sia 'l giorno, et 'l mese, et l'anno, et la stagione, e 'l tempo, et l'ora, e 'l punto, e 'l bel paese, e 'l loco ov'io fui giunto da'duo begli occhi che legato m'anno…" *Oh, blessed be the day, the month, the year, the season and the time, the hour, the instant, the gracious countryside, the place where I was struck by those two lovely eyes that bound me…* He paused, then shook his head. "There is more, but I cannot remember."

"I don't need another word," she whispered. "I just need you… tonight."

"You're awfully quiet," Ryan observed. Jamie was driving, devoting one hundred percent of her attention to the road, about twenty-five percent more than usual.

"Just…thinking."

"About your mom."

Jamie turned quickly and Ryan saw the tiny smile on her lips. "Yeah."

"What's on your mind? Are you worried about her? 'Cause she seemed like she was in control."

"Mmm…no, I'm not exactly worried. I'm…oh, I don't know what I am. I guess I just hate that he exists." She shivered roughly enough for Ryan to see her body shake in the dim light.

"That's pretty extreme." She put her hand on Jamie's thigh and stroked it gently. "What's up with that?"

There was irritation in Jamie's gaze when she looked at Ryan again. "How would you like to meet the man your mother had an affair with?"

"Damn," Ryan said, feeling ill. "Do you have to put it that way?"

Clearly angry, she spoke quickly. "Yes, I do. I know she's single-ish now, but she wasn't when this started. I'm not happy about that."

"Have you ever told her that?"

"Are you nuts?" Jamie didn't say a word for a long time, and Ryan judiciously kept her mouth shut. Finally, Jamie broke the silence, speaking in a quiet, thoughtful tone. "We had a distant relationship for twenty-one years. She trusts me now, Ryan. She tells me things and I tell her things I never dreamed we'd be able to share. I don't wanna screw that up by busting her for telling me something she's ashamed of."

Ryan thought about that for a minute. "I can see that. But you ought to talk about it if it's bugging you. You don't have to call her out. You can just say that…I don't know…something like…" She made a face. "I see your point."

"I wanna be close. And I want her to feel like she can tell me anything."

"Jamers," Ryan soothed, "maybe that's not such a good idea. She's your mom, not your pal. It's nice that you've gotten so close, but you still have to be able to treat her like your mom. And no one wants to hear her mom talk about her lover. It's way high on the ick scale."

Jamie smiled briefly. "I know. But I'm not sure how to handle this."

"Well, she'll get rid of him and you won't have to worry about it. You can talk to her when you're not feeling upset about it."

Jamie nodded, not adding the thought that was poking at her. *If I was sure she was going to get rid of him, I wouldn't be so upset.*

On Monday after practice, Ryan walked home, going out of her way to stop by Top Dog. Walking home with the scent of a hot link and a calabrese sausage wafting up to tickle her nose, she planned her evening. *Gotta spend at least an hour doing my progress report on my independent study…then I could work on that funky little problem I've been having with that polynomial…or I could read the latest JAMS…but that's fun to read when Jamie's home.* She smiled. *It always cracks me up to tell her about some math discovery so esoteric that no one could really care about it and have her try to act interested.*

She couldn't resist the smell of her dinner, so she stuck her hand in the bag and came up with the hot link. *Mmm…it's kinda nice to be able to eat something so spicy and not have Jamie's eyes cross when I kiss her. Course, I'd eat nothing but vanilla pudding to keep her home.* Her mood began to darken, even as she munched on her fabulously hot sausage. *Ahh…screw it. I'll do what I always do when I'm feeling down—I'll write to Aisling.*

After depositing her gym bag in the closet, Ryan went into the kitchen and got a beer to wash down her dinner. Going to her bedroom, she kicked off her shoes, and spent a long time writing to her cousin, venting every small, medium and large thing that had been bothering her. Jamie repeatedly suggested that Ryan call once in a while, but Ryan couldn't bear the thought of spending money so blithely, so she continued to write.

She was still a little hungry, so she went downstairs and stared at the meager contents of the refrigerator. The only thing that looked appealing was another beer, so she popped the top and took a long gulp. *Damn, that washes down a sausage better than anything.*

After walking into the living room, she sorted through the mail, finding nothing of interest for herself. None of the magazines or journals looked interesting, either. She considered listening to a CD, but quickly dismissed that idea. She needed contact. Human contact.

She knew she couldn't go see her father, since he'd notice the liquor on her breath and not like what drinking alone implied—much less the tongue lashing she'd get from driving after having more than an ounce of alcohol. Going down her list of old friends, she considered calling Alisa, one of her frequent sex partners. They'd been more than fuck buddies, and Alisa was a great listener. But she knew it would send wrong message if she called.

Suddenly, she smiled and grabbed the phone in the living room. Pressing one of the speed-dial buttons, she waited a few seconds until a soft soprano voice answered. Ryan felt tears in her eyes, but she cleared her throat and said, "Hey, stud. Boomer."

"Boomer! Where the hell have you been?" Jordan asked. "Mia's on the phone with Jamie every two minutes, but I never hear from you."

"My phone hasn't been ringing, either." She laughed softly. "Do you hate to talk on the phone as much as I do?"

"More," Jordan said, laughing along with her. "But I should still call you. I just never know when you're home, girl."

"Neither do I." She lay down on the sofa and draped her legs over the arm. "Is this a good time to talk?"

"Yeah. Sure. We're just sitting in my room watching TV."

Ryan heard Mia call out, "Love you, sweetie."

"Tell her I love her, too."

Jordan did so, then she and Ryan chatted for a long time, filling each other in on all of the details of their respective sports.

During a pause, Ryan said, "Hold on a sec. I need to get something to drink." She went into the kitchen, took a look in the fridge, and grabbed another beer. Taking a few big swigs on the way back to the phone, she belched loudly and picked up again. "Sorry about that."

"What? The burp or making me wait?"

"That was a pretty good one, wasn't it?"

"All-world," Jordan agreed. "Hey, we've got a new game going. We keep track of every error we make during practice, then we take our dirty practice clothes and put 'em in a big laundry bag. Each woman gets hit as many times as she screwed up."

"Does it hurt? Doesn't seem like it would."

"It does when you add shoes!"

"Not bad. Maybe we should take a swing at each other with a bat for every strikeout. That'd make people look alive out there."

"I don't know if you could get away with that in college," Jordan said, seemingly serious. "The stakes are so much higher here. There's none of that 'nice try' stuff. If you screw up you hear about it from the coaches and your teammates. It's a lot more like a job."

"I guess it would be," Ryan said, feeling an overwhelming sense of relief that she hadn't tried out for the Olympic team. "I think I'm gonna like playing in a beer league after this year. I don't think I'd like to feel like I was working while playing."

"It's not bad. It's put up or shut up time. This is what I've always wanted, and I'm willing to put up with whatever I have to in order to get the job done."

"They wouldn't be able to have the Olympics without people like you. I admire how focused you've been on this, buddy. I know what you're giving up."

"I haven't given up much. Mia, on the other hand, isn't getting anything from this deal except getting to see me for a few hours a day. She's the one who should get a medal."

"She's got you," Ryan said. "You're better than a medal, any day."

"Are you okay? You're being kinda…sappy."

Ryan took a sip of her beer. "I'm all right. Jamie's gone…you know."

"Ooh. How long's she been gone?"

"Since Sunday. She'll be back Wednesday night."

"Sucks," Jordan said.

"Sure does. It's…I'm…" She blew out a breath and didn't even try to finish.

"You need your woman," Jordan said. "I know just how you feel. When I was here by myself, it felt like every day was just a...a blank. You know what I mean?"

"Yeah."

"I didn't need anyone before I met Mia. I mean, I had friends, and I loved hanging out and stuff, but I didn't need anyone. It's been hard to get used to."

"That's it," Ryan said, nodding emphatically. "It's hard to get used to. I used to be able to fill up an evening without giving it another thought. But now...if Jamie's not here..."

"I know, Boom. I really do."

Ryan yawned loudly. "I think I'm just gonna go to bed early. I'm pretty tired."

"That's a good idea. You'll feel better if you sleep more while she's gone. Then you'll be ready to rock when she gets home."

"Thanks," Ryan said. "Felt good to talk to you."

"You too, Boom. I'm here anytime."

"Same goes for me. Give that girlfriend of yours a kiss for me."

"No way," Jordan said, laughing. "If you wanna kiss her, you've gotta come here. I'm not doing it for you."

"Fair enough. I love you, buddy."

"Me, too. Now get to sleep."

"Will do. See you." Ryan hung up and finished her beer on the way to her bedroom. By the time she'd brushed her teeth she was ready for bed, and a few minutes after she lay down she was sound asleep.

Chapter Twenty-Nine

Ryan was nearly enthusiastic when it came to her turn in therapy on Tuesday morning. Smiling, she said, "Jamie's out of town, and I'm doing a lot better than I thought I would."

Most of the members made approving noises, and Ellen said, "Tell us how it's been."

"Well, Jamie left on Sunday night, and I got through that night pretty easily. There was a big party down at her mom's house and I went to sleep twenty minutes after I got home. Felt great."

"That is great," Ellen said

"Last night, I called my friend in Colorado and we talked for a long time. It felt good to admit that I was still having trouble. She was very supportive."

"Way to go," Arlene said. "It almost always helps to tell someone you trust that you're scared."

Ryan's gaze flitted past the woman. "Yeah. Right."

"Anything else?" Ellen asked.

"No, I'm good. Jamie will be back on Wednesday afternoon and I'll be home late Wednesday night. I just have to get through tonight."

"Do you need any suggestions...support?"

"No, I'll just do what I did last night. I had a couple of drinks and that relaxed me."

Several women shifted in their seats and a few looked like they wanted to jump in. "Barb?" Ellen said.

"You might want to think of some other coping strategies. Using alcohol to get through your fears is an easy way to wind up in AA."

Ryan scowled at her. "I had two drinks, not twenty."

"It's not the amount as much as the fact that you used it instead of facing your feelings," Barb said.

Ryan consciously relaxed her jaw and tried to look like she was open to the suggestion. "Okay. I get that. It would be easy to get into the habit of drinking yourself calm."

Ellen gave Ryan a small smile and asked, "Anything else?"

"Nope. Next," Ryan said, looking to her neighbor.

Late Wednesday afternoon, Jamie and Juliet were playing in the last group of their tournament in El Cajon. Their round had been delayed by lightning, and their opponents were playing so slowly they'd been warned by the officials. Scott ran up to them as they stood on the seventeenth tee. "We're going to have to leave if we want to catch the plane. Can you two take a cab to the airport?"

"Sure," Jamie said, looking at Juliet for agreement.

"Can't you wait just fifteen minutes?" Juliet asked.

"No. We're barely gonna make it as it is. A cab might be able to make better time. Do you need some cash?"

"I've got it," Jamie said. "Don't worry about it, Scott."

He handed her two envelopes. "Here are your tickets. If you miss the plane, the next one is just an hour later." Looking very apologetic, he started to back away, shrugged his shoulders and ran for the group in front of theirs, obviously to deliver the same news.

Juliet shoved her cap further down on her head and crossed her arms over her chest. Jamie was about to wrap a nine-iron around her neck, but she tried not to let her feelings for her teammate interfere with her concentration. She walked to the back of the tee box and quietly took some practice swings, trying to keep warm by knocking the heads off clover.

Forty-five minutes later, Jamie and Juliet loaded their golf bags and suitcases into a taxi. "That sucked," Jamie said after telling the driver their destination.

"Sure did," Juliet said. "The damned green wasn't rolling true at all."

"I meant the part about being left behind." Jamie idly wondered if Juliet had a part of her brain that wasn't dedicated to golf.

"Oh. Right." She leaned against the opposite door and stretched her legs out as well as she could in the cramped back seat. "Think we can upgrade to first class?"

"What are we booked on?"

"Mmm..." Juliet looked at her ticket. "United Express."

"I have a lot of United miles. I could get us both upgraded if there's room."

"Eh...it's no big deal. Short flight."

"I don't mind. I usually wind up donating some miles to charity every year."

"If they offer an upgrade I'll take it, but I don't want you to spend your miles."

"I wouldn't offer if I minded," Jamie said, looking at Juliet closely, trying to read her.

"Sorry I brought it up. It's really nothing."

Jamie was in just a bad enough mood to confront her. Her voice took on a sharp edge. "Why don't you want my miles?"

Juliet shifted in her seat. "It's not a big deal. The flight's just over an hour. Why waste 'em?"

"That's not the point. They're mine to waste. You wanted an upgrade and I offered one. You'll take United's upgrade, but not mine. Why?"

Juliet expelled an aggrieved breath. "Does this have to be a big deal? Just let it go."

"I'm sick of letting things go with you." She was glaring at her, and Juliet looked like she'd rather get out and walk than be in the cab. "The players from the other team are friendlier to me than you are. I'm sick of your treating me like we've never met. What the fuck is going on with you?"

Juliet rolled her eyes, much in the way Jack used to when Jamie pressed a point he didn't want to discuss. "I'm not here to make friends. I've told you that before. I'm here to play golf and work on my game before qualifying school. Sorry you don't like the way I treat you, but that's your problem."

"Are you afraid to be seen with me?" Jamie asked, refusing to let go.

"No," Juliet snapped. "I'm not afraid. I just...there's no benefit to being around you. Everybody knows you're a lesbian," she whispered. "And I don't want people to assume the same about me."

Jamie didn't say another word. She turned her face to the window and watched the traffic crawl by. They arrived at the airport a good ten minutes after their flight had left. Jamie hefted her golf bag over her shoulder, then took her rolling bag and set it on the sidewalk. She paid the driver, asked for a receipt, and started to walk, ignoring Juliet, who passed her and kept going.

Jamie stood right behind her teammate at the ticket gate, and she heard the agent say, "Yes, I can upgrade you to first class." Juliet finished with her transaction, then went to sit down and wait for boarding.

Jamie pushed her ticket across the counter.

"I can upgrade you, too, Ms. Evans."

"No, thanks," Jamie said. "I like the people in coach much better."

It was nearly nine p.m. when Ryan opened the front door of her home. She dropped her bag loudly, then stood still, looking up the stairs expectantly. Her expression changed into a luminous smile when Jamie bolted out of their bedroom and ran down the stairs.

With a very brief warning, she leapt from the second step and flew into Ryan's arms, hanging on tight when they banged into the wall.

"Miss me?" Ryan asked. Without waiting for a response, she kissed her partner while slowly lowering her to the floor.

Jamie held onto Ryan's strong body with all of her strength. Her eyes were closed and she murmured into her jacket, "I can't even tell you how much I missed you."

Ryan grasped her shoulders and pushed her just far enough away to see into her eyes. "What's wrong?"

Jamie shook her head and burrowed back into Ryan's warm body. "Nothing. Just the usual."

Reveling in holding her lover again, Ryan just leaned against the wall and ran her hand through Jamie's soft hair for a long time. When Jamie sighed heavily and moved away, Ryan grasped her hand. They walked into the kitchen together, in silent acknowledgment that Ryan always needed a snack when she returned from a game.

Ryan poked her head into the refrigerator and looked for just a moment before she realized that Jamie had been gone since the previous week and couldn't have refilled the larder. "Did you have dinner?"

"Yeah. I got a burger on the way home. I had the taxi go through the drive-through window at McDonalds."

Ryan stood up and looked at her. "What? Why were you in a taxi?"

Jamie moved past her, opened the freezer and took out a bagel. "Cream cheese and tomato?"

"Yeah. That'd be great." Ryan watched her move to the microwave to defrost the bagel, wondering when Jamie was going to tell her what was on her mind. She jumped onto the counter, content to be in the same room for the first time in a few days.

After setting the timer on the microwave, Jamie turned around. "Happy to be home?"

"Yeah. Not very happy to be leaving tomorrow. How about you?"

"I'm not very happy about leaving, either. But I'm gonna like my traveling companion. Unlike today." She went to the cutlery drawer and took out a knife. Leaning against the counter, she slapped the flat of the blade against her hand. "If I'd had this knife this afternoon, I'd probably be in police custody right now."

"Will you please tell me what's bugging you? I'm tired of being patient."

Jamie smiled at her. "Sorry, babe. I just hate to bitch about that idiot again."

"Juliet rears her ugly head again?"

"Yep. We were paired today and our round was delayed because there was lightning in the area. We had to take a cab to the airport, and we missed our flight."

"Uck. So you had to fly home with just her, huh?"

"No, two other girls were on the flight with us, but we didn't sit together 'cause we got to the airport at different times."

"So you had to sit with Juliet and that bugged you?"

Her expression conveyed her frustration, and Jamie finally said, "I'm sorry, honey. I'm just...I'm sick of her. She's...damn, she's so fucking frustrating!"

Ryan got up and put her arms around her. "You don't have to talk about it if you don't want to. I'll just assume she was being a jerk and got to you a little bit."

Jamie smiled up at her. "Just as well. She isn't worth the trouble."

Even though she knew Jamie always felt better when she vented, Ryan let her keep her feelings to herself. They gently held each other until the microwave beeped and Ryan's empty stomach took precedence.

Mia stood in the surprisingly spacious kitchen and loaded the dishwasher. Jordan always wanted to help, but she worked so hard during the day Mia hated to ask her to do any work around the house. Their meals were always simple, due to Mia's inexperience in the kitchen and Jordan's dietary requirements, so cleanup was equally simple. She dried her hands and went into their room, to find Jordan dozing lightly.

Jordan tried to be lively in the evenings, but Mia knew it was a struggle for her. Having never seriously participated in a sport, Mia didn't truly understand how demanding a world-class sport was—but she saw the results of those demands. She knew that Jordan would snooze all evening long if she wasn't there, and she occasionally wondered if that wouldn't be the best thing for her. But Jordan wouldn't hear of it. As soon as Mia entered the room, she was awake, trying to look like she was ready-for-action. "Wanna do anything tonight?"

"I don't have a need to," Mia said, even though she did. Jordan frequently offered, but Mia knew her heart wasn't in going out. And neither of them knew where to go or what to do, since neither had spent any time investigating Colorado Springs. Mia knew it was her responsibility to search around, since she had a car and plenty of time, but she didn't want to do touristy things by herself. She stretched out on the bed and cuddled up to her partner. "I wish I'd brought Jamie's bike with me. I know she's not using it, and it would be great exercise to ride it on the hills around here."

"Mmm…she'd send it to you if you asked," Jordan said. "But I know you wouldn't ask."

"Never. I looked into joining a gym, but every one I called charged a fairly expensive fee just to join. I hate to pay a fee for a local club that I won't be able to use when we go home."

Jordan gave her a weak smile. "It might be a while before I go home permanently, baby. If we do well in Sydney, I don't think I'll be able to walk away."

Mia patted her on the stomach, feeling the depression where her belly used to be. "Let's stay in the present, okay? We don't know what the future's gonna hold."

Jordan rolled onto her side and regarded Mia with a concerned look. "Are you sorry you came?"

"No!" She slapped her gently on the hip. "Never, never, never. I'm very, very happy that I'm with you."

"But you're bored. You have to be."

Mia smiled and gave her a tickle. "I'd be a pretty boring person if I were perfectly content, wouldn't I? But I'll find my groove. It's just gonna take a while. I was thinking," she said, drawing patterns on Jordan's side, "that we might consider moving to a smaller place."

Jordan's eyes grew wide and she scanned the room. "Smaller than this?"

"No, silly. A one bedroom. For just us. Even a studio would be okay."

Nodding, Jordan said, "You don't like it here."

"Do you?"

"I don't *dis*like it. It's a place to sleep, and that's all that I need. Heck, I had to be talked into this. I was happy to stay in the dorm at the training facility."

Mia knew her partner was more than frugal, but she couldn't let the point pass. "I think I'd be happier…I know I'd be happier if we had our own apartment. I hate the lack of privacy, and I hate sharing a bathroom with two other people. It's depressing to be here all day, honey, and there are only so many hours I can sit in a library or bookstore."

Jordan sat up abruptly. "I knew you weren't happy," she grumbled. "I just didn't wanna admit it."

Mia grasped her T-shirt and pulled her down, then kissed her tenderly. "I *am* happy—with you. I just want some privacy—to be with you."

Blowing out a breath, Jordan asked, "Do you know how much a studio would cost?"

"I haven't done any research. But I could."

"All right." The lines on her forehead showed that her feelings didn't match her words.

Mia touched her chin and looked into Jordan's eyes. "What's on your mind? Talk to me."

Jordan shrugged away from the contact and stood up. She ran her hands through her hair and stood motionless for a few seconds, obviously thinking. "It's almost the end of March. We'll probably move out of here at the beginning of September. It doesn't make financial sense to move when we'll just be here a few more months, but I'll do it if you're unhappy."

"What?"

"I said I'll do it if you're unhappy."

"I heard you," Mia said. "I just don't understand what you're talking about. Why would we move in September?"

Looking puzzled, Jordan said, "Jill rented this place last September, so the lease is up in August."

"But I thought you wanted to stay with the team after the games."

"I probably will...kinda."

"What in the hell does that mean?"

"The team disbands after the games. Everyone goes her own way until the 2004 team is chosen. I mean...it's kind of a given that you'll be offered a spot if you do well in Sydney and keep playing, but it's not a lock."

Mia stood and put her hands on Jordan's hips. "I'm thoroughly confused. Where would you play?"

"Depends. I have to see how I do, and see who's interested in me."

Nearly yelling, Mia demanded, "Who might be interested?"

"Some European team. That's the only place that has professional volleyball. I thought we could kinda look around when we start to travel. See where we might like to live."

"See where we might like to live." Mia repeated the words, but they didn't make sense to her.

"Yeah. We start our European tour in three weeks. I've got close to ten thousand dollars that I've put aside for you to travel with me. We've gotta start shopping for airfare to Madrid. That's our first stop."

"It is?"

"Yeah." Jordan smiled. "See how time flies?"

"I...I had no idea. You've never mentioned travel plans."

"Really?" Jordan gave her a perplexed smile. "We have to travel to get in shape for Sydney. But it's gonna be cool! We're gonna see the world, honey. Spain, Japan, Eastern Europe. That's why I've tried to watch my spending. We'll need every bit of the money I've saved for airfare and hotel rooms."

Mia tried to keep her smile bright, but all she could think of was sitting in a hotel watching television in a foreign language while Jordan practiced and played. "Do many other spouses or boyfriends go on these trips?"

"No, I don't think so. Most people can't get the time off." She put her hand under Mia's T-shirt and flicked her belly-ring. "You don't have that problem."

"No, I sure don't," she said. "I'm free as a bird." *In a really boring cage.*

Chapter Thirty

The next morning, Jamie woke and immediately smiled. She snuggled deeper into her partner's embrace while checking the clock. They'd decided to take the day off to reconnect a little as well as help Catherine move into her new house, and she was determined to enjoy every minute.

They had an afternoon flight to Los Angeles for Ryan's weekend games with UCLA and USC, and Ryan had promised that they'd spend as much time alone as possible. Jamie had taken the liberty of making dinner reservations for just the two of them on both Friday and Saturday nights—just so Ryan didn't have the chance to suggest a pizza with the other girls.

As soon as Jamie moved, Ryan's eyes opened and she tilted her head just enough to be able to kiss her. They each shifted to have more skin contact while the kiss deepened. "Is there a better way to wake up?" Ryan asked when they broke apart, her voice deep and a little raspy.

"No. This is the best way in the whole world. Time for love?" she asked, not having looked at the clock. She moved her hand up and down her partner's body, drawing a little purr from Ryan.

"Easy, cupcake. We've gotta leave in half an hour."

"Not a problem," Jamie said, pulling her into a deep, sultry kiss. As her hands roamed, Jamie felt her libido surge. She was so intent on her body's needs that she didn't notice Ryan's tepid response. Easily, she flipped Ryan onto her back and started to move down her body when the phone rang. Jamie gave the phone a deadly glare and focused again on Ryan's body—which wriggled away from her. Jamie looked up in shock as Ryan reached for the phone.

"H'llo?"

"I'm at the bakery," Catherine said. "So don't eat breakfast. I'll have enough to fill even you up."

"You sound pretty excited," Ryan said. "Most people dread moving."

"I'm about to squeal! I can't wait until you two get here."

Ryan's brow furrowed. "Are you in Hillsborough?"

"No, I'm in Pacific Heights. I can't wait."

"We'll be there as soon as we can," Ryan said, giving her partner a swat on the seat and mouthing, "Heat up the shower."

But Jamie didn't follow instructions. She was lying on her stomach, her eyes boring into Ryan, who hung up and stared back at her. "What?"

"Why did you answer the phone?"

"Uhm…because it rang?" Her smile was sweet, and clearly contrived to charm.

But her charms were wasted on Jamie this morning. "We have an agreement. We never answer the phone or the door when we're making love."

"I know that." She slipped out of bed, leaned over and shook her head, trying to get some of the tangles out. "But we weren't making love. We were just waking up."

"Cut the bull."

Ryan's eyes opened wide. "What bull?"

"If you don't wanna make love, that's fine. But don't act like we weren't starting to."

Ryan walked into the bathroom and turned on the shower, then came back to the bedroom and ruffled Jamie's hair. "I didn't pick up your signal, babe. My mind was on what we had to do today."

Jamie's eyes never left her partner's. Ryan gave her another smile and shrugged her shoulders. "I'm sorry. Sometimes we just don't click."

"Right," Jamie said, unsmiling.

Ryan went back into the bathroom and called out, "Your mom's waiting for us in the city. Wanna get in the shower with me?"

"No, thanks. I'm not in the mood." She rolled over and scooted up and put her head on her pillow. She was certain that Ryan would turn off the shower and come back into the room to smooth things over. But she heard her lover get into the shower and start to wash her hair, singing quietly.

What in the hell is going on with us? She's never intentionally ignored me when she knows I'm angry. And she knows *I'm angry. That smile might have gotten her out of disagreements with her fuck buddies, but it's not going to work with me.*

Even though she was still angry, Jamie deliberately ignored the issue. She knew they had to talk, but having an argument on the way to help her mother move wasn't a good idea.

They got to the BMW, which was behind the Boxster. Ryan stood near the rear bumper, looking a little like a sloth. "Wanna take your car?"

"Because it's more difficult?" Even though she didn't want to fight, it was hard to be civil.

"No." Ryan yawned ostentatiously. "I'm not feeling very sharp. I thought you could drive."

"Give me the keys. I can manage to drive a big car."

"Don't screw up my seat settings."

Grumbling to herself, Jamie got into the driver's seat. She moved the seat and the mirrors, knowing that Ryan's settings were set in the computer module. Several times she started to say something about their morning, but she bit her tongue, reasoning that they'd have time alone on the weekend. Ryan hummed a soft tune during the whole trip, irritating Jamie all the more. Other than the humming, Ryan didn't say a word all the way to Pacific Heights.

She was able to find a parking space quite close to the house, and when they approached the front of the dwelling both young women rocked back on their heels and gazed up at the structure in wonder.

The pristine, white-painted residence was absolutely gorgeous. A combination of understated elegance and pure, simple lines, it had such tremendous curb appeal that both Jamie and Ryan were perfectly content to just stare at it.

"Don't you want to come inside?" Catherine asked, her voice carrying down from the balcony.

Shielding her eyes against the sun, Ryan called up, "It can't get much better than this. What a perfect view of the Bay!" She turned to watch an assortment of sailboats dotting the bright blue water, and sighed deeply. "I'd give a lot to have a view of the Bay from my house."

"We can have that," Jamie reminded her.

"Not until they move the Bay closer to Noe," Ryan said regretfully, shaking her head. "Family before view."

"Well, you're my family, and I'll share my view with you any day,"

Catherine promised. "Now get in here and start looking around."

They walked up a few steps, then entered a small, covered entryway. Catherine threw the door open.

"Holy crap!" Ryan cried out as they entered, earning an elbow to the gut from her partner.

"Behave."

"You don't have to behave," Catherine laughed. "It's nice to hear an honest reaction once in a while. It is impressive, isn't it?"

"It's not just impressive," Jamie said, looking around. "It's absolutely breathtaking, Mom. Who in the world designed it?"

"The former owner is an art director who works in Hollywood. He certainly used all of his talents here, didn't he?"

"I'm confused," Jamie said. "Did you buy it furnished?"

"Yes. I've never considered buying a furnished home, but the pieces were made for this place, and it seemed silly to try to replicate the feel that I got when I walked in here. It's the whole mood that I fell in love with, so I made my offer contingent on the inclusion of every stick of furniture."

"Then how is this moving day?" Ryan asked.

"My personal furnishings are on their way. Everything for the kitchen, small appliances…linens…clothing."

"Just two trucks, huh?" Ryan asked, getting another elbow.

Jamie did another spin, amazed at how lovely the room was. "Hard to imagine a guy owned this. It doesn't have a masculine feel at all. It's very rich and sumptuous, isn't it?"

"Yes," Catherine agreed. "It feels like a warm cocoon."

She was smiling broadly, and Jamie saw a peacefulness in her expression that had been missing for quite some time. "I'm so glad you were able to buy it, Mom. I think it's really going to suit you." She turned to say something to her partner, but Ryan was missing. "Where did she run off to?"

"I think we'll be able to find her. The house isn't very large."

"How many rooms?"

"Living room, dining room, kitchen, bath and study on this floor, and five bedrooms with four baths upstairs. It's obviously bigger than I need, but the rooms are rather compact. The dimensions really appeal to me."

"I see what you mean. The smaller sized rooms add to the lush feeling you get in here."

"One room that isn't small is the kitchen," Catherine said. "Marta's going to love it."

They walked into the large space and Jamie spent quite a few minutes oohing and ahhing over every one of the top-quality appliances. "Just perfect. And made for entertaining."

"Yes. It will be nice to have you two over for meals. We can all sit in here together. I might even learn a thing or two about cooking."

Jamie took advantage of the fact that they were alone. She lowered her voice and asked, "How did it go with Giacomo? I…uhm…thought you'd call me while I was gone."

Catherine looked nonplussed. "Oh. I…suppose I should have. I just didn't…think."

"So…?" Jamie looked at her mother carefully, seeing how evasive and skittish she seemed.

"Well, we worked some things out. I had some…concerns…and we talked them out. I think we…settled some things."

Jamie smiled at her and waited for her to continue, but Catherine just smiled back, not offering another word. The younger woman pursed her lips, then rocked back on her heels and looked around. There was an uncomfortable silence, then she said, "Where's that girlfriend of mine? Are you sure she didn't leave?"

Looking relieved, Catherine said, "No, but I have a feeling she's outside. Let's go find her."

As predicted, Ryan was sitting on one of the chairs on the deck, watching the Bay with a peaceful expression on her features. "What a great spot," she sighed. "Can I come over every morning to have my coffee?"

"I'd be delighted," Catherine said. "Actually, nothing would make me happier than to see you two on a daily basis."

"I think that can be arranged," Ryan said, smiling brightly. "We'll be over so much, you'll change the locks."

Jamie surveyed the entire space, murmuring her approval. "You're going to be very happy here, Mom. Just the place for a fresh start."

"That's exactly how it feels to me, honey. I've lived in the Bay Area my whole life, but I've never lived in the city. I'm going to take advantage of all this place has to offer."

"Look out San Francisco," Ryan called out to the city below. "Catherine Evans is takin' over!"

Chapter Thirty-One

That evening, Jamie lay on the king-sized bed at the Westwood Holiday Inn, waiting for Ryan to take a shower so they could go out to dinner. Her partner was puttering around the room, obviously in no hurry. So Jamie picked up her cell phone and dialed the third position on her speed dial. "Guess where I am?" she asked.

"Paris," Mia said. "Or Cairo."

Jamie laughed. "You're not even trying."

Mia let out a breath. "Okay. You're in some boring college town. Playing golf or softball. Better?"

"Mostly right. But we're in L.A., and I made reservations for just the two of us at the hottest new restaurant in town. And if I can keep her awake, I'm gonna drag my sweetie to a big lesbian club. That's not too boring, is it?"

"Ooo...L.A.," Mia sighed. "I have some great memories from L.A."

"Me, too. I was just lying here thinking about when all of us were here this past fall. Wasn't that a great weekend?"

"Sure was. Jordy and I were just starting to fall in love. Damn, it seems like it was years ago, James."

"I know it. Years and years. But it's only been about six months...if that."

"I'd love to be there with you guys. These roommates suck so bad."

"Not any better, huh?"

"Nope. I've gotta pin Jordy down and figure out what's going on. She knows a hell of a lot more about her plans for the next few years than she's told me. I just have to find the time to get her alone and awake."

Jamie groaned. "How'd we get into the same fix? Jack was a pain in the butt, but he was always sitting on the couch where I could find him."

"Whoo! Ryan's in deep shit if you're comparing her to Jack. What did she do?"

"Oh...nothing...really. We're both too busy and we're not taking time to talk like we usually do."

"All you do is talk and have sex."

"Those were the old days. Now all we do is travel and study and try to keep some family obligations. May can't come soon enough for me."

"It'll be nice to be finished with school, but Jordan has me scheduled to do a world tour with her."

"Really? That sounds cool."

"It kinda does," Mia said. "But I'll go to all of her games, and they're anytime from nine in the morning until eight at night. That'll screw up my tourist schedule. I mean, I know I shouldn't bitch, but there's a difference between traveling with Jordan and traveling as a tag-along with the team."

"You don't have to tell me," Jamie said. "It's been nice to go to softball matches with Ryan, but when I went along on basketball games it sucked. Of course, we were in Pullman and Corvallis and not Paris and London."

"I want to travel with Jordy, but..." She let out a sigh. "I can't complain about this. This is what makes Jordy happy, and I've gotta be a trooper. I'll just have to enjoy the travel."

"You always had fun when you traveled with your parents, and I know you didn't hang out with them the whole time."

"I was looking to hook-up, James! It's great to go to Madrid and meet a hot guy in a club. But I've gotta go visit cathedrals and museums now."

"Oh, you poor thing. You're gonna have to see the stuff regular tourists see, rather than stranger's bedrooms."

"It's a bitch!" Mia agreed, laughing.

"Does Jordan know how you feel?"

"Hell, no. She's oblivious. You know how jocks are. As long as she gets enough sleep and enough to eat, she's happy."

"Ryan jokes that Conor only has four emotions; hungry, thirsty, tired and horny. But she doesn't have a whole lot more, so she shouldn't talk."

With an evil-sounding laugh, Mia said, "The horny part makes me put up with a lot. Thank God Jordy isn't too tired for that."

"The roommates listening doesn't bother you any more?"

"You can get used to anything. But we've learned to be very, very quiet."

"You?"

"Well, Jordan usually claps a hand over my mouth, but I think I should get some credit."

"I miss you, buddy," Jamie said, on the verge of tears.

"Me, too. Being here has really shown me how much I love Jordy. She's the only good thing about being here, but it's been enough. She's enough for me."

"I'm very glad to hear that. I worry about you a lot."

"I'm fine, babe. I've been studying my ass off, out of sheer boredom. I want to make Dean's list just to show my parents that I'm not a total flake."

"Have you spoken to them much?"

"Nada. Not since the time I told you about. They both have my cell phone number, but my mother must have ordered my father not to call. He tends to follow her lead."

"What about Peter?"

Mia laughed again, and Jamie could hear her fondness for her brother. "He does what he wants. He calls me at least once a week. He's a very good brother."

"I'm glad you have at least one person in the family who's reasonable. Thank God for Peter."

"Yeah, he's been great. I don't think he believes Jordan's the one for me, but he doesn't ever say so. That's all the support I need."

"Really? That shocks me."

"He seems to think I'm more straight than gay. I think he assumes I'll get tired of chick-love and run back to hetero-land."

"That doesn't bother you?" Jamie asked, thinking that she wouldn't like it at all if she were in Mia's position.

"Nah. I have been a flake for most of my life. I can't blame him for thinking I'm still like that."

"You're not a flake," Jamie said firmly, her protective streak rising to the fore.

"I'm not any more. Love changes you in many ways, James. It's made me grow up a lot. Peter will see that over time. And so will my parents… if they ever speak to me again."

"Your mom loves you too much to let this last long. I'm sure it's driving her crazy."

"Short drive."

"Oh, Ryan looks like she's on the verge of being ready. I'd better go."

"Give Ryan a kiss for me and remind her that she has everything in the world she needs to be happy—your love."

"I love you, Mia. Kiss Jordan for us."

"Repeatedly," Mia agreed, before hanging up.

"How are our children?" Ryan asked.

"Okay. Mia's bored beyond belief, but Jordan seems happy."

"Aren't you glad that I made one intelligent decision in my life?"

"Uhm...besides choosing me?"

"Right," Ryan said. "That's a given. But aren't you glad I didn't try out for the Olympic volleyball team? You know with my luck I would have made it."

"Yeah. You're just unlucky enough to be chosen as one of the top fifteen volleyball players in the country." Jamie got up and walked over to her lover. "But your luck is about to change."

"It is? How?"

Jamie picked her phone back up and scrolled through her phone book. Finding the number she wanted, she dialed and waited for an answer. "Hi, this is Jamie Evans. I need to cancel my reservation for seven thirty. Sure. You're welcome." She hung up and smiled at Ryan. "Mia reminded me of something."

"Never to make me go out to a nice restaurant again?"

"Nope. That we have to concentrate on the things that are important. Going out to dinner isn't important." She put her arms around Ryan's waist. "Talking about what's going on in our relationship is what's important right now."

Immediately, Ryan looked terrified. "What's wrong? What'd I do?"

Jamie stroked her bare skin, then kissed her chest. "You didn't do anything, love. We just have to talk through some things. It's early, we're both awake, and we don't have to be anywhere. It's time."

Ryan rubbed her arms, and Jamie saw the goose bumps. "I'm freezing. Let me put some sweats on."

"Okay." Jamie sat down on one of the two club chairs that flanked a small table. When Ryan had donned some sweatpants and a T-shirt, she took the chair opposite her. As usual when they had a serious discussion, Ryan looked like a schoolgirl trying to show that she was paying rapt attention. Her eyes were fixed on Jamie's and she didn't move a muscle.

"I'm not going to lecture you. We just need to talk."

"I hate those words," Ryan said. "They're always code for 'you screwed up.'"

Reaching out to squeeze her knee, Jamie said, "Not this time. We've both screwed up a lot of things lately, but everything is repairable."

Eyes wide, Ryan said, "Shit. This sounds worse than I thought."

"Calm down." Jamie tenderly stroked her leg, and looked at her for a moment. "I haven't been doing a very good job of taking care of you."

"What?" Ryan visibly relaxed and ruffled her partner's hair. "You take better care of me than Da did, and that's saying a lot. You have the house cleaned and my car washed and you make dinner for me almost every night. You come to every one of my games if you're in town. What more could you possibly do?"

Jamie didn't smile back. She kept her gaze locked on Ryan. "That's not what I'm talking about. I'm talking about the big stuff. Things like making sure you feel secure and safe and protected. I've let you down, baby, and I'm gonna try to do better."

Ryan looked completely befuddled. "What are you talking about? It's not your job to do things like that. I'm an adult. I have to take care of myself."

Grasping both of her hands, Jamie squeezed them. "It *is* my job. It's my job to take care of you and it's your job to take care of me. That's why we're together."

Still giving her a curious look, Ryan said, "Okay, I agree. But you can't make me feel secure when I'm insecure. I have to work through that kinda thing on my own."

"No, you don't!" Her frustration finally exploded. "That's where you're wrong. You're so wrong! I can help you, but you have to trust me. You have to tell me how you're feeling."

"I do," she said, not meeting Jamie's eyes.

"You do not! I didn't know you were only going to your group because I want you to."

"Rory," Ryan mumbled under her breath. "Can't keep a secret to save his life."

"I didn't know you've been unable to sleep when I'm gone."

"Aisling! She's a traitor, too?"

"I didn't know something happened at softball practice that made you run away from Coach Roberts."

"Heather! Jesus, I thought she was intimidated by me. I can't believe she went behind my back."

Jamie grasped Ryan's chin and held it tight. "I didn't know you'd gone to a shooting range."

Ryan's lips pursed, and Jamie said, "American Express. You can't use your charge card if you're doing things you don't want me to know about."

"I wasn't hiding anything."

"That's lie, Ryan. A boldfaced lie."

"It is not!"

"You went on a night I was away. I'm sure I asked you what you did that night."

"No, you didn't," Ryan said, looking like she was about to cry. "You turned off your cell phone and went to sleep."

The words struck Jamie like a knife. She held it together for a moment, then broke down, sobbing piteously. Ryan wrapped her in her arms and rocked her, asking, "What's wrong? What did I do?"

Jamie shook her head, her tears keeping her from speaking. Finally she gasped out, "Nothing, you big dope! You haven't done anything. I'm the one who's let you down. I should have known your group wasn't helping you. I should have known you weren't sleeping. I should have known you were so…whatever it was that made you go to a shooting range and spend fifty dollars on ammunition. You normally wouldn't spend fifty dollars on getting a broken leg set without telling me about it!"

Ryan disentangled herself and stood up, holding onto the wall for a second to get her balance. "I'm sorry," she said. Her head was hanging down and her voice shook. "I've been trying to fight my way through this, but nothing's working."

Jamie jumped to her feet and wrapped her arms around Ryan, holding her from behind. "I understand that. That's why you should have talked to me. You should have been telling me all of the little things that have been adding up. All of them. That's why I'm here."

"I didn't wanna bother you. Your schedule is as busy as mine. It's bad enough that you've had to travel with me on your few weekends off."

Jamie grasped her by the shoulders and turned her around so they were face-to-face. "Are we partners, or aren't we? Are the morons who voted for Prop 22 right? Maybe we don't deserve to be married."

"What?" Ryan put her hands on Jamie's waist and shook her. "What?"

"You heard me. Do you want to act like we're dating, or do you love me enough to marry me?" She held up her emerald ring, putting it right under Ryan's nose. "You spent all of the money you had on this ring. What does it mean?"

"It means I love you and want to spend the rest of my life with you."

Jamie's hands went to Ryan's shoulders and shook her hard. "When things are good, or all of the time?"

"All of the time. What kind of question is that?"

Jamie held her tightly and stared into her eyes. "You act like I should only love you when things are good. You want to be there for me when things are bad, but you won't be honest with me when things aren't good for you. That's never going to work, Ryan. I will not marry you if you don't trust me enough to be honest with me. I'm sorry, but I won't."

Ryan sank to the bed and blinked slowly. She looked utterly stunned. "Jesus Christ. I've never seen you so upset."

Sitting right next to her, Jamie took her face in her hands. "We have to work on our relationship. If we're not ready to commit to each other in good times and bad, I'm going to postpone the wedding. I won't listen to an empty promise."

"You're serious? You really mean that?"

"Deadly. I've never been more serious."

Stunned, Ryan just stared at her. "What do I do? How do I convince you I'm ready to marry you?"

"It's going to take some time, and some effort."

Ryan nodded mutely.

"The first thing we're gonna do is get you some individual therapy. You've got issues from the carjacking that aren't going to go away if you don't get some real help—and your therapy group doesn't seem to be cutting it."

"Okay. I…I guess you're right."

"Then we're going to have some couples therapy. Maybe not right now, but as soon as school's over. We have to work on some things before we get married. I don't wanna put more pressure on you, but we have to agree on how we're going to interact as partners."

"I'll do whatever you want, Jamie. Just don't give up on me, please!"

Her eyes were wide with fright, and Jamie put her arms around her and held her tightly. "How can you ask if I'm giving up on you? I love you with all my heart. I just want to make sure that we're happily married, Ryan. We can't be happy if we're not honest…if we don't trust each other…if we're not vulnerable with each other."

"Vulnerable? Jesus! I cry every two seconds. I've never let a woman see me cry like I do you."

Jamie got up and walked across the room to stand in front of the air conditioner. She felt like she had a fever, but she knew she was just upset. "Here's what you do. You keep things inside until you're ready to explode. Then, something happens and you can't hold it together anymore. Then, you cry. That's not what I'm talking about. I need for you to talk to me before you're ready to explode. I need for you to tell me about your fears, about your weaknesses, about the things that you're ashamed to admit. That's what being vulnerable is."

Ryan looked across the room, her eyes hooded, her expression guarded. "You don't tell me things you're ashamed of."

Stalking across the room, Jamie dropped to her knees in front of her lover and grasped Ryan's hands. "You wanna know what I'm ashamed of?" Her eyes were nearly glowing with emotion.

Looking like she regretting having asked the question, Ryan nodded slowly.

"I'm worried that our marriage is gonna turn out like my parents'."

"What?" The word was so slow and drawn out that it sounded like it had three syllables.

"I'm ashamed to admit that," Jamie said quietly. "But one of the things that destroyed their marriage was that they didn't talk to each other about the important things. If my father had talked to my mother when he first felt tempted to be with another woman…" She cast her eyes to the floor, her cheeks reddening.

Ryan jumped up, sending Jamie onto her butt. Bending to help her up, Ryan spoke with childlike incredulity. "You think I'm going to cheat on you."

Jamie bit her lip and nodded—almost imperceptibly. "I don't want to. You've never given me any reason to think you will. But I don't think my father planned on cheating on my mother. And I know damned well that my mother didn't expect it."

Ryan stood, her eyes wide and unfocused. They she started to speak. Softly at first, then with greater volume as each word tumbled out. "He lies. He cheats. He manipulates the people he claims he loves. He threatens people. He intimidates people. He tried to bribe me to get me to break up with you. He hired a fucking private investigator to make up shit about me! He cheated on your mother. He cheated on the women he was cheating with." She stopped, breathing hard, sweat showing on her forehead. "I wanna know how in the fucking hell you think I'm going to start acting like him? Am I gonna start controlling you like a puppet? Or will I just whore around on you?" She pushed past Jamie and ran her hands across the dresser, clearly not finding what she sought quickly enough, so she swept her hand across the surface, papers flying in the air before fluttering to the floor. "Where's my goddamned room key?"

Jamie stood, motionless, her gut telling her to be afraid, but her mind unable to believe Ryan would ever hurt her.

Ryan turned and glared at her, then something seemed to snap. She whirled around and pushed the dresser with all of her strength, banging it hard against the wall. Then she grabbed the chair and hurled it onto the bed, picked it up by two legs and threw it again and again, the heavy piece thudding mightily. Lifting it over her head, she snapped her arms down, sending the chair crashing to the floor where it cracked and broke into pieces, sending shards of wood flying everywhere. She stood there, breathing heavily, sweat staining her shirt. A tentative knock at the door seemed to reach her, and she turned to stare, wild-eyed at Jamie—who cowered in the corner of the room, crying silently. Their eyes met and Ryan collapsed, crumbling slowly to the floor, where she sat, staring into space.

The knock became louder, and Jamie finally moved to answer it. She cracked the door open and saw Jackie, Ryan's regular roommate. Jackie looked like she'd rather be anywhere else, but she stood there, trying not to look at Jamie's tear-streaked face. "Is…everything okay?" She took a long look at Jamie. "Are you okay?"

Jamie opened the door and stepped into the hall. She was still wearing the dress she was going to wear to dinner, and she looked perfectly fine except for her red-rimmed eyes. "I'm fine, Jackie, and Ryan's fine. Or…" She looked at the door. "She will be when she calms down."

Looking into her eyes, Jackie asked again, "Are you sure? It sounded like she was tearing the place apart."

"She was," Jamie admitted. "She's really, really angry, but she's just venting. She'd never hurt me."

"That's what most women think," Jackie said, her eyes dark with warning.

Jamie put her hand on her arm. "Thanks for caring about us, but the only person who has to be afraid of Ryan is Ryan. She's brutal with herself sometimes—but only herself."

Jackie looked very uncomfortable, but she stayed right in front of the door, shifting her weight from foot to foot. "Want me to talk to her?"

"No. Please. She's embarrassed enough. She hates to cause a scene. I swear we're fine, and if you hear any more noise, feel free to call the police. I guarantee this is all over."

Jackie nodded. "I will call the police if I hear furniture flying around again. I don't want either of you to get hurt."

Jamie put her arms around the sturdy woman and gave her a hug. "Thanks for looking out for us, Jackie. I really do appreciate it."

"Ryan's my bud, but I'd call the police on her in a second if she raised a hand to you."

"She never has. She never will. I know her." Her stomach flipped and she worked those words over in her head. She patted Jackie and went back into the room, immediately going to Ryan's side. Kneeling next to her, she held her in her arms and whispered, "I know you. You're my faithful, loving partner. You'd break your own arms before you'd cheat on me."

Ryan looked at her, her normally clear eyes clouded with doubt and pain. "I don't know...what happened?"

"You lost it, baby. I told you my deepest fear and you...just lost it."

"Fuck, fuck, fuck," Ryan muttered. "I'm so sorry." She straightened out her legs, kicking away some of the broken chair. "I don't even know who I am anymore."

"I do," Jamie said, her voice full of confidence. "You're my sweet, sweet lover, and you're so stressed that you're about to snap. We're going to get you some help, Ryan. And I'm going to be there for you. And we'll do anything...anything it takes to let you get back to your old self."

"Maybe it's gone," Ryan said disconsolately. "Maybe it's just...gone."

"No, it's not. It's not, baby. Every time we have a couple of days at home, you're just like your old self. We have to figure out how to use all of our resources to make your world safe again."

Ryan smiled sadly. "I don't think my world will ever be safe again."

"Yes, it will. We'll make our world as safe as we can. We can do it," she insisted, putting her hands on Ryan's shoulders. "My love for you is enormous. It's massive. It's everlasting."

"That's how I feel about you," Ryan said, her blue eyes showing so much sadness that Jamie's heart ached.

"We've made some mistakes lately. I shouldn't have stayed on the golf team after the carjacking. You shouldn't have joined the softball team. You shouldn't have agreed to do this massive independent study. But we're in too deep to turn back now. We just have to figure out a way to struggle through the next two months—together."

Ryan nodded soberly. "I know I shouldn't have joined the team—even though I really like the guys. The travel's killing me."

"That's how I feel about golf…well, expect for the liking the guys part."

"You at least get to play," Ryan said, a tiny smile showing.

"True. And that's the part I like. But it's not worth it. I should have chucked it. But…I didn't. And I don't feel right quitting now. We're doing well, and I've contributed a lot of wins. I'd be letting too many people down to quit now."

"I wouldn't be letting anyone down, since I never play."

"Yes, you would," Jamie insisted. "You're the first person off the bench. One injury and you're a starter, honey. That's important."

"I know, I know. I just wish…I wish I had a lot of things to do over again."

"So do I," Jamie said. "But one thing I've never regretted is being with you. You're my compass, Ryan. You're always there when I need you. I just need to know that you feel the same way about me."

"I do," Ryan said, whispering the words into Jamie's ear. "And I'm gonna try to show you I mean that from now on."

Jamie stroked her cheek. "Any other secrets I should know about?"

"Uhm…did I mention that I went to the lesbian bar one night and sat there like a big loser for a couple of hours?"

Jamie looked up at the ceiling. "Good lord, is there anything else?"

"I'm afraid to drive when you're in the car," she said, her voice trembling. "I have to be on the lookout. I don't ever want anyone to sneak up on us again."

Jamie held her tightly, murmuring into her ear, "No one will, baby. No one ever will."

Chapter Thirty-Two

After Jamie called the front-desk to arrange to pay for and have the broken chair taken from the room, she looked over to see her partner devouring the contents of the mini-bar. Ryan drained a bottle of water in moments, then peeled the wrapper off a candy bar and started to gobble it down. Holding up another candy bar, she asked, "Want some?"

Jamie rubbed her eyes. "I must be hallucinating. You're willingly raiding the mini-bar?"

"Gotta be cheaper than the restaurant you were gonna take us to," she said, giving her a toothy grin. "I'm gonna eat the macadamia nuts next, and that's way out of my comfort zone."

"Bring me something sweet...besides yourself." Ryan grabbed a diet Coke, more candy and the nuts and sat on the edge of the bed. "You're always a surprise, Ms. O'Flaherty."

"It was either this, or room service. And that's no bargain, either. At least this was fast."

"But not enough to fill you up."

"No, but it'll keep me until breakfast. I can load up then."

"Really? You don't want a sandwich or something?"

"Yeah, I'd love one." Ryan held her second candy bar up to Jamie's lips, letting her take a generous bite. "But I don't wanna wait."

Jamie put her hand on Ryan's leg. "Do you think I'm odd?"

"Huh? You're sitting next to a woman who just destroyed some pretty substantial furniture, had her teammate come by to check that she wasn't a wife-beater...and you wanna know if you're odd? I'm nearly ready for the men in the white coats."

Jamie slapped her arm. "You're a long way from that."

"What makes you think you're odd?"

"I wondered if you thought it was odd that I get…interested…after we have a big blowout fight?" She ran her hand up Ryan's leg, then leaned over to kiss her ear.

"Interested in what?" Ryan asked, looking puzzled.

"Okay, O'Flaherty," Jamie said, standing up to stare at her lover. "What's going on with your sex drive?"

Ryan giggled playfully and pulled her partner back down. "It's kinda broken. But I got that clue."

"Is it broken from stress?"

"Maybe. But I think it's probably still left-over junk from the carjacking. I don't feel the drive I used to feel."

"You do seem to do better if it's really spontaneous," Jamie agreed. "And you seem to need to be in control."

Grinning like a wolf, Ryan purred. "I always wanna be in control."

Jamie gave her a tickle. "Not always. But recently you really seem to need it."

"Well, maybe I can take a hint and still be in control." She stood up and whipped off her shirt, then dropped her pants. Taking Jamie by the hand, she helped her to her feet. For the first time that night, Ryan seemed to step back and take a look at Jamie's clothes. "God, you look fantastic."

Jamie could see just how sincere the compliment was when her partner's nipples started to harden. "Do I look better in clothes?"

"I'm not sure. I'd better check." Ryan had a playful smile on her face, one that Jamie desperately missed. Ryan urged her into the remaining chair, then bent to remove her shoes. She knelt and let one cool hand slide up a thigh, touching the band of lace that held the stocking up. "These are so damned hot." She bent over and rested her cheek on Jamie's thigh, taking in a few deep, relaxing breaths while Jamie ran a hand through her hair. They stayed just like that for a few minutes, letting their bodies get used to being intimate again.

Ryan's fingers couldn't stay idle for long, and they slipped up another couple of inches. Jamie's thighs were closed and Ryan couldn't quite reach her goal. She looked up, eyes sparkling with interest. "Panties?"

"Uh-huh." Jamie ruffled her hair. "Disappointed?"

"Never. I'm always pleased with your underwear decisions." She put both hands on a thigh and slowly peeled the stocking off one leg, then the other. Smiling sexily, Ryan ran her hands up and down the silky-smooth legs. "Nicest skin in the world. Truly a work of art."

As a reward, Jamie returned the smile and spread her legs just a little, letting Ryan playfully rest her chin on the chair to take a peek. "Looks nice from here."

"Thank you. Want more?"

"Much more." Ryan got up and held out a hand. Jamie accepted it and they stood facing one another. They kissed, lengthily and sensually, their bodies pressing against one another. Ryan's hands slid down her partner's back and grasped her ass, pushing it so her hips pressed forward. Then her fingers climbed back up and tugged at the dress's zipper, sliding it down soundlessly. Her thumbs and index fingers gripped the fabric and pulled, sliding the dress off and letting it pool on the floor.

Now that Jamie was clad in only her underwear, Ryan held onto her hungrily, wrapping her in a nearly-painful hug while they kissed with a passionate intensity. They stood in the quiet room, the whir of the air-conditioner accompanied by the soft sounds of their lips touching.

"God, you're good at this," Jamie murmured between kisses.

Ryan smiled, then kissed down her neck, peppering the edge of her bra with a moist line of kisses. "Good at what?"

"Making me hot. Very hot."

"This makes you hot?" Ryan slid her hands inside Jamie's pearl pink panties, palming her ass and squeezing the cheeks tenderly. She continued to kiss her, exploring her mouth with her tongue.

Jamie finally pulled away, pausing to catch her breath. "That makes me sizzle. Everything you do makes me hot. Am I just easy, or are you really good?"

Ryan laughed softly. "Maybe both." She bent and picked Jamie up, effortlessly carrying her to the bed. "Or maybe you just make me so hot that some of my heat rubs off on you." She placed her in the center of the bed and climbed on top of her, dipping her head to kiss her again.

Jamie wrapped her arms around Ryan, pressing their breasts together. They rolled around on the bed, briefly fighting for position, but Ryan was intent. Jamie let her win and lay passively on her back—for the time being.

Magically, Jamie's bra had been unfastened while they wrestled, and Ryan slipped it from her shoulders. Sliding down, Ryan started to feast on her breasts, catching Jamie by surprise with her intensity. But surprise quickly gave way to total satisfaction, and Jamie started to writhe under her, her hips pressing against Ryan's pelvis.

Soon, Jamie started tapping on Ryan's shoulders, urging her down. But Ryan clearly wasn't in a hurry, and she obviously didn't want to be directed. She stayed right where she was, laving Jamie's breasts with bouts of tender care alternated with lusty sucking and delicate kisses. She was truly insatiable, and Jamie gave up trying to promote her own agenda. She simply lay there, her hands wrapped in Ryan's hair, letting her lover fulfill her need.

Ryan started to turn up the heat, her desire slowly becoming more and more voracious. Jamie reached down and grabbed her ass, clutching the flesh, squeezing hard each time Ryan sucked firmly.

Finally, Ryan pulled away, breaking the suction with a loud pop. She looked thoroughly dazed and rolled onto her back, panting. Jamie leaned over her, smoothing the hair from Ryan's eyes. With a smoldering look, Ryan murmured, "My mouth. Your clit. Now."

Instantly, Jamie yanked at her panties, unable to get them off fast enough. She carefully put one knee on either side of Ryan's head and ever-so-slowly lowered herself until she hovered just above her partner's waiting lips.

Ryan reached up and gently spread her open, then growled in satisfaction the moment her mouth touched the delicate flesh.

Jamie cried out some unintelligible sound, then reached up and grasped her own breasts, pulling on her nipples just to distract herself. Every time she felt herself start to go over the edge, she pinched herself hard—the pain sensors redirecting some of the pleasure from her clit. But Ryan was devouring her so magnificently, reaching every nerve-filled spot, that she couldn't hold out for long. Far sooner than she wished, she came hard, nearly humping Ryan's face.

Her hips finally stilled, and she tried to pull away, but Ryan held her firmly. "More," she demanded. "I need more."

Jamie wanted to gather her wits, to get herself under control. But she realized that she didn't need to be in control with Ryan. She could let her partner take over completely. So she lowered herself onto that eager, waiting mouth and let the pleasure wash over her again and again.

It was after ten when they'd finally had all of their needs fulfilled. They were exhausted, their bodies covered in sweat, the bed a mess. "This might sound crazy, but I feel better than I have in months," Ryan said.

Jamie snuggled closer, kissing Ryan gently. "It sounds perfectly logical to me. We both got a lot off our minds tonight. I feel more optimistic than I have in a while."

Ryan looked at her, her clear eyes taking on a childlike innocence. "Will we really be able to get through this?"

"We will." She could feel her confidence grow as she hugged her lover tightly. "I'm gonna change my priorities and make them what they should have been all along. Our relationship comes first."

Ryan touched her nose. "You come first."

"That's true. But if you've got a little more energy...you could come last."

Ryan spread herself out on the bed. "Do me," she growled. "Do me good."

Chapter Thirty-Three

In Hillsborough, California, a big, black Ram truck pulled into the stately, circular drive of a very impressive home. When Conor rang the bell, Helena answered promptly and escorted him into the living room. Catherine came down just moments later, sweeping down the long, broad staircase in a long, beaded gown, the brilliant blue color nearly matching that of her escort's eyes. The dress was strapless, with a square cut to the bodice, and a full, gathered skirt. Her hair was arranged in her usual casual, layered style, and it served to contrast nicely with the elaborate, formal, sapphire and diamond pendant that graced her throat. Matching drop earrings—sapphires surrounded by diamonds—nestled against her ears, and a substantial sapphire solitaire ring was on the third finger of her left hand, supplanting the diamond that had occupied the space for the previous twenty-two years.

She glided into the room, unconsciously making an entrance after all of her years of practice. "Conor, you look marvelous in that suit."

He turned from the photos he'd been studying and tried to make his mouth work. Before he knew it, he was slowly circling the woman, nodding his head as he took her in. "I'm speechless," he finally said, and the look on his face gave credence to his claim.

She leaned over and kissed his smooth cheek, noticing just a bare hint of cologne. "That's the nicest compliment I've had in years. Thank you."

Giving her a broad smile, he said, "You know, I really like Jim. He's been very nice to me, and he seems like a sharp guy, but letting you get away makes me doubt both his intelligence and his sanity."

"You're just the antidote for my bruised self-esteem," she chuckled, linking her arm in his to head for the door. She took a black silk stole and a black beaded bag from the table by the front door and handed Conor her keys.

"What kind of a statement do you want to make?" he asked playfully. "We can take my truck."

She considered his offer for a moment and then admitted, "I can't imagine getting out of your truck without falling on my face. Other than that, though, it would be a kick."

As he drove along the highway in the usual, heavy traffic, Conor gave Catherine a glance. "How do you want to play it tonight? Am I a friend, a date, or what?"

"What do you feel comfortable with?" she asked carefully. "I suppose my goal is to shake people up a little and make them not approach me with their false sympathy over my divorce."

"Oh," Conor said, a smile covering his handsome face. "So you'd like everyone to think we're..." Turning slightly, he gave her a waggling eyebrow grin, the original his sister had stolen from him years before. "Works for me."

Catherine placed a hand on his forearm, briefly wondering if he was wearing armor under his Armani. "I don't want you to be uncomfortable. No one will come out and ask if we're dating, of course. They're far too polite for that. But I certainly wouldn't mind if my erstwhile friends thought I could attract a handsome young man." She paused briefly then asked, "How are you at acting interested in a woman old enough to be your mother?"

"Catherine," he said softly, his crystal clear blue eyes landing on her briefly, "you're barely thirteen years older than I am, so the mom thing doesn't work." His eyes darted to her once again as he said, "I hope this doesn't make you uncomfortable, but I find you devastatingly attractive, and if you weren't Jamie's mother, I wouldn't have to *act* interested in you. You'd know just how interested I was." His smile returned. "This is honestly the first time that I regret having Jamie as a sister-in-law."

Squeezing his arm once again, Catherine said, "I can't imagine that's true, but I'm going to convince myself that it is. Thank you."

"Almost a year ago, I had a conversation with my sister. She was talking about her new friend, and about how great she was, and how much she liked her. I remember that she said, 'Conor, this woman is so special, but she's with a guy who doesn't have the brains to see it.' The same thing applies to you. It's gonna be a very lucky guy that finally snares you."

She didn't comment, feeling like she might cry if she even tried to speak. Her stomach flipped when she thought of the huge compromise she'd made to keep Giacomo in her life. She patted Conor's arm and sank back in her seat, wondering if she'd compromised her morals as well as her future.

The first few minutes were difficult. Catherine's heart was beating so wildly it was nearly audible, and her hand was so cold and clammy that not even Conor's warmth took the chill off. No sooner had they stepped into the venue than she had second thoughts, even though it was far too late to turn back. The startled looks her friends and acquaintances were giving them were making her stunningly uncomfortable, and she had a momentary thought to slip out before she and Conor caught anyone else's attention.

Catherine's stomach clenched, and she was stricken with panic as she considered that she might follow Jamie's tactic when it came to stress and lose the insubstantial contents of her stomach. The feeling intensified as her former friend, Laura Martin, made a beeline for her. Catherine gripped Conor's hand so tightly that he winced, but before she could warn him, the woman was in their faces, looking smug and superior, as always.

"Well, this is a surprise," she said, her eyes roaming over Conor with thinly veiled distaste. "For a minute I thought you'd brought Jamie's 'friend', but then I realized that this must be her brother." She smiled sweetly at Catherine. "It must be hellish to try and find a suitable escort for an affair like this. It's nice that you have some…options." She gave Conor a look like the one she would have given a spilled load of trash.

As her ire rose, her stomach calmed, and in seconds Catherine's discomfort abated. "Laura Martin, this is Conor O'Flaherty." Turning to Conor she added, "Ryan and Jamie know Laura's daughter, Cassie. She's the young woman who gave that delightful interview to the National Inquisitor." She actually took a step back as she said this, just to make sure she wasn't hit with blood or bone fragments when Conor decked the woman.

Laura's already pale face paled further, then flushed as she spluttered, "Cassie didn't say one thing that wasn't the truth."

Conor's blue eyes had narrowed to slits, and his posture became very aggressive. He was leaning toward the small woman with malevolent intent when Catherine put her hand on his arm to draw him back. She didn't get a hand over his mouth, however, and he started to let the woman have it.

"First off, my sister is not just Jamie's friend," he growled. "She's her lover...her partner...her spouse."

Laura's eyes widened at his words and his tone. In her circle, people didn't speak the plain truth.

"My sister's told me all about your daughter," he spat, his eyes sparking fire. "It's clear that the apple doesn't fall far from the tree." He turned and draped one long arm around Catherine's waist and guided her away from the obnoxious woman, not stopping until they were on the opposite side of the room. His expression was contrite as he gazed at her and said, "I'm sorry I lost my temper. I just get so pissed off when people are cruel, especially where Ryan's involved."

"Conor," Catherine said, squeezing his large hand, "you have nothing to apologize for. There was a large part of me that wanted to see you knock her across the room." His big blue eyes widened at her statement, and she insisted, "I'm being perfectly honest. She's an evil woman, and if I didn't feel so guilty for spending as much time with her as I have, I'd feel justified to hit her myself."

He gave her a gentle squeeze. "Thanks," he said softly. "I thought I'd ruined your night."

Catherine laughed. "You're the highlight of my night. The only way my evening will be ruined is if you don't enjoy yourself."

"Not a chance. Let's not let the idiots get us down, okay?"

"It's a deal." Looking around, she commented, "It didn't dawn on me that people would recognize you, but it makes perfect sense. I guess my little scheme didn't work. Everyone will think I've had to resort to bringing family members to events. That's rather like bringing your cousin to the prom."

Conor gave her a studied look. "Even though you're a member of our family, there's no legal or moral reason that you and I couldn't be dating. I'm only going to look like your cousin if we act like cousins." His eyes twinkled with mischief. Catherine blinked at him in surprise as he continued, "Let's take a turn on the dance floor and show 'em a thing or two."

"Wha...what do you want to show them?"

"I wanna show 'em how to dance."

"You…know how to dance?" She'd assumed Conor's talents lay in swinging a hammer rather than a partner.

"Sure do. I'm pretty darned good, if I do say so myself. My Granny's main purpose in life was to make sure we had a little class. After our mother died, she got even more focused…since she considers us orphans. She's very big on knowing how to dance, and how to use the proper utensils at a meal, all that crap." He grinned, charmingly.

"You're just full of surprises." She beamed as Conor led her to the dance floor.

"That's what makes life interesting." He took her hand in his and led her seamlessly around the ballroom. Their height difference did not impair their gracefulness in the least, even though he was somewhere around six foot five and she was a hair under five foot four. His hair was so black that it matched the obsidian studs in his starched shirt, hers so fair that it shone like the sun. His skin was burnished to a rich, dark warmth, hers was nearly alabaster. His body was beyond sturdy, filling his well-made suit out perfectly; hers was nearly frail, only her months of following Ryan's workout program having caused some beginning signs of definition in her exposed shoulders and arms.

Even with the striking differences in their bodies, their coloring, and their ages, there was something so complementary about the pair that they not only didn't appear out-of-place, they looked absolutely perfect together, and their relaxed, smiling faces only served to highlight their connection.

"I don't often dance with someone who moves as well as you do," Conor murmured into her ear as they moved gracefully around the floor.

"I had lessons also. My mother and your grandmother sound like they'd get along perfectly. I was taking some kind of dance or piano class from the time I was in third grade."

"It doesn't seem like it when we're young, but those lessons really can pay off. If I didn't know how to dance, I'd feel like a dope out here, trying to keep up with you. I should write to my grandmother and thank her." He turned Catherine gently to lead her around another couple who were not having an easy time keeping up with the music.

"You should add a thanks for teaching you about the proper way to use flatware," Catherine said. "I didn't mention this because I didn't want to scare you off, but we're at the head table."

"Ooh...you are Jamie's mother," he teased. "Ryan says that's just what Jamie does to get her to do things. She springs 'em on her when it's too late to turn back."

Batting her eyes, Catherine asked, "You're not angry, are you?"

"Of course not. I'm perfectly comfortable here." They danced a little more, moving across the floor with enviable grace. "One thing puzzles me," Conor said a few moments later.

"What's that?"

"You didn't know that I knew how to dance, and you didn't know that I knew how to behave at a formal dinner. Why didn't you ask me? It would have been kind of embarrassing for you if I ate with my hands and wiped my mouth on my sleeve."

"I've had many meals with you, and it's obvious that you're a very well mannered man."

"Yeah, but there's a difference between being couth and fitting in with this crowd," he said, twitching his head in the direction of the other guests.

Catherine thought about his question for a moment, giving it her full concentration. "I've been worried about this night. I didn't want to come alone, but I also didn't want to be with some stranger, or someone I'd have to entertain. I knew that I'd feel perfectly comfortable with you, and no matter how awful the evening was, we'd still have fun. That's been very reassuring to me," she said, tilting her head as she gazed into his eyes.

He gave her a gentle hug, pressing her body into his. "I'm very glad that you asked me." With an even wider smile, Conor added, "The cousins are all jealous."

She laughed. "Oh, surely they wouldn't enjoy hanging around with this crowd."

"You just don't get it, do you?" Conor smiled to himself as he picked up speed and whirled Catherine around in a tight spiral.

The dinner portion of the evening went better than Catherine had dared to hope. Conor was the definition of suave, thoroughly charming the elderly woman who sat to his left, managing to make her giggle her way through her entire meal, to her husband's great displeasure.

Catherine was able to tend to her social obligations, knowing that her escort was perfectly able to fend for himself. The only near disaster was when Conor leaned over at one point and commented, "Most of the women at this table are as brittle as a fifty year old shingle." Catherine had just taken a spoonful of soup into her mouth, and it was through sheer will that she didn't spew the bisque onto the table.

Conor gave her a sheepish grin. "Sorry about that. We always try to make each other spit. I lost my head there for a minute."

She tossed her head back and laughed, a full-throated, genuine, belly laugh. Every other person at the table turned to look at Catherine, none of her long held acquaintances having ever heard anything even remotely approaching a real laugh come from her mouth. Finally getting herself under control, she clapped a hand on Conor's arm and leaned in to whisper, "I guarantee you're the only man in this entire room who's tried to make his date spit." Giving him a squeeze, she added, "I am so glad that you agreed to come with me. You know how to show a woman a good time."

As soon as the dinner service had ended, the board members all went to the podium to say a few words about their particular area of expertise. Conor was favorably impressed with Catherine's smooth delivery. Not one trace of nerves showed even though the crowd numbered over five hundred. Since she was the president of the society, she was the last to speak, and he noted with approval that her speech was shorter and more to the point than any of the others. As soon as she concluded her remarks, the band started to play again, and without even resuming her seat she tapped Conor on the shoulder. "Dance with me?"

He nodded agreeably and got up to join her on the dance floor, which was populated by just a few other couples. "Nice job," he smiled as he grasped her right hand in his left, and placed his right hand on her waist.

"Thank you. Public speaking isn't my favorite thing, but I've gotten over my nervousness by doing it often."

"If you were nervous, it was impossible to tell."

Catherine smiled at him, having to lean back in his embrace to see his eyes. "I wasn't nervous tonight," she said, as though that fact was a surprise to her. "I'm not sure why, but I am remarkably unconcerned about what people think of me tonight." She moved closer and rested her head on his chest as the music slowed and segued into a gentle rhythm. "Right now I should be making small talk with everyone. I normally make sure I speak with every person who attends one of these events."

She sighed heavily as she added, "I honestly don't care tonight. I just want to enjoy myself."

"You deserve to have fun," he said, giving her a squeeze. "You obviously do a lot for this organization. Tonight should be a time for you to relax and feel good about your contributions. All of the people here saw you... they all heard your speech...you've done enough. They don't own you."

Once again Catherine leaned back in his arms and gazed at him for a long minute. Something clicked in that moment and she blinked up at Conor, maintaining the look for so long that he eventually gave her a puzzled smile and asked, "What's going on behind those brown eyes?"

"What you said," she murmured, her voice distant and faint. He leaned down closer so that he could hear her as she said, "They don't own me."

He stood tall and cocked his head at her, his puzzled smile still in place. "No, of course they don't. No one owns you, Catherine. You're your own woman." This was so obvious to him that he didn't think it merited comment, but it was clearly a revelation to Catherine.

"I am, aren't I?" Her voice held as much question as certainty.

"You are," Conor said more forcefully. "You're a strong, determined, decisive woman."

Catherine blinked up at him and asked in a small voice, "Do you really see me that way?"

He smiled at her and gave her another gentle hug. "It's not a matter of seeing you that way. That's what you are. Everyone sees you that way." He gazed into her eyes and saw the fragile, wounded woman that lurked just under the surface of her competent, controlled exterior. "You're the only one who sees a different image," Conor said softly, closing his eyes as he gave her a warm hug. "I don't know why you don't believe in the you we all know and love, but I hope that someday you will."

Blinking away her tears, Catherine took Conor by the hand and led him onto a small balcony and let the cool March night help her regain control. She took in a few deep breaths, with Conor's powerful arm covering her exposed shoulders, his heat keeping her surprisingly warm. "I was my father's daughter," she said softly, the words floating from her lips on small clouds of vapor. "Then I was my husband's wife." She looked up at Conor with a warm, confident smile. "One day I'll be known as my daughter's mother." She shivered in the cold night, her body finally reacting to the chill. "But for now...for right now...I'm my own woman." She wiped the tears from her eyes, amazed at how cold the drops became as they slid down her cheeks.

"Catherine Evans is gone. She's a thing of the past." Warm brown eyes, overflowing with tears met Conor's. "I'm giving up the Evans name," she said with surprising decisiveness. "I wasn't going to do it…I thought it would cause too much controversy…but I'm not an Evans any longer." She snuggled closer, her skin so cold that it was painful, but she couldn't bear the thought of going back inside. Conor saw her shiver and took off his jacket and placed it around her shoulders.

"Thank you," she sighed, the residual warmth surrounding her like a blanket warmed by the fire. "I'm a double Smith, you know."

"No, I didn't." His cocked head urged her to go on.

"My great-grandmother was a Smith and she married my great-grandfather, who shared the same last name. They met at Stanford," she said wistfully, "just like Jim and I did. My great-grandfather was a member of the Pioneer Class—the first class to be admitted as freshmen. My great-grandmother was two years younger. She was a biology major." She smiled up at Conor. "Just like Ryan."

"Wow. It must've been hard for a woman to even go to college then, much less major in a science."

"She was extraordinary." Catherine smiled. "She became a medical doctor, the only woman in her class. My great-grandfather was an engineer, and he developed a tabulating machine that in some ways was a precursor of the modern computer. He sold the rights for a substantial amount of money, as well as stock. That's how the Smith fortune was created." Cocking her head at Conor, Catherine said, "Everyone in the family looks up to my great-grandfather for having had the idea and the business acumen to amass the kind of wealth he did, but in my mind, the larger figure of the pair is my great-grandmother." She blinked back another few tears. "I'm reclaiming the Smith name for her."

"I'm sure she'd be pleased with that decision." Conor paused a moment and added, "I'm sure she'd be pleased with you, too."

Catherine gazed up at him as her eyes focused sharply. A determined, intense look settled on her face. "I'm not sure that would be true up to this point. I've wasted many, if not all of the gifts I've been given." She shook her head firmly, the fire in her eyes growing brighter as she declared, "Those days are over! I've been looking at my life and counting the losses and the disappointments, rather than looking at the gifts and the opportunities I've been graced with. I swear that I'm going to stop that nonsense today. I'm going to make something of my life. I'm not sure what, and I'm not sure how to go about it, but I swear that I won't rest until I've made a positive contribution to this world. I'm going to be proud of myself," she declared fiercely.

Conor wrapped his arms around Catherine, a warm smile gracing his features. "Your family is already proud of you. You never have to prove a thing to us."

They stood together on the moonlit balcony, the cold wind playing havoc with Catherine's fine blonde hair. She looked out into the black night, her mind playing over the events of the last few months that had led her to this place. Her mind was overwhelmed with the details of the past year, and she consciously put them aside, not interested in looking back. Focusing her vision, she gazed at a bright star near the horizon and let her mind idly dream, her wishes for the future suddenly sharper and brighter than her memories.

The End

By Susan X Meagher

Novels

Arbor Vitae
All That Matters
Cherry Grove
Girl Meets Girl
The Lies That Bind
The Legacy
Doublecrossed
Smooth Sailing
How To Wrangle a Woman
Almost Heaven
The Crush

Serial Novel

I Found My Heart In San Francisco

Awakenings
Beginnings
Coalescence
Disclosures
Entwined
Fidelity
Getaway
Honesty
Intentions
Journeys
Karma
Lifeline
Monogamy
Nurture

Anthologies

Undercover Tales
Outsiders

To purchase these books and eBooks visit
www.briskpress.com

To find out more, visit Susan's website at
www.susanxmeagher.com

You'll find information about all of her books, events she'll be attending and links to groups she participates in.

All of Susan's books are available in paperback and various e-book formats at www.briskpress.com

Follow Susan on Facebook.
www.facebook.com/susamxmeagher